Readers LOVE *The C[...]*

'My new favourite c[...]'
★★★[★★]

'Truly, this was one of the best starts to a new British cosy series I have read in a while'
★★★★★

'I loved it, and I hope this is the start of a long series of Cherrywood books!'
★★★★★

'I loved this British cosy mystery . . . the characters were so good!'
★★★★★

'I absolutely loved everything about this . . . Packed full of intrigue and humour, this entertaining story held me from beginning to end'
★★★★★

'I was hooked . . . The humour in this had me laughing out loud'
★★★★★

'I absolutely loved this book . . . unexpected twists and turns along the way. Brilliantly written'
★★★★★

'Everything about this book has been brilliant . . . I loved [it] from beginning to end'
★★★★★

'Compelling, hilarious and cosy with lashings of sass. More please'
★★★★★

Penny Blackwell grew up in rural West Yorkshire. After university she spent time in several different cities, but eventually returned to settle in Brontë Country. Penny Blackwell is a pen name for Lisa Firth, who also writes award-winning contemporary romantic comedies as Mary Jayne Baker and World War II fiction as Betty Firth. *Murder at the Bonfire* is the second novel in The Cherrywood Mysteries series.

Also by Penny Blackwell:

The Cherrywood Murders

MURDER at the Bonfire

PENNY BLACKWELL

Copyright © 2023 Penny Blackwell

The right of Penny Blackwell to be identified as the Author of
the Work has been asserted by her in accordance with the
Copyright, Designs and Patents Act 1988.

First published in 2023 by Headline Accent
An imprint of HEADLINE PUBLISHING GROUP

1

Apart from any use permitted under UK copyright law, this publication may
only be reproduced, stored, or transmitted, in any form, or by any means,
with prior permission in writing of the publishers or, in the case of
reprographic production, in accordance with the terms of licences
issued by the Copyright Licensing Agency.

All characters in this publication are fictitious and any resemblance
to real persons, living or dead, is purely coincidental.

Cataloguing in Publication Data is available from the British Library

ISBN 978 1 0354 0011 9

Typeset in 11.75/15.75pt Dante MT Std by Jouve (UK), Milton Keynes

Printed and bound in Great Britain by Clays Ltd, Elcograf S.p.A.

Headline's policy is to use papers that are natural, renewable and recyclable
products and made from wood grown in well-managed forests and other
controlled sources. The logging and manufacturing processes are expected
to conform to the environmental regulations of the country of origin.

HEADLINE PUBLISHING GROUP
An Hachette UK Company
Carmelite House
50 Victoria Embankment
London EC4Y 0DZ

www.headline.co.uk
www.hachette.co.uk

For my three four-legged copy editors:
Minky, Millie and Gemma.

Prologue

The first thing I notice is how little has changed.

That doesn't feel right. That this place should have remained the same, when everything inside me is different. My face, my voice, my body... nothing is as it was when I left. I am someone else now – transfigured, as if by magic.

I look around at the familiar buildings as the leaves shatter underfoot. The apothecary, with its antique bottles of coloured glass casting rainbows across the main street. The bakery, with its delicious autumn fragrance of ginger parkin and spiced pastries. The village hall, decked with orange and black bunting. It's such a homely place, it's hard to believe this was a village that could chew a person up and spit them out – so thoroughly disfigured as to be unrecognisable, even to themselves.

Cherrywood. It makes me feel nauseous to be back here, drowning in memories of the past. But needs must when the devil drives – or so the saying goes.

I bend my steps towards the park. The bunting on the village hall is flapping in the wind. On an impulse, I reach up and yank one of the strings down. Stupid thing to do, but I can't help myself. It seems so inappropriately merry. Seeing the forlorn flags twitching pathetically among the fallen leaves makes me feel a little better.

I turn into the park, which, with its floral clock and Victorian bandstand, seems to be pretending to a civility it hadn't been entitled to in my time when the village teens had used the place as a smoking and make-out spot. Perhaps they did still.

In the centre of the park stands a mountain of branches, old pallets, broken-up furniture and other junk, arranged into a high pyre ready for Guy Fawkes Night. Against it leans an effigy that in daylight might be quite comical, but now, as the sun starts to sink behind the high fells, looks more than a little macabre. Its black witch's hat is pulled low, casting a shadow over its face, and it leers up at me from under the broad brim. If I dipped my head, the figure's ridiculous ping-pong-ball eyes would be visible and the effect would be ruined. But now, standing above it so only the crone's bloody smile can be seen, she seems to mock; to taunt. I don't mind, though, and nod to her with something like bonhomie. We're two of a kind, she and I. I know her taunts are not for me.

I take the envelope from my pocket and slip it into the pocket of her robe. Then I smile. Soon, it will all be over.

Chapter 1

Tess Feather would never have believed something so truly horrible could occur in Cherrywood. And now it was all over the papers, visitors from far and wide would soon arrive to witness the ghoulish spectacle.

'Would you look at that?' she observed to Roger, her flatmate Raven's cockapoo. The little dog had one leg cocked against Neil and Sally Hobson's garden fence as he answered an apparently urgent call of nature – his third in the ten minutes they'd been out.

Roger deigned to glance upwards at the poorly stuffed figure in Puritan dress that had taken up residence in the Hobsons' front garden, its sad papier-mâché head lolling pathetically, and Tess was sure she saw him grimace. Practically every garden in the village was now host to a similar dummy as Cherrywood geared up for the opening of the Penny for the Guy Trail this afternoon, one week before Bonfire Night.

It was while examining the dummy that Tess noticed a suspicious figure peeping furtively around the corner of Royal Row. As she watched, it sidled out and broke suddenly into a run, before stopping short and proceeding to jog in a meandering zigzag in the direction of the park.

'What's he up to?' Tess gave Roger's lead a tug. 'Come on, trusty canine sidekick. It looks like the game's afoot.'

Tess eventually caught up with the figure in the park. It was lurking behind the bonfire pyre, peering around the side.

'What's going on, Liam? Are you on a case?'

'Yes, Tess, I'm on a case,' Liam whispered. 'Look, can you keep your voice down? You'll scare her off.'

'I knew it! Are you chasing down a perp? What did they do, what's their MO? Come on, tell me.'

'You really need to stop watching so many cop shows.' Liam Hanley, the village's first – and almost certainly last – private detective-cum-freelance gardener, turned to face her. 'It's an escaped dog, all right? Fred Braithwaite's border collie bitch, Molly. She's in season and he wants me to track her down before she gets into trouble. I had her in my sights a minute ago, then she got the scent of something and was off in the other direction.'

Tess felt a surge of disappointment that Liam wasn't working on anything more exciting, then instantly berated herself. She knew it wasn't right, selfishly wishing for drama. The events of this spring, when a number of the village's old guard had found themselves either dead or under suspicion of murder, had sent shockwaves through the tiny community that it was only now beginning to recover from. Still, Tess couldn't forget that working on the Women's Guild murder case with Liam had given her the sort of mental stimulation she struggled to find in her everyday life.

'Another missing dog?' she said. 'You've had nothing but missing dog cases since you moved here, Lee. I swear it's only errant canines and rose-bush pruning keeping you in business.'

Liam looked wounded. 'I don't just find missing dogs. I get other cases.'

'What other cases?'

'Well . . . there was that missing ferret two weeks ago.'

'Wow.'

'Hey, I found him, didn't I? And he was a third of the size of a dog.'

'Again I'm going to have to say, wow.'

He sighed. 'I am starting to wonder what I was thinking when I decided to relocate here from London. I must've been mad to think I could get enough work to keep me busy in a sleepy little place like this.'

'What were you thinking?'

He glanced at her. 'I have absolutely no idea.'

Tess lurched forward suddenly as Roger lunged to the full length of his lead, sniffing frantically at the air. A flash of black and white appeared in the hedge surrounding the park, then just as quickly disappeared.

'Aha!' Liam glanced down at Roger. 'Now there's an idea. A honey trap.'

Tess shook her head. 'I refuse to allow you to pimp out poor Roger just to catch Fred Braithwaite's sheepdog.'

'Oh, come on. She only needs to get a whiff of him and she'll be bounding over. Don't worry, I'll grab her before Randy Rodge can take it any further.'

'Hmm. Do we get a fee?'

'A G&T and a dog biscuit at the pub?'

'I'd hardly call that a fee, but all right.'

Tess followed Liam to the bushes where the streak of black and white had been seen. Roger was practically pulling her arm off to get ahead. With Liam's encouragement Tess walked back and forth with him, letting Molly pick up the scent. Sure enough, it wasn't long before a twitchy canine nose appeared out of the bushes.

'All right, just a little further,' Liam muttered. 'Come on, Molly. Come out where I can grab you.'

Roger was wagging his tail like mad now his lady friend had shown herself. Tess felt guilty that she was going to have to scupper his amorous intentions. Canine bachelor life must be frustrating.

She let the cockapoo edge a little closer. It worked, and Molly shuffled out of the hedge fully. As soon as her collar was visible, Liam made a grab for it, fished a lead from his pocket and clipped it on her.

'Gotcha!' He gave the dog a stroke between the ears. 'Sorry to ruin your fun, girl, but your dad thinks you're not ready for a family just yet. Time to go home, eh?' He looked at Tess. 'You going my way?'

'I'm due to meet Raven for the Guy Trail opening in a bit, but I'll walk through the village with you. Roger needs the exercise.'

She walked beside him, being careful to keep the two dogs separate. Roger was determined to get to Molly and she seemed equally intent on making his acquaintance, so it felt like Tess and Liam were perpetually tripping over dogs, leads, each other or themselves as they tried to navigate the main street.

'So it looks like – whoops, sorry Molly – I solved yet another case for you,' Tess observed to Liam.

'Were you born this smug or did you have to practise?'

She shrugged. 'Bit of both.'

Liam bent to guide Roger out of his way. 'I'd say Rodge ought to take the credit for this one. He was a top-notch honey trap.'

'Do you think you'll ever get a case that isn't to do with missing pets?'

'I could have a juicy infidelity sting lined up, since you ask. Potential philandering wife.'

Tess's ears pricked up. 'Anything I can help with?'

Liam shook his head. 'Tess, we've talked about this. The Clemmie Ackroyd case was a one-off, all right? I'm not letting you get involved in my work again.'

'Why? Worried I'll show you up by solving your cases before you do?'

'No, because it could put you in harm's way. I wouldn't have involved you before if I hadn't needed someone on the inside at the Women's Guild.'

'Oh, right. Just because I'm a lass you think I'm some delicate bloom who needs protecting from all the big, bad men in the world.'

He laughed. 'I promise you, Tess, I've never thought you were a delicate bloom in my life.'

'Well, then why so reluctant to let me help?'

'Because it's not your job, is it? I get paid to put myself in that kind of danger; you don't. We're not partners.'

'That wasn't what you said last time.'

'I told you, that was different. You ought to focus on your singing. It's great you've been getting some paid gigs outside the pub. Put your efforts into that.' He glanced at her. 'I do owe you a fee for helping with Molly, though. What about coming for that drink with me? Roger's more than welcome to tag along and claim his biscuit.'

'Lee, I told you—'

'I know what you told me. What I don't understand is why.'

'I just think, with everything that's happened between us . . . it's for the best if we steer clear of anything that feels like dating.'

'I wasn't suggesting a date. Just some nice, platonic socialising where we're both on the same side of a bar for once, that's all.'

'Anything that *feels* like dating, I said, which means anything that involves just the two of us, alone. You're trying to build your business, I've got my singing career to focus on, and then . . . well, there's our history. It isn't the right time.'

'Will there ever be a right time?'

Tess looked away. 'I'm not sure. Maybe not.'

Liam sighed. 'OK, forget it. Apparently I have to bump someone off around here for you to want to spend time with me.'

'That isn't fair, Liam.'

'I like being with you, Tess, and I think you like being with me. I know there's still the Porter case looming over us, but after everything we went through this spring I don't understand why—' He swore as he tripped over Roger's lead. 'Bloody dogs!'

Tess looked at her watch. 'I don't have time to go over this again. I'm meeting Raven soon. See you later, Lee.'

Liam didn't reply. He just marched off in the direction of Fred Braithwaite's place, ignoring Molly's protestations as she pulled on her lead to get back to Roger. Tess sighed, wondering when everything had become so horribly messy.

She did like being with Liam. That was the problem – she was worried she might start to like it a little too much. Tess hadn't forgotten that there'd been another time when she'd allowed herself to grow too fond of Liam Hanley's company, and it hadn't led anywhere good. In fact it had led right here to Cherrywood, the village she'd grown up in. It was thanks to Liam that she'd found herself back here eighteen months ago, her high-flying London job kaput, nursing a broken heart and propping up the wrong side of a bar for minimum wage. That was the sort of thing that made you cautious about men generally, let alone the exact same one who'd landed you in the mess. Yes, she'd forgiven Liam to an extent when they'd worked together to solve Clemmie Ackroyd's murder in the spring. But forgiving wasn't forgetting, and Tess wasn't about to repeat the mistakes she'd made in her dealings with Liam Hanley the first time around.

She was still early to meet Raven so she sauntered in leisurely fashion back to the park, stopping to examine some of the other contributions to the Penny for the Guy Trail.

It had all been the idea of Angela Campbell, the new

president of Cherrywood Women's Guild, who'd moved here from Scotland three months ago to take a job on the local paper. Traditionally Cherrywood held a scarecrow festival in the autumn months, but as Angela had pointed out, they were becoming pretty old hat these days. The Penny for the Guy Trail was more original and it served a double purpose in celebrating both Bonfire Night and Halloween, since most of the guys had been dressed in appropriately spooky costumes.

Angela had guaranteed them some column inches in her paper if they went ahead with the idea, which had won over the publicity-hungry village bigwigs who tended to decide these things (and who felt it might be nice, after the spring, to be in the papers for something other than yet another murder). She'd promptly been elected head of the Guy Trail organising committee and swept through the village like a cyclone, gathering volunteers up in her wake. Somehow Tess and Raven had found themselves recruited, along with their best friend Oliver Maynard. As village vicar, Oliver tended to find himself on committees whether he volunteered for them or not.

Nearly every building in Cherrywood now had some form of guy in its garden. As she walked to the park, Tess observed devils, witches, spooky dolls, plague doctors, evil clowns and all sorts of other horrors – horrors in the badly-made-and-a-bit-naff sense rather than being genuinely frightening, although she wasn't fond of walking through the village at twilight now, when the guys became spooky silhouettes against the setting sun. Every dummy had a money box next to it, raising funds for this year's chosen charity. Villagers were happy to leave the cash unattended, trusting to people's honesty for its safety. In spite of the spate of murders earlier in the year, this was, after all, still Cherrywood.

Tess wondered again how she'd ended up getting dragged into this guy business. Angela hadn't so much invited her and Raven to join the committee as commanded them, and Tess had found the firm 'no' she'd been planning to give turning into a grateful 'yes' even as it travelled from her brain to her vocal cords.

This always seemed to be happening to her. If she wasn't accidentally joining Guy Trail committees, she was accidentally volunteering to do refreshments for the am-dram society's *Mamma Mia!* production or finding herself a member of the Cherrywood Women's Guild. Clearly there was a part of her that longed to be public-spirited and it would keep popping its irritating little do-gooder hand up. Surely, at thirty-one, she was too young for this level of civic duty? Still, it was something to fill the chill autumn days – at least until Liam got himself a nice juicy case she could inveigle him into letting her help with.

Chapter 2

Tess had stopped outside the Cartwrights' place to examine their dummy when she felt a chummy elbow in the ribs. She turned to face Kennedy Hamilton, the new village GP.

'The Cartwrights have gone a bit daring with the political satire,' Kennedy said, nodding to their guy. One of the better-made dummies, it was clearly supposed to be their local MP. He was shown sitting on a toilet with his trousers round his sock suspenders, guzzling a pie.

'It's not very scary, is it?' Tess observed.

Kennedy shrugged. 'I suppose that depends which way you vote.'

'What do you think the pie represents? Taxes or something?'

'No. Sometimes, Tess, I think a pie is just meant to be a pie.'

Kennedy wasn't so much a newcomer to the village as an oldcomer. She'd lived here with her parents as a kid but the family had moved down south when Kennedy was sixteen, leaving her grown-up siblings behind. Her mum and dad had passed away now, and Kennedy, having no family of her own, had moved back to Yorkshire to be closer to her brother and sister.

Tess, Raven and Oliver had been friends with Kennedy at school. Tess had been pleased to see her old classmate back in Cherrywood, her accent rather different now, but otherwise slotting into village life again as if she'd never been away. Still, Tess always felt slightly intimidated by Kennedy and her siblings. The Hamiltons were a family of high achievers, to such a daft extent that it would make anyone feel intimidated. Kennedy was a GP, her older sister Seana a university professor and her brother Nicholas a Church of England bishop, for God's sake. Mr and Mrs Hamilton must have been very proud to have three children all answering to the title Doctor.

Being reminded about the existence of the Hamilton siblings couldn't help but make Tess reflect soberly on her own achievements. At school, there'd always been a healthy academic rivalry between her and Kennedy as they'd competed for the top grades. Now Kennedy was the village doctor, fixing people's ailments, while all barmaid Tess could offer them was a pint of something warming at the bar of the Star and Garter. After her career as a London PA had tanked following Liam's exposure of the Porter scandal, which had seen her boss go to jail for embezzlement, Tess had found herself working as a barmaid-cum-singer whose ambition soared no higher than that one day she might become known as a singer-cum-barmaid. And as for Tess's siblings, her three older brothers . . . well, the less said on their career choices, the better. Certainly none of them was going to be offered a bishophood any time soon.

Kennedy glanced into the garden next door to the Cartwrights'. It was one of the few not to be graced by a guy, although it wasn't empty. Outside the house was a painted sign, decorated with pentangles and other symbols. It read:

Peg Bristow (Ms), Wiccan and foreteller
The Cunning Woman of Cherrywood
Spells, palmistry, tarot, astrology
Readings from £8 (student and OAP concessions)

'No guy for Peggy Bristow, I see,' Kennedy observed.

'No, she says the burning of effigies is offensive to her people. I don't think she's keen on that witch the am-dram society contributed for the big bonfire in the park.'

'I thought that was to plug their December production of *Macbeth*.'

'Yes, but Peggy's decided to take it as a personal slight. I guess modern witches are sensitive to that whole burning at the stake thing.' Tess turned to face Kennedy. 'Are you coming to the park for the trail's grand opening, Kenn? I'm meeting Raven there, and I guess Oliver will be on his way with his mum and dad. They're staying at the vicarage for a couple of weeks.'

Kennedy laughed. 'Poor little Oliver. You should see the terror in his eyes when he sees me. Ever since Nick was appointed bishop of our diocese, Ol lives in fear that I'm going to tell tales to his boss.'

Tess shook her head. 'It's so weird your brother's the new bishop. It's so weird your brother's a bishop! I still remember him as that lanky student who worked a summer job at HMV when we were in primary school.'

'Oh, right, it's weird for you. How do you think I feel?'

'Did it put a lot of pressure on you growing up?' Tess asked, genuinely curious. 'I mean, having a brother and sister so much older who were these academic high flyers. Your parents must have expected a lot from you.'

Kennedy shrugged. 'I never felt that way. Having me later in life did seem to make my mum and dad more protective, though. They wrapped me in cotton wool in a way they never had the older two.'

Roger started pulling at his lead, and Kennedy smiled.

'Looks like your friend wants to get to the park,' she said. 'I'll walk with you. I was headed to the opening ceremony anyway.'

As they passed the village hall, Tess noticed some Halloween bunting had come loose and was skittering among the leaves like an escaped ferret.

She frowned at it. 'Who's done that? People are heading over there for buns and hot chocolate after the trail's been opened and now we've got bunting flapping about, making the place look untidy. I'll have to ask Benjamin to sort it out.'

Kennedy laughed. 'Get you, Miss Pillar-of-the-Community. First the Women's Guild, now the Guy Trail committee. Is this the same young rebel who once got our entire patrol drunk at Guide camp with a stolen bottle of her aunty's Archers?'

'I know, I don't know what happened to me. I swear I'm one step away from a tweed twinset.'

A yip from Roger reminded them where they were bound.

'Peggy's wrong, you know,' Kennedy observed as they carried on walking. 'About witch-burning, I mean. We hardly burnt any witches in this country – or alleged witches, I should say.'

Tess frowned. 'Didn't we? I thought we spent most of the Middle Ages hunting them down.'

'We did, but in England they were mostly hanged. Only a few were burnt at the stake. In Scotland they burnt quite a lot, but only after they'd strangled them first. I know it's the first thing we tend to think of when we imagine the Witch Trials, but burning alive was more of a European thing.'

'You seem to know a lot about it.'

'I've picked up bits from my sister over the years,' Kennedy said. 'Seana lectures in the history of magic, folklore and witchcraft. Pretty interesting. I keep telling her she ought to write a book – one us normal people can read, not something in that opaque style academics are expected to write up their research in.' She glanced at Tess. 'How's the singing going?'

Tess tried not to flinch. Of course, Kennedy didn't know how she was feeling. She certainly wasn't trying to make Tess dwell on the gap between her own career and that of the high-flying Hamiltons. But that was the effect of it, all the same.

'Yeah, not bad,' Tess said, trying to sound bright. 'I'm performing at a hotel this weekend. The lead singer with their house band is ill so they've booked me to fill in.'

'As Cher?'

Again, Tess tried not to wince. It was bad enough that she was the village pub's resident singer without being one half of an unbelievably naff tribute act into the bargain. The costumes she was forced to wear while impersonating either Cher or Dolly Parton did nothing for her already fragile dignity.

'No, as Dolly. It's for a wedding. The grooms are fans.'

Kennedy squeezed her arm. 'That's great, Tess. Your voice is too good to waste doing duets with Ian Stringer at the Star.'

Again, Tess knew her friend was just trying to be nice. Kennedy really would be happy to hear that Tess's career prospects were improving. Still, that didn't make her feel any better.

They'd reached the park now, and Roger was straining towards a couple embracing near the bonfire pyre.

Tess nodded to them. 'Check out love's young dream.'

Kennedy laughed. 'Raven and Benjamin. Locked at the lips again, I see.'

'Yeah, you get used to it. We'd better go tell them to pack it in before they make it to second base.'

They approached Raven and her boyfriend. Raven detached herself from Benjamin's lips to look at them.

'Oh,' she said. 'It's just you two. That wasn't worth interrupting a snog for.'

Tess shook her head at Kennedy. 'You see what I'm forced to live with?'

'You're just jealous,' Raven informed her in a superior tone,

'It's a pleasure to see you as always, ladies.' Benjamin gave Raven a nudge. 'See that? Chivalry, they call it. I've been practising.'

'I'm glad one of us is a gentleman, darling.' Raven beamed at Roger, who'd jumped up to put his front paws on her legs. 'And here's my other favourite boy. Come here, handsome.'

She crouched down to make a fuss of him, and he wagged his tail vigorously.

'You nearly became a granny today, Rave,' Tess told her. 'I bumped into Liam on the trail of that sheepdog of Fred Braithwaite's: Molly. She's in season. Lee recruited Roger to act as a honey trap.'

'Oh, my little boy's far too young and innocent for that sort of thing,' Raven crooned while Roger rolled over for a belly tickle.

'He's getting to be a right dirty old man. You're going to have to have him snipped, before the village is overrun with half-cockapoo pups.'

'Not yet. He's still growing, aren't you, darling?' Raven shot her a look. 'All he really needs is for Aunty Tess to keep a proper eye on him instead of getting distracted by pretty detectives.'

'I'm going to ignore that remark.' Tess turned her attention to Benjamin, who was an electrician and general odd-job man for the village hall. 'Benjamin, have you got time to get your ladder out and reattach the bunting that's come loose from the hall? We're going to have half the village there in a little while, not to mention the Lord Mayor. We don't want the place looking scruffy, do we?'

'Anything for you, Tess.' Benjamin turned to give Raven a kiss. 'I'll be back soon, gorgeous. Don't miss me too much.'

'Now don't ask me to make promises I can't keep, Benjy.'

'Keep her warm for me, girls,' he said to Tess and Kennedy before he strode off. Raven watched his broad figure with what could only be described as a simper on her face.

Kennedy shook her head. 'I'd never have believed it. Raven Walton-Lord, in love with someone nice.'

Raven flicked her black hair. 'You've been gone a long time, darling. I grew out of that bad-boy phase years ago.'

'She didn't,' Tess mouthed to Kennedy.

'Oi. I saw that.' Raven beamed in Benjamin's direction as he exited the park. 'He is wonderful, though. I've never been with someone like Benjy. All warm and considerate and . . . well, sweet. And of course Grandmother's thrilled we might be moving to the heir-producing stage of the relationship any day now.'

'She approves of him then?'

'They haven't been formally introduced yet, but she approves of the fact I'm dating someone. I mean she'd definitely prefer to see me with one of the chino-clad Hooray Henry types she was always trying to set me up with when I was single, but she's getting desperate now.'

At eighty, Raven's grandmother Candice lived in dread that the last of the Walton-Lords would fail to provide an heir to the family estate in her lifetime. When her granddaughter had been a teenager, Candice had disapproved of Raven's boyfriends as a matter of principle. Now that Raven had reached her early thirties, as soon as any relationship got serious Candice was drawing up guest lists, seating plans and lists of baby names.

Kennedy raised an eyebrow. 'You're not talking babies yet, are you? It's only been two months.'

'Of course we're not.' Raven smiled a soppy little smile. 'But you know, girls, for the first time in my life, I can actually see it going that way.'

'Really?'

'I think so. I don't want to rush things, but I've got high hopes for Benjamin.'

Tess, who had heard all about Raven's high hopes for Benjamin already, was only half listening. Her gaze had drifted towards the witch that had been given pride of place in the park as the village's official guy, ready to go up in smoke on Bonfire Night. Not that it was better than the others, but it had been donated by Cherrywood Players to promote their forthcoming production of *Macbeth* and since Angela Campbell was both the chair of the Guy Trail committee and a keen member of the am-dram group, she'd wangled it the star position.

As dummies went it was pretty basic: just a stuffed sack with a couple of sausage legs shoved into stripy tights, with a papier-mâché head stuck on top. Some of the junior am-drammers had helped to make it, and the cartoon-like face had been crudely scrawled by the kids. The witch had a couple of protruding ping-pong-ball eyes and a wide lipstick grin that the Joker would've been proud of.

Still, it always drew Tess's eye. Clothed in an old black dress and a cape that flapped, Dementor-like, in the keen autumn breeze, pointed hat pulled low over its face . . . caught at the right time of day, the witch seemed almost otherworldly. Tess was rather looking forward to watching the thing burn.

When she tuned back in to the conversation, she found that Kennedy and Raven had moved on to the subject of families.

'I know this is rather a personal question, Rave, but do you actually want kids?' Kennedy was asking. 'I suppose in your family it's sort of expected, and your grandmother's obviously mad keen, but I've never heard you express an opinion one way or the other.'

Raven looked thoughtful. 'I honestly don't know,' she said. 'You're right, it was expected – the great and glorious Walton-Lords must have an heir, right? Still, I've never been in any hurry about it. I suppose the idea rather scared me.'

'Why?'

'Well, I've not been set much of an example in that respect, have I? Of course, I barely knew them myself, but by all accounts my parents hated one another.'

Tess was listening now. It was rare for Raven to volunteer information about her parents. All Tess knew about them was that Raven's father had been a racing junkie who'd died at the wheel, and that her mother, who was rumoured to have been very beautiful, had dumped Raven with her grandmother shortly after her husband's death – supposedly for a handsome fee, if you believed village gossip. After that, Raven had been raised at Cherrywood Hall by her grandmother, Candice, and her nanny, Marianne Priestley.

'Did they hate each other?' Tess asked. 'I never heard that.'

'I don't know for sure. That's just the impression Grandmother gave me.'

'Do you know much about your mother?' Kennedy asked. 'I don't think I ever heard her name, even.'

'Oh yes, I know everything about her,' Raven said breezily. 'At least, as much as I ever wanted to know. Eva Russo, she was called.'

'Did she live here in the village?'

'No, she lived in London with my dad. I think the only time she was ever in Cherrywood was when she dumped me at the hall on her way through and never looked back.'

Tess's gaze was drawn to Raven's jet-black hair. 'Italian, was she?'

'Possibly, although Eva Russo might have been a professional name – something to make her sound exotic. She was a model, I think, or an actress or something like that.'

'Do you ever think about tracing her?' Kennedy asked.

'Not really. Why should I? She made her views about me pretty clear when she walked out of my life.'

'If it was me, I'd feel like I had to know. It's hard not to be curious about someone who contributed half your DNA.'

'I can't say I've ever felt that way myself. I'm me. No one else gets either the credit or the blame; DNA be damned.' Raven glanced thoughtfully at Benjamin, who was making his way through a now sizeable crowd of villagers. 'Although I do think about her sometimes. Well, not her personally. About mothers. Whether I'd make a good one.'

'I didn't know you worried about that,' Tess said.

'Well, darling, I don't tell you everything, you know.'

'Do you think you will have kids?' Kennedy asked.

'If I do, it'd have to be with the right guy. I'm not doing it just because Grandmother thinks it's my duty as a Walton-Lord to donate my ovaries to the family.' Raven smiled as Benjamin reached them and took her in his arms again. 'What took you? I missed you something rotten.'

'Sorry. I wanted to make sure it was going to stay put this time.'

'Cherrywood doesn't deserve you, Benjy.' Raven treated him to another kiss while her unromantic friends rolled their eyes at one another.

'I hope I stayed away long enough for you girls to have a good gossip about me,' Benjamin said.

'You certainly did. We've been hearing all about Raven's plans for you.' Kennedy smiled when Raven shot her a warning look. 'Don't worry, Benjamin. All good things, I promise.'

Chapter 3

Raven nudged Tess. 'Look who's just arrived.'

Tess followed her gaze and laughed. It was hard to miss the flushed face of their friend Oliver, shining like a beacon through the crowd. With him were his girlfriend Tammy and parents Annette and Paul, who were visiting for a fortnight while their seaside park home was being refurbished. Tess waved to him, and Oliver waved rather frantically back. After whispering something to Tammy, he made his way through the crowd towards them.

'His mum and dad are driving him round the bend,' Raven murmured. 'They're here for another ten days yet, and it sounds like he's already at breaking point. If there's another murder in Cherrywood, Liam won't have to look far to find out whodunnit.'

'What are Ol's parents doing to drive him mad?' Tess asked.

'Oh, I can't tell you, darling; it's too good. You have to hear it from the horse's mouth. It's nowhere near as much fun otherwise.'

Oliver looked so happy to see them, Tess thought he might actually fall on her neck and weep.

'Thank goodness you lot are here,' he said feelingly. 'I was desperate for an excuse to get away for ten minutes.'

'Nice to see Tammy with you,' Raven said, waving at the girl through the crowd. 'You haven't brought her out with us for ages. I thought you two would want to be spending as much time together as possible before she leaves on her big trip.'

'She's been busy. She's got a lot still to do before she goes.'

'What's the matter, Ol?' Tess asked. 'You look stressed.'

He glanced back at his parents, who were talking to their old friend Bev Stringer, the landlady of the Star and Garter. 'God's testing me, Tessie. I'm a modern-day Job. I really wish He'd stuck with the more traditional excruciating physical agony and plagues of unsightly boils, though.'

'I know just how you feel, Rev,' Benjamin said, patting him on the back. 'I love seeing my mum, but three days of her criticising my furnishings and interrogating me on my love life are plenty. Two weeks and I might just crack.'

'Is that it?' Tess asked Oliver. 'Have your mum and dad redecorated the vicarage for you? Or are they more interested in rushing you and Tam to the altar?'

'Neither.' Oliver winced. 'Kennedy, please don't mention what I'm about to tell you to your brother.'

Kennedy laughed. 'Oliver, I have not been planted back in Cherrywood as a spy for your new boss. To choose a metaphor you'll understand, you can consider anything you utter in my presence to be as sacrosanct as what's said in the confessional.'

'Wrong denomination, but thanks.' Oliver took a deep breath. 'Well, Mum and Dad are having a great time on holiday, seeing old friends and revisiting haunts from their younger days. It's . . . restoring their youth, you might say.'

Raven snorted. 'Sorry,' she said to the others. 'It's just, I've heard this story.'

'What's wrong with that?' Kennedy asked Oliver.

'Nothing. Nothing.' Oliver sounded pained. 'I mean, I like to think of myself as being pretty progressive, you know? Certainly I'm not a prude, and I'm under no delusions as to how the babies I baptise have come to be here – or how I came to be here, for that matter. But I could do without being reminded of it in quite such a . . . tangible way.'

Tess's eyes widened. 'You didn't walk in on the pair of them . . . you know?'

'No.' He closed his eyes. 'But I heard them . . . you know.'

'Oh my God!'

'And the worst thing is, so did the eight members of the women's Bible study group who were having tea and biscuits in my living room at the time.'

Raven burst out laughing, and Oliver flashed her a hurt look.

'Oh, darling, I'm sorry,' she said, putting an arm around his waist. 'I know it isn't funny. Well, not for you. But objectively it is sort of hilarious.'

'I ought to have known I could expect nothing but mockery from the likes of you.' He let out a sound that was something between a whimper and a groan. 'It wasn't just that one time either. Honestly, they're like a pair of hormonal teenagers. I always suspected those park home retirement estates were hotbeds of sexual intemperance and swinging.'

Tess raised an eyebrow. 'Did you?'

'Well, no, but I do now. I mean, every day, Tessie! I have to keep making excuses about needing to show round potential buyers so I can hide at Ling Cottage until they're done.'

'I thought the estate agent showed potential buyers round.'

'No one shows potential buyers round. There are no potential buyers. But my mum and dad don't know that, thankfully.'

When Prue Ackroyd's will had been read out following her death earlier that year, Oliver had discovered to his great surprise that he'd inherited Ling Cottage, her gloomy house on the hill. The place was currently up for sale, but the brutal murders of several previous occupants were not proving to be a selling point.

'They're not even embarrassed about it,' Oliver muttered. 'My dad walks around the vicarage with his silk dressing gown wide open, tighty whities proudly on display. If they think I handed in my parent sex cringe reflex when I got ordained, they're very, very wrong.'

'It's sort of sweet though, that they still have a healthy sex life after all those years of marriage,' Kennedy said. 'After all, desire doesn't just stop when you get older, does it?'

'I know it doesn't. In an objective sort of way, I'm happy for them. I just don't see why they can't stick to having a healthy sex life in their park home and leave my vicarage out of it. At the very least, they could try to restrain themselves during Bible study classes. You should see the smirks I got at communion on Sunday.' Oliver shot Kennedy a wary glance. 'Goodness knows what Nick would make of it.'

'Oh, my brother's pretty liberal about these things – you know, as bishops go. I wouldn't worry about that, Oliver.'

'Nick's hardly going to have you struck off or defrocked or whatever it is that happens to naughty vicars just because your mum and dad are still shagging,' Raven said. 'It's not your fault. Besides, they're married, aren't they? Surely even the traditionalists of the Church don't object to sex between married people.'

Oliver's attention was still on Kennedy. 'You won't tell him though, will you?'

Kennedy smiled. 'No, Ol, I won't tell him.'

Oliver glanced back at Tammy making conversation with his parents and Bev. He winced when he noticed his dad's hand fondly caressing his mum's bottom.

'I'd better go rescue Tam,' he said. 'I dread to think what they're saying. Bev'll only be encouraging them. If I start looking like I've given up the will to live, one of you come and save me, can you?'

Tess patted his arm. 'Of course.'

Oliver pointed out Angela Campbell and the Lord Mayor, who were making their way towards the bonfire. 'There's Angela with our guest of honour. Looks like we're about to get started. See you later, gang.'

Tess noticed Peggy Bristow standing a little way from them, alone. She had a disapproving look on her grey, bespectacled face as she watched Angela and the mayor.

'She doesn't look very happy, does she?' Tess observed to her friends.

'I'm surprised she turned up,' Kennedy said. 'She's been complaining about this Guy Trail ever since Angela came up with the idea.'

'I'll see if I can make peace on behalf of the committee. I'd hate to genuinely upset her. She's not a bad old stick.'

She approached Peggy and nodded a greeting.

'Everything OK, Peg?'

'You tell me.' Peggy cast a dark look at the witch effigy propped against the bonfire. 'You're the one hosting this celebration of the execution of persecuted minorities by narrow-minded bigots who couldn't understand any mode of living that differed from their own.'

'You know, they didn't actually burn witches in this country,' Tess said. 'Kennedy was telling me. Her sister Seana's an expert in the subject.'

'Who mentioned witches?' Peggy turned to look at her. 'I always did think Plot Night was rather bleak, when you know the history. Religious persecution, torture, and then that horrific mode of execution: hanging, drawing and quartering. Apparently that's what we call "fun for all the family".'

Tess frowned. 'I've never really thought about it.'

Peggy gave her a dry smile. 'People rarely do.'

'We forget how it all began, I suppose – or at least, we forget the darker parts. Nowadays it's just a good excuse for treacle toffee and sparklers. Something bright and colourful to cheer us up in the months between summer and Christmas.'

'Well we've no right to forget. I know the Guy Trail's for charity but it leaves a pretty nasty taste.' Peggy lowered her voice. 'Not to mention that burning people in effigy whiffs of dark magic, whatever the excuse for it. We could be stirring up all kinds of turbulence.'

'Mystical turbulence, you mean.'

'I do, and you can take that cynical tone out of your voice, young lady. Mark my words: nothing good's going to come of all this.'

'That's why you don't have a guy in your garden? I thought you were upset on behalf of your fellow Wiccans.'

'Well, I'm not too happy about the witch we're going to be burning either.' Peggy deigned to flash Tess a smile. 'Although not nearly as unhappy as the mugs who've bought tickets to the Players' awful production of *Macbeth*.'

'How do you know it's going to be awful?'

'They always are, aren't they?' Peggy patted Tess's arm. 'Now you mustn't think I blame you for the Guy Trail. I know Angela Campbell is a hard woman to say no to. She's bullied half the Guild into joining her new committee.'

'If you're so angry about the Guy Trail, why did you come to the opening?'

'Answer that yourself. You've known me long enough.'

'Because there's nothing that goes on in this village without you knowing about it?'

Peggy gave her a thin smile. 'How right you are, young Teresa.' She nodded towards Angela, who was standing in front of the bonfire waiting for silence. 'Here we go.'

Conversation quickly died down. The first time Tess had

ever clapped eyes on Angela Campbell, she'd observed that the woman had Presence – with a very capital P. Here was someone who could silence a crowd with nothing more than a slightly raised hand.

Angela was a striking woman in her mid-fifties, very tall – around six foot, Tess would have guessed – with hair dyed the colour of the flames that in one week's time would consume the Players' witch effigy: orange at the roots, melting into a vibrant red at the tips. Her outfits were equally eye-catching: daring ensembles in red, orange and black, all handmade by herself. Tess liked Angela – she was a lot of fun, and Tess admired her confidence – but she did sometimes find her faintly terrifying. She'd never met anyone who could fill a room quite the way Angela Campbell could.

'Welcome,' Angela said to the crowd in her brisk Scottish tones. 'I'm very proud to be here with the Lord Mayor as we open the first annual Cherrywood Penny for the Guy Trail. The guys will be available to view from now until our big bonfire event on the fifth of November, and I'm grateful to all those villagers who have chosen to take part.'

It seemed to Tess that Angela flashed a brief but resentful look at Peggy here. Far from being offended, Peggy looked rather smug.

'All the money raised will go to charity, so please give generously,' Angela continued. 'In the past a guy would fetch a mere penny, but we do ask that you allow for inflation.'

There was a ripple of muted laughter, and Angela paused graciously to allow it to die down.

'Now I have just one more thing to announce before

I hand over to the Lord Mayor,' she said, smiling beneficently at the crowd. 'As you know, there will be a prize for the best guy, and I promised the committee that I'd use my press influence – such as it is – to recruit us a celebrity who would not only act as judge but also do us the honour of setting light to this year's bonfire. I'm now in a position to announce who that will be.' She paused to let this sink in. 'I'm very happy to announce that I have, in fact, been able to get us two celebrity judges for the price of one. We will shortly be welcoming to the village the renowned disc jockey Ade Adams – "Screaming" Ade Adams, as those of a certain age will remember him – and his chart-topping wife Leonie Abbott.'

A hum of surprise and concern passed through the crowd.

'Yikes,' Tess muttered to Peggy. 'I think that mystic turbulence you mentioned is about to be unleashed.'

Chapter 4

It was late evening when Liam Hanley locked up the flat above the chip shop that was both his home and the offices of Cherrywood Investigations and Gardening Services.

He wasn't sure why, but he felt anxious about having missed the opening of the Guy Trail. It hadn't seemed that important to attend, but now Liam found he couldn't relax until he found out what had occurred. Even when he wasn't on a case, he couldn't seem to switch off the detective part of his brain – it simply insisted on knowing everything that was going on. That was why he was now heading to the Star and Garter, hopeful he'd be able to pick up on any important gossip.

And of course it was Sunday, one of Tess's nights to serve behind the bar. That wasn't the main reason he was going in for a drink, but . . . well, it was a reason.

Liam had realised pretty soon after arriving in Cherrywood that he was far from over Tess Feather. When they'd first met in London two years ago, while she was working as a PA and he was undercover investigating an embezzlement scam within her company, Porter Investment, he'd known she was something special. All right, he'd only discovered that after he'd started dating her as a way of finding out more about her boss, but it was how he felt. Then his investigation had brought Porter down and Tess had ended up back here – jobless, heartbroken and hating his guts. It was hardly surprising that it was going to take time for her to learn to trust him again, and Liam knew he needed to be patient.

But how could he be, when she was refusing to see him? It was so frustrating! He knew Tess enjoyed his company, and working together on the Clemmie Ackroyd murder had gone a long way to making them at least friends again. More than that, the kiss they'd briefly shared during the case had confirmed Liam's secret hope that Tess might still have feelings for him, even if she was trying to deny them. The possibility of a future with Tess had been a major reason for his frankly ludicrous decision to up sticks and move his business here three months ago.

Yet when he'd finished tying up his affairs in London and returned to Cherrywood full of optimism about making a new start, he'd found Tess had withdrawn into herself again, all her previous trust issues back in force. She was friendly enough when they bumped into each other, but the only time she actively sought Liam's company – puzzle junkie that she was – was when he was on a case.

Liam had sworn he wasn't going to put her in harm's way again – not that he had any cases on which would allow him to do so, unless it involved a nasty nip from an escaped ferret, but he stood by it. He knew Tess could look after herself, but it worried him that she saw his cases more as a game or a puzzle to be solved than anything genuinely dangerous. Besides, they weren't partners. This meant the only conversation he tended to have with Tess Feather was over the bar of the Star and Garter, and he increasingly found himself in there on the nights she was working.

When he pulled up his usual barstool, he found Tess chatting with her boss, Bev Stringer.

'Well, I never thought *he'd* dare show his face here again, did you?' Bev was saying.

'A lot of people won't be right happy to see her again either,' Tess replied. 'I know I won't.'

'I suppose it's a bit rich for me to comment, with my romantic history, but to do what he did when that poor woman was on her deathbed . . . it was a cold, cruel act by any standard.'

'What are you two gossips chattering about?' Liam asked.

'Evening, Officer.' Bev gave him a cool nod and started pulling a pint of his usual beer.

'I'm not a copper any more, Bev. Come on, what's the story? I knew I'd miss something if I didn't go to the Guy Trail opening.'

'Why didn't you go?' Bev asked.

'I wasn't in the mood.'

'He means he was sulking with me,' Tess told Bev.

Bev raised an eyebrow. 'Lovers' tiff?'

'Very definitely not.' Tess nodded to the pint Bev had left to settle. 'I can top that up, if you want to take your break. You've been due one for ten minutes.'

Bev smirked. 'Like that, is it? Right you are then.'

She fished her cigarettes out of her balconette bra and went outside to have a smoke.

'Sorry about earlier,' Liam said when they were alone. 'I shouldn't have stormed off like that.'

'No you shouldn't.' Tess topped up his pint. 'You're going to have to stop coming in so often, Lee. People are starting to talk.'

'If you mean Bev, she's been talking about us since I got here. Nothing I do is going to change that.' He took his pint. 'You could always let me take you somewhere on your night off, you know. I know a nice Italian restaurant.'

'Stop asking, can you? You know I can't.'

'Why not, when you want to?' He met her eyes, which held an expression both determined and a little sad. 'You do want to, right?'

'No.'

'Once more with feeling, Tess.'

She sighed. 'All right, maybe I do. But it isn't that easy, is it?'

'Are you ever going to forgive me for what happened when I was investigating Porter? I've said I'll do anything to make it up to you. Just tell me what.'

'I'm not sure there is a way to make it up to me.' Her voice became quiet. 'Anyway, it isn't only that.'

'What is it then?'

'Lee, there are things . . . things you don't know about me. Let's just stay friends and leave it at that, eh?'

Liam frowned. 'That sounds ominously mysterious. What are these things?'

'I can't tell you. Suffice to say, me and you . . . it's not as simple as you think it is.'

'It could be. If we let it.'

'No. It couldn't.'

There was silence for a moment.

'So what were you and Bev talking about?' Liam asked after a while, sensing Tess was waiting for him to either change the subject or drink up and leave.

'Oh right, that.' Tess glanced around the pub and lowered her voice. 'It's some old Cherrywood business Angela Campbell's managed to stir up.'

'Journalist Angela?'

'Yeah. You know she promised to get us a local celebrity to judge the Guy Trail?'

'Yes?'

'Well, Cherrywood's only ever had one celebrity resident. Do you remember Screaming Ade Adams?'

Liam frowned. 'That cheesy DJ from the nineties? Known for making prank calls on air?'

'That's him. He had a TV show on Sky too, *Screaming Laughs*, but it only ran for one series.'

'I remember. A poor man's *Beadle's About*, pranking the public. He's got a wife young enough to be his granddaughter who was on some reality show recently, right?'

Tess nodded. 'Leonie Abbott. She was a three-hit wonder about thirteen years ago and now she's the sort of rent-a-gob who seems to pop up whenever a TV show needs a minor celeb. She's more famous than Ade now, but she was nobody when they married. Her husband launched her career.'

'Was Screaming Ade from Cherrywood, then?'

'No, but he and his wife lived here for a while when I was a teen – his previous wife, I mean. They were in the village for about a year, after his career started declining and he had the breakfast slot on Aire Valley FM.'

A customer approached, and Tess broke off while she served him.

'You were saying about Ade and his wife?' Liam prompted when she was done. He was interested in the story, and it was nice to have Tess chatting to him in that easy, friendly way, sharing secrets. Reminded him of old times.

'There was a big scandal locally,' she said in a low voice. 'The wife, Sarah, was terminally ill, and it was discovered Ade had been messing about with someone else – a schoolgirl too, just a year above me in the sixth form at our local secondary. She was barely eighteen when it all came out.'

'Bloody hell! Dirty old bastard.' Liam took a sip of his pint. 'I don't remember hearing about that. Surely messing about with a schoolgirl while his wife was on her deathbed would be front page news, even if the guy's career was on the wane.'

'You'd think,' Tess said. 'There would've been plenty of people happy to spill the beans too. The village en masse was appalled, obviously, and a lot of people got hurt by it. Sarah found out, poor soul – people said the shock probably brought the end on sooner. And the girl Ade had been screwing around with had a devoted boyfriend who went right off the rails when he discovered she'd been cheating. God knows what sort of contacts Ade's got in the press but there was never a sniff of it in the papers.'

'Why would he agree to come back here?'

Tess shrugged. 'For the money, I suppose. Fifteen years is a long time, and there's no one still in the village who was involved in the business. Besides, what's the worst that could happen? He kept it out of the press then, and no one cares enough to make it public now.'

'Still, it sounds like he won't be made very welcome. Why come back just to open the Guy Trail? The fee can't be much.'

'Perhaps he owes Angela a favour,' Tess suggested. 'Like I said, he must have some press contacts to have kept the scandal off the front pages. Angela's been in the biz a while, and she's worked for bigger papers than our local rag.'

Liam sipped his pint, which he'd almost forgotten about while he'd been caught up in Tess's story.

'Did Angela know about any of this?' he asked.

'She must do by now, at any rate. People have been talking about nothing else since it was announced.'

'You say there's no one left in the village involved in the scandal? What about this schoolgirl Ade was messing about with?'

Tess gave a tight smile. 'The schoolgirl was Leonie Abbott.'

'Leonie Abbott!'

'Yep. Helen Judson, as she was then. Leonie's a stage name.'

Liam was about to ask more, but he stopped himself when the door to the pub opened and Angela Campbell came in. She was dressed in her jodhpurs and riding gilet, obviously having just come from a ride on her pony Meg, which she paid Raven to board in the stables at Cherrywood Hall. She seemed to be looking for someone.

'Evening,' Tess said. 'Who is it you're after, Angela?'

'I was hoping I might find young Benjamin in here,' she said. 'I spotted some unsightly graffiti on the bandstand just now. The language used was rather . . . crude.'

'Wasn't the park shut up after the Guy Trail was opened? Peggy or Benjamin usually lock the gates once it gets dark.'

'It was. I let myself in after I put Meg away, to make sure whoever locked up had remembered to chuck the tarp over the bonfire.'

'I didn't know you had a key.'

Angela nodded. 'The parish council gave me one as chair of the committee so I could make the preparations for Bonfire Night. I suppose the graffiti must've happened this afternoon during the opening. I was going to ask Benjamin if he could make it a priority for removal tomorrow before any kiddies spotted it.'

Tess smiled. 'He'll be at my flat doing something unspeakable with Raven, I shouldn't wonder. I'll text him if you like.'

'Ach, no, let the two of them enjoy themselves. I'll try him on his cell later.' Angela glanced at her watch. 'Well, I suppose nine isn't too late to stay for a drink, although I seem to struggle to stay awake much after ten nowadays.'

Tess laughed. 'It's only eight, Angela. Clocks went back last night, remember? You must've forgotten to change your watch.'

'No, it's next weekend.' She blinked. 'Isn't it?'

'Nope. Always the last weekend in October.'

Angela tutted as she reset her watch. 'I really must get one of those smartwatches that does it automatically. I'm far too forgetful these days. Lucky my iPhone magically adjusted itself and popped up a reminder about the Guy Trail opening or I'd have missed the whole thing.' She took a seat on the barstool next to Liam. 'Well, just the one then. I have to look after the old ticker these days – doctor's orders. I'll have a double whisky please, Tess. Straight up, no ice.'

'This crude graffiti in the park,' Liam said. 'Was it about Screaming Ade Adams, by any chance?'

Angela frowned. 'Now, who told you that?'

'Just a guess.' Liam nodded to Tess. 'I've been hearing all about his stint as public enemy number one around here. I suppose you've been filled in yourself by now, have you?'

'Oh, I knew already.' Angela paid for her whisky and took a tentative sip. 'Bev Stringer told me.'

'But then why book him?'

She turned to Tess. 'Tess, what's been the big topic of conversation in the pub tonight?'

'Well, Screaming Ade opening the bonfire.'

'Exactly. And since the announcement we've sold . . .' She took out her mobile phone and opened up the app the committee used for online ticket sales. 'Another forty tickets for Bonfire Night – more than double what we'd sold so far. Does that answer your question, Liam?'

'I don't get it,' Liam said. 'People round here hate the man, don't they?'

'That's what I was counting on. There's only one thing more fascinating to people than celebrity, young man, and that's notoriety. Mark my words: now Ade and Leonie have been announced as judges, our Guy Trail's going to make a killing.' She took another sip of her whisky and pulled a face. 'The odd bit of graffiti is a small price to pay if the bonfire sells out at five pounds a ticket. It's for charity, after all.'

'Wow. That's...kind of evil.' Tess nodded. 'I'm impressed.'

Angela laughed. 'Well, if that isn't the nicest thing anyone's ever said to me.'

'Do you know Ade, then?'

'Not well but yes, a little. He was an acquaintance of my late husband's.'

'Something wrong with the whisky?' Liam asked Angela when she sipped it and pulled another face.

'Oh. No, it's fine. I just can't get used to the taste.' She smiled at the look on his face. 'I know, a Scot who doesn't like whisky. Hard to believe, isn't it?'

'If you're not a whisky fan, why are you drinking the stuff?' Tess asked.

'The *Gazette*'s got me working on a piece comparing whiskies served in the local area. I tried to explain to my editor that I wasn't a whisky drinker, but all he hears is the accent. He'll have me reporting on caber-tossing and porridge-making next week, I shouldn't wonder.' She took another sip and coughed. 'What is this one, Tess? I'd better make some notes about its woody undertones and bouquet of chocolate-chip cookie dough, or whatever sort of thing I'm supposed to write.'

Tess turned to read the name of the distillery from the bottle. 'Highland Barrel.'

'Right. Another one I can check off.' Angela took out a notepad and scribbled down the name.

'What others have you tried?' Liam asked. 'I like a good Scotch. If you've got any recommendations, you can send them my way.'

'See for yourself.'

Angela handed him her pad, which was covered in doodles, shorthand symbols and scrawled notes. Under the title 'whiskey feature', seven brands were listed in a table. Each column had the name of the pub that served it, some notes on the scent and flavour and a score.

'You've given them all one out of five,' Liam pointed out.

Angela shrugged. 'They all tasted like a one.'

'Wow. You really don't like whisky.'

'All right, all right, keep your voice down. If sales of Scotch plummet because I've been badmouthing the stuff down here in Sassenach country, I'll never hear the end of it.' She nodded to Liam's pint. 'If I wipe the lipstick off my glass, what do you say to a swap? I'll trade you the rest of my whisky for the rest of your beer.'

Liam laughed. 'Deal.'

Angela grinned and took out a clean tissue to wipe the rim of her tumbler.

'I remember what I was going to ask before,' Liam said to Tess. 'What happened to that man you mentioned?'

Tess frowned. 'What man?'

'The boyfriend. The one who went off the rails when Leonie Abbott left him for Ade.'

'Him?' Tess shrugged. 'I couldn't tell you. He left the village a while ago, much to everyone's relief. No one's seen him for years.'

Chapter 5

'You're glum tonight,' Tammy observed as Oliver tramped moodily beside her early one evening a couple of days later.

It was Halloween, and the village was thronged with legions of adorable little ghouls and goblins as they followed lit jack o' lanterns from door to door, trick-or-treating. Oliver knew some of the kids from St Stephens' Messy Church group and tried to summon a bright smile for them as they passed by, but bright smiles felt like an effort tonight.

He'd offered to take Raven's dog Roger for a walk, mainly to escape his parents. His mum and dad weren't engaged in any bedroom activity, thank God, but they'd invited Bev and Ian Stringer and some other old friends over for wine and nibbles and the party had become increasingly raucous. When they'd started trading sex stories, Oliver had hastily made his excuses.

Oliver roused himself. 'Sorry, Tam. I'm the worst sort of company tonight. I bet you wish you'd stayed at home.'

'No, I'm glad you called me.' She looked up at him. 'Sorry I've not been around much lately.'

'That's OK. I know you've been busy getting ready for Thailand.'

He glanced down at her hand, wondering if he ought to take it. They'd held hands a lot when they'd first got together in the spring. Now . . . somehow it didn't feel quite natural any more.

'So why all the glum?' she asked. 'Stressing about your parents?'

'I am a bit worried wine and nibbles might have descended into a full-scale orgy. It felt like they were one bottle of Mateus Rosé away from car keys in the fruit bowl.'

She laughed. 'I think you're lucky. I'd love to have fun parents like yours.'

'Fun parents are all very well when they're being fun somewhere else. When they start doing it in my vicarage, it's not nearly such a laugh.'

'It's sweet, though. A lot of people who went through what they went through . . .' Tammy looked awkward. 'I mean, losing your brother. That sort of thing puts a lot of strain on a marriage.'

Oliver closed his eyes, thinking back to when they'd lost his older brother Archie. Archie had been just eighteen when he'd died of a heart condition, a side effect of his Down syndrome.

'It's the sort of thing that makes or breaks it, I guess,' Oliver murmured. 'It could have gone either way, but in the end I think sharing that grief made Mum and Dad's relationship stronger. God knows I was no help to them. They were worried to death about me after Archie died.'

'What did you do to worry them? You never did tell me.'

'No, and I'm not going to now.'

'Oh. OK.'

'Maybe one day,' Oliver said in a gentler voice, noting her hurt tone. 'But . . . not yet. When I'm ready. Sorry, Tam.'

'If that's what you want.'

There was an uncomfortable silence before Tammy changed the subject.

'So is it your parents getting you down?'

'Partly.' Oliver sighed. 'But . . . no. Not only that.'

'What is it, then?'

Oliver looked at her hand again. 'I don't know. Life, I suppose.' He forced a smile. 'Are you all packed for the big trip, then? Not long to go.'

'Nearly.' She smiled, although the smile looked a little wistful. 'I can't believe I'm finally going to do it, can you?'

'I'm so pleased for you, Tam. I know this is what you've always dreamed of.' He glanced at her. 'Not that I won't miss you, obviously.'

'I know. I'll miss you too.'

'Well, it's only six months. Email when you can, OK? I want to hear all about your adventures.'

They'd reached the grounds of Cherrywood Hall now, and Oliver bent to let Roger off his lead. There was a 'No Dogs on the Grass' sign, but since Raven owned the place and Roger was her dog, Oliver guessed it was allowed. Roger immediately ran to the pagoda-style summerhouse and cocked his leg to mark it as his property.

Tammy turned to face him. 'Oliver, look. I was glad you

asked me to come out tonight, because . . . well, I've been meaning to talk to you.'

Oliver sighed. 'I was afraid you were going to say that.'

'Were you?'

'I suspected it was on the horizon.'

She smiled sadly. 'You've felt it too, right?'

'Yes. But I thought, if we could just get through this trip . . .'

'I like you, Oliver. I really like you.' She looked away, touching a fingertip to the St Christopher medallion around her neck. 'But it isn't just going to be this trip, is it? I want to travel – see places. Not just this one time – for the rest of my life, maybe. It isn't fair to expect you to be waiting for me every time I come home.'

'I like waiting for you.'

'What I'd really love is a boyfriend who'd want to come with me,' she said quietly. 'I get that you can't, though, when your parish is here, and your friends. I'd never ask that of you.'

She took his hand, and Oliver pressed his eyes closed. 'You don't have to say it,' he whispered.

'Oliver, being with you these past few months . . . I wouldn't change it for anything. But this, us – it isn't right, is it? We've both felt it. It's not only that we want different things out of life. We just don't work, somehow.' She squeezed his hand. 'You deserve something better – we both do. Something . . . something like what your mum and dad have got.'

He gave a wet laugh. 'You had to remind me.'

'I know you must want that. The sort of love that lasts a lifetime; that can weather all of life's tragedies. The sort where you can't keep your hands off each other, even after forty years.' She swallowed. 'And I know you can never have that with me.'

Oliver pulled her into his arms when he heard her sob. He kissed the top of her head.

'Not going to try to talk me out of it?' she whispered, nestling against his chest.

'Do you want me to?'

'No. But I'm going to miss you like crazy, all the same.'

'Likewise. You'll still email, won't you? I want to hear about everything.'

'Of course. I won't forget you, Ol.'

'I won't forget you either.' He kissed her again and let her go. 'Goodbye, Tam. And . . . thanks for the memories.'

*

When Oliver had finished saying his last goodbyes with Tammy, he dropped Roger back with Raven. If she and Tess had been alone at home, he'd probably have sobbed out the story of his latest love-life failure, staying over for an evening of wine and tears as per break-up tradition. But Tess had a singing gig tonight at some hotel's Halloween do and Raven was spending a cosy evening in with Benjamin, so he'd kept the story of his break-up for another day and gone home to check his parents hadn't caused a major scandal by having a full-on orgy on the vicarage lawn.

When he got back, the other guests had disappeared.

His mum was washing-up while his dad stood behind with his arms around her, kissing her neck.

'Has the party broken up?' Oliver asked, trying not to look at where his dad's hands were.

'No, just relocated,' his mum said. 'The others have gone to the Star. I didn't want to leave you with all our mess so I said I'd tidy up before we joined them.'

'That's all right.' What Oliver really wanted was the house to himself as he brooded on his unhappy return to singledom. 'I don't mind finishing off the washing-up.'

'Oh, nonsense. I won't have it said we don't earn our keep.' His mum glanced at him. 'You OK, sweetie? You look worried.'

Oliver forced a smile. 'Just preoccupied. I . . . can't think of a topic for this Sunday's sermon.'

'That still sounds so strange to me. My baby boy, giving sermons at church.' His mum giggled as his dad nibbled her ear. 'Give over, Paul. You'll embarrass the lad.'

'Not him. He's a man of the cloth now, love. They're like doctors: professionally detached from the sins of the flesh. It's impossible to embarrass them.'

'What a vivid phrase that is, the sins of the flesh,' Oliver murmured. 'So graphic and . . . haunting.'

Paul let his wife go and turned to grin at Oliver, spreading his arms wide to display the apron he was wearing. 'Remember this old thing, lad? Ian found it in his garage. I wondered where it had got to.'

Oliver winced at the apron, which bore the torso of a scantily clad and generously bosomed French maid. The thing had been the bane of his childhood, when his dad – convinced this was the absolute height of comedy – had insisted on wearing it to every family barbecue.

'I was sort of hoping it'd been burnt,' he said.

'Best purchase I ever made, this.' His dad winked. 'This, my young apprentice, is the secret of my success with women. If you can make 'em laugh, they're yours. You remember that.'

'All right. I'll borrow it to wear for Sunday service, shall I?'

'Now you're talking like a son of mine.' Paul nudged his wife. 'Come on, love. You can finish the washing-up later.'

She glanced at Oliver. 'You're sure you don't mind?'

'Not at all. Actually I'd appreciate a night to myself. It'll give me a chance to work on that sermon.'

'All sorted, then.' Oliver's dad slapped his wife on the backside. 'Get your coat, Nettie. You've pulled.'

'Erm, Dad? You're not wearing that apron to the pub, are you?' Oliver called as they left the kitchen.

'Course,' his dad called back. 'It's Halloween, isn't it? Besides, I bet they need a bit of livening up down there.'

Oliver grimaced as he heard them leave the house. He'd spent so much time cringing since his mum and dad had come to stay that he was surprised he had any grimace left, but apparently he was in no danger of running out.

He was heading to the living room, privately resolving that this Sunday's sermon would be about 'moderation in all things' in the hope his mum and dad would take a hint, when there was a knock at the door.

Typical. Trust someone to turn up just when he'd been

looking forward to a night by himself, coming to terms with his break-up over a few glasses of red.

Oliver glanced at his watch. It was after nine, so he doubted it was anyone wanting to consult him professionally. His parents had the spare key. Was it Raven? Tammy?

But when he answered the door, Oliver discovered the person outside was neither Raven, Tess, Tammy nor anyone else he might have expected to see there. Instead, in the stark illumination of the vicarage's security light, he found himself looking at the haggard, unshaven features of someone he hadn't seen in a very long time.

Oliver didn't pause. He didn't even think. Pulling back his arm, he punched the man full in the face.

Chapter 6

Tess let her mind wander as she belted out 'Jolene' for the patrons of the hotel she'd been hired to sing at, none of whom were paying the slightest bit of attention.

She'd much preferred the wedding she'd played at on Saturday. The grooms and their guests had been true Dolly fans and Tess had loved geeing them up in her best Southern drawl, getting everyone singing along. Anyway, it had impressed the hotel manager, who'd engaged her for tonight's Halloween shindig too.

There wasn't much of a party atmosphere, however. A couple of guests had made a half-hearted attempt at fancy dress – there was a mummy decked out in what was probably a week's supply of his suite's loo roll, chatting to a couple of sickly-looking zombies – but the bar was mostly filled by the unfortunate attendees of a work conference, still wearing their business suits and name badges after the day's sessions. The music was just background to them as they got drunk, chatted and tried to convince fellow conference-goers to accompany them back to their rooms. Still, they weren't actively jeering her, the money was good and it was another singing gig to add to her CV, so Tess was content.

'What shall we give them to finish, Tess?' the guitarist asked. 'One more, then that's us done.'

'Let's have a bit of Dusty Springfield. You've got the music for "Spooky", haven't you?'

'Well, yeah, but that's not Dolly.'

'What does it matter? They're not listening. Besides, it's Halloween.'

The man shrugged. 'You're the boss.'

Tess gave herself free rein to enjoy herself as she belted out the song. After eighteen months impersonating Dolly and Cher at the pub, she was a bit sick of their back catalogues. It was nice to do something different.

It was while she was leaning forward with the mike that she spotted a familiar face sitting at the bar. He was all dressed up in a smart shirt and blazer – a far cry from the mud-splattered jeans he tended to be wearing when she spotted him on a gardening job or chasing down another escaped dog.

Liam. And he wasn't alone. He was talking to a gorgeous dark-haired woman who was obviously flirting with him, resting her long fingernails on his arm and laughing. Tess couldn't see the woman's face fully, but she was certain it was no one she knew. She'd remember someone with a figure like that.

So this was how Liam spent his weekends, was it? Every time Tess saw him, he tried to convince her to go on a date with him. Whenever he flashed those big, sad brown eyes at her he seemed to be endeavouring to convey the impression that he spent his evenings languishing alone at home, dreaming of the day she'd give him a second chance. And all the time he was gadding about in hotel bars, getting touched up by beautiful, seductive women who didn't smell of beer, never had to dress up in rhinestone jumpsuits and knew how to contour properly.

Well, she didn't care. Liam was a free agent, and so was she. She'd told him on multiple occasions that she wasn't interested in romance with him, so it was fair enough if he chose to go looking for it elsewhere – or looking for something elsewhere, at any rate. She was only surprised, that was all.

Tess pulled her gaze away, trying to focus on her singing, but her eyes soon drifted back.

Was she a girlfriend, this woman? Surely not. It was only a couple of days ago that Liam had been trying to convince Tess to let him take her out for a meal. Liam Hanley could be a tricksy bugger, but would he really play two women at once?

There was only Liam and his date at the bar. As Tess watched, Liam's friend stood up and appeared to make her excuses. Liam kissed her hand before she left, looking deeply into her eyes, but as soon as she was gone his expression changed. The flirtatious smirk disappeared, replaced by a hard, determined look, and he took out his phone.

Had she been reading it wrong? Perhaps it wasn't a date but a case that Liam was on. What had he said when she'd bumped into him while walking Roger? Something about an infidelity sting?

When the song had finished, Tess said a hasty goodbye to the band and made her way over to Liam.

He glanced up when she approached, fixing his face into the flirtatious simper again, but he dropped it immediately when he saw it wasn't his lady friend.

'Tess? What the hell are you doing here?'

'I might ask you the same question.' She took a seat on his girlfriend's barstool.

'You have to go,' he said in a low, urgent voice. 'Seriously. You're drawing attention to me.'

'Don't be daft. How am I drawing attention to you?'

'Tessie, you're dressed as Dolly Parton.'

'Oh.' Tess glanced down at her rhinestone jumpsuit. 'Right.'

'Are you going to go?' Liam demanded. 'That huge blonde wig must be visible from space.'

'Tell me what's going on first.' She lowered her voice. 'Are you working?'

'Yes, I'm working. And you're about to ruin my whole operation.'

'I knew it! Is it the infidelity case you told me about?'

'Yes it is. Now can you go? She only went to fetch her handbag.'

'After you tell me what you're doing. Are you a honey trap?'

Liam nodded. 'I've got it arranged with Helen's husband. He's upstairs in the hotel room I booked. All I need to do is get her up there, and I very nearly had it cracked when you showed up. Trust me to pick the one hotel where I was going to run into an ex.'

'I'm not a real ex.' She raised an eyebrow. 'You look like you're enjoying yourself, anyway.'

'Are you kidding? I'm bored stiff.' Liam took a morose swig of his Martini. 'She's obsessed with crystals and astrology and all that woo-woo bollocks.'

'Really?'

'Yeah, it's like being on a date with Peggy Bristow. Look, Tess, I love you but please can you bugger off? I need this job.'

Tess tried to suppress the relief she felt on learning Liam was only acting the part of an interested lover. 'All right. But if I can help—'

'For the hundredth time, Tess. We. Are not. Partners. Go sing "Nine to Five" or something.'

'No, I'm going home. That was our last number. See you later, Lee.'

She was about to leave when she spotted the woman Liam was with coming back and did a double-take.

Tess hadn't been able to see the woman properly when she was on the stage, but now she had a full view of her face. She was wearing a wig and it looked like she'd had some work done since Tess had last seen her in the flesh, but she knew full well that the woman's name wasn't Helen – not any more.

It was Leonie Abbott.

*

The man now splayed across the vicarage's front lawn got unsteadily to his feet.

'Jesus Christ, Maynard!'

'Watch the mouth,' Oliver growled. 'This is Church property.'

'Watch the mouth! The one you just socked me in?' The man rubbed his fast-bruising jaw. 'Would never have believed you could throw a punch like that.'

'Mikey Feather.' Oliver shook his head. 'I never thought I'd see you again. What the hell do you think you're doing here?'

'I could ask you the same question, mate.'

'I'm very, very far from being your mate, Mikey.'

'All right, I get it. Time heals all wounds except one. But what . . .' Mikey trailed off as for the first time he seemed to register Oliver's dog collar. 'You've got that on for trick or treating, right?'

'I have not. This is my parish. And you've got some nerve showing your face in it again, after the stunts you pulled.'

'You think I don't know that?' Mikey looked like he was still struggling to come to terms with Oliver's vicarship. 'But . . . where's old Springer?'

'Dead. Two years since.'

'Oh.' Mikey paused while he processed this. 'And you're really the vicar here? You?'

'I'm standing in the vicarage doorway wearing a clerical shirt and dog collar, Mikey.'

'But . . . I mean, how?'

Oliver laughed. 'I graduated from theological college, did six years of curacy under Reverend Springer, then he passed away and I applied for his parish. The usual way. Is it really so hard to believe?'

Mikey considered this.

'I guess it must be true then,' he said finally. 'Shame about Springer. He was good to me, the old Rev. Came to see me inside and everything. I never had much time for religion but he was one of the good ones. I mean he believed it, all that love your neighbour stuff. Lot of them say it, but they don't give a shit about you when the chips are down.'

Oliver's brow unknitted a fractional amount.

'Is that what you came for?' he asked. 'To see Reverend Springer?'

'Yeah.' Mikey ran a hand over his brow. 'Been out three months and I'm struggling, Maynard – I mean, your reverence. Father.'

'It's just Oliver. What are you struggling with?'

'Work. Somewhere to stay. Thought the vicar might be able to put me in the way of a job. I'm going straight.'

Oliver smiled dryly. 'We've heard that before.'

'On my life this time.' Mikey looked bashful, which didn't suit him. 'I met someone while I was inside – a woman. We'd been talking to each other online and I hoped we'd have a future together, once I was out. A proper fresh start.'

'Can't this girlfriend put you up?'

'It's a bit complicated. Bels has got a housemate who doesn't want the likes of me around the place, which is fair enough, I guess. We want to find a place together, but I need to be working first and no one wants to employ an ex-con.'

'Where've you been staying for the past three months?'

'Hostel. Sometimes an old mate's sofa, if they can spare it. Bus shelter when there's nowhere else.'

Oliver was silent, thinking this over.

'Couldn't Caleb give you sofa space for a bit?' he asked. 'He's been straight for a while.'

'Caleb doesn't want his big brother around. Told me as much. He's got a wife and young family to consider.' Mikey laughed bleakly. 'Not the sort of influence you want around the kiddies, is it? Uncle Mikey turning up to teach them the old family trade.'

'Well, your sister, then.'

'After the funeral? Tess won't want to see me.'

'Neither do I, yet somehow here you are on my doorstep.'

'Yeah, I get that.' Mikey looked at him. 'Look, I'm sorry, Oliver. About Archie. I never meant . . . but that doesn't matter. I guess I had that punch coming.'

Oliver felt his anger rise again, just thinking about it. 'You knew he didn't understand,' he said, his voice rising in pitch as he spoke. 'Archie only saw the good in people, and he thought you were his friend. He didn't know you were asking him to break the law. You took advantage of him because he was a better person than you, and because . . . because you knew no one would suspect a lad with Down syndrome of doing something like that. It was a wicked thing to do.'

'I was young,' Mikey muttered, looking at the ground.

'Nineteen is a long way from being a child. Of all the shitty things you've done in your life, Mikey, I hope you know that the way you exploited my brother was one of the worst.'

'Oliver, I've got nothing,' Mikey said quietly. 'I'm destitute here. All I want is help to make a decent start. Springer was my last hope.'

Oliver closed his eyes. A battle was raging inside him.

He hadn't realised his anger towards Tess's older brother was still so raw, until Mikey had shown up tonight and he had instinctively reacted with his fists. It must be sixteen years since it had happened, but that hadn't dulled the edge.

Archie hadn't understood that his supposed new friends, Mikey's little gang, were getting him to break the law when they asked him to steal vodka from a local shop. Only Oliver and his parents knew how distressed Archie had been when the police had come to their home to confront them with the CCTV evidence of his shoplifting, and the awful conversation which followed as his mum and dad had tried to explain that sometimes people who seemed to be friends were actually following their own agenda. No charges had been brought, but Archie had been so hurt when he realised his new friends had tricked him. A little bit of his trust in the world disappeared that day. Then less than two months later, he was dead. Remembering how this incident had marred his brother's last few weeks on earth made Oliver want to hit things; to swear aloud and cry tears of rage.

But he couldn't, could he? A now thirty-five-year-old Mikey was here on his doorstep, desperate, nowhere to go, and Oliver had a Christian duty to forgive his brother unto seventy times seven even if a more basic human instinct was urging him to lash out. If these things were always easy, there'd be no need for faith. He ought to help the man, no matter what had happened in the past. Even the Mikey

Feathers of the world were entitled to a second chance. More than all that, Oliver knew it was what Archie would want him to do.

'What about your dad?' Oliver asked, although he had little hope from that quarter. The answer, when it came, was exactly what he expected.

'Inside.'

'Matt's still abroad?'

'Yeah, out in Oz.'

Oliver sighed. 'You realise Tess is going to kill me for this?'

Mikey brightened. 'You'll help me?'

'I'll . . . see what I can do. Come inside and we'll have a talk.'

Chapter 7

It was four days after the incident at the hotel that Tess next ran into Liam. She'd been dying to find out what had happened that night. Tess had fled the scene as soon as she realised who Leonie was, anxious not to be identified. Thankfully her heavy makeup and Dolly wig meant her old acquaintance was unlikely to have recognised her at a distance.

Leonie certainly wasn't the fresh-faced teen Tess remembered, back when she'd left the village with Ade fifteen years ago to launch her pop career. These days, even in disguise Leonie was pure showbusiness. Her lips were plump, her face shiny, her eyebrows shaped and waxed, and her chest looked to have doubled in size. Of course Tess had seen Leonie on TV, minus the black wig she'd been wearing on her date with Liam – usually she was an elfin blonde – but people never looked quite the same under the cameras as they did in real life.

It had been Leonie's eyes that had allowed Tess to figure out who she was. Everything else about her might have changed, but they were the same: a distinctive cloudy green. They held a certain little-girl-lost quality at odds with her seductive sex-kitten appearance; a look that belonged not to Leonie Abbott but to Helen Judson, the person she'd once been. Tess remembered Helen as a pretty, vivacious, fun-loving girl, with a vulnerability she tried to hide under a bubbly personality. She'd been the singer in a band that had included Tess's brother Caleb on drums as well as some other sixth-form kids, and Tess in the year below had admired her like nobody else in her little world.

They hadn't been friends exactly – school was a time when you'd as soon think to cut off your own foot as form a friendship with someone in a lower year – but Leonie had taken Tess under her wing in an almost sisterly fashion when she'd discovered she had a set of pipes on her and had given her tips for strengthening her voice.

Tess sometimes wondered what life would have been like for Helen Judson if Ade Adams had never come into her life. Probably she'd have married the boyfriend she'd seemed so deeply in love with, bought a home in Cherrywood, started a family. Perhaps she might have kept up the singing in her free time – with a proper job to pay the bills, of course. Perhaps she'd even have been happy.

But Helen had been ambitious. Cherrywood wasn't enough for her – she had talent and looks, and she wanted to be a star. So when Screaming Ade Adams – married and nearly forty-five years her senior – turned up offering her everything she'd ever wanted, it was too much for the eighteen-year-old girl to resist. She'd kicked the dust of Cherrywood off her heels, apparently sparing little thought for the dying wife Ade left behind him and the boyfriend whose heart she broke, and gone to her new life as Leonie Abbott without a look back. She was someone else entirely now – at least, Tess had thought so, until she'd seen the expression in her eyes that night at the hotel.

Anyway, Ade had been as good as his word. He'd got Leonie everything she wanted – the recording contract she'd so desperately craved; wealth; celebrity. But was she happy? Tess doubted it, if she was spending her free time picking up men in hotel bars while her jealous husband hired private detectives to catch her out.

Tess had texted Liam as soon as she was out of sight to let him know who his client really was, but she had no idea if he'd picked up the message in time. He hadn't texted back, and he hadn't been into the pub since either. As keen as she was to know what had happened, Tess was too proud to text him demanding details.

It was while she was walking to the village hall on Saturday afternoon that Tess spotted Liam on a gardening job, raking leaves in Dot Hobson's front garden. Quickly she altered her route, crossing the road like that had been her plan all along. She pretended to stroll nonchalantly past, then did a double-take as if seeing him for the first time.

'Oh. Hiya. You OK?'

Liam straightened up to face her. 'Since you ask, I've been better.'

She stared at the black eye he was sporting. A florid purple bruise had appeared around his half closed right eye. 'Bloody hell, Lee!'

'I'd like to say you should see the other guy, but it was me who copped it.' He touched the area gingerly. 'I feel a proper plum.'

'Who did that to you?'

'Your pal Leonie Abbott. She really socked me one.'

'You're kidding!' Tess took a seat by him on the garden wall. 'Come on, what happened?'

'Well, I got your text. Read it while she was ordering us another couple of drinks. Anyway, I didn't see that it was any reason to change my plans. A case is a case, and if her husband doesn't trust her then who am I to turn down a fee? She was obviously up for a bit of infidelity so it seemed to me she only had herself to blame.'

'You didn't know it was Ade who hired you?'

Liam shook his head. 'He gave a fake name. Everyone seems to be at it.'

'Then what?'

'I flirted a bit more, waited until she seemed nicely chilled, then I invited her up to my room. Soon as we got there, Ade jumps out of the en suite with an "Aha!" like the jealous husband in an Edwardian farce.'

Tess settled herself more comfortably on the wall. 'Go on.'

Liam frowned. 'Not if you're going to sit there looking like you're enjoying it.'

'Sorry.' Tess tried to fix her face into an expression of abject sympathy. 'How's that?'

'Hmm. An improvement. But you'd better mean it.'

'Oh, I do, I do. Get to the punching bit.'

'All right.' He glanced around, as if worried someone

might overhear. 'Soon as she sees him, Leonie says, "For God's sake, Ade, not this again." Then she turns to me and says, "Get your thirty pieces of silver, did you?" Next thing I know, she's taking a swing. Tell you what, for a skinny girl she's got some right hook on her.'

'She's a black belt in judo. She was on our school team.'

'Is she? You could've mentioned that in your text.'

'What happened then? Did they have a blazing row?'

'That was the weirdest bit,' Liam said. 'Ade started laughing. Like not a "ha ha ha, gotcha" sort of a laugh, but all merry, as if he genuinely found the whole thing hilarious. Then he held out his arms to her, and – what do you think?'

'Did she punch him as well?'

'Nope. She burst into tears and went to him for a hug. It was all a bit sick really.'

'That's weird,' Tess murmured. 'Did he say anything to her?'

'Something like, "Don't forget, I can always find him." I left then. Told him my invoice would be in the post. I felt weird hanging about watching their marriage collapse.'

'Or not, by the sounds of it.' Tess pondered. 'I wonder what that meant. Who can he always find?'

'Any lovers she decides to entertain, I suppose.'

'But he didn't say *them*, he said *him*. That sounds like someone specific.'

'It was bizarre, no doubt about it. There was no sense of threatening her with divorce if it happened again or anything. It was like Ade just wanted her to know he could always catch her out.' Liam touched his sore eye. 'Anyway, not much point speculating. I got my fee. Not sure it was worth it really, but cash is cash.'

'You should send Ade an additional invoice for all the bags of frozen peas you must be getting through.' Tess hopped off the wall.

'Where are you headed?'

'The village hall.' She smiled. 'You might want to keep your head down if you want to spare your remaining good eye.'

'Eh?'

'I'm going to meet the pair of them – Ade and Leonie. A few of us from the committee have been volunteered by Angela to give them the tour of the guys so they can judge the winner before the bonfire tomorrow.'

'How well did you know Leonie Abbott, Tess?'

'We weren't best friends or anything, but I suppose you could say we were part of the same gang,' Tess said. 'She was in my brother Caleb's year at school. They were in a band together.'

'How many brothers and sisters have you got?'

'Three. I'm the youngest. The only girl.'

'Three big brothers! I bet no boys ever dared to mess you about, did they?'

She smiled tightly. 'Only one.'

'Where are all these brothers?' Liam asked, choosing to ignore that dig.

'Oh, here and there. We don't see much of each other now we're grown up.'

'Will Leonie remember you, do you think?'

67

'I'd be surprised if she didn't. She was always round at our house.' Tess paused. 'It'll feel weird to see her again after the way she left.'

'Will you say anything to her? I mean about this big scandal fifteen years ago?'

'No. Probably not.'

'Probably not?'

'I have to admit, there are a few things I'd be curious to know. But in the interests of keeping the peace, I should probably keep my mouth shut.'

Liam smiled. 'Now, if I were a betting man . . .'

'No. No, I'm going to be good. That was all a long time ago.'

*

Tess made her way to the village hall meeting room where she and some other members of the committee were due to meet Ade and Leonie. She found Angela and Raven already there, obviously in the middle of a pretty salacious gossip.

'You never!' Raven was saying.

'Swear on my life.' Angela crossed herself solemnly.

'You locked him out without a stitch on him?'

Angela nodded. 'Man had a face like Buster Keaton after a house had just fallen on him, wearing nothing but a bow tie and some whipped cream in places I'd rather not go into detail about. That protected his modesty pretty well. There really wasn't much to hide.'

Raven laughed. 'What did he do after you shut him out of the house?'

'What could he do? He had to drive buck-naked to the

other girlfriend's place to beg her for a pair of pants. What he didn't know was that she and I were in cahoots to catch the two-timing bastard out. He found all his clothes in pieces in the front yard.'

'I was going to ask what you two were talking about, but I'm not entirely sure I want to know,' Tess said.

'Tessie, I swear this woman needs to write a book,' Raven said, turning to her. 'She was just telling me how she got her own back after she found out her boyfriend was cheating.'

Angela smiled. 'Oh, I'm sure you young people have got stories of your own that could shock even an old reprobate like me.'

Raven shook her head. 'Not like yours. I can't believe the stuff you've done, Angela.'

'Well, that was in the good old days, before the docs told me my heart wouldn't stand too much fun of that kind. After that I took up riding instead. I hope I'll never be so broken I have to give that up, even if I am fifty-six.'

'I was serious, though – you really ought to write your memoirs. I bet you could be a bestseller within a week.'

Angela laughed. 'Maybe when I'm in my dotage and everyone I'd want to mention in them is gone. For now, I think features on whisky and interviews with *Emmerdale* stars for the *Gazette* are better suited to a quiet life.'

'I always wanted to do that as a kid,' Raven said wistfully. 'Become a journalist, I mean. I was going to apply for the NCTJ Diploma after uni.'

'How come you didn't?' Tess asked. 'You used to write up a storm for that little school paper we had.'

'Oh, story of my life. Grandmother wasn't keen. I'm sure she had this image of me in a dirty mac and fedora, slumming it with the gutter press in a way quite unbefitting a Walton-Lord. Anyway, she managed to talk me out of it as usual.'

'At least you've ended up doing something creative, I suppose.'

'Writing copy for posters and greetings cards? They'll have me replaced with an AI bot within the next year, I shouldn't wonder,' Raven said. 'You know, sometimes I feel like my life to date is just a series of missed opportunities. I wish I could've been more like you, Angela.'

'Ach, I'm sure you don't,' Angela said. 'It wasn't all fun and games, you know.'

'Even so, I'd have loved to be that sort of free spirit. I ought to have stood up to Grandmother more when I was younger.'

'Don't you and your grandmother get along, then?'

'No, we do – well, sort of,' Raven said with a sigh. 'I mean I couldn't bear to live with her, but Grandmother's sweet in her old-fashioned, upper-class way. It's just that our views of the world are so very different. I try to make my own way but at the same time I hate to think of hurting her. I feel like I've made too many compromises.'

'Well, kiddo, it's never too late for a change,' Angela said, clapping her on the shoulder. 'If you've still got a hankering for journalism as a career, why not come along to the *Gazette* offices with me one day and see how it all works? I can introduce you to some people who can give you advice.'

Raven brightened. 'Would I be allowed to do that?'

'Sure you would, if I tell the editor you're with me. OK, so you're a little older than the usual work experience kids we have, but I think you'd get a lot out of it. Then if it's still something you feel like you want to pursue, you're armed with all the facts you need to tackle Candice.'

'Thanks, Angela. I'd genuinely love to.'

The door opened and Oliver came in.

'Hi everyone. Sorry I'm late.'

'Are you all right?' Angela asked, frowning at him. 'You look worn out, Oliver.'

Oliver rubbed his eyes. 'Yeah. Just a busy few days, that's all.'

'Right.' Angela looked at him curiously. 'Well, shall we walk to the park?'

'Are we not meeting them here?' Tess asked.

'That was the original plan. I thought we could have a cuppa and a chat before going to look at the guys, but Leonie sent me a message asking if we could meet at the bonfire instead.'

'Why?' Oliver asked.

Angela shrugged. 'Wants to get it over with, I expect.'

The four of them left the hall and headed towards the park. While Angela was deep in conversation with Raven, sharing another anecdote from her misspent youth, Tess plucked Oliver's elbow.

'Sure you're OK?' she said in a low voice. 'You're very pale, you know.'

'I'm fine. It's just having my mum and dad over. Visitors

can really take it out of you, especially when they're perpetually randy.' He grimaced. 'They're having such a wonderful time, they've decided to stay another week.'

'Poor Oliver,' Tess said feelingly. 'Any time you want to hide at ours you can. Or I'm sure Tam would be glad to give you sanctuary.'

Tess was sure she saw her friend flinch.

'Thanks,' he said. 'I might take you up on that.'

She frowned. 'What's up, Ol? Are you fretting about Tammy's trip to Thailand?'

'No. Not exactly.' He sighed. 'We broke up, Tess.'

'Oh no. I'm so sorry, love.' She pressed his arm. 'When did it happen?'

'Tuesday. Halloween night.'

'Tuesday? That was four days ago. Why didn't you say before?'

'It never seemed to be the right time. You've been working, Raven's been busy with Benjamin, and I've had Mum and Dad to think about. And then there was—' He stopped.

'What?'

'Nothing. Some work stuff I've had to deal with.' He glanced at her. 'How's your family, Tess?'

She blinked. 'My family?'

'Yeah.'

'Same as they ever are. Why do you ask?'

'It's been a while since you mentioned them. I wondered if everything was OK.'

'When is it ever OK with the Feathers?' She shrugged. 'Our Caleb's doing well, at least, working as the caretaker for a community centre. Having Jess and the kids in his life really seems to have straightened him out.'

'I'm glad. And . . . the others?'

'Matt's out in Oz, working in construction apparently, although God knows if it's legit. As for Dad and Mikey . . . your guess is as good as mine.'

'You don't hear from them?'

'Dad phones when he remembers I exist and asks me to visit him at whichever of His Majesty's finest institutions he's currently being put up at. Mikey . . .' She scowled darkly. 'He hasn't been in touch since Mum's funeral. He wouldn't dare.'

'You're not curious to know if he's doing OK?'

'Why should I be? He never gave a monkey's peanuts about whether I was doing OK, did he?' She glanced at him. 'I'm surprised you're asking after him, after what he did to your Archie. You never brought him up before.'

'I suppose he's been on my mind lately – all of them, I mean,' Oliver said. 'I'm a vicar, Tess. It's part of my job to worry about people.'

Tess sighed. 'I've been thinking about them recently too. I'll ring Caleb this weekend and see if he's heard from Dad or Mikey. It'd be good to know where they are, at least.' She looked at Oliver. 'You're not asking about my family just to change the subject, are you?'

'Why would I be?'

She squeezed his arm. 'I know you had high hopes for you and Tam, Ol. If you're not ready to talk that's fine, but . . . here if you need me, eh?'

'Thanks, Tess.'

They'd entered the park now, where two figures were standing by the bonfire: one a woman in her thirties with cropped hair of dyed golden blonde, immaculately if not very appropriately dressed in a short, skintight dress and high heels. The other was a man in his seventies wearing a tasteless polka-dot suit with wide lapels that just screamed 'look at me, I'm whacky!', with a mane of long white hair. Anyone who didn't know the pair might assume they were grandfather and granddaughter, but Tess knew better.

'There are our guests of honour,' Tess murmured to Oliver. 'Let's go renew old acquaintances, shall we?'

Chapter 8

It was only 3.30pm, but the light was already beginning to fade as the welcoming committee approached the two VIPs.

Tess noticed immediately that Ade's expression was distinctly at odds with the forced jollity of his trademark whacky suit. It was clear he would far rather be somewhere else. Leonie, on the other hand, was prodding the witch guy as if she found it rather fascinating.

'How does its head stay on?' she was asking Ade.

'How should I know how its bloody head stays on? Who cares?'

Leonie gave a high-pitched, girlish giggle, and he turned a look of contempt on her.

'How much did you take, Leonie?' he muttered.

'What do you care? You've taken enough in your time.'

'I can't bear to see a woman in that state. It's disgustingly unattractive.'

'I pay for the stuff, don't I?' she said, sounding petulant now. 'I pay for it just like I pay for everything. I'll take as much as I like.'

Ade grabbed her arm. 'And who've you got to thank for

your money, you ungrateful bitch? You'd have nothing, be nothing, without—'

He broke off when he noticed the group approach and dropped his wife's arm, but he didn't change his expression. Tess thought back to what Liam had told her. The warning Ade had given his wife; the macabre hug . . .

'Mr Adams. Miss Abbott,' Angela greeted the couple, assuming her businesslike chairperson voice. 'Welcome to—'

'Let's just get this over with,' Ade said. 'Show us the damn scarecrows so we can all go home and climb into a drink.'

Tess nudged Raven. 'Not quite the jolly prankster he pretends to be on air, is he?' she observed under her breath.

'He's a charmless wanker,' was Raven's more frank assessment. 'I hope we can get this done quickly. I've got a date with Benjy and a bottle of gin tonight.'

Tess glanced at Leonie. It was evidently something far stronger than gin that had turned her pupils into pinpricks as she wobbled the witch's head from side to side in fascination. Tess made a sound to attract her attention. Leonie looked up at her, but with no sign of recognition.

'Of course,' Angela said to Ade. 'We ought to make the most of the remaining light – it gets dark so early now the clocks have gone back.'

Ade had turned to sneer at the witch while he fired up his vape.

'Reminds me of my ex-wives,' he said. 'Now there's a coven of witches. With one spell, they've made all my money disappear.'

'How many ex-wives have you got, Mr Adams?' Tess asked.

'Huh. Enough to keep me poor.'

A cloud of pungent menthol steam from Ade's vape enveloped them, making Angela cough.

'Let's go see the other guys, shall we?' she said, with forced brightness. 'Follow me.'

Angela cast a glance at Oliver, who took the hint and tried to instil new life into the conversation.

'I think you'll be impressed by the guys, Mr Adams,' he said. 'Every group in the village has contributed one, even the littlies from the nursery, and most of the houses have one in their garden. You'll find it a difficult job to choose a winner.'

Ade didn't give any response to this except a grunt.

'You'll be wanting to make notes and things, I suppose,' Oliver said doubtfully, observing the absence of any sort of notepad.

'Don't you worry about that, padre.' Ade tapped his temple. 'I keep it all up here. Like a steel trap, even if I am seventy.'

Leonie snorted, and Ade shot her a filthy look.

'For Christ's sake, girl, sort yourself out,' he muttered aside to her, although not quite under his breath enough to make it inaudible to Tess, who was nearest them. 'We're not at home now.'

Leonie gave a harsh laugh. 'Who cares? You'll still be a lying old goat of seventy-seven, no matter where we are.'

'Do you want to take this back to the hotel?' he said

between his teeth. 'We can go now, if you want, and see what happens. I'm not too old to make you sorry for that.'

Leonie fell silent at once, dropping her gaze.

'Um, we're very excited to have you judge the Guy Trail for us, Mr Adams,' Raven said, following a look from Oliver that clearly passed the conversation baton to her. 'A lot of newer village residents had no idea we'd ever had a television star living here. There's been a lot of buzz about it.'

Ade look rather gratified at the reference to his short-lived career in television. He turned to look at Raven, and for the first time his face kindled with interest.

'What's your name, honey?' he asked, moving closer.

'Er, Raven. Raven Walton-Lord.'

'Walton-Lord, eh?' He looked enquiringly at Angela. 'Knew a couple of those once. Richer than sin. Same family?'

Angela nodded. 'Same family.'

'I suppose you married in, did you?' he said to Raven.

'No.' Raven looked uncomfortable at the old man's proximity. 'I was born in. I'm not married.'

'Aren't you indeed?'

Angela cleared her throat, edging between them. She gestured to the first guy. 'Well, Mr Adams, here we have Mr and Mrs Cartwright's guy, which I think you'll agree is rather daring. It's a caricature of our local MP, who was involved in a cash for access scandal recently. It's been in all the papers.'

Ade gave the pie-eating MP on the toilet a calculating look.

'Looks like he chose the wrong friends,' he said quietly.

'Miss Walton-Lord, perhaps you could show me the next one?'

Leonie, who'd been staring with fascination at the Cartwrights' guy, turned sharply to look at her husband as he walked to the next garden with Angela, Raven and Oliver. He'd slipped one arm around Raven's waist and she was leaning uncomfortably away from him. Tess was about to follow, but something made her hang back.

'Are you all right?' she asked Leonie.

'He's either getting blind or greedy,' she muttered, apparently to herself. 'That one's far too old.'

The others were well out of earshot now, and only Tess and Leonie remained outside the Cartwrights' place.

'Um, if you don't mind me saying, your husband's quite different in real life to his radio persona,' she observed.

Leonie snorted. 'Don't I know it?'

'You and him . . . are you . . . you know, all right?'

Leonie took out a vape of her own, switched it on and inhaled deeply. 'No need to worry about me, hon. Fun and games. Virginia Woolf.'

'Virginia Woolf?'

'As in, nothing to be afraid of.' Leonie trilled a false-sounding laugh. 'What I mean is, my husband and I understand one another well enough.'

Tess had promised herself she wasn't going to bring up the past tonight. But now she had Leonie all to herself, a mystery wrapped in an enigma inside a deep fake tan, she couldn't resist.

'You don't remember me, do you?' she said.

'You? How would I know you?' Leonie gave her little false laugh again. 'I'm sure we don't mix in the same circles.'

It was odd, that laugh. Helen Judson had never laughed in that juvenile, artificial way. Whatever her faults had been – her drive for success whatever the cost being chief among them – Helen had still been bright and confident and . . . well, real. Was it the drugs Leonie had obviously taken that made everything she said and did feel like a performance?

'We did once.' Tess nodded to the rest of the group, who were now a couple of gardens down. 'My friends Oliver and Raven too. We were at Plumholme together. You were in the year above us.'

'Plumholme? My God, that appalling hole.' Leonie exhaled steam from her vape. 'I was another person then.'

'So I see,' Tess murmured. 'You don't remember me at all, then?'

Leonie looked Tess up and down with her odd, glazed eyes. 'Why, were you someone important?'

'No. I've never been anyone important. Just plain old Tess Feather.'

'Then why on earth should I remember you?'

'I thought you might recognise the name. My brother? You were round our house all the time.'

Leonie blew two columns of steam from the corners of her mouth, making her look a little like a dragon. 'Sweetie, I've known a lot of brothers.'

'What happened to you, Helen?' Tess asked quietly.

Leonie shrugged. 'I levelled up.'

'Really?' Tess nodded in Ade's direction. He was now sneering at the guy made by the village Brownie pack. 'You think being married to that abusive old perve is levelling up? I heard how he was talking to you. I bet there are bruises on your arm from where he was holding you.'

Leonie gave her a sharp look. 'Who even are you? Are you anybody worth noticing? I don't remember you, or your friends, or your brother. I don't remember anything about this dump except that I hated it and it hated me. Oh, and the names. Whore. Homewrecker. Gold-digger. Far worse things than Ade was called for his part in it, although he was old enough to be my grandad and I wasn't much more than a kid – that's what this village did to me. So do me a favour, whatever your name is, and keep your boring, ordinary, jealous nose out of my life.'

*

The next day was Sunday the fifth of November – Guy Fawkes Night. It marked the end of Cherrywood's first Penny for the Guy Trail, culminating in the bonfire pyre in the park finally going up in smoke.

Tess would be rather relieved to see the end of the Guy Trail. The dummies that had taken up residence in Cherrywood, casting long and not quite human shadows down quiet streets and into dark corners, had given the place a haunted feel. And it wasn't only the guys she'd be glad to see the back of. The dramatic return of Leonie and Ade had brought back memories of the past that had unsettled her too.

However, she found her spirits improving as she prepared

food for the bonfire. The little kitchen in the flat had filled with delicious scents: fresh-baked pork pies; syrupy ginger parkin; rich treacle toffee. She hummed as she stirred a vat of sugar and golden syrup destined for toffee apples, occasionally dropping some decadent little treat on the floor for Roger as he sat optimistically at her feet.

Tess had been a big fan of Bonfire Night as a kid. She hadn't known, then, about the grisly history she'd been reminded of recently by Peggy Bristow. She'd only known that it was an exciting night of sound, colour, delicious food and breathtaking spectacles that had brought warmth and light to the otherwise dreary period between going back to school and the Christmas holidays. It had been something to look forward to in the autumn months, when she and her brothers were young and the family at least relatively happy. That was a long time ago, but the joyful memories evoked by the sweet, spicy smells couldn't help but lift Tess's mood.

'You're up early,' Raven observed when she appeared in the kitchen in her pyjamas.

'Only by your standards. It's ten a.m., Rave.'

'Well, it's early to be making toffee anyway,' she said, nodding to the bubbling pan. 'Weren't you working last night? I thought you'd need a lie-in after a late shift.'

Tess left off stirring to fix her flatmate with a stern look. 'Maybe I did, but some pillock volunteered us to contribute to the food tent tonight, didn't they? Some pillock who I notice has been conspicuous by her absence this morning while I've been toffeeing my fingers to the bone.'

Raven shrugged. 'It's only fair that you do the cooking after I made our Guy Trail contribution.'

'You mean that thing?' Tess said, nodding to the four-inch-high dummy stuffed with pins on the windowsill. Raven had constructed it last week using an old tea towel, a Sharpie and some very average sewing skills. 'That's not a guy, Rave, it's a voodoo doll.'

'Exactly. In keeping with the spooky theme.' Raven picked the thing up and stroked it fondly. 'I call him James-Dave-Joe-Tyler-Kyle-Zach.'

Tess turned back to stir her toffee. 'Aww. You named it after all your most twatty exes. That's sweet.'

'Yep.' Raven casually repositioned the pin sticking in the dummy's heart to its groin. 'I've already warned Benjy that there's room for another name if he steps out of line.'

'Where is Mr Loverman? Still in bed?'

Raven hopped on to a stool at the breakfast bar. 'No, we had to cancel last night's date. He'd had a job on that overran so he wanted an early night. It was just me and Rodge with a bowl of popcorn.'

'That's a shame.'

'To be honest, I was relieved.' Raven shuddered. 'I wasn't in the mood for sexy fun after having that creepy old bastard's wandering hands all over me yesterday. I stayed in the shower until I'd practically shrivelled up and I still felt dirty.'

Tess's lip curled. 'God, wasn't he awful? I'll be glad when he's out of the village again.'

'I don't know how Helen or Leonie or whatever she calls herself these days stands him.'

'Well, Helen's got her own secrets,' Tess murmured, bending to check on the parkin pigs she had baking in the oven.

Raven lifted an eyebrow. 'Oh?'

'Swear you won't tell anyone? Liam'll kill me.'

Raven licked her finger and crossed herself. 'Hope to die and may demons stick hot pokers up my bottom for all eternity if I tell. Come on, spill.'

'Lee was on a case the other day at the hotel I was performing at.' Tess took her parkin pigs from the oven and started arranging them on a wire rack. 'Infidelity sting – a cheating wife. And who should that wife be but . . .?'

'No!'

'Yep. Ade hired Liam under a fake name to catch her out. Lee said it was really weird. As if Ade didn't want to stop her cheating; he just wanted to make some big power play, show her who was in control.'

'After the way he was with her yesterday, I can believe it.'

Tess turned the toffee apple syrup down to simmer. 'I'd promised myself I wasn't going to bring up the past but I couldn't help it. I had to know if she recognised me.'

'And did she?'

'Nope. Not at all.'

'What did she say?'

'Oh, she was determined to do her rich bitch impression.' Tess paused with her hand on the cooker. 'Somehow it didn't quite ring true, though. Almost like it was a defence mechanism rather than something real.'

'She really didn't remember? I thought if she recognised any of us, it'd be you.'

'She didn't even react when I told her my name.' Tess shook her head. 'I thought at least that would get some sort of response.'

Raven hopped off her stool to help herself to one of the parkin pigs.

'Oi.' Tess slapped her wrist. 'That's charity parkin, that is. You can pay for it just like everyone else at the bonfire.'

'It's only a burnt one. No one wants to pay for that.'

'My parkin pigs are not burnt.'

'Whatever you say, darling.' Raven finished the pig in double-quick time before Tess could snatch it back and proceeded to lick the ends of her fingers. 'I'd be surprised if Leonie remembers anything much these days, to be honest. Did you see her eyes?'

'Yeah. What does that to someone?'

'Ketamine? Cocaine? Something illegal and expensive, no doubt.'

Roger jumped up at her leg, annoyed that his humans weren't involving him in the conversation, and Raven crouched to pet him.

'I hope this little guy will be OK tonight,' she said to Tess. 'I feel awful leaving him when there'll be fireworks going off.'

'Peggy's an animal lover. She'll know how to reassure him.'

'I hope so.' Raven tickled the dog's ears thoughtfully. 'I know she hurt a lot of people, but you have to feel sorry for her, don't you?'

Tess blinked. 'Peggy?'

'Don't be daft. Leonie.'

'Oh. Her again.' Tess shrugged. 'She sold her soul to the devil and discovered her heart's desire was also her worst nightmare. That's the thing about Faustian pacts – there's always a catch. Leonie Abbott got exactly what she bargained for.'

'Still. She was so young, Tess.'

'I know. But whatever Helen Judson had in life, she always seemed to want more.' Tess stirred her toffee thoughtfully. 'There but for the grace of God, eh?'

Chapter 9

The bonfire started that evening at seven p.m. Tess and Raven, having done more than their fair share of the organising, had been given the night off by Angela so they could enjoy the festivities. After taking Roger to spend the evening with Peggy Bristow and her cat-slash-familiar Nelson, they made their way to the park.

It had been raining earlier, but now the night was chill and crisp: perfect bonfire weather. The air was filled with the smell of woodsmoke and Tess hummed as they made their way through the village.

'You're in a good mood,' Raven observed.

'Not exactly. More sort of . . . nostalgic. I always get that way on Bonfire Night.'

'How come?'

'I suppose it reminds me of when the family were all together. We used to go to the big village bonfire, then later we'd have a miniature one in our garden with sparklers and parkin pigs. The Feathers were never what you might call functional, but we were happy for a while.'

Raven reached out to squeeze her friend's hand, and Tess, smiling, squeezed it back.

'So what's the plan for the night?' Raven asked after a little silence.

'Angela's going to give a speech, then Ade will announce the winning guy and set light to the bonfire.'

Raven smiled. 'It's funny how different Angela is when she goes into head-of-the-committee mode. She's such a laugh when she's off duty, it's hard to remember it's the same person.'

'I know, she's like Jekyll and Hyde. I mean if Hyde was less evil and more, just, really bossy and well-organised.'

'I'm dying to see her in *Macbeth*. I can't imagine it, can you?'

Tess took a piece of the bonfire toffee she'd made from its paper bag and popped it into her mouth. 'She's playing one of the witches, isn't she?'

'Yep.' Raven laughed. 'The idea of her dancing round a cauldron chanting about fillets of fenny snakes is pretty hilarious. Can't wait for my sneak preview.'

'What sneak preview?' Tess mumbled as her teeth struggled to get to grips with the chewy toffee.

'On Tuesday night. She invited me to watch the first dress rehearsal.'

'Right. Because you guys are bestest mates now. I knew you'd trade me in one day.'

'Oh, don't start being jealous. Angela's cool, that's all. The sort of cool I want to be when I'm her age.'

'It's early for a dress rehearsal, isn't it? They're not performing for two months.'

'Angela organised an early one under performance conditions as a practice run for the new Players, and to get some advance feedback from a few people. I suppose she's nervous about her stage debut.'

Tess laughed. 'Angela nervous?'

'I know, hard to believe.' Raven helped herself to some treacle toffee. 'You ought to come along too. I'm sure she won't mind, as long as we still buy tickets for the real thing.'

Tess groaned. 'You mean sit through a Cherrywood Players production – twice? You know I only go to them because otherwise I get mucky looks from Bev in the pub.'

'Go on, keep me company. You're not working; I'm not seeing Benjy: we can make it a proper girls' night. With Ol too, of course. He's an honorary girl.'

Tess smiled. 'Don't say that to him, for God's sake.'

'Oh, he knows full well.' She took another piece of toffee. 'I guess he told you about Tammy?'

Tess nodded soberly. 'Poor lad. I think he really believed this was it.'

'Did you think it was?'

'I suppose. Why, didn't you?'

Raven shrugged. 'At first, maybe. Lately . . . I don't know. She's a lovely girl, perfect for him in a lot of ways, but something always felt like it was missing to me.'

'What was missing?'

'I don't know. Chemistry. *Je ne sais quoi*. Whatever the thing is that makes someone the person you're destined to be with.' She tapped her nose. 'Trust me, I can smell incompatible couples. It's like a sixth sense.'

'Yeah? Then why's it taken you so long to find the right guy?'

'Sadly it only works on other people.' Raven glanced at her. 'So is Liam coming tonight?'

'Why'd you ask me that right after mentioning your sixth sense thing?' Tess asked, narrowing one eye.

'Just moving on to another subject. It's called the art of conversation, darling.'

'Well, I've got no idea. I'm not the man's keeper, am I?'

At the park, they handed their tickets to the committee member on the gate and joined the already sizeable crowd.

'Seems like Angela was right about notoriety selling tickets,' Tess said. 'There must be a hundred people here already.'

'There's Kennedy, look, with Angela,' Raven said, pointing to their friend standing by the barrier tape that encircled the bonfire. 'Who's with them?'

Tess squinted. It was night, but a lot of people had torches and the refreshment marquee was giving out some light so they weren't completely in darkness. She could just make out a woman in a large, shapeless coat and bobble hat standing at Kennedy's other side.

'Kenn's sister, I think – Seana, the university professor. I haven't seen her since I was a kid.'

'Me neither.' Raven laughed. 'So that's two potential spies for the bishop in our midst. Oliver's going to be thrilled.'

'Let's just hope his parents manage to keep their clothes on. You know how bonfires bring out that primordial human urge to get starkers and dance around. Come on, we'll join them.'

They pushed through the crowd until they reached Angela, Kennedy and her sister.

'Evening all,' Tess said. 'Are we ready then, Angela?'

Angela cast the bonfire an irritated look. 'As long as we can get the damn thing to light.'

'Why do you say that?'

'Some pillock, pardon my French, yanked the tarpaulin off sometime today. The wood's been sitting there saturating in the rain all afternoon.'

Tess frowned. 'I thought we were keeping the park gates locked all day.'

'We did, but someone's still been in. And if I find out who it was they'll be getting the sharp end of my tongue.'

'I wouldn't worry,' Raven said. 'It was only a bit of drizzle. The wood can't be too damp.'

'Hmm.'

Someone tapped Angela on the shoulder, and she turned around to face Oliver and Liam.

'Oh,' she said. 'It's just you two.'

Oliver laughed. 'No need to sound quite so pleased to see us.'

'Sorry. I thought you might be Ade, that's all. He and Leonie should've been here by now.' Angela squinted at Liam's black eye in the light of her head torch. 'What happened to you?'

'That's a story to rival even one of your racy anecdotes,' Liam said as he joined Tess. 'It's got everything. Beautiful women. Jealous husbands. Dolly Parton. But since you're obviously stressed out, I'll save it for another night at the Star.'

'Stressed out is right. It's funny, isn't it, how you can plan something to the nth degree and things still go wrong at the last minute?' Angela cast Oliver a suspicious look. 'It wasn't you who moved my tarp, was it, young Reverend Maynard?'

'Why would I move your tarp?'

'Because there's only me, you and about three other people who've got a key to access this place, which puts you on my very short list of suspects.' She nodded to the witch dummy, which had been hoisted to the top of the pyre and seated in a little wicker chair. 'Unless you think our guy did it.'

'Well, it wasn't me.'

'It's a funny thing, isn't it?' Liam observed, glancing at the pyre. 'Humanity's fascination with fire.'

Kennedy laughed. 'You'll wish you hadn't said that, Liam. Now you're going to get a TED talk from Seana about the mystical and ancient rite of the bonfire. That's one of her specialisms.'

Tess remembered Seana Hamilton from childhood as a shy, earnest, studious young woman, and the passage of time had done little to change that. Seana had been standing quietly while the conversation flowed around her. Now, she treated the group to an uncertain little smile.

'It is rather fascinating, the dual nature of fire,' she said in her soft, childlike voice. 'I mean when it's considered as a totem for us as a species. It was used in the most ancient of rituals. It gives warmth, it cooks food, it can cauterise a wound. We need it to live, and yet we fear it. It gives life and takes it on a whim, and it's in thrall to no one, not even its creator. We can make it, but we know we can never master it.' She laughed awkwardly. 'Sorry. I know I must be very boring, but I just can't help talking about it.'

'No, it's quite fascinating,' Angela said politely.

'The bone fire,' Kennedy said. 'That's where the word comes from, right, Seana?'

Her sister nodded. 'It's the most likely etymology, yes.'

Kennedy glanced at the witch on top of the pyre, its hands folded demurely in its lap, and gave a little shiver. 'God knows what grisly rituals are at the root of that.'

'It's a creepy thing, isn't it?' Seana observed as she too looked up at the dummy. 'Where did it come from?'

'Cherrywood Players donated it to promote their next play,' Tess said.

'You know, in this light you could almost believe it was real.' Seana shivered. 'Sends a chill down your spine.'

'The eye of childhood fears a painted devil,' Angela said quietly, her gaze also fixed on the witch.

Her voice sounded odd. Raven stared at her, and Angela tore her eyes away.

'Sorry,' she said, forcing a smile. '*Macbeth* on the brain.'

Murmurings were beginning as people waited for something to happen. It was now quarter past seven.

'Where the hell is Ade?' Tess asked Angela. 'We should've had the thing blazing by now.'

'Hmm.' She checked her phone. 'Not a word. He hasn't responded to any of my texts or calls, nor Leonie either.'

Kennedy took out a tub of chewing gum and popped a pellet into her mouth. 'Well, what can we do? People are getting antsy.'

'Oh, I'll light the damn thing myself. We can announce the Guy Trail winner after the fireworks, assuming Ade and Leonie have turned up by then. We can't have weans standing here in the cold all night.'

'I hope they do turn up,' Tess said. 'We've sold a lot of tickets on the back of the pair of them opening this thing. We could be facing an angry mob if people feel they haven't got their money's worth.'

'Ade'll be here. He wouldn't dare let me down.' Angela beckoned to Liam. 'You look like a lad who knows how to handle fire. Give me a hand lighting it, will you?'

Liam nodded and followed her under the safety barrier.

'How come he gets given all the manly jobs?' Oliver demanded.

Raven shrugged. 'I wouldn't take it personally, darling. She probably thinks it's against your calling to set fire to things.'

'Huh. I'm just as entitled to set fire to things as the next man. In Old Testament times, half the priest's job was setting fire to things.'

'Oh, here.' Tess took a long packet from her bag. 'Shut up and have a sparkler.'

It seemed Angela had had nothing to worry about, in spite of the untimely removal of the tarp. The bonfire had been stacked well and tightly. She and Liam got to work with their wax tapers, and flames were soon licking around the base of the pyre.

Above the crowd came the high-pitched *wheeee* of a firework from someone else's celebration, and a shower of golden sparks burst out of the sky. Tess found her gaze drawn once again to the witch. It was partially illuminated by the flames now, strange shadows dancing across its body.

She could see why all eyes were drawn to it tonight. It looked even creepier than usual, the hat pulled so far down its face that no features were visible at all. Its knobbly legs in their stripy tights hung heavily, and the hands folded in its lap . . . the hands . . . the . . .

The hands!

'Stop!' she yelled.

Raven blinked. 'What's wrong, darling?'

'Stop the fire! We have to stop it, now! Get water, can you? The buckets . . .'

Tess's gaze darted frantically around the park until it landed on one of the emergency water buckets. She fought her way through the crowd to get to it, then ducked under the safety barrier.

'Put it out!' she shouted to the crowd. 'There's someone up there! Get the other buckets!' But no one seemed to hear her.

Liam was still setting light to kindling. He stared at Tess as she threw her water bucket on the base of the fire.

'Tess? What're you—'

'Liam, we have to put it out! There's someone up there!' She gestured frantically to the top of the pyre.

'What? No there isn't, there's just—' He stopped. 'Shit! Are you joking?'

'I saw its hands, Lee. That's no dummy.'

The next moment he was running for another bucket,

calling to the crowd to help. They didn't ignore Liam. He still had too much of the policeman in his tone. Within seconds, Angela was on the phone to the emergency services and it was all hands on deck. The fire had climbed higher now, reaching a point where the crowd couldn't douse it without the aid of a ladder. Flames had already started to lick at the bottom of the witch's cape.

'Is there a ladder?' Liam called to Angela.

'There should be.' She looked around rather wildly. 'It must have been moved into the refreshment marquee.'

'Hurry. We're running out of time.'

Angela nodded. 'Tess, come help fetch it.'

Tess did as she was told. They soon found the ladder that had been used to get the guy to the top of the pyre and carried it back between them.

'What are you going to do?' Tess asked, watching Liam extend the ladder and prop it against the bonfire.

'I'm going up, of course.'

'It's dangerous, Lee. The fire's still going. Shouldn't we wait for the fire brigade?'

'Whoever's up there, they're either dead or unconscious. If it's the latter, I need to get them down now if we're to have any chance of saving them.'

Before she could stop him, Liam was clambering up the ladder. On his way up, he grabbed a long piece of pallet wood from the base.

'This is as high as I can get,' he called down when he reached the flames. 'I'm going to have to push whoever's up there down for people to catch. Has anyone here got a blanket?'

Several people came rushing forward with picnic blankets. A space was cleared, and a couple of the largest blankets were soon suspended between willing volunteers.

'OK,' Liam called. 'Here we go. One. Two. Three . . .'

He stretched as high as he could, trying to tilt the wicker chair forward without either losing his own grip or touching the tongues of flame that licked above him. On the third attempt, he managed it. The figure went toppling off the chair and volunteers rushed forward with their blankets to catch it.

'Wrap the body in the blanket and roll it on the ground until the flames are out,' Tess instructed them. 'Kennedy! We need a doctor over here.'

'I'm here.' Kennedy appeared at her side, pale but determined. 'Show me where I'm needed.'

The flames had been extinguished now. Tess took Kennedy's elbow and guided her to the blanket.

'Who is it?' Kennedy whispered.

'I don't know,' Tess said, but even as the folds of blanket were pulled aside, she knew that wasn't true. She knew, although she wasn't sure how, that she'd be looking into exactly that face: instantly recognisable in spite of the ghoulish red smile painted over the mouth in lipstick.

The white, staring face of Screaming Ade Adams.

Chapter 10

'Oh my God,' Kennedy whispered. 'What did we do? We killed him!'

'It was an accident. It must've been an accident.' Tess looked at her. 'Can you do anything for him?'

'I . . . Let me see.'

'Everyone stand back!' Tess called to the people surging around, trying to get a look at the body. 'Give the doctor some space.'

Kennedy knelt by Ade and put her ear to his mouth, feeling for a pulse at the neck.

'Is he alive?' Tess breathed.

'I can't say for sure without a stethoscope. If there's a pulse it's very weak.' She moved her fingers to his wrist.

While Kennedy was examining Ade, Tess noticed a singed envelope lying between the witch's cape and the blanket the body was stretched out on. She picked it up and drew out the contents.

Playing cards?

No. Not playing cards. These were tarot cards, weren't they? Three of them. Tess stared at the image on the top one. A child, riding a horse under a blazing sun . . .

'Tess?'

Tess stuffed the cards into her pocket and turned her attention back to Kennedy.

'Can I help?'

'I need you to hum for me.'

Tess frowned. 'Hum?'

'Yes. I need you to hum "Nellie the Elephant".' Kennedy gave her a weak smile. 'It sounds ridiculous, but it's got the right tempo for CPR. I need it for the rhythm.'

'Oh. Um, all right.'

Feeling rather foolish, Tess started humming 'Nellie the Elephant' while Kennedy pumped her hands over Ade's heart. When she was done she covered his mouth with hers, cupping his jaw with the heel of her hand. She repeated the process several times, then checked his pulse and breathing again.

'You can stop humming now,' she said to Tess, letting Ade's wrist drop.

'Did it work?'

Kennedy shook her head.

'Sorry, Tess. No pulse, not even a faint one. He's gone.'

*

Emergency services arrived not long after: a triple bill of fire, police and ambulance. The fire engine didn't stay long once the fire was out, this being their busy night, but the police remained to examine the area.

Liam was sitting on a bench, watching the police officers sniffing around. The paramedics had checked him over for burns and smoke inhalation, and when they'd released him no one had seemed to care that he was still hanging around. His friend Della was part of the police team scouring the park, he noticed.

Tess approached and sat beside him.

'Well, here we go again,' she said.

'We don't know it was murder.'

Tess lifted an eyebrow. 'So you think Ade accidentally dressed himself as a witch, climbed to the top of a bonfire pyre and dropped dead?'

'What's the alternative? Someone did him in and felt the best way to cover up this perfect murder was by dressing him as a witch, heaving him to the top of a bonfire – I'm assuming you've never moved a dead body, but that means we must be looking for at least two good, strong murderers here – on the same day everyone in the village would be gathering to see the thing set alight?'

She shrugged. 'Could be.'

'Right. And who'd do that?'

'Someone with a taste for the theatrical.' Tess shuffled to face him. 'Did you breathe in too much smoke or something? Normally you're the first person to suspect foul play. I'm surprised you're not accusing half of Cherrywood of being in on it.'

'Even if I did suspect foul play, it's not my case, is it?' He nodded to the police, who were picking through the remains of the fire and putting things into little plastic bags. 'Let them handle it.'

'Now that is out of character.' Tess squinted at him. 'Did the paramedics look at you?'

'Yeah.'

'You're OK then? You must've breathed in a fair bit of smoke, climbing up that flaming bonfire like a twat.'

'I believe you mean like a brave hero who knows no fear.' He smiled at her. 'It's nice to know you care, though. Yes, I'm OK.'

Tess let out a snort of laughter.

'What?' Liam said. 'Are my death-defying escapades amusing to you?'

'Sorry. You just look so funny. Your face is covered in soot.' She put a hand to her head. 'I shouldn't be laughing, should I? I feel a bit light-headed.'

'Did you see the paramedics yourself?'

'No need for that. It was the shock of seeing him, that's all.' She shuddered. 'That mouth!'

'What was wrong with it? I didn't see the body close up.'

'Not his actual mouth. Someone had drawn on a Joker smile, like the one the witch had. That's what I'm going to see in my nightmares – that blood-red grin on a staring white face.'

Liam reached out to take her hand. Tess didn't push him away.

'How come you're still here?' he asked. 'I thought the police had cleared everyone.'

'I have to answer some questions, since it was me who noticed the body. Della's just talking to Kennedy, then it's my turn.' Tess lowered her voice. 'Lee.'

'What?'

'Look at these. I found them by the body. I think they fell

from the pocket of that witch costume when Ade was being rolled in the blanket.'

Tess removed an envelope from her pocket and drew out the contents.

Liam frowned. 'Tarot cards?'

'Three of them. One with a sun and child, one an angel blowing a trumpet above a load of naked people, and the other looks like the devil.' She glanced at him. 'Still think it was an accident?'

'Tess, you have to give these to the police.'

'I was going to. I forgot I had them, in all the chaos.'

Liam nodded to Della, who was approaching the two of them. 'Hand them over now, before you get accused of withholding evidence.'

'Right.' Tess hesitated, then took out her phone. 'Hang on.'

She took a photo of each card before tucking them back into their envelope.

'What did you do that for?' Liam asked.

'Just . . . you know, in case they turn out to be important.'

'Oh, no. No.' He turned a stern look on her. 'It's not my case, Tess, and it's definitely not yours. Don't interfere in things that don't concern you.'

'I want to find out more about what they mean, that's all. To satisfy my own curiosity.'

Liam was about to remonstrate when Della reached them. She laughed when she saw Liam's face.

'What happened to you?' she asked.

He rubbed his sooty cheek. 'I've been performing impressive feats of derring-do, if you must know.'

'I mean the soot I can understand, but how'd you get the black eye?'

'Ah. Well, that's another story.'

Della smiled. 'I'll take your word for it. Now sod off while I have a talk with Tess.'

★

Liam left and Della took his place on the bench.

'We really must stop meeting like this, Tess.'

'I'd be more than happy to, if people would stop getting murdered for ten minutes.'

Della raised an eyebrow. 'You think it was murder, do you? Why's that?'

'Perhaps I've just come to expect it.' Tess hesitated, then took out the envelope with the tarot cards. 'Although . . . I did find these.'

She handed them to Della, who examined them.

'Where were they?' she asked.

'Sort of by the body, as if they'd fallen out of a pocket.'

'Hmm.' Della frowned at them. 'An odd selection. The Sun, Judgement and the Devil.'

'You know about tarot?'

'My sister does. She's into all that hippy-dippy New Age stuff.' Della continued to frown thoughtfully at the cards. 'So I suppose the big question is, did these belong to Ade Adams or the witch?'

'Do you know the answer?'

'Not yet, although I know it was the witch's actual costume he was wearing and not a duplicate. We found the dismembered dummy – what was left of it. It had been stripped, taken apart and stuffed into the heart of the fire, along with Ade's clothes.' Della tucked the tarot cards away. 'How did you know it was Ade up there and not the guy, Tess?'

'The hands. Once the flames started getting higher, I could see they weren't stuffed mittens. I could see the fingers.' Tess shuddered. 'Do you think that was the plan? To burn Ade's body up in the bonfire where no one would think to look for his remains?'

'A pretty stupid plan if it was. Burning up a body and leaving no trace is the sort of thing that might well happen in the movies, but in real life it's not that simple. I won't go into graphic detail but the barbecue smell would have given the game away rather quickly, once the flames started to consume it.' Della glanced at the blackened and partially dismantled bonfire pyre. 'What it may have been is an attempt to hide the victim's identity – or to destroy evidence, perhaps.'

'Evidence?'

'Yes. We found the remains of Ade's wallet and what looks like a vaping device in the fire, but the damage means that whatever they might have been able to tell us before, they're worthless now. Still, it's a clumsy way of going about it. Hardly the perfect crime.'

'Do you know how Ade died?'

'At the moment we don't know how, when or why, although your doctor friend and the paramedics agree it probably had nothing to do with the fire. Whether Ade was dying or already dead when you spotted him we won't know until we have the coroner's report.' Della turned to her. 'But none of this needs to concern you, Tess. The best thing you can do is go home, climb into bed and have a hot drink. Is there a friend who can stay with you tonight?'

'My flatmate will be at home. You remember Raven?'

'All too well,' Della said, smiling.

Tess stood up and prepared to leave, but her gaze was drawn back to the bonfire. 'I don't get it,' she murmured. 'Liam said it would've taken two strong men to get a dead body up that pyre.'

'Yes, I'd tend to agree. Getting a fourteen-stone man to the top of a bonfire pyre without disturbing it would be practically impossible.' Della gazed thoughtfully at the charred heap of wood. 'No, it seems perfectly clear to me that there's only one way Ade Adams could have got to the top of that bonfire, and that's by climbing up there himself.'

Chapter 11

The week following the death of Screaming Ade Adams was an eventful one for usually sleepy Cherrywood. His bizarre death quickly thrust the largely forgotten former celebrity back into the limelight. Journalists and photographers descended on Cherrywood in a pack, and for a few days Screaming Ade was front page news again. No doubt he'd have been thrilled, Tess reflected – if he hadn't been rather too dead to enjoy it.

Leonie's profile enjoyed a boost too. Tess hadn't realised she was still producing music. The only time she saw Leonie these days was on reality programmes and panel shows, but apparently she was still bringing out albums. Now every newspaper wanted to talk to her. Leonie, far from being prostrate with grief, basked in the attention – and of course made sure she mentioned her forthcoming album to every journalist she gave an exclusive to.

However, once it was clear that no fresh lurid details were going to emerge, the journalists started to disappear from the streets of Cherrywood. The police, while still investigating, had told the many enquiring reporters that Ade's death was likely to have been by misadventure – one of his infamous pranks gone tragically wrong.

The cause, apparently, had been a heart attack. It was no secret that Ade had been a cocaine user, as well as being a heavy smoker for many years. The idea that he might have dressed himself in the witch's costume in order to prank the village and then suffered a heart attack while waiting to spring his surprise wasn't too much of a stretch. It was exactly the sort of thing he might have staged in an episode of his short-lived TV show, *Screaming Laughs*.

Tess felt uneasy, though. There were the tarot cards she'd found under the body, for one thing. Had they belonged to Ade, or been planted on him? And what was the significance of the cards chosen: the Devil, Judgement and the Sun? Liam had told her to let the police handle it, but Tess couldn't help pondering.

Raven nudged her as she, Tess and Oliver took Roger for a walk up on the moors. 'Why so quiet?' she asked.

Tess forced a smile. 'Sorry. Just thinking.'

'You're not trying to puzzle out those tarot cards again?' Oliver shook his head. 'You're obsessed.'

'Leave it for the police, Tess,' Raven said. 'This isn't like when Aunty Clemmie was killed. We didn't even know Ade, except briefly as an unpleasant, abusive letch. Sorry, but I'm finding it hard to get too emotionally involved.'

'Aren't you guys curious about what the cards were doing there? What they mean?'

'Nope,' Raven said firmly. 'Ade Adams is dead and based

on my experience of him I'd say it's no great loss to the world. Now I'd like to forget all about him and get on with my life.'

Oliver smiled in Tess's direction. 'Not our Tessie, though. You know when there's a puzzle to solve, she can't let it go.'

'I hate unanswered questions,' Tess said. 'Those tarot cards must've been there for a reason. They must *mean* something.'

Raven shrugged. 'Google them then.'

'I did, but I couldn't make much sense of how tarot readings work. There was all this stuff about Major Arkana and Minor Arkana and what it means if you draw them in this order or that order, which way round they are and things. I need it explained to me by someone who knows what it all signifies.' She paused. 'I'm going to talk to Peggy about them.'

Raven frowned. 'You don't think she put them there, do you?'

'God, no, I'm not saying that. She'd know what they meant though, wouldn't she?'

'You'd better be careful,' Oliver said. 'She's probably a bit wary of people turning up to ask her about murders after you and Liam practically accused her of killing Aunty Clemmie.'

'That was all Lee,' Tess said. 'He's the most clodhopping interviewer of suspects I've ever met. God knows how he manages his cases when he doesn't have me to help him.'

Roger had stopped to do his business, so they paused outside Ling Cottage while Raven fumbled for a poo bag.

'Still not found a buyer for the old place?' Tess asked Oliver, nodding to the 'For Sale' sign outside.

'I'm not sure I ever will, after what happened there.' Oliver shivered as he looked at the old stone cottage. 'Even without the murders, I bet it'd struggle to sell. Look at the place. It's the sort of cottage you see on the cover of thriller novels with one lighted window.'

'OK, I'm done,' Raven said, tying a knot in the poo bag. 'Let's turn back, shall we? The wind's freezing my buttocks off.'

They started to walk back, but Tess stopped when she thought she saw a movement from the corner of her eye. She turned to look at the cottage.

'You've not got a viewing today, have you?' she asked Oliver.

'No. Why?'

'I just . . . thought I saw something moving inside.'

'I didn't see anything,' Raven said.

'It was just a shadow through the curtains.' Tess stared at the cottage, which was perfectly still now. 'I thought it was.'

'What did it look like, this shadow?'

'I didn't see it clearly. I just got an impression of long hair.'

Oliver frowned. 'Long hair?'

'Yeah.'

'Well, I suppose it could be the estate agent.'

'You said there wasn't a viewing today, though. Anyway, there's no car. I don't suppose they're in the habit of walking clients up here.'

'Maybe it's that pesky Ling Cottage Ghost again,' Raven said, laughing. 'You'll have to do another exorcism, Oliver.'

Tess massaged her temples. 'I'm probably imagining it.

After what happened at the bonfire, my brain's been a bit . . . well, you know.' She glanced at Oliver. 'Have you got your key? Just to make sure.'

'No, it's back at the vicarage.'

'Try the door, can you?'

He shrugged. 'All right, if it'll make you feel better.'

Oliver went to the front door and jiggled the handle. Then he went to try the back.

'All locked up,' he said when he came back.

'Hmm.'

'Would it make you feel better if I came back later with the key?'

Tess hesitated.

'No. No, don't make a trip up just for my sake,' she said, finally. 'I'm probably being daft.'

'Let's go to the cafe and get a hot chocolate each, shall we?' he said, taking her arm. 'Raven's right, it's freezing up here.'

'OK. That sounds nice.' Tess took a last look at the forbidding cottage, now as still and silent as the grave, before accompanying her friends down the hill.

*

At the desk in his office, Liam opened his email client so he could stare at his empty inbox.

He'd rarely struggled to get cases in London. There was always someone who needed the services of a detective – a wife who wanted her cheating banker husband exposed; a boss worried one of his employees was on the take. But here in

Cherrywood, even a missing dog case was a boon. Tess was right: gardening work and lost dogs were the only things keeping him in business now, and then only just. He was living off his savings and the rent he got from letting out his old office down in London. And that was about to become empty.

And now, for once, there was actually something going on around here. Ade Adams's death was a mystery he could really get his teeth into . . . and it had nothing to do with him. All Liam could do was sit back and watch Della and her colleagues run off in entirely the wrong direction.

They'd been questioning the wife. If he was on the case, he'd have started with the journalist – Angela. He liked the woman, but there were a lot of things that stood out as odd.

Angela Campbell had been the one who'd set this whole thing up. Why would Ade agree to come here, back to this sleepy village that hated his guts, just to judge a scarecrow competition? His fame might've waned but he could still get better gigs than that. Did Angela have something on him? Why had she been so determined to lure him to the village? And then there was her notebook . . .

But there was no point speculating. It wasn't Liam's case and there was an end of it. He picked up his mobile and pulled up the number of the woman who managed the block where his old London office was located.

'Hi, Teri,' he said when she answered.

'Liam! Not heard from you in ages. Still living the dream out in the countryside?'

'Yes and no. I just wondered, when is my office becoming vacant?'

'They're moving out this week. Why?'

'Just something I was pondering.'

'You're not thinking of coming back to us, are you?'

Liam hesitated. 'I'm . . . not sure. Maybe.'

'I'm seeing someone about renting the empty space tomorrow, but I can hold it if you want some time to think about it? You own the space so you're welcome to keep it empty as long as you like.'

'No . . . no, don't hold it. I need the rent. Or actually—' Liam broke off as someone knocked on the door. 'Sorry, I have to go. I'll call you later, OK?'

'Sure. See you, Liam.'

He hung up and called for the person waiting outside to come in. The door opened, and in strode the last person Liam expected to see.

It was Leonie Abbott.

Chapter 12

Liam pretended to finish arranging some papers before coolly greeting his visitor.

'Miss Abbott. Or is it Helen today?'

'Very funny.' She glanced at his eye. 'That looks sore. You should get some steak on it.'

'You know I was just doing my job, right? I've got bills to pay, same as everyone.'

'Some might say that setting people up by pretending you want to sleep with them is a pretty dirty way to make a living.'

'And some might say that cheaters deserve to get caught.'

'That's a rather sweeping generalisation, Mr Hanley. No two situations are ever the same.' She gestured to a chair. 'Am I welcome to sit down?'

'Certainly. I don't hold grudges. Can I take your coat?'

Leonie was wearing a long coat with the hood pulled right up, presumably to avoid any unwanted attention from fans. She removed it and handed it to Liam, who hung it on a hook on the wall.

She wasn't exactly in widow's weeds underneath, although she was wearing black: a short, tight dress that just skimmed her thighs, with a pair of very high heels. She smiled, cat-like, when she noticed Liam taking this in.

'As you can see, since my husband's death I've been in deep, deep mourning.'

She took a seat on the other side of his desk and crossed her long legs.

'Why are you here, Miss Abbott?' Liam asked, resuming his own seat. 'If this is about the infidelity sting—'

'It isn't.' She took out her vape. 'Do you mind?'

He shrugged. 'If it helps you relax.'

Leonie turned on her vape and took a deep drag. Liam tried not to cough in the cloud of vanilla-flavoured steam.

'That's better.' She looked at him appraisingly. 'I won't lie to you, Mr Hanley. I don't like you. I don't like any of your kind, scrabbling around in the gutter for your dirty money on behalf of people like my late husband. But of all the detectives he's sent after me, you were the one who showed the most smarts. Usually I see through them before we get anywhere near a suite.' She took another draw on her vape. 'That's why I'd like to hire you.'

Liam frowned. 'Me? What for?'

'What else? To investigate my husband's murder.' She fumbled with the vape, scowling. 'The police think I'm behind it. I've been hauled in twice for questioning. They've got a man trailing me too – you'll see him outside if you look.'

Liam went to look out of the window. Sure enough, there was a man sitting outside the tearoom opposite who had 'undercover copper' written all over him. Police officers always looked uneasy when they worked in plain clothes.

He sat back down. 'Why hire me? I'm only a humble backwater detective.'

'I told you: you impressed me. Besides, I'm aware of your record. Uncovering the Porter Investment scandal was your doing, wasn't it?'

'Yes, that was me.'

She smiled. 'Ade lost some big bucks on that. So will you take the case?'

Liam hesitated. He needed work, and as he'd reflected earlier, this was just the sort of case he could get his teeth into. Still, something was unsettling him about it. Possibly it was Leonie herself, sitting there so calm and collected. She wasn't at all like the person he'd met that night at the hotel. She was some actor, which meant she was some liar too. Cases weren't easy when you had a client you couldn't trust.

'It'll cost a bit,' he said. 'It's a messy business. A lot of work involved.'

'I expect so.' She took a long drag on her vape, not taking her eyes off his face. 'How does forty grand sound?'

Liam choked, then batted at the vape steam to cover for his shock.

Forty grand! Even in London, that was more than he'd earned in a year.

'Make it fifty and it's a deal,' he said, as coolly as he could. 'Plus expenses, of course.'

'All right, fifty it is.' She took out her chequebook. 'Shall we say half now and half on solution of the case?'

Liam nodded assent, and Leonie started writing the cheque.

'I'll need to ask you some questions before I start,' he said.

Leonie's calm, cool facade seemed to wobble for a moment, and she rubbed her forehead. 'I'm so tired of questions,' she said wearily. 'But if that's what you need, so be it.'

'You seem very different from the last time we met,' he said. 'I believe you're a clever woman, Leonie Abbott. Why did you go out of your way to persuade me you were an airhead?'

She shrugged. 'When I set up these liaisons, I try to be as little like myself as possible. It's a fantasy. I play a part – it's more fun for me that way.'

'Were you often unfaithful to your husband?'

'Is that relevant?'

'It may be.'

'Ade had been impotent for the past four years, if that answers your question,' Leonie said. 'Drugs, and his age. It was a big relief. He was less dangerous when all he could do was look.'

'Was there a voyeurism element to it?'

'If I could find a willing partner. Sometimes Ade would watch, or he'd hide himself away and listen without the man ever knowing.' She smiled at his expression. 'I know what you're thinking.'

'I'm certain you don't.'

'You think I'm no different from a sex worker, giving in to Ade's sick fancies. Certainly I got no personal pleasure out of them. Believe me, Mr Hanley, I've been called all the names you can imagine and then some in my time.'

'I wasn't thinking that at all,' Liam said. 'My thoughts had a far more practical bent.'

'Oh?'

'I was wondering, if you had your husband's blessing to have sex with other people, why did he hire detectives to catch you out?'

'Ade liked to watch me with men but he hated the idea of any of them owning me,' Leonie said, carelessly buffing a manicured fingernail. 'He'd stage these little traps, just to remind me that anyone I chose to sleep with could be working for him. To remind me whose property I really was.' She looked up at Liam. 'I've been called a gold-digger many times, and it's fair to say that's what I was. It was a transaction on both sides – Ade's money and influence for my youth and looks. But while I may have got involved with Ade Adams for the sake of my career, I was still a child. I didn't understand the price when I made a deal with the devil. I didn't kill my husband, but . . .'

'You did wish him dead,' Liam finished for her.

'Yes,' she said quietly. 'I'm not hiring you for my husband's sake, Mr Hanley, I'm hiring you for my own. It's been said that there's no such thing as bad publicity and Ade's death has worked in my favour so far, but a murder charge is the last thing my life and career need – still less a conviction. Still, as for grief . . . Adrian Adams was an obsessive, misogynistic, controlling, violent, evil son of a bitch and I hated his guts. Whoever killed him did me a favour.'

'And yet you claim that in spite of your feelings, it wasn't you who killed him.'

'Would I be hiring you if I had?'

Liam shrugged. 'It's happened before. Murderers get arrogant, and it can be a useful screen. Why do the police think you did it?'

For the first time, Leonie looked hesitant.

'I need to know all the facts, Miss Abbott.'

'Well, for one thing, they're not satisfied with my alibi,' she said after a pause.

'Which is? You weren't at the bonfire.'

'I'm not proud of it, but the day of the bonfire . . . I'd blacked out.' Her cheeks coloured. 'In mine and Ade's hotel suite. We'd argued, he'd said some cruel things, and I'd spent the day drowning my sorrows in vodka and . . . other things. I didn't wake up until the police banged on the door to break the news he was dead.'

'Can anyone vouch for that?'

'The girl on the front desk said she didn't see me leave the hotel. The CCTV backs her up, but the police still aren't satisfied. They think I could have sneaked out in disguise or via a fire exit.'

'Disguises you have, of course. You were wearing a black wig the night you met me at the hotel. Do the police know that?'

'Yes. I own a range of wigs, if you must know.'

Liam scribbled this down on his notepad. 'And your husband. You say you argued. When did he leave the suite?'

'Early. Very early. I'd been out the night before. Got back around five a.m. That was when the fight broke out.'

'Where had you been?'

'A few bars, then a club.'

'Any witnesses?'

'I wasn't with anyone. A few bartenders could probably back me up. I can email you a list of places.' She switched on her vape again and took a drag. 'Although since my husband was very much alive at that point, I don't see the significance.'

'Did your husband say where he was going?'

'No. He never did, although I was expected to account for every second of my time when we weren't together.'

'Any affairs you know about?'

'Plenty, in the early days. But now . . .' She gave a hard laugh. 'Let's just say his eyes were bigger than his belly in that respect. Even if everything had been working downstairs, there was little to tempt the sort of girl Ade liked in an elderly has-been DJ with a drug problem and no money. He'd have been bankrupt years ago if he hadn't been on the Leonie Abbott gravy train.'

'What sort of girl did he like?'

'Young,' Leonie said quietly. 'Late teens, early twenties. No older than twenty-five. The thing is, celebrity can only carry you so far when the women you're chasing weren't even born back when you were a name.'

Liam wrote this down.

'What about motive, Miss Abbott?' he asked. 'You've been up front about the fact you hated your husband, but it sounds like he had other enemies. Lovers he'd abandoned. This ex-boyfriend you dumped years ago.'

Leonie frowned. 'Ex-boyfriend?'

'I hear the boy you were dating took it very hard when you left him for Ade.'

'Did he?' she said vaguely. 'I suppose I would've been dating someone.'

'You don't remember? I'm told he was besotted with you.'

'That was another life, Mr Hanley. Another girl. There may well have been a boy, but I couldn't tell you his name. Anyway, I doubt he's still holding a grudge after all this time.'

'Well, there are others who might be. And yet the police seem convinced you did it. Why?'

She flushed slightly. 'Ade believed I had a lover. Not just a casual partner but someone I cared for. He came to believe, at the end of his life, that I was planning to leave him for this other man.'

'Did you have a lover?'

'Not a regular one. It was just an impotent old man's paranoia.' She smiled bleakly. 'But the police found references to it after they seized his laptop so now they're convinced it must be true. Hence my shadow at the teashop outside.'

'Why would you kill your husband though? You weren't financially dependent on him. Why not just leave him?'

'Because he never would have let me,' Leonie said quietly.

'You don't know what he was like. I tried to leave him once, years ago, and . . . the foulest things came from his mouth. Threats, against me and the people I loved. I could never have left Ade while he was alive.' She glanced up. 'I know how that sounds. But I didn't kill him.'

Liam focused on making some notes. He wanted to believe her – there was something in the woman's eyes that seemed genuine, and rather vulnerable in a way that invited protection. And yet . . . he couldn't forget how convincing she'd been in her other personality, that night at the hotel. The first rule of this job was 'trust no one'. He'd be in a fine pickle if he started ruling out suspects just because they were attractive women who laid a sob story on thick while they fluttered their false eyelashes at him.

'Your husband was a drug user, you said?' Liam enquired.

'Yes – we both were. Cocaine mostly. Ade was a fool to still be taking them at his age, but he always did believe he was invincible.'

'The police still think it was murder, though, not an overdose?'

'Apparently. They must have found out something that makes them suspicious.'

'Any legal medications your husband was taking? Known health issues?'

'Only a heart arrhythmia his doctor picked up recently, but he wasn't being medicated for it. Other than that, he was as strong as a horse. I've got the bruises to prove it.'

'He was physically abusive to you?'

Leonie nodded, averting her eyes.

'It's not how he died so much as the circumstances that I can't get my head around,' Liam murmured, half to himself. 'He must have climbed the bonfire himself. Could it have been a prank that went wrong, or is that what the murderer wants us to think? And why would they want the murder revealed in such a public way? It's bizarre.'

'Well, that's what I'm paying you to find out.' Leonie stood up. 'I have to go. If you have any more questions, I've written my contact details on the back of that cheque.'

Liam stood too. 'Before you leave. Do you know anything about tarot?'

'Not really. Why?'

'Three cards were found near Ade's body.'

Leonie was silent while she processed this.

'What cards were they?' she asked.

'I didn't see them closely, but I think one was a child, another an angel and the third was the devil.'

She laughed. 'Well, that one certainly fits.'

'Was your husband into anything occult?'

'Not as far as I'm aware. But . . . there is this. It might be relevant.' She took out her purse and produced a business card. It was completely black, and at first Liam thought it was blank, but when he examined it under his desk lamp he could see that there was a small symbol and a London address embossed in one of the corners.

'What is it?' he asked.

'Your guess is as good as mine. I found it in Ade's desk. The address is for a bookshop in London, but I thought the symbol looked like it might be occult.'

Liam turned the card in the light, looking at the symbol. It was a sort of upside-down triangle with two diagonal lines within it forming an X. The bottom of the triangle curled outwards, incorporating a V shape.

'I've seen this before somewhere,' he murmured.

'Is it any help?'

'It gives me a starting point, at least. If you find anything else that might be relevant, let me know.'

Chapter 13

Tess came home from an afternoon shift at the pub a few days later to find Raven sitting in front of the TV, staring at her mobile while Roger snoozed on her lap. There was a mystery series on: the sort of thing that Tess loved but Raven always referred to disparagingly as 'granny telly'.

'What're you watching this for?'

'Hmm?' Raven glanced up at the TV. 'Oh. I hadn't noticed the programme had changed.'

'Something up?'

'Nothing.' She glanced at the phone again. 'Probably nothing.'

'Probably nothing?'

Raven sighed. 'Boy problems.'

Tess threw herself down on the sofa. 'Don't tell me you and Mr Perfect have had a row.'

'Not a row. More a sort of... communication issue. Unless I'm imagining it, which isn't unheard of.'

'What happened, Rave?'

'It was a couple of days ago. We were walking Roger and

spotted Kennedy in the playground with her brother's kids, pushing them on the swings. We stopped to chat and Benjy offered to help with the pushing. Then I joked that he'd make a great dad one day.' She grimaced. 'Ugh, what was I thinking? That's not three-month-relationship banter. The words spilled out before I could think.'

'He's not ghosting you, is he?'

'Not exactly. But he's been slow to respond to my messages, and he forgot to put a kiss on the last two. Plus he's cancelled our date tomorrow.'

'I'm sure it's nothing,' Tess said, squeezing her shoulder. 'He could be stressed with work or . . . or any number of things. I sincerely believe Benjamin's too nice a guy to hurt you on purpose.'

'But he is still a guy. Even the nice ones can get freaked out when new girlfriends sound like they're getting baby fever.' Raven frowned at the phone. 'And he hasn't met Grandmother yet. That'll send him running for the hills if nothing else does. She'll probably start lecturing me about freezing my eggs again.'

'She wants you to freeze your eggs?' Tess shook her head. 'She's really getting bad.'

'It's a lot of pressure, being the last of a dynasty. You start feeling like your womb's public property.' Raven glanced listlessly at the TV. 'What rubbish have I got on?'

'It's *Murder, She Wrote*. And don't knock it till you've tried it.' Tess grabbed the remote and changed the channel. 'There. Watch the news, that'll cheer you up.'

'In a schadenfreude sort of way maybe.'

There was a woman on screen being interviewed by a reporter, her face in shadow to hide her identity.

'I was fourteen when I met him,' she was saying. 'He was a friend of my uncle's. Oh, he stayed on the right side of the law. Waited until I was sixteen before he let anything physical happen, but he knew what he was doing. Bringing me presents of clothes and makeup; telling me how much it suited me, "becoming a young woman". I didn't know the word grooming in the nineties, but I do now.'

'His fans might say it's easy to accuse the dead when they're no longer here to defend themselves,' the interviewer said. 'The fact you waited until he was dead before speaking out might be seen as an attempt to make a fast buck. What would be your response to that?'

'I'd remind them of the techniques these people have at their disposal to brainwash the young and inexperienced,' the woman said. 'How they convince them they won't be believed, gaslight them into thinking what's happening is acceptable, make them feel ashamed. Not to mention the powerful friends who can make it all go away with a click of their fingers. I'd ask these defenders if they have daughters of their own, or sisters or nieces, and if they'd accuse them so casually of lying about abuse.' Her voice broke, and she struggled to speak. 'Ade Adams robbed me of my youth and destroyed my mental health. I can promise you, there's nothing imaginary about that.'

'Bloody hell,' Tess muttered.

Raven frowned. 'Did she say Ade Adams?'

'Yeah.' The interview ended, and Tess muted the sound. 'I mean, I knew he was a despicable old letch but fourteen! That poor woman.'

Raven shuddered. 'Eurgh. To think he had his horrible hands on me. Do you think there are others?'

'Almost certainly.' Tess was silent for a moment. 'That certainly increases the number of potential murderers. Seems like Ade's got a dark history. For all we know there could be hundreds of people who wanted him dead.'

'I wouldn't blame them either.' Raven roused herself. 'Well, forget about him. Are we still having our girls' night tonight? Ol's got something on but me and you can go out. I thought we could stop by the *Macbeth* rehearsal, take Roger out for a wee, then have a couple of drinks at the Star. That's about as wild as our nights out seem to get since we became a puppy-owning household.'

Tess grimaced. 'I forgot about the dress rehearsal. Did you promise Angela?'

'I think she'll be disappointed if we don't show up. She's rounded up a few of the Women's Guild ladies to be a test audience. Kennedy's invited too. We can ask her to come for a drink with us.'

'Who else is going?'

'Grandmother and Marianne,' Raven said, counting on her fingers. 'Bev's in the play, of course, playing Lady Macbeth. Peggy's going as well. Probably as chief witch consultant.'

Tess's ears pricked up. 'Peggy?'

Raven shook her head. 'You're not going to interrogate her about your daft tarot cards. We're supposed to be having a fun night out. I don't want Ade Adams spoiling it from beyond the grave.'

'I only want to ask what they mean. I won't tell her where I found them.'

'Leave it, Tess. Ade's dead and after what we saw on the news, I can't say in all good conscience that he didn't have it coming. Let the police sort it out.'

'But what if they get the wrong person? Terry Braithwaite spent time in custody for Aunty Clemmie's murder when he had nothing to do with it, and Peggy only narrowly avoided getting charged too. The police aren't infallible.'

Raven rolled her eyes. 'And you are, I suppose, having seen every single episode of *Murder, She Wrote*.'

'Not just *Murder, She Wrote*. *Columbo* too.'

'Oh, well. I'd march right down to the police station and ask if they've got an opening for a new detective inspector.'

'I'm just going to ask. No harm in asking, is there? Come on.'

*

'Seems daft that the Players have got Bev Stringer playing Lady Macbeth when they could have had Angela,' Raven observed as they walked to the village hall. 'Surely they should have their only genuine Scot in the lead role?'

'You just think that because of your mega girl crush on her. She might be the world's most awful actor.'

Raven shrugged. 'Is it so wrong to want to be Angela when I grow up? She's a feminist icon. Besides, she can't be a worse actor than Bev.'

'True. But as long as Bev's the president she'll keep giving herself and Ian the star parts.' Tess frowned as she spotted Liam under the lamp post by the park gates, shaking the bars. They'd been kept locked since Ade's death, at the request of the police. 'Why's he trying to get in there?'

'Who knows? Who cares? Come on.'

'Yeah. OK.' They started to walk on, then Tess looked back. 'Actually, you go ahead. I'll see you in there.'

Raven frowned at her. 'Tess . . .'

'I just want to know what he's up to. Maybe no one's told him the police want it keeping locked.'

'For God's sake,' Raven muttered. 'For a man you want nothing to do with, darling, you really seem to struggle to stay away from him.'

Tess ignored that remark and left Raven to walk to the hall while she crossed the village green to accost Liam.

'Trying to break in?'

Liam jumped. 'Tess. Do you have to creep up on people like that?'

'Well, you were in the act of committing a felony. As a public-spirited Cherrywooder, it's my duty to question you and potentially make a citizen's arrest with the pink fluffy handcuffs Raven keeps in her knicker drawer.'

'Promises, promises.'

'So why are you trying to get into the park?' Tess asked, leaning against one of the gate supports.

'I'm not.' Liam looked up at the large metal gates with their big padlock. On either side of them was a high fence of spiked iron railings that encircled the park. 'I just wanted to test how secure these were.'

'They look pretty secure to me.' Tess glanced at the spikes. 'I doubt anyone could shin over the fence either. I mean, I assume you're thinking about Ade's murder.'

'I might be. Just recreationally, you understand.'

'Did you see the news tonight?'

'Yep. That widens the pool of suspects a bit, doesn't it? I don't envy Della's job. With the number of people who might have a motive to want Ade dead, finding his killer could be like looking for a needle in a haystack.'

A circle of bushes around eight feet high were planted on the other side of the fence, which meant there was a limited view of the park from outside. In daylight you'd have been able to see the bandstand and the corner of the kiddies' playground, but the bonfire pyre at the far end would have been hidden from view completely.

'My mum used to say that all you really need to find a needle in a haystack is a magnet,' Tess murmured.

'Which would be very helpful, if one knew where to get hold of this metaphorical magnet.'

'I wonder how long Ade was up there?'

'I've been keeping an ear open for gossip and no one seems to have seen him or anyone else come in that morning, although we know the tarp must have been moved sometime between the marquee going up the evening of the fourth and when the drizzle started late morning on the fifth. The park was locked all day as well as overnight, wasn't it?'

'Yes, to stop anyone messing with the marquee.'

'The only people anyone saw going in and out were the Guy Trail committee, but that was later in the afternoon.' Liam looked at the big padlock. 'Has this place always been locked up at night?'

'It never used to be, but it'd become a hangout for kids. When we were teens, me, Rave, Oliver and Kennedy used to come down here with a gang of others to get up to mischief. Harmless enough, really – the odd elicit fag, some heavy petting behind the bandstand.'

Liam raised an eyebrow. 'Oliver?'

'He wasn't born a vicar, you know,' Tess said, laughing. 'Back then he was just an ordinary reprobate teenager like the rest of us. Anyway, some of the kids had started smoking something a bit jazzier than Marlboro Lights, if you get my meaning. That was when the parish council cracked down on us and started locking the place at night.'

'I should've known your bad behaviour would be behind it,' Liam said with a smile. 'What time does it get locked up?'

'Around six, although like I said, on the fifth it was locked all day until around half an hour before the bonfire.'

'So no one could have got in without a key?'

Tess shrugged. 'Looks that way. No sign of the lock being forced.'

'Who has keys?'

'Oliver has one, as chair of the Friends of Cherrywood Park. Peggy and Benjamin – the village hall is responsible for upkeep of the bandstand, so as the hall's cleaner and handyman respectively, those two are keyholders. Albert Whistler, chairman of the parish council. Oh, and Angela had one temporarily as chair of the Guy Trail committee. She'll have handed it back to the parish council now, I guess.'

'Angela,' he murmured. 'Interesting.'

Tess frowned. 'You think one of them was involved?'

'Not necessarily, but I do think whoever was involved must have had a key. I've been all around the fence and there's no way through. I think we've established that it would be practically impossible to go over.' He turned to look at her. 'Where are you headed?'

'Cherrywood Players' dress rehearsal for *Macbeth*,' Tess said, pulling a face. 'I imagine it's going to be as dire as their performances usually are, but Angela roped Raven in, which means Raven roped me in.'

'Angela's in it, is she?'

'Yeah, she's playing a witch. She wants a test audience before they perform it for the whole village next month.' Tess squinted at him. 'What do you care?'

'I'm just surprised. I can't see her treading the boards, somehow.'

'I'm not sure Cherrywood Players really counts as "treading the boards".' Tess nodded goodbye. 'See you then.'

'Hang on.' He put a hand on her shoulder. 'You mind if I tag along too?'

She hesitated.

'It's hardly a date, is it?' he said. 'I'm nosy, that's all. I've never seen a Cherrywood Players Shakespeare production and I want to see if they're as bad as everyone says.'

'I promised Raven we could have a girls' night, though.

It's in breach of our Sisters Before Misters contract if I bring a boy. What's more she'll smirk, and I get enough of that from Bev.'

'As soon as we get there I'll pretend I don't know you, I promise,' he said, putting his hand on his heart. 'Come on, what's the worst that can happen?'

Chapter 14

The performance had already begun when Tess and Liam reached the hall. They crept in quietly and joined the group of people watching. Peggy was there, as well as Raven's grandmother Candice and her companion Marianne, and of course Raven herself, who was sitting with Kennedy and her sister Seana. She beckoned Tess over, but Tess opted to take the seat beside Peggy Bristow. Hopefully, when the cast stopped for a break, she could find a way to introduce the subject she wanted to discuss.

To her annoyance, Liam entirely forgot his promise to pretend he didn't know her and took a seat on her other side.

It was the big opening scene, and Angela, along with Dot Hobson and her husband Barry in a drag role, were standing in front of a painted backdrop showing not a blasted heath but an empty ballroom. This was the Players' big innovation: to set the play in the Roaring Twenties. This probably accounted for the fact that rather than the traditional black robes and pointy hats, Angela, Dot and Barry were dressed in tatty fringed dresses and pearls as faded flappers. Angela looked like a cross between Miss Havisham and Morticia Addams.

'When the hurly-burly's done, when the battle's lost and won!' Angela was screeching, skipping around her bubbling cauldron, as Tess settled in her seat.

'Bloody hell,' Liam murmured in Tess's ear. 'And the award for hammiest acting goes to . . .'

Tess nudged him to be quiet, but she was forced to agree. Even by the standards of Cherrywood Players, there was a cringeworthy level of overacting going on. It was surprising really. She wouldn't have pegged Angela Campbell as a ham.

She cast a sideways glance at Liam. Why had he wanted to accompany her? He often tried to find ways to spend time with her – as long as they didn't involve letting her help him with cases – but he'd only developed an interest in amateur theatre when Tess had mentioned that Angela was in the play. Did he suspect her of being involved with Ade's death?

Tess couldn't imagine why. There was no obvious motive for Angela to kill Ade, and as for opportunity, she'd been with the Guy Trail committee nearly all day on the fifth, and most of the evening of the fourth, when they'd put the marquee up. That didn't leave much of a window for murder. Of all the potential leads, Angela was the last person Tess would have thought of.

Nevertheless, she couldn't help noticing that the crimson lipstick Angela was wearing on stage was the exact same shade as the ghoulish smile smeared across Ade Adams's mouth . . .

It soon became clear that even by the standards of Cherrywood's notoriously awful am-dram group, this wasn't good. Ian Stringer's Macbeth seemed to have forgotten he was a Scot as he waded through his lines in a sort of mid-Atlantic drawl, probably aping some Hollywood adaptation. Ian spent far more time focusing on getting the vowels right in his weird new accent than infusing any emotion into his performance, and consequently had the opposite problem to Angela in that he barely acted at all. Even when Macbeth began his descent into crazed paranoia, Ian's expression didn't shift from the earnest, slightly constipated look he'd worn throughout the play. Bev, meanwhile, played Lady Macbeth as a pouting sex kitten in a low-cut, skintight red dress. It was so painful that Tess was tempted to plead a headache and sneak off, except she was still determined to talk to Peggy.

When the first half ended and the lights came back up, Tess took her chance.

'What do you think then, Peg?' she said to her neighbour. 'Are you offended on behalf of witchkind?'

'I'm offended on behalf of Will Shakespeare. Honestly, I wonder how they keep going.'

'Angela was certainly . . . enthusiastic,' Liam said tactfully.

'Angela was the worst of the lot, which in a production involving Bev and Ian is no mean feat,' Peggy said. 'Did she think it was pantomime?'

'It's definitely not her best work,' agreed Candice, who was on the other side of Peggy. She spotted Raven at the drinks table, talking with Marianne. 'Ah, there's my Raven.

Excuse me, ladies and gentlemen. I need to have some words with my granddaughter.'

The cast started filtering into the little auditorium as Candice left to join Marianne and Raven. Meanwhile, Peggy fixed her face into a simper when Angela approached, looking pleased with herself.

'Prepare to lie through your teeth,' Peggy whispered to Tess.

'Well, what did you think?' Angela demanded of them immediately.

'Well done, Angela, dear,' Peggy said smoothly. 'You were wonderful.'

Angela beamed at them. 'You really enjoyed it?'

'I was glued to my seat,' Tess said, feeling this was at least some degree of honest.

'I hope you don't mind me tagging along, Angela,' Liam said. 'Tess told me about it and I couldn't resist a sneak preview.'

'The more the merrier. Although I hope you'll still buy a ticket for the real thing.'

'Certainly. You know, it takes a lot of guts to perform in public like that. I don't know how you do it.'

Liam was being extra charming tonight, Tess noticed. He was definitely after something. What was that line of Bev's from the play? *Look like the innocent flower, but be the serpent under it . . .*

Angela didn't seem to notice anything amiss, however.

'Oh, you know. Screw the iron balls in place and don't be afraid to make an eejit of yourself.' Angela glanced around the room. 'There's young Raven, I see, with Candice and Marianne. I'd better say hello, since I was the one who invited them. Excuse me.'

'I'll come with you,' Liam said. 'I'd like to say hello too.'

He followed Angela, leaving Tess alone with Peggy.

'That's how they keep going,' Peggy said to Tess in an undertone. 'No one's got the heart to put them out of their misery. We all blow smoke up their bottoms because we're too British to tell them to their faces that they stink.'

'It keeps them out of trouble, I suppose.' Tess nodded to the beverages table. 'Shall we get a cuppa?'

'A very good idea. Shame there's nothing stronger available. I feel like I need it after that.'

They approached the table and Peggy made them both a tea. Tess helped herself to a biscuit.

'I was hoping to ask you for a bit of professional advice, if you wouldn't mind,' Tess said, nibbling her Digestive.

Peggy raised an eyebrow. 'You're after a reading? I thought you were a non-believer.'

'No. I just wondered if you could tell me what some tarot cards mean.'

Tess took out her phone and skimmed through her photos to the three cards she'd found on the night of Ade's death.

Peggy took the phone for a closer look. 'This is an unusual deck.'

'Is it?'

'Well, the illustrations are from the Rider-Waite deck, which is one of the oldest and most widely used, but it's unusual for them to carry pictures without a label or number. Where did they come from?'

'I found them. In the park. I wondered if they meant something particular.'

'Is there any reason why they should?'

'Not that I'm aware. I'm just being nosy really. What can you tell me about them?'

Peggy flicked between the pictures. 'Well, these are all cards in the Major Arcana – twenty-two cards collectively known as the Fool's Journey, which represent major milestones through life. It would be unusual for three to be drawn together in the same reading.'

'Is the number significant?'

'The three-card spread is a popular reading technique. What the cards mean would depend on who the querent was and what they were focusing on when the cards were drawn so I can't give you too much insight, I'm afraid.'

'Generally speaking, though, what do they symbolise?'

Peggy skipped back to the first photo. 'This card, with the child riding a white horse under a blazing sun, is called the Sun card. The child represents joy, purity and innocence, the horse stands for strength, and the sun is for illumination, warmth or new beginnings. The card overall is associated with optimism and positivity.'

Tess frowned. 'Optimism?'

'That's right. There could be a numerological interpretation too. The Sun is the nineteenth card of the Major Arcana, which gives it a base number of one or ten. That means it might refer either to beginnings or to endings. In terms of the four elements it's a fire card – a positive force when you're in control of it but destructive or even fatal if you lose that control.'

This reminded Tess of what Seana had said the night of the bonfire, about the dual nature of fire. Was there a connection?

'There seem to be a lot of layers,' she observed. 'I didn't realise the cards could have so many meanings.'

'Absolutely. The elements, the astrological sign of the person seeking the reading, the seasons, numerology, the position and order of the cards, even the weather – these can all influence what a reading means. You see why it isn't as simple as just telling you what each one symbolises.'

'What about the angel blowing the trumpet?' Tess asked. 'That's called the Judgement card, right?'

Peggy nodded. 'That represents awakening and rebirth – a spiritual awakening, perhaps, or a realisation of destiny. It could refer to letting go of your old self and embracing the new, or coming to a crossroads that will require you to make a major decision.'

'What about the last one? The devil?'

'The Devil card can represent seduction by the material or physical, or it can represent your own dark side. It might denote an addiction to hedonism and instant gratification, or a desire for reputation and status. And it can symbolise individuals too – perhaps a person in one's life who is abusive or controlling.'

'How do they all link together?' Tess asked. 'I can't see

how optimism and positivity links to spiritual awakenings or hedonism.'

'Like I said, I can't make any guesses on that point without knowing more about the person involved.'

Tess paused. 'All right, suppose . . . suppose a specific individual had drawn these cards,' she said hesitantly. 'Ade Adams, for example.'

Peggy gave her a sharp look. 'Ade Adams? Have these got something to do with him?'

'No. That was just . . . a hypothetical example.'

Peggy regarded her through narrowed eyes. 'Where did you say you found these cards?'

'In the park.'

'When, exactly?'

Tess flushed. 'Well . . . it might have been on Bonfire Night.'

'And where are the originals?'

'They, er . . . they might be with the police.'

Peggy glared at her. 'This is the second time you've got information from me under false pretences, missy, and I'm no greater fan of it now than I was before.'

'Sorry,' Tess murmured. 'I knew you could tell me, but I didn't want you to think I was . . . you know, implying anything. It's all innocent, Peg, I promise.'

Peggy glanced at Liam, who was deep in conversation with Angela. 'Your young man will have put you up to it, I suppose. He's a slippery one, that Liam Hanley. You never know what he might be trying to get out of you. And frankly, Tess, you're getting just as bad.'

'He hasn't put me up to it, honestly. It isn't his case, it's mine. I mean it isn't, but I was the one who found the cards.' Tess knew she was blathering. 'Sorry, Peg. I genuinely didn't mean to offend you.'

Peggy didn't seem to have registered this. She was still glaring at Liam.

'I wasn't asking because I think the cards have anything to do with you,' Tess reassured her. 'Everyone knows you do tarot readings. It'd be a pretty dim move for you to leave some on the body, if you were involved in the death. Which of course you weren't.'

Peggy turned back to her. 'So the cards were found on the body, were they?'

Tess grimaced. This was not going well. She'd only wanted to know what the cards meant. It hadn't been part of her plan to reveal so much information.

'Not on it,' she murmured. 'More sort of . . . by it. But they looked like they'd fallen from Ade's pocket. The witch's pocket, I mean.'

'I suppose I can expect another visit from the police, can I? It's not so long ago they were hammering on the door to arrest me for poor Clemmie's murder.'

'I doubt they'll bother for something like this. Tarot cards are common enough, aren't they? There's no reason for anyone to think they could be connected to you.'

Peggy smiled dryly. 'Don't you think so? I can think of one, as much as I've spent the past thirty-five years trying to forget it.'

'I'm sorry?'

'Well, you might as well know,' Peggy said with a sigh. 'It'll be common knowledge soon enough, if the police are sniffing their way back to me. You see, Tess, I was Ade Adams's second wife.'

Chapter 15

Tess stood, dazed, as Peggy strode out of the hall.
There was obviously more to this story than she'd realised. She hadn't been aware that Ade had another connection to Cherrywood. Neither he nor Peggy had given any hint of it, either in connection with his recent visit or when he'd lived in the village before. And yet there was no reason for Peggy to invent it – considering the revelations about Ade on the news, she had every reason to want to keep it quiet.

It was over sixteen years since Peggy had arrived in the village. She'd moved here with her husband Ian Stringer in her early forties, and the couple had lived quietly until the scandal two years ago when Ian had left Peggy for his current wife: her best friend Bev. Then came the second scandal when, earlier this year, it had been discovered that Ian was now having an affair with his ex-wife. Peggy, it turned out, had a talent for BDSM that Ian's new bride couldn't match, and he'd gone running back into her PVC-clad arms. The Bev–Peggy–Ian love triangle had been complicated enough without throwing Ade Adams into the mix.

How many times had Ade been married? Before Leonie there'd been Sarah. At some point before her, there'd been

Peggy. That had been thirty-five years ago, Peggy had said. Had there been others in between? Ade had talked about a coven of ex-wives. And under what circumstances had Ade and Peggy's relationship ended? There seemed to be any number of women with a reason to hate Ade Adams – perhaps even enough to kill.

Tess glanced at Liam, who was talking to Angela in a little group that included Raven, Kennedy, Seana, Candice and Marianne. A suspicion had started to grow.

Was Peggy right? Was Liam speculating about Ade's murder through more than idle curiosity – had he been hired to investigate? If so, he'd be bound to want to know what she'd just discovered. She wandered over to find out what they were talking about.

'Whereabouts are you from, Angela?' Liam was asking. 'I'm finding your accent a little hard to place.'

'Oh, I've moved around some in my time,' she said. 'I was born in Aberdeen, but I spent a lot of my working life in Glasgow, and later down in London. My accent's something of a mishmash now.'

'Have you ever lived abroad?'

'Nowhere outside Great Britain. I like to think I've led an exciting sort of life, but it hasn't involved much wandering.'

OK, now Tess was definitely suspicious. Liam rarely made small talk, and from the perspective of someone who'd seen him interview suspects before, the questions he was asking seemed pointed. He was looking for a secret . . .

'I must say, it's nice to be part of a conversation that isn't about something grisly,' Marianne observed.

'It's nice to be part of one that isn't about my reproductive system,' Raven said in a undertone, shooting a look at her grandmother.

Candice ignored her and nodded in agreement with Marianne. 'This village has been talking about nothing but murder since it happened. It's all rather mawkish.'

'Has it been awful?' Seana asked. 'Of course I've seen it in the newspapers, but I live far enough away that we haven't seen much disturbance.'

'We had a lot of journalists, but things have mostly settled down now,' Kennedy said. 'People are still talking about it, though. Especially after what was on the news today.'

Seana's brow lowered. 'Poor woman. No wonder somebody wanted that man dead.'

'Well, we don't know it was murder,' Angela said. 'I'm inclined to support the idea it was a prank that went wrong. It would certainly be in character, wouldn't it? Ade died as he lived, it seems to me.'

Seana shuddered. 'It's a nightmarish image: him at the top of the bonfire with the flames licking around. Almost like a human sacrifice.'

Kennedy smiled. 'You spend too much time in your books, Seana. Let's get another coffee, shall we? It'll be time for the second half soon.'

'Ah, now there's a suggestion,' Marianne said. 'I could murder a biscuit. Let's go, Candy.'

They left, leaving Angela, Raven, Liam and Tess.

'Don't you need to get back to the wings?' Raven asked Angela.

'No, the witches aren't on for a while. There'll be plenty of time to fix my makeup before my next scene.'

Tess nodded to a little card Liam was twiddling idly between his fingers. It looked like a posh business card, completely black with some text embossed in one corner.

'What's that?' she asked.

'Oh, this?' Liam looked at it as if he'd forgotten he was holding it. 'I'm not sure where I found it, to be honest. Actually, I brought it along to ask Angela if she knew what it was all about.'

Angela frowned. 'Me?'

'Yes.' Liam showed it to her, moving it around so the light caught the embossed area. 'This symbol: the one that looks like an inverse triangle with an X incorporated. Do you recognise it?'

Angela squinted at it. 'I don't think so. Why did you think I might know?'

'I remembered seeing a similar symbol in your notebook that night in the pub, when you handed it to me to look at your whisky ratings.'

Angela still looked puzzled, but did she also seem a little fearful? Tess was finding it hard to tell from her expression.

Raven leaned over to have a look. 'Oh. I know this symbol.'

Tess blinked. 'You do?'

'Yeah, it's the logo for a gentlemen's club down in London. A Masonic type of thing.'

Tess shook her head. 'How can you possibly know that? You're not a gentleman. You're barely even a lady.'

'For your sake I shall choose to ignore that remark,' Raven

said with mock hauteur. 'It belongs to something called the Fifteen Club. My dad was a member.'

'How do you know that?' Angela asked. 'I thought he died when you were a baby.'

'There was some stationery with this symbol and the address in a box of his stuff I found.' Raven looked smug at being the one to solve the mystery. 'The address is for a bookshop but I guess that must be a front. I thought it was sort of exciting, my dad being in a secret society. I almost went down there to see if I could find out any more about it, but it was right before all that drama with Aunty Clemmie's murder so it went right out of my head. I'd love to go there, though.'

'It'll be a glorified boys' club, as all those sorts of things are,' Angela said dismissively. 'It's probably in a treehouse with a sign on the door saying "No Girls Allowed". I wouldn't give it any further thought.'

'Don't you think it would be exciting to sneak in and find out what it's all about?'

'Please don't try it, Raven. It might be dangerous.'

Raven, who'd clearly been hoping to find an ally in her adventurous new friend, looked put out. 'I thought you said it was just a glorified boys' club.'

'Yes, but even the most pathetic overgrown schoolboy can be a threat if he's got power on his side. You don't know who you might be dealing with.'

'So you don't recognise the symbol, Angela?' Liam asked. 'I'm sure it's the same as the one in your notebook.'

'Oh, I doodle all sorts of rubbish.' Angela glanced at the

symbol again. 'I should think what you actually saw was some scribbling in shorthand.'

'Do you still have your notes?'

'No, they're long recycled. That piece was published a week ago.'

'Shame. Still, if you don't recognise it then I guess you're right.' Liam tucked the card away. 'Well, ladies, I'm going to excuse myself and leave you to enjoy the second half. I want to save myself some surprises for the final performance.'

Angela laughed. 'Not to give any spoilers, but I wouldn't come hoping for a happy ever after.'

Liam smiled. 'Break a leg, Angela. See you later, gang.'

He nodded to them and left.

'Hang on,' Tess said to Raven and Angela. 'I just . . . I won't be long.'

She followed in Liam's footsteps, catching sight of him again outside the building.

'Oi!' she called.

He turned back. 'What? I thought you wanted rid of me.'

'Don't give me that.' She jogged up to him. 'You're not just curious about how Ade died. All that stuff about accents and symbols – you're on a case, aren't you?'

'No.'

'Don't lie to me, Lee. I've worked out your tells.'

He sighed. 'Tess, I told you: I'm not letting you get involved in my cases again.'

'So you are investigating Ade's murder!' she said triumphantly. 'I knew it.'

'That doesn't concern you. Go watch the rest of the play.'

'Where did you get that card? Your client? Who is it, Leonie Abbott?'

'That's confidential.'

'You never care about confidentiality when you need me for something, do you?' she said. 'Come on, let me help. I've got information for you. A lead.'

He squinted at her. 'No you haven't.'

'I have, I swear.'

'All right, what is this lead?'

She folded her arms. 'Not telling.'

'Don't be childish. Tell me what it is, if it's so important.'

'I will if you let me help.'

'Fine. Forget it then.' He turned to go.

'All right, all right.' She paused. 'Let's just say that you might want to look further into Peggy Bristow's romantic history.'

He frowned. 'Peggy?'

'Yeah.'

'What's this got to do with Peggy? Were they her tarot cards you found?'

'Nope.' Tess was rather enjoying keeping him in the dark. 'I'll tell you what. If you tell me why you were interrogating Angela, I'll tell you what I know about Peggy.'

'Or I could ask Peggy directly and cut out the middle man.'

'That won't help. She's still annoyed at you for suspecting her of Clemmie's murder.' She grinned. 'You see, you need me, Lee. People around here know me and I know them. You're still too much of an outsider.'

'Hmm.'

'Look, I promise I won't put myself in any danger,' Tess said, sensing he was starting to crack. 'I won't even ask for a cut of your fee. You can just treat me as . . . a consultant. Your expert in all things Cherrywood. Admit it: you'd never have cracked Aunty Clemmie's murder without my help.'

'I would eventually.'

'Before Marianne was murdered?'

'Possibly not,' he admitted. 'But that was just a one-off.'

'You don't know that.' Tess met his eyes. 'We work well together, Lee. We made a good team last time.'

'Why does this mean so much to you?' he demanded.

'I suppose . . . because I feel like I'm good at it. Pulling at loose threads and seeing where they take me; using my brain.'

'You see, this is what worries me. This isn't a puzzle-solving exercise for hobbyists, Tess – we're dealing with killers here. This is my job, and I can't guarantee it won't be dangerous.'

'But if I'm only a consultant I won't be in any danger, will I? You need someone to bounce ideas off. Someone who knows this place. Who else if not me?'

'Well . . .'

'Look, this time six months ago you were begging me to help you on a case. Because you knew I could solve it.'

'No, because it involved the Women's Guild and I was lacking the required attributes to go undercover myself.'

'You can't just pick me up when you need me and drop me

when you don't, Liam. You said you'd do anything to make things up to me. Let me help, then.'

Liam sighed. 'All right, if you're going to lay on the emotional blackmail. Since I'll clearly get no peace otherwise, I guess... you can help with some of the research. Just remember, we're not partners, OK? If there's any hands-on stuff to be done, you're to keep out of it.'

Tess beamed. 'Thanks, Liam. I knew you'd see sense.'

Liam consented to smile back. 'You do make a pretty good Watson. I'm still offended it takes a murder for you to want to be in my company, though.' He nodded to the village hall. 'Are you going back in? If not you can walk me home.'

She raised an eyebrow. 'Scared of the dark?'

'A bit. There's still a few of those dummies about.'

Tess smiled. 'All right, I'll text Rave and ask her to make my apologies – I can meet her in the pub when it's all over. Luckily we've got Roger to use as an excuse when we need to escape torturous social events. Will you tell me why you were interrogating Angela if I tell you what I know about Peggy?'

'I suppose I might as well say yes, since you'll only hound me until I agree. You can come up to the office and have a look at my whiteboard if you want.'

Tess clapped her hands. 'Ooh, yes please.'

'It's weird how excited you get about this,' Liam muttered. 'Listen, you can't tell anyone you're helping, OK? If someone in the village was behind this, I don't want them making you a target.'

'I'll wrap my feeble female frame in cotton wool and bubble wrap just as soon as I get in. Now, tell me why you're suspicious of Angela.'

Liam glanced around to make sure they weren't being overheard. 'Let's just say I've got good reasons to suspect that Angela Campbell isn't who she claims to be.'

Chapter 16

Well, somehow he'd done it again.

Liam had promised himself he wasn't going to let Tess get involved in any more of his cases. She was right when she said they worked well together, but Tess could be impulsive, and she lacked the sense of jeopardy that Liam had honed through years as a cop. That could lead to her wandering blindly into situations that might be dangerous to her, and there was a killer on the loose. His first priority had to be keeping her out of harm's way.

But Liam had to admit, the idea of spending time with her was difficult to resist. They'd started to grow close when they'd investigated Clemency Ackroyd's murder, and Liam had been longing to develop that closeness. Only Tess's insistence on pushing him away – in spite of her admission that she enjoyed his company – had prevented him from building on the relationship they'd started to develop.

Nevertheless, he needed to be firm. Wanting to be with Tess was no excuse for putting her at risk. If they were working together then he had to set boundaries. Tess needed to understand that any maverick sleuthing meant she'd be out on her ear.

They didn't talk much as they walked to Liam's office. Tess seemed lost in her thoughts, no doubt turning clues over in her mind. It was true she had a natural talent for this sort of work, speedily making connections and spotting patterns in a way Liam was rather envious of. He was quiet too, stealing the odd glance at his companion as he wondered where this new collaboration might take them.

It was probably for the best that they didn't discuss the case much out in the open. It would be impossible to hide from the village that he was investigating Ade's death – Angela and Raven had probably already started putting two and two together – but he did want to conceal Tess's involvement if possible.

'Well, step into my parlour,' he said when they reached his flat. 'Sorry about the mess. When I've got a case on it always looks like a bombsite.'

'Don't worry about that. I live with Raven, I'm used to it.'

Still, Liam felt rather self-conscious about the unwashed coffee mugs and crumpled paper that littered his office as he showed Tess in.

While Liam hastily gathered up a few mugs and chucked his waste paper into the basket, Tess glanced around the bare walls and at the unshaded lightbulb overhead. 'Love what you've done with the place, Lee. Guantanamo chic, I think they call it.'

'Yeah, I should probably get some pictures up. I've been putting it off. Wondering if I was going to be staying.'

Tess frowned. 'Why, where were you thinking of going?'

'Back to London,' he said with a shrug. 'I still own some

office space down there. I've been renting it out, but when I was struggling so much for cases, I did think maybe that was a sign I was wasting my time up here.'

Tess walked to his whiteboard, where he'd stuck up the names of people of interest relating to Ade Adams.

'Well, you've got a big case now,' she said, gesturing to it. 'I guess that means you'll be sticking around.'

'We'll see. One big case is better than no big cases, but it's still only one.'

'You'll get more,' Tess said, with more confidence than Liam was feeling. 'You just need to get your name out and about. Ade's case has been all over the papers. That'll help.'

'Yeah, if I can solve it.'

'You will. I mean, we will.'

'I'm glad you think so.'

Liam, rarely ill at ease around the opposite sex, felt uncharacteristically awkward at having Tess here in his living space. Well, his working space, but the bedsit he slept and ate in was just next door. He never had created proper boundaries between his personal life and his work.

'Um, you want a glass of wine or something?' he asked Tess. 'Actually, no, I haven't got any wine. But there's beer in the fridge.'

'Better not. I'm going to the pub with Raven after the rehearsal.' She glanced at him, and her expression relaxed a little. 'Well, I guess one can't hurt.'

Liam smiled and went to fetch a couple of bottles from the fridge in his bedsit. He joined Tess at the whiteboard and handed her a lager.

'So, what do you think?' he asked, nodding to the board.

There were images of the three tarot cards found on the body, plus the weird symbol the Fifteen Club used as its logo. There were also photos of Angela Campbell and Leonie Abbott, and cards with question marks for anonymous suspects: the woman who'd recently come forward as having been groomed by Ade as a teenager; his drug dealer; Leonie's ex-boyfriend; her current lover.

'Is that it for Ade's nearest and dearest?' Tess asked, taking a sip of her beer. 'Any kids? Family?'

'Not as far as I can find out. Just an older sister, but she's in a care home in New Zealand. She's eighty-four so I think she can be eliminated. Nephew and niece and their families, also in New Zealand. That's it.'

'You haven't got Peggy on there.'

'I'm not sure why I should. All right, tarot cards were found by the body, but I don't think—'

'Not because of the tarot.' Tess turned to look at him, with the smug air of someone who has a great secret to share. 'You'll never guess what I found out.'

'You're right, I won't. What is it?'

She took a sip of her beer, obviously relishing having her audience in the palm of her hand.

'OK, I'll tell you,' she said when she'd kept him waiting for as long as dramatic impact required. 'Peggy was Ade's second wife.'

'You what?'

'She told me tonight – said she'd spent thirty-five years trying to forget about it. I had no idea they had a connection.

Still, I can't see why she'd invent something like that, can you?'

'Well, no,' Liam said, feeling dazed. 'That's something I hadn't reckoned on. She's not still spending her free time whipping her most recent ex-husband in the village-hall boiler room, is she?'

Tess shook her head. 'The affair with Ian's over. He's all loved-up with Bev again. Don't ask me the details, but I did notice Bev has started getting parcels delivered to the pub from a company called Fifty Shades of Wahey.'

'Oh.' Liam thought about this and pulled a face. 'Eesh.'

'I know, right?' Tess turned back to the whiteboard. 'I think Ade must've been married a few times. The night he viewed the Guy Trail, he referred to *ex-wives* – plural. Called them a coven of witches.'

'How very *Macbeth* of him.'

'That does suggest three,' Tess said thoughtfully. 'Sarah's dead and Leonie he was still married to. Wife number two we know was Peggy. I'd see if you can track down another two.'

'Right.' Liam made a note of this. 'I hadn't thought the tarot cards had any connection with Peggy – far too obvious – but coupled with this and the fact she was one of the few people with a key to the park, it does make you wonder . . . Did you talk to her about the cards?'

'Yeah. She didn't seem furtive at all. She was quite happy to talk about what they meant, until I mentioned Ade's name.'

'Be careful, Tess. I really don't want it getting out that

you're helping. I'd rather you left interviewing witnesses to me.'

'I didn't know you were investigating then, did I? I just wanted to know more about the cards.' She smiled. 'Besides, you're a terrible interrogator. You need me to play Good Cop for you.'

He shrugged. 'I did all right tonight. I found out what that symbol meant.'

'Oh yeah. The weird triangle thing.' Tess looked thoughtful. 'Rave never told me she'd found out this stuff about her dad. You don't think he was connected to the murder, do you?'

'I can't see how. Hasn't he been dead thirty years?'

'About that, yeah.'

'Who was he?'

'Raven hardly ever talks about him. All I know about Dominic Walton-Lord is what everyone in the village knows: that he was a racing junkie who died at the wheel. He was one half of a pretty glamorous couple. Raven's mum was a model, I think, or an actress. Possibly both.'

'Is she still around?'

'I imagine she is, somewhere. She cut off contact with Raven when she was a baby. Sold her, basically, to be raised by Candice. By all accounts she never had been the maternal type, and when her husband died she decided she was done with motherhood. Drove up from their place in London, ditched the baby at Cherrywood Hall and disappeared. No one knows what happened to her after that.' Tess paused. 'I do know her name, though. Raven mentioned it recently, something Italian . . . Russo, that was it. Eva Russo.'

Liam went to his desk to jot this down.

'Do you think Raven's parents are significant?' Tess asked.

'Probably not. Still, it's worth knowing, since Raven's dad was a member of this Fifteen Club. I'm guessing Ade must have been too. Leonie found the card in his desk.'

'So she is your client.'

Liam nodded. 'Which isn't to say she can't be a suspect. The police certainly have her firmly in their sights.'

Tess's gaze ran along the cards stuck to Liam's board. 'Her lover's a suspect too, it says. How do you know she has one? Did she tell you?'

'No, but the police think there's someone, and so did Ade. Leonie denied it, but something in her manner made me think she might be hiding something.' Liam looked at the board. 'And then there's the ex-boyfriend.'

'What ex-boyfriend?'

'The one you told me about. Leonie was seeing him when she cheated with Ade and he went off the rails as a result.'

'You can't think he was involved. He left the village yonks ago, and I very much doubt he's still pining for Leonie Abbott after all that time.'

'Yeah, I was padding the suspects list a bit with him,' Liam admitted. 'Still, it's good to explore all avenues. How exactly did he go off the rails, this man?'

'He fell in with a bad gang and ended up doing some dangerous stuff. Illegal stuff. I don't remember all the details.'

'Do you know his name?'

'God, Lee, it was years ago. He was just another local lad, that's all.'

Liam gazed thoughtfully at the card on his whiteboard. No one seemed to remember the man's name – not even Leonie, who he had apparently been so in love with that he'd thrown his whole future away after losing her. Was that significant?

Tess had gone to Liam's desk, where he'd tossed the black card for the Fifteen Club. She picked it up.

'If you ask me, this is the avenue you ought to be exploring next,' she said, waving it at him. 'I'm guessing the connection with Angela's notebook is behind your bit of espionage at the am-drams tonight.'

'You mean *thesp*ionage.' He shrugged when Tess gave him a look. 'What? Just because this is a murder investigation doesn't mean we can't enjoy a quality pun.'

'Your definition of "quality" must be very different to mine.' Tess flapped the card again. 'Well? Is this the reason Angela's on the suspect list?'

'One reason, although I can't say for certain that was the symbol in her notebook. There were plenty of squiggles, and my memory's not perfect.'

'What are the other reasons? You said you didn't think Angela is who she says she is.'

'Ah, now that's where it gets interesting.' Liam went around the other side of his desk and sat down. 'I've been suspicious ever since that night at the pub, although I couldn't see why she'd be lying until Ade was murdered. Still, I was certain she was.'

'How were you certain?'

'Because of her spelling.'

Tess frowned. 'Her spelling?'

'Her spelling of one word in particular. Whisky. I noticed right away that she spells it with an E.'

Tess took a seat opposite him. 'I can't see what's significant about that. Being a journalist doesn't make you an expert on spelling. Just the opposite, judging by some of the clangers I've spotted in the *Gazette*.'

'Yeah, but she's a Scot – at least, she claims to be. At the risk of invoking the No True Scotsman fallacy, no genuine Scot would spell whisky with an E. They just wouldn't. Americans and the Irish spell it like that, but no Scot ever would.'

'You're that certain?'

'Trust me.' He steepled his fingers and rested his chin on them. 'Anyway, that set me thinking. I've got family in Scotland, and I'd thought before that Angela had a sort of mixed-up accent. I couldn't pinpoint where in the country she might come from.'

'You think the accent's fake?'

'I do. Didn't you notice tonight, when she was hamming it up playing that witch? No matter how good someone is at faking an accent, they nearly always lose it when they have to shout. There were places where it sounded more like New England than old Scotland to me.'

Tess frowned. 'Now you mention it, I did notice some strange pronunciations. Still, Ian was doing some weird quasi-American thing too. I reckon he was imitating someone he'd seen playing the part on TV. Maybe Angela watched the same film.'

'But Ian's accent sounded fake, and consistently so too. Angela sounded realistically American in places, then suddenly it was back to Scottish. And then there's her habit of occasionally using phrasing or slang that doesn't sit right with where she claims to be from, not to mention forgetting which weekend the clocks went back. You remember she thought it was the first weekend in November? That's when they go back in the States – a week later than they do here.'

'Do they? I didn't know that.'

'Yep. I'd say she was either American or that she'd lived there for a long period – long enough to absorb the spelling, the accent and some of the slang. Yet she told us tonight she'd never lived outside Great Britain.'

'So she did,' Tess said. 'Is that not quite whatchamacallit though – circumstantial? Everyone sounds a bit American these days, with the influence of social media and Hollywood.'

'Not to that extent. Besides, it isn't only that. I'm also struggling to corroborate what Angela's told people about her life. She's mentioned a few newspapers she's worked for, but I've searched their archives and there's no record of her byline. The only one with any record of her is the paper she was working for in Glasgow before she came here.'

'That does seem suspicious. But what's her connection to Ade?'

'I'm not sure yet,' Liam admitted. 'Let's not forget she was the one who invited him here, though.'

'I didn't get the sense they knew each other particularly well the night we showed Ade round the village,' Tess said.

'Mind you, Angela did tell us Ade was a friend of her late husband's so they must have had some level of acquaintance. Do you think it is definitely murder? It's not totally unbelievable to think it was a prank that went wrong. We know he must've climbed the pyre himself.'

'If it was then there are a lot of loose ends that don't make much sense. Tarot cards, previous relationships, people lying about who they are . . . There's something going on, Tess.'

'But how did they do it? I mean, that bizarre method of death. The bonfire, the witch's costume, the tarot cards . . . how, and more importantly, why?'

'That I don't know yet,' Liam admitted. 'At this point I'm planning to follow the leads I do have and hope method, motive, means and opportunity will slot into place when I know more.'

'What will you do next?'

'Three things. I'll try to sweet-talk Della into sharing the results of the post-mortem, first of all. Then I'll see what I can learn about Ade's ex-wives, and I'll find out more about this Fifteen Club.' Liam picked up the business card. 'I wonder if the symbol is supposed to be a stylised way of writing the number fifteen. It does look a bit like it's designed to incorporate Roman numerals, with the X and the V. Why fifteen, though, I wonder?'

'Could be the year the club was founded?' Tess suggested. 'Or the number of members?'

'Perhaps.'

'I take it you've reverse image-searched that logo?'

Liam frowned. 'Reverse whatted it?'

Tess shook her head. 'I swear you're an eighty-year-old trapped in a thirty-five-year-old's body. You know if you go to Google and click the little camera icon in the search bar that you can do a search for similar images, right?'

'That's a thing?'

'Honestly, I don't know what they teach you kids at detective school these days. Hang on.'

She went to his whiteboard to take a photo of the symbol, then sat back down to do the search. Her eyebrows lifted.

'What? Did you find out something about the club?' Liam asked.

'Now this is interesting.' She turned her phone around to show Liam the website she'd discovered. 'Here's your squiggle in a table of occult symbols. Read the description.'

' "A symbol used in ritual magic, known as the Sigil of Lucifer, or the Seal of Satan," ' Liam read. ' "First recorded in the sixteenth-century Italian volume *The Grimoire of Truth*. For those who worship Satan as a god, this symbol can be used to call him forth." '

Tess shuddered. 'The devil again, just like on that tarot card I found. This case is getting creepy, Lee.'

'Did Peggy tell you what that card meant?'

'She said it usually symbolised a person's dark side, or an addiction to hedonism.'

'That certainly fits Ade Adams. He was all about sex, drugs and rock and roll, according to his most recent wife. Let's see if we can find out any more.'

Liam opened his laptop and did a Google search for 'tarot card devil'. He clicked on the top link.

'What does it say?' Tess asked. 'Anything we don't know already?'

'"Symbolising our own baser animal instincts, the Devil is the fifteenth card of the Major Arcana" – fifteen!'

'The Fifteen Club,' Tess said. 'Do you think there's a connection between the club and the tarot card we found by the body?'

'"Tis the eye of childhood that fears a painted devil,' Liam murmured.

'Pardon?'

'It occurred to me when Bev said it in *Macbeth* tonight, how Angela had quoted that same line as she was looking up at Ade's body on the bonfire. There's a connection here, Tessie. Painted devils all over the place. I'm sure Angela Campbell must be involved somehow.'

'How does it all link to this Fifteen Club?'

'Only one way to find out.' Liam closed his laptop. 'Can you ask Raven to call me? It's time I did a bit of undercover work.'

Chapter 17

Oliver's mum was in the kitchen cooking when Oliver emerged from his study one late November afternoon.

'Here he is. My little God-botherer.' She wiped her hands on her apron and went to peck his cheek.

'Please don't call me that, Mum. I'd hate for it to catch on.' Oliver nodded to the oven. 'What are you making?'

'Something to put hairs on your chest and vim in your engine. Shepherd's pie, your favourite. We can't have you wasting away from a broken heart, can we?'

Ever since his mum had heard about the breakup with Tammy, she'd been feeding him up like she was a witch in a gingerbread cottage. She seemed convinced that the only cure for a broken heart was the sort of stodgy fare that made you feel like your stomach was lined with lead.

What's more, his parents were still showing no sign of wanting to go home. They couldn't leave while their boy needed them, his mum said – entirely failing to recognise that Oliver was a grown man of thirty-two who in fact needed nothing more than a bit of space. He couldn't even use Ling Cottage as a refuge any more. He was trapped in the vicarage with his perpetually randy parents, who seemed intent on staying until they'd either seen him safely to the altar with a suitable mate or put on five stone, whichever happened first.

But his mum meant well, and it was comforting to know his parents still worried about him. Oliver knew he should be grateful to have two loving parents, whatever their foibles. It wasn't something any of his friends had, young as they all still were. Tess's mum was long dead and her dad had been in and out of prison throughout her life. Raven, too, had lost one parent to death and another to abandonment. Kennedy, who'd been conceived when her mum and dad were already middle-aged, had lost her parents far younger than most people expect to.

'My heart's not broken, Mum, I promise,' Oliver said, putting an arm around her shoulders. 'I mean I'm sad that it ended that way, but Tammy was right when she said we didn't quite fit. You really don't need to keep looking after me.'

'Oh, indulge an old lady, Oliver. Someone has to look after you until you find a wife to do it, don't they?'

Oliver smiled. 'I like to think I'm enough of a modern man that I can look after myself without any female intervention. I'm not Dad, you know.'

'You should get a housekeeper,' his mum said, ignoring him. 'Vicars always have housekeepers on the telly.'

'I don't need a housekeeper.'

His mum raised an eyebrow. She ran a finger over the top of the cooker and showed him a fingertip covered in dust.

'All right, so I ought to dust more often,' he conceded. 'Where's Dad?'

'Gone to fetch a paper.' She quirked her head at the sound of the front door opening. 'That'll be him.'

Paul appeared a moment later with a newspaper tucked under his arm.

'Evening, sexy. Miss me?'

His wife giggled. 'You were only out quarter of an hour, you daft beggar.'

Paul pulled her into his arms. 'Quarter of an hour's a long time when you're a virile young man.'

'Or a lecherous old man,' Annette said, tapping his nose.

'Come on, Nettie, give us a kiss. I demand some steaming hot conjugal rights.'

'Ahem,' Oliver said as they melted together for a snog.

His dad glanced round. 'Can we help you?'

'I actually came in to let you know I'm expecting the bishop in ten minutes.'

'Nick's coming, is he?'

Annette and Paul had been friends of the Hamiltons and had known their son Nick as a young lad. This meant they found it even harder to get their heads around him being a bishop than they did accepting that their own son was now the village vicar.

Oliver nodded. 'We'll be going into my study for a chat.'

'Send him in to say hello, won't you?'

'Well, it's a work call rather than social. I don't want to keep him when he's busy. Could you manage not to, um . . . I mean, I'd be grateful for a bit of quiet while I talk to him.'

'We'll be like church mice, won't we, Net?' Paul said, pinching his wife's bottom.

Oliver glanced at the paper under his arm. 'Any breaking news, Dad?'

Paul's brow lowered. He unfolded the paper and tossed it on the worktop. 'Another poor lass has come forward to tell her story. God knows how many more there might be.'

'They were talking about it on breakfast TV,' Annette said. 'One of the presenters saying how it's easy to accuse someone once they're dead. No wonder these girls are scared to come forward when all they get for their trouble is accused of lying.'

'Makes you wonder how they'd react if it was a daughter of theirs.'

Oliver glanced at the front of the newspaper. It was a national redtop, not the *Gazette*, and bore the headline *Sick Adams abused me on radio work experience*.

'How many is that?' he asked.

'Four.' His dad grimaced. 'This one was just fifteen. Tell you what, if that bastard was still alive . . .' He glanced at Oliver. 'Not a very Christian attitude, you're going to tell me, I suppose. But it's kids, Oliver.'

'I wasn't going to say that.'

'I should think we know better than to question whether he was guilty, at any rate,' Annette said. 'It makes me sick to my stomach that it never came out while he was alive. And that poor child . . .'

'Well, Leonie was eighteen,' Oliver said. 'Not that that makes it all right, but she wasn't a minor so there'd have been no reason for the law to take an interest.'

'That wasn't who I meant.'

Oliver frowned. 'Were there other girls in Cherrywood with stories about him back then?'

'No. I mean, it's not for me to say. Forget I mentioned it.' The doorbell rang. 'That must be your friend.'

'Right. I'll see you both in a bit.' Oliver went to answer the door.

'Do you want some tea or pop bringing in?' his mum called after him.

Ugh. Pop. She'd be making up party bags for them next.

'That's fine. I can fetch him a drink if he wants one,' Oliver called back. 'You guys just chill out. You're on holiday, don't forget.'

Oliver ushered Nick into his study hurriedly, before his mum could jump out and start pressing bowls of jelly and ice cream on to them.

'Thanks for coming,' he said when they were both seated. The walls lined with mahogany bookshelves and the leather wing-backed armchairs went some way to making him feel like a grown-up again.

Nick leaned back in his chair. He was a pleasant, open-faced man, still youthful-looking at forty-three, with rumpled sandy hair, kind eyes and a mouth that suggested humour and understanding. Oliver had been pleased when Michael, his stern elderly bishop, had retired and Nick had been appointed in his place. This felt like someone he could talk to.

'I was surprised to get your message,' Nick said. 'I hope there's nothing wrong, Oliver.'

'Not wrong exactly. I've been having something of a crisis.'

Nick frowned. 'A crisis of faith?'

'No, my faith is . . . good. Fine. Strong, I mean.' Oliver pressed his eyes closed. 'There's something I've been worrying about, though. I was hoping you could give me some advice.'

'Well, that is my job,' Nick said with a warm smile. 'Is it a moral dilemma that's worrying you?'

'You could call it that.' Oliver hesitated, his gaze drifting to a painting of Jesus delivering the Sermon on the Mount. 'I've just been thinking lately . . . What if you can't forgive someone for something they've done? What if you try and try, but you can't do it? That's wrong, isn't it?'

'I know what's brought this on.' Nick leaned forward earnestly. 'Of course it's natural to feel that way when the crimes were so abhorrent, and when the person is no longer with us to show any remorse or repentance.'

Oliver frowned. 'No longer with us?'

'Well, yes. It is Ade Adams you're thinking of, isn't it? I assumed, because of his connection with the village, that you had some angry parishioners on your hands and were seeking help in giving them guidance.'

'Oh. Yes, well, people are very angry – you can understand why, when children were involved. But this is more of a . . . personal dilemma.'

'I see.' Nick steepled his fingers and regarded Oliver over the top of them. 'Who is it you're trying to forgive?'

'I'd rather not say, if you don't mind. It's someone I've been helping in a professional capacity and he's asked me not to reveal he's back in the area for the time being. There's a troubled history involved, which includes a wrong done to someone I cared about very deeply.' Oliver pressed his fingertips to his temples. 'I reacted badly when he appeared back in my life and I'm ashamed of that, but I've been going through all the right motions since. I've found him somewhere to stay, I'm helping him look for work, I've kept his presence secret as he asked. But I can't *mean* it, Nick. I'm still really, really angry about this thing he did. I'm helping him because I'm a Christian and it's my duty, but in my heart I haven't forgiven him. I'm not sure I ever will be able to. And I should be able to, shouldn't I?'

Nick looked thoughtful. For a long time he didn't speak.

'You know the thing that worries me in what you just told me?' he said at last.

'What?'

'It isn't that you haven't forgiven this person. Anger is natural, especially when the issue was left unresolved for such a long time. It's that you said you're not sure you ever will be able to. That sounds an awful lot like you've made up your mind not to try.'

'Perhaps I have,' Oliver said. 'Does that make me a bad person?'

'No. But it can make you a very unhappy one, if you let your resentment grow instead of working on a way to finally let go of it. This person – are they sorry for what they did?'

'They say so.'

'And do you think they're telling the truth?'

Oliver was silent, picturing Mikey's face the day he'd turned up on the doorstep.

'Yes,' he said quietly. 'He hasn't always been honest with the people who've wanted to help him, but I think that this time he's genuinely put his cards on the table.'

'In that case, I believe the best thing you can do is have a talk with God, and with yourself. Try to get to the root of your anger, and why it feels so insurmountable. Then I think you ought to talk with the person who caused it to see if you can break the link. Above all, don't feel guilty. No one can forgive instantly and easily when someone's caused them pain, no matter how sincere the repentance – not even Christ, when He was as human as you and I. You are as God created you, Oliver, and what makes you a good man is that you strive to do what's right even when the going gets tough.'

Oliver's face relaxed into a smile. 'Yes. Thanks, Nick.'

But his smile soon faded when he heard a familiar giggle from upstairs, and the sound of the bed in the spare room creaking.

He pressed his eyes tight closed. 'Oh no. Not again.'

Nick frowned. 'Something wrong?'

Oliver sprang to his feet, speaking extra loudly to try to mask any further disturbing sounds from upstairs, although his dad's dirty laugh could cut through anything.

'Well, thanks for coming!' he said, shaking Nick's hand rather manically. 'I don't want to keep you. I know how busy you are. Let me walk you to the door.'

Nick looked rather dazed as he was unceremoniously pulled from his seat and practically jogged to the front door.

'I did wonder if a cup of tea might not be out of the question,' he said. 'I haven't had a sip since breakfast.'

'Er, well, I'd love to but . . . the kettle's on the blink. Um, the teashop's open in the village.' Oliver fumbled in his trouser pocket and pressed a pound into Nick's hand. 'Here. On me.'

The grunting had started now. Oliver almost pushed Nick through the door, followed him out and closed it behind them. He leaned back against it and let out a low whistle of relief.

'Oliver, what is the matter?' Nick asked.

'It's just . . . my mum and dad are staying. I don't want them to feel they have to hide themselves away while we're chatting.'

'Ah.' Nick smiled. 'Annette and Paul are here, are they? I thought I heard something from upstairs. I was told they'd been up to their old tricks.'

Oliver grimaced. 'Kennedy told you?'

'Oh, I have other sources than Kennedy. I bumped into Bev Stringer at Morrisons.'

'Right,' Oliver said, not sure how he ought to feel about this. 'Also, um . . . old tricks?'

Nick laughed. 'I'm sure you were too young to have picked up on it, but they always had a reputation. Still, I won't tell tales.' He patted Oliver's arm. 'There's no need to be embarrassed, Oliver. Sex isn't a dirty word, even in the Church – at least, not any more. But, er, I think I'd better have my tea at the cafe all the same, don't you?'

Oliver laughed. 'Well, thanks for the advice. And sorry about all the . . . parents.'

'Glad to be of help.'

The bishop was preparing to go when a thought crossed Oliver's mind. 'Nick?'

Nick turned back. 'Yes?'

'You were living in the village when the scandal broke, weren't you? Ade Adams and Leonie Abbott, I mean. Helen Judson as was.'

'My parents were, and Kennedy – that would've been right before they moved down south. Seana and I had long left home, though. I'd have been in my late twenties by then. Why?'

'Just something my mum said, about a girl he might have had a history with. I wondered if you remembered anything. I had my own stuff going on at the time so it's all a bit of a blur.'

'Sorry, can't help you. I was long gone. Is there a reason you're asking?'

Was there? He must have been spending too much time around Tess.

'Not really,' Oliver said. 'I just like to keep abreast of what's going on in the village. Make sure I'm aware of anyone who might need my help.'

'I'd have thought you, Kenn and the other kids would have known about it, if anyone did. I'm assuming this girl was as young as the others.' Nick shook his head. 'Nasty business, isn't it? Let's hope there'll be justice for all of Ade's victims now it's out in the open at last. I'll be asking my congregation to pray for them this Sunday.'

'Yes, that's a good idea. I'll add it to my service sheet too. See you later, Nick.'

Oliver watched Nick go, the bishop's last words flitting around his brain. *Let's hope there'll be justice for his victims, now it's out in the open at last . . .*

Could one of Ade's victims have decided to seek justice in a rather more immediate fashion?

Chapter 18

Tess was in front of the TV with a notepad, watching videos on YouTube, when Raven came home from a date with Benjamin. Roger was snoozing on the sofa, but he bounced up to greet his mum when she came in.

'Hello, darling,' Raven said to Tess when she'd finished making a fuss of Roger. 'I thought you'd be at work.'

'No, I'm not on till eight.' Tess paused her video. 'You're home early. Everything OK?'

'I'm tired, that's all. A drink'll help. You want one?'

'Better not before work.'

'Suit yourself.' Raven went into the kitchen to pour herself a large gin.

'What's this you're watching?' she asked when she came back in, throwing herself down beside Tess.

'An old episode of *Screaming Laughs*. They're all up on YouTube. I've watched three so far.'

Raven shook her head. 'I wish you'd get a new hobby, Tess. It's all very well for Liam. He gets paid to do this stuff. I don't like him taking advantage of you, especially when there could be a killer running around.'

'Taking advantage? I was practically crawling on the ground begging him to let me get involved. He very grudgingly said I could help with the research, but if I tried to take on any of the practical stuff he'd take me off the case straight away. Where he gets this idea that I'm a delicate little bloom who'll swoon into Granny's picnic basket as soon as she sees a big bad wolf I have no idea.'

'That's something, I suppose. At least he's not the one throwing you to the big bad wolves.' Raven cast a listless look at the TV. 'So have you discovered anything?'

'I have, actually. I knew the business with the witch rang a bell. Take a look at this.'

Tess navigated to one of the episodes she'd watched earlier, skipping to a point about halfway through.

Ade Adams appeared on screen in one of his trademark loud suits. His TV persona was very different from the personality they'd caught a glimpse of the night he'd judged the Guy Trail. He spoke in the bouncy, bunged-up mid-Atlantic accent beloved of old-school DJs, revealing to the audience in a confidential tone just how the prank he was about to set up was going to work.

'Can you believe the guy was ever a star?' Raven said. 'Aside from what we now know about his personal life, he's so *annoying*. Why did DJs from the olden days have to do that stupid voice?'

'Hush and watch.' Tess nodded to Ade, who was getting into costume. A time-lapse sequence showed his transformation as he became a pretty convincing scarecrow, his suit stuffed with straw and a head created from sacking and a length of rope. When it was done, only his hands gave him away as being someone of flesh and blood. Once the costume was complete, Ade was transported to a nearby farm, where he took the place of an identical scarecrow and prepared to give the unsuspecting farmer the fright of his life.

'Seems familiar, right?' Tess said.

'So it was a prank gone wrong. Then why are the police still investigating?'

'There must be more to it. Don't forget the tarot cards, and that Fifteen Club Liam's looking into.' The doorbell rang. 'That'll be him now.'

Raven raised an eyebrow. 'You invited him over?'

'Don't look like that. It's not a date,' Tess said. 'I want to compare notes on what we've both found out. Besides, he wants to talk to you. He's been trying to ring you for days about those papers of your dad's.'

Raven sighed. 'Yeah, I've been ignoring him. I'm not in the mood for talking to detectives. Or men generally, for that matter.'

'This is important, Rave.'

'It might be important to Liam. Personally I couldn't give a monkey's if they never catch who murdered Ade Adams – if he even was murdered.'

Tess stood up. 'I know you're angry. Everyone is. I am. But the killer still needs to be caught, don't they? If you start turning a blind eye to murders just because the victim was a nasty piece of work, where does it end?'

She went to answer the door.

'Evening.' Liam held out a bottle of wine he'd brought.

'To make up for my previous deficiencies as host. I thought we could have a glass while we sleuth.'

'Oh. Thank you,' Tess said. 'I'd better not though. I'm working in an hour.'

Liam looked disappointed. 'Right.'

'Come on in. Raven's here too. She brought those documents over from Cherrywood Hall for you.'

Liam followed her to the living room. He took a seat in the armchair, and Roger, as the man of the house, flashed him a resentful look.

'I've been watching old *Screaming Laughs*,' Tess said as she resumed her seat, nodding to the video paused on the TV. 'My hunch was right: there was a prank similar to the witch thing on one episode. Ade disguised himself as a scarecrow to frighten a farmer.'

'Interesting.' Liam glanced at Raven. 'Can you spare me five minutes, Raven?'

'If you must, darling, but make it quick,' Raven said dispassionately. 'I've got an appointment with my duvet and the remains of my bottle of gin.'

'What's up with her?' Liam asked Tess.

'She thinks we should let the murderer get away with it because Ade had it coming. Oh, and that you're exploiting me as slave labour.'

'Exploiting you? I can't get rid of you.'

Tess grinned. 'I like to think my persistence is endearing.'

'You can ask what you like, Liam, but I don't know much,' Raven said. 'Hang on. Let me fetch the bits I found.'

She went to her room and came back with a card folder.

'Most of this stuff seems to be menus,' she said, shaking out a wad of documents on the coffee table. 'It all carries the same branding: the club name and that weird symbol. I guess my dad must've been in charge of catering or something.'

Liam picked up a sheet. 'Foie gras, oysters, lobster thermidor, Dom Perignon champagne . . . sounds like these guys know how to live. Anything else?'

'There were a couple of docs relating to governance. Details of how membership works, the agenda for a meeting. All pretty mundane. I was kind of disappointed. It was quite exciting to think my dad had been in a secret society, but it seems to be not much more than a glorified dining club.'

'Can I see the agenda?'

She shuffled the papers until she found the relevant sheet and handed it to Liam.

Liam glanced at it. 'Act of worship, reading of minutes, treasurer's report, balloting of new members, yawn yawn yawn, moment of silence for departed members, any other business.'

'Doesn't sound enthralling, does it?' Raven said. 'No different than the parish council, except with foie gras instead of tea and biscuits.'

'Anything else?' Tess asked.

'Well, there's this. It wasn't with the papers, but the robes made me think it must be connected.' Raven drew out a photograph and handed it to her.

The photo showed seven people, all in long red robes.

Three had their cowls up so their faces were partially obscured by shadow, but the other four looked jolly enough, smiling a little drunkenly. Tess handed it to Liam so he could have a look too.

'Which one's your dad?' she asked Raven.

Raven pointed to one of the uncowled members, a handsome man with dark hair smiling – or rather, smirking – on the right of the photo.

'Good-looking chap,' Tess observed. 'Obviously it must've skipped a generation.'

'Ahahahaha.'

'Hang on,' Liam said slowly.

'What?' Tess asked.

He held the photo up and squinted at it. 'This one in the centre, with his cowl up. It's Ade Adams, I'm sure of it.'

Tess looked at the figure. It had the cowl of its robe pulled so far forward that the face was in almost complete shadow, with only the mouth visible.

'How can you tell?' she asked.

'The mouth.' Liam stood up to hold the photo next to the image of Ade paused on the TV screen. 'Thin and sort of sneering, with those deep lines at the corners. Don't you see it?'

'Oh my God! He's right, it is him.' Raven grimaced. 'The night we met him, Ade told me he knew the name Walton-Lord. I suppose that must have been because of my old man. I've never held the guy in particularly high esteem, but to know he was the sort of person who could be friends with Ade Adams . . .'

'He won't have known what he was like,' Tess said.

'I guess no one did, or he'd have been exposed while he was still alive.'

'Unless this is the sort of club that can stop things being exposed,' Liam said. 'There must be a reason Ade was never found out. He doesn't seem to have been particularly discreet.'

Raven finished the remains of her gin. 'You know, the more I learn about my parents, the more I'm disappointed in them. Makes you wonder why we bother, doesn't it?'

'Bother with what?' Tess asked.

'Well, procreation. I'm starting to feel quite Philip Larkin about the whole business.'

Tess frowned. 'You're sure you're all right, Rave?'

'I'm fine.' Raven stood up and whistled to Roger. 'I ought to take his Lordship out for his walk. I'm sure you two have got important murder-related business to discuss.'

Chapter 19

'Is she OK?' Liam asked Tess when Raven had left.

'She's seemed a bit down lately. I think she and Benjamin might be having some issues. Plus Candice keeps putting pressure on her to freeze her eggs, which probably accounts for the sudden prejudice against procreation.' Tess shook her head. 'Tell you what, I'm glad I'm not an heiress. What you gain in financial security you lose in uterine autonomy.'

'Actually, I'm glad she's gone. I have been looking into this Fifteen Club. I didn't like to talk about it in front of Raven, knowing her dad was a member.'

Tess frowned. 'Why, is it bad?'

'Well it's not exactly the Rotary Club.' Liam gestured to the meeting agenda Raven had left on the coffee table. 'Let's just say this collective act of worship they schedule into their meetings isn't Sunday School hymn-singing.'

'What, you mean . . .' Tess's gaze was drawn to the strange symbol in the club's letterhead: the Sigil of Lucifer. 'You're kidding me!'

'Why would I be? There's not much about the club online. What there is is tucked away in the darkest corners of the web, but the link with the devil is mentioned in all of them. It's pretty old, apparently, and very, very exclusive.'

'But it's . . . daft. I mean it's nonsense, all that black magic stuff. Hocus pocus and fairy tales.'

'Is it? As a concept, selling your soul for wealth and success is as old as time. As old as the notion of a dark power who can make that happen.' Liam picked up the photograph of the hooded members. 'Wealth, success . . . and perhaps in exchange for covering up any sinister proclivities that society and the law might frown upon.'

'But there's no such thing as the devil.'

'You know that, do you? What does your friend Oliver think?'

Tess felt a bit dazed. 'All right, some people believe there is, but a devil who trades souls for power? That happens in stories, not real life.'

'Thousands of women were executed as witches because they were accused of doing just that.'

'That was misogyny and mass hysteria. There are no real witches.'

'Peggy Bristow wouldn't agree, would she?'

Tess shook her head. 'You're just playing devil's advocate – I mean, literally. If Ade Adams was murdered, there has to be an earthbound explanation. Witches and devils weren't behind this; people were.'

'I know,' Liam conceded. 'Still, these ideas are powerful. Like you said, they can whip up hysteria – hysteria that can kill.' He picked up the Fifteen Club agenda and examined it thoughtfully. 'And now here's a whole club built around the sort of person who thinks the darkest side of human nature isn't something to fear but to admire. To worship, even. We can't rule out a ritualistic motive now we know Ade Adams was involved.'

'Lee, I don't like this,' Tess said in a low voice.

'I told you, I'm not going to let you get into any dangerous situations. Whatever goblins and ghouls are out there, you'll be safe from them.'

'But you won't be.' Tess shuddered. 'A secret society that worships the devil. It sends a shiver down your spine. You're not still thinking of going undercover at this place?'

'I have to, don't I? These guys aren't giving anything away. Not to anyone but their fellow Brothers in Satan.'

Tess shivered again. She'd never thought of herself as a superstitious person, but she felt an instinctive, visceral repulsion at the idea of the Fifteen Club.

'What exactly are you going undercover to uncover?' she asked.

He shrugged. 'Whatever there is to uncover.'

'You really think these guys might be involved?'

'I think Ade was a member of this club, and now he's dead. That feels like a coincidence worth investigating.'

'How will you get in?'

Liam looked through the papers for one that Raven had mentioned: details of how membership worked. '"All prospective members must be introduced by an existing member or be a close relative of a deceased member",' he read. '"Priority will be given to prospective members who can contribute significant skills and influence. Prospective members will be subjected to a secret ballot of existing members before being granted the status of Novice."'

'So you're scuppered then,' Tess said, experiencing a wave of relief. 'You don't know who the other members are.'

Liam glanced again at the photo. 'But I know a couple of deceased ones.'

'You're going to pretend to be related to Ade?'

'Not Ade. Dominic Walton-Lord.' He smiled. 'Raven's about to get herself a big brother. She's going to be thrilled when she finds out it's me.'

'Well, you can't go alone. Who knows what weird stuff these guys are into?'

'I'm thinking at worst there might be some unpleasantness with chicken blood and at best an orgy involving a bevy of Satanic supermodels. I'll be fine, Tess.'

'Stop joking. You said yourself this might have been a ritualistic murder.'

'It's a possibility, but with the costume and the tarot cards, it all feels a little . . . well, gaudy. I'm no expert but that doesn't sound like the way true Satanists would go about things. No, I'm definitely leaning towards a more human motive.'

'Still, it might be dangerous. You're always worrying about me being in danger. Worry about yourself for once.'

He smiled. 'Well, it's sweet that you care.'

'Let me come with you.'

'Tess, I think there's something in the phrase "gentlemen's club" you haven't quite grasped.'

'You have to take someone. They might . . . they might sacrifice you or something.'

Liam laughed. 'If it's a virgin they want, they're about eighteen years too late. Honestly, I'll be fine.'

'Hmm. I don't like it,' Tess murmured. 'What do you want me to do while you're guzzling demonic foie gras and getting pentangles tattooed on your bum-cheeks, then?'

'I had a thought about that. There's a lot of symbolism at work here. The tarot, the bonfire, the witch, the devil . . . do you not feel like the murderer's trying to send us a message?'

'Is that something murderers usually do?'

'Depends what they want out of the crime. Let's say we go with the most likely motive, which is that one of the many people Ade wronged is now out for revenge. Ending his life might only be one aspect of why they did it. They might be just as focused on exposure – not only destroying his life but his reputation too.'

'I don't understand.'

'Getting away with murder might not be on their agenda at all. You said it before: the way the murder was carried out does point to someone with a flair for the theatrical. Someone who wants all eyes on the crime. Someone who knows what grabs people's attention – a journalist, perhaps.'

'Angela?'

He shrugged. 'She does fit the bill. When there's a clue at the scene of a crime, it's usually been dropped by accident or planted there to misdirect. Personally, I don't think the tarot cards fit into either of those categories. I think the killer is quite deliberately trying to tell us why Ade was murdered with all this heavy-handed symbolism, and if we can tease out the meaning then it might help us figure out where to look next.'

'So what do you want me to do?'

'Look into it. I feel like the bonfire and the witch are as much a part of it as those cards you found. Stay out of trouble and do some desk research, and when I get back from investigating the club we'll hopefully know more.'

Tess shook her head. 'Desk research? Come on. You're fobbing me off with a fluff job.'

Liam held his hands up. 'I'm not, honestly! We need to know how this stuff ties together. Detection can't be all undercover work and chasing down suspects, Tess.'

'It can for you, apparently,' Tess said, folding her arms. 'So I'm to sit here trawling Wikipedia while you're being sacrificed in a Black Mass, am I? Wouldn't I be better off trailing Angela, or Leonie? Or I could investigate if any of the park gate keyholders are missing their keys, or if they—'

'Nope,' Liam said firmly. 'I told you before, Tess: if you don't follow my rules about staying away from the practical stuff, you're off this case. You don't know who around here could be the killer. The last thing you ought to be doing is going off on your own trailing suspects.'

'At least let me talk to Peggy Bristow. We know she can't have done it, even if she does know something.'

'How do we know that?'

'Because we established she wasn't a murderer once

already. When we were investigating who killed Aunty Clemmie.'

'No, we only established she wasn't *that* murderer.'

Tess shook her head. 'What it's like living in your head, suspecting everyone all the time? I bet you'd even suspect me, wouldn't you?'

Liam shrugged. 'I might, if you gave me good reason to. Any secret connections to Ade Adams?'

'Look, I've known Peg for years. She likes me – most of the time. I can't be in danger from her.'

'You'd known Clemmie Ackroyd's murderer for years too, hadn't you?'

'Well, yes, but . . . that was different.'

'Sorry, Tess, but it's desk research or nothing. Somewhere out there is a murderer and I don't want you anywhere near them.'

'If it definitely was murder,' Tess said, her eyes flickering to Ade disguised as a scarecrow on TV. 'We haven't totally ruled out the prank gone wrong thing. There could be other explanations for the tarot cards.'

'Nope. This is definitely a murder. A poisoning, in fact.' Liam reached into his pocket for a document and unfolded it. 'You can't tell anyone about this, OK? Not even Raven.'

Tess sat up straighter. 'What is it?'

'Toxicology report showing how Ade died. Della shared a redacted version in exchange for that titbit about Peggy Bristow.'

'What does it tell us?'

'That Ade had a pretty impressive cocktail of substances

in his system at the time of death. Alcohol, nicotine – I guess from vaping – diazepam and digoxin.'

'Diazepam . . . why does that sound familiar?'

'You'll know it better as Valium – sleeping pills. The report also tells us he must have died within two hours of being discovered. He may even have been alive when I got him down. The cause of death was a heart attack brought on by a high dose of digoxin.'

'What is digoxin?'

'Heart medication. It's used to regulate heart contractions, but an overdose can prevent the heart contracting properly and induce cardiac arrest. Just a few times over the normal dose can be fatal.'

'Was Ade taking heart medication?'

'Not according to his wife. He'd been diagnosed with arrhythmia but he wasn't being medicated for it.'

'Then how did it get into his system?'

'Well, I had a theory about that. Ade was a cocaine user, right? Powdered digoxin would look very similar. The murderer makes a switch, Ade goes to do a line and . . . instant heart attack. There was no coke in his system at the time of death, but there was a large amount of digoxin.' He lapsed into thoughtful silence. 'What's interesting is that here was an opportunity to make it look like an accident. If the murderer had laced his cocaine instead of switching it, it could have looked like his dealer was at fault. But they didn't; they introduced it another way. That makes sure of two things: firstly that he was getting an undiluted dose which meant death was certain, and secondly that there was no way it could look like an accident. The person we're searching for isn't putting much effort into covering their tracks.'

'Interesting,' Tess murmured. 'What about the Valium?'

'I asked Leonie and apparently Ade didn't take any sleeping drugs. The police didn't find any among his possessions either, yet there was a high dosage in his system. That suggests he might have been drugged before he was murdered.'

'Why, though? If you're right and the murderer swapped his cocaine for something lethal, they knew it was going to stimulate cardiac arrest. All they had to do was sit back and wait.'

'You remember my theory, that this was about exposure as much as murder? If Ade had died in his hotel room, he wouldn't have been on the front page of every national newspaper. I doubt we'd have all these women coming forward to tell their stories. It'd slip totally under the radar.'

'So they drugged him, dressed him as a witch, dragged him up to the top of the bonfire and then killed him? Or they convinced him to dress as a witch and climb the bonfire somehow and then drugged and killed him?'

'I still think he must've climbed up himself. The alternative is too messy to go unnoticed in broad daylight.'

Tess shook her head. 'That makes no sense, though. They could've just killed him outright. Why drug him first?'

'I know. I can't work it out either.' Liam glanced again at the report. 'According to Della, an examination of the crime scene shows the ladder I used to climb the bonfire was the same one that got Ade up there. It was pushed down after him – there was an indentation by the pyre that shows it had lain there for a time – and at some point moved to the refreshment marquee, probably by one of your committee. Could the murderer have climbed up after Ade and forced him to swallow a load of Valium?'

'What, while he just sat there and submitted? If he'd cried out, someone would have heard. He'd have disturbed the pyre too if there was a struggle. Fallen, probably.'

'Yeah, it doesn't quite add up. And that still leaves the other question – who murdered him, and when?'

'He died within two hours of the bonfire,' Tess said slowly. 'But Angela said the tarp had been moved that morning. That's why the wood had been wet, because it drizzled all afternoon.'

Liam nodded. 'And Leonie said he left their hotel suite in the early hours after a row. So he mounted the bonfire sometime in the morning but he wasn't killed until late afternoon at the earliest. Why the big gap?'

'It's baffling,' Tess agreed. 'Does it feel to you that every time we find out something new, it answers one question and raises two more?'

'Welcome to the wonderful world of detection.'

'Is there a clue in the substances? Who on your suspect list would have access to digoxin?'

'It's not helping Angela's case. She has a heart defect, doesn't she?'

'Yes. She had a pacemaker fitted a few years ago. She's on medication too, I think.'

'And I'll just bet it's digoxin.' Liam stood up. 'I'd better go. I guess you need to get ready for work.'

'OK.' Tess glanced up at him. 'Think about what I said, though. I'd feel a lot happier if you took someone else when you went down to London.'

'What do you want me to do, hire a bodyguard? That'll give the game away before I've got through the door.'

'No. Just . . . leave it with me. I might know a guy.'

Chapter 20

'Hey, Rev,' Mikey said when he opened the door of Ling Cottage. He was in his dressing gown, hair rumpled as if he'd just woken up.

'Evening.' Oliver tried not to sound too stern, but he couldn't help it. His voice naturally tended towards sternness with Mikey. 'Can I come in?'

'Your place, isn't it?' Mikey stood aside and Oliver went through to the front room.

Ling Cottage had always made him shiver, long before it became associated with the grisly events of the spring. However, Oliver was surprised to find it looking almost homely today. Colourful new touches – a scented candle here, a plush throw there – seemed to give the place a whole new vibe. Now they were in early December, even a little Christmas tree had appeared, glistening with glass baubles. Oliver pushed aside the cherry-red cushions that now adorned the sofa so he could sit down.

'I hope you don't mind,' Mikey said. 'I know they're a bit girly, but Bels wanted the place to be cosy for me.' He smiled fondly. 'You have to let them have their fun, don't you? It might be a while till we can play house for real.'

Bels, Oliver had learnt, was the girlfriend – or fiancée, rather – who Mikey had connected with in prison. She'd been an old friend who had got back in touch via social media, and the bond between them had quickly grown.

'No, they look nice,' Oliver said. 'It's good you should make the place your own.'

'I'll pay you rent, now I'm working.' Mikey glanced down at his tatty dressing gown – an old one of Oliver's. 'Sorry I'm not dressed. The warehouse has got me on night shifts.'

'Don't worry about it.' Oliver turned away slightly. He found it hard to look long at Mikey.

As a lad, Mikey had been good-natured, cocky and rather handsome – at least, all the girls had seemed to think so. A sort of loveable rogue, when he was still in his mid-teens. Still, aside from the odd slap on the wrist, during his schooldays he'd stayed more or less on the right side of the law.

Four years older than Tess, after leaving school Mikey had become their dad's protege in the family business – if you could call it that. Dan Feather's 'trade' involved the buying and selling of dodgy goods, along with other illicit activities. Under the influence of his father and the unsavoury group of friends he'd found himself among, Mikey's criminal activities increased in both frequency and severity. His occasional prison sentences had lengthened, until finally a serious GBH conviction landed him behind bars for two years. He could have been out in one – if it hadn't been for an ill-judged escape attempt while on compassionate day release.

Mikey hadn't been given a chance really – none of the

Feathers had. Only Tess had managed to avoid that sort of life. Oliver would have pitied the man, if it wasn't for what he'd done to Archie.

'You don't mind Bels staying over sometimes, do you?' Mikey asked. 'She's only been a couple of times. It's hard for her to get away.'

Oliver forced himself to look at the man. 'I don't, but you need to be careful, if you're serious about keeping it a secret that you're up here,' he said. 'The curtains are only thin. Tess spotted someone through them last week. Bels, I guess.'

Mikey frowned. 'Tess? What was she doing up here?'

'Going for a walk. It's not unheard of for people to do that, especially the ones with dogs.'

'Has she got a dog?'

'Raven has.'

Mikey smiled. 'Well, I'm glad. She was forever pestering our mum and dad for a dog.'

'What I'm saying is, don't assume you're undiscoverable just because you're a little way from civilisation and you keep the curtains closed. All right?'

'All right.'

Oliver realised he was frowning, and his voice had taken on a harsh tone. He endeavoured to soften it. 'Anyway, no need to pay rent when you're only temping,' he said. 'If you want to pay me back for putting you up, you can consider talking to your sister.'

Mikey looked down at his hands. 'I told you. She won't want to see me.'

'I think you might be wrong about that.'

'I went on the run at our mum's funeral, Oliver. It's not something she's likely to have forgotten.'

'Why did you do it? You had a record of good behaviour. You could've been out in another two months.'

'I don't know. They let me out on day release, no cuffs, only one cop keeping an eye on me, and it was like . . . a moment of madness, I suppose. I wasn't much more than a kid then.'

'Not as much of a kid as your sister. She was seventeen. She needed you, Mikey.'

'I know.' Mikey rubbed his forehead. 'If it was Matt or Caleb . . . but our Tess is the only one of us who managed to make something of her life on the right side of the law. I don't want to drag her down.'

'If you mean it about going straight, she could be a big help.'

'I don't deserve help from her.' Mikey glanced up. 'Or from you either. If you weren't a man of God, I reckon you'd have chucked me out on my arse when I turned up like that.'

'Well, I did punch you in the face.'

'But then you put me up, and you gave me a reference for the warehouse job.' Mikey met his eyes earnestly, and Oliver tried not to shudder. 'I won't forget it, Rev.'

Oliver stood up. 'Just don't let me down. You've got a lot of people putting their faith in you this time, Mikey. Make it count.'

'I will.'

'And remember what I said. You really ought to talk to Tess.'

'Well, I'll see. Maybe when I'm properly back on my feet.'

'Any progress looking for a place with Bels, or is she still stuck with the unsympathetic housemate?'

Oliver was greatly looking forward to the day when Mikey Feather was no longer his responsibility.

'The housemate's gone but we can't just move in together. Need to be able to afford my share, see. I don't want Bels to think I'm leeching off her. Maybe if I can get a permanent contract.'

'Well, let me know how that goes. Need anything else?'

'You've done more than enough for me already.' Before Oliver knew what was happening, Mikey had grabbed his hand and was pumping it vigorously. 'Thanks, Oliver. Like I said, I won't forget it.'

As soon as he could politely disengage himself, Oliver jerked his hand away. 'Um, thanks. See you, Mikey.'

*

Oliver wandered back to the village deep in thought.

His intention in visiting the cottage had been to have the conversation with Mikey that his bishop had advised him to have. He'd been putting it off for a week now, but he knew it had to be done. But when it came to the crunch, he hadn't been able to trust himself to raise the subject without getting angry.

The irony was, if Archie had been here he'd have forgiven Mikey like a shot. He could never bear a grudge for long. But Archie was gone, and Oliver knew full well that his unresolved anger went hand in hand with his unresolved grief.

His anger at Mikey was just an extension of his anger at the unfairness of losing his brother too young and too soon. He was self-aware enough to realise that, but he still had no idea how to move past it.

The vicarage loomed in the distance. Oliver gave it a morose glance. He really didn't feel like going home. His parents had gone now, finally returning to their refurbished park home, and Oliver finally had the solitude he'd been craving. His own space, with the peace and quiet to process the changes that had happened in his life recently. It must be the perverseness of the human brain that he found himself rather lonely now that his mum and dad had gone. Now he was alone again he felt his singledom keenly, seeing his future stretching out with no friend and companion to share it with. Embarrassing as their antics were, he couldn't help envying what his parents had together.

His phone buzzed and he took it out.

Tess. He felt a wave of guilt on seeing her name, knowing he was keeping the presence of her brother a secret from her. But what could he do? He couldn't betray the man's confidence.

'Ol, I need a favour,' Tess said when he answered. 'Actually, I need two. One's small and fun, the other's big and dutiful.'

'Whatever you need,' Oliver said, wincing immediately as he realised he'd let his guilt volunteer him for unknown favours.

'Firstly, can you go round to the flat and give Roger a walk if it's convenient? Rave's got a date with Benjamin and

I totally forgot I had another gig at that hotel tonight. He'll be stuck in until after midnight otherwise. You know where we hide the spare key.'

'Under the plant pot by the front door,' he recited. 'What's the other thing?'

'Ah. Well, this is going to sound weird, but I promise it comes under the heading of battling the powers of darkness.'

Oliver blinked. 'It's not another exorcism, is it?'

'No, but it is in the name of crime-fighting. I need a man of strong moral fibre to help Liam with some undercover work.'

'You need a man of what to do what?'

'I want you to put on a red robe and go undercover at a gentleman's club. Oh, and if you possibly can, because I do quite like the guy in spite of everything, could you make sure Liam doesn't get human-sacrificed?'

*

Oliver didn't actually need the spare key from under the plant pot. When he inserted it into the lock, he discovered the door to Tess and Raven's flat was unlocked. He gave a tentative knock. All was quiet apart from a few yips from Roger so he pushed it open. Had Raven gone out without locking up?

He soon found out when he discovered her in the living room, watching TV in an oversized fleecy hoodie with a large glass of gin in her hands.

'Oh. Hiya, Rave,' he said. 'I thought you were out. Hey, I've just had the weirdest call from Tess.'

Raven sniffed and looked round. Her face was streaked with mascara-coloured tears.

'Raven, hey.' Oliver sat down and put an arm around her shoulders, which earned him a suspicious glance from Roger. 'What's happened, love? Tess said you were out with Benjamin.'

'It's over, Ol,' she murmured, resting her head on his shoulder. 'What nice guy wants to be with a mess like me, right?'

'You broke up with him?'

She took a deep swig of gin. 'He broke up with me. Of course he did. It was only ever a matter of time.'

'Don't talk like that.' He planted a gentle kiss on top of her head. Unlike the job Tess wanted him to help Liam with, this, at least, was charted territory – seeing his friends through break-ups. 'Any man would be lucky to be with you. I've been telling you that for years.'

'Perhaps you ought to tell a few of them too.' Raven lifted her glass and blinked at it. 'I know you have to say that, though. It's the duty of best friends to lie when you're upset.'

'Not me,' Oliver said, tapping his dog collar. 'Not allowed, am I?'

'Not even the little white ones?'

'Nope. I'm compelled to tell the truth, the whole truth and nothing but the truth at all times.'

Raven summoned a weak smile. 'What happens if you don't? Does the man upstairs send a thunderbolt for you?'

'That's right. And since I clearly remain unsmote, I must be telling the truth. See?'

'I don't believe you.'

'Here. Look at me.' Oliver bent his head so she could look into his face. 'You've known me since I was three years old, Raven. Now tell me if I'm lying.'

Raven studied his face for a moment, then smiled. 'I'm glad you came,' she said, snuggling against him.

'I'd have been here sooner if I'd known you needed me. You should have called.'

'I didn't want you to see me in this state. I look like a panda.'

'Well, yes. But a very pretty panda.'

She laughed and blew her nose on the handkerchief he passed her. 'Sorry, Ol. I still owe you a shoulder to cry on, don't I? You haven't cashed in your break-up night of tears and tissues for Tammy yet.'

'To tell the truth, I feel more philosophical than sad about it. Tam's great, but she was right when she said we weren't meant to be.' He sighed. 'The scariest thing is wondering if that was it, relationship-wise. My last shot.'

'Tell me about it. I thought me and Benjamin were meant to be. He was the first genuinely nice guy I ever dated.' She gave a bitter laugh. 'Who was I kidding? It was only a matter of time until he found out what a screw-up I really am.'

'You're not a screw-up.' Oliver gave her a squeeze. 'You're perfect. I mean it, Rave. If the men you've dated are too blind to see that, it's on them.'

Raven smiled. 'You know, darling, you're the perfect girlfriend I never had. You're much better at saying the right thing than Tess.' She glanced up at him. 'Although in her favour, she does bake for me when I'm upset.'

'I could rustle you up some chocolate cornflake buns? Unfortunately all my baking skills were learnt helping at the kids' Messy Church group.'

She laughed. 'No, that's OK. Go get yourself a drink, though. I'm refusing to let you leave yet.'

'Like I'd leave you in this state. I'll stay until Tess gets back.'

Oliver went to the kitchen, helped himself to a glass of Tess's red wine and sat back down.

'Want to tell me about it?' he asked gently as Raven snuggled back against him.

'Oh, it was so stupid. The decline started a few weeks ago when I made this throwaway comment about him making a good dad. Benjy went quiet for a bit afterwards, and I thought I'd freaked him out. Turned out that wasn't it at all. Totally the other way round.'

'How do you mean?'

'Once he'd thought it over, he was mad keen on the whole family thing. Couldn't wait to get started – I mean, he was like the answer to all Grandmother's prayers. Then it was me who freaked out, thinking about what a state I'd be as a mum.' Raven laughed. 'Can you imagine?'

'Imagine what? You'd make a great mum.'

'Oliver, I'm a gin-soaked overgrown child who can barely take care of herself, let alone anyone else. The only way I manage to muddle through as a grown-up is by relying on you and Tess. Not to mention that genetically I'm predisposed to be the worst parent ever.'

'In what way?'

'Well, my mum was so horrified at the idea of parenting that she gave me away rather than try, and my dad was a debauched playboy who spent his time guzzling foie gras at dodgy clubs with perverts. I'm the last person who should be allowed to pass on their genes.' Raven knocked back the last of her gin. 'Angela Campbell's got the right idea. No ties, no kids: just living life the way you want without inflicting humanity on another generation of poor saps. Let me be the last of the Walton-Lords. The family's had its time.'

'That's pretty bleak, Raven. Is that what you said to Benjamin?'

'Words to that effect. Needless to say he couldn't ditch me fast enough, after that little outburst.'

'You're not your parents, you know,' Oliver said quietly. 'You're you. Beautiful, ridiculous, perfectly imperfect you. And one day you'll meet someone who really, truly gets that.'

Raven smiled and pressed his hand. 'Come on. What chance have I got, if even someone like you can't meet The One? You're literally the nicest person in existence.'

'I'm really not,' Oliver said, thinking of his feelings towards Mikey. 'I try to be a good person, but it's hard sometimes, you know?'

'But you never stop trying, do you? That's what makes you special.'

Oliver took a morose sip of his wine. 'After what happened to Archie, I could've been lost for ever. I was trapped in a cycle of self-destruction that year. I might've ended up like . . . well, like . . .'

'Like Mikey?'

He turned to look at her. 'How did you know that's who I was thinking of?'

She shrugged. 'Who else would you be thinking of? Anyway, me and Tess wouldn't have let that happen.'

Oliver smiled. 'You never gave up on me.'

'Of course we didn't. And then look what happened,' Raven said, tapping his dog collar. 'What's it like, Ol?'

'What?'

'You know. Faith. Believing with that intensity.'

'I don't know if I can describe it to someone who doesn't have it. But I don't like to think about where I might have ended up without it.'

'It must be comforting,' Raven said with a sigh. 'To feel there's someone always looking out for you.'

Oliver pressed his lips to her hair. 'There is someone always looking out for you, Rave.'

*

It was early morning when Oliver was awoken by the sound of Tess arriving home from her gig. He blinked, trying to get his bearings.

He wasn't on the living-room sofa. Where was he? He was . . . in bed, with a duvet over him. Someone was next to him . . .

Damn! Now he remembered.

Oliver lifted the duvet and peeped under it, and a word he rarely used escaped his lips.

'Oh . . . bugger,' he muttered into the darkness.

Chapter 21

It was three days later, and Tess was buttering bread in the kitchen while a Babelesque tower of sandwiches teetered on the bread board next to her.

'What are all those for?' Raven asked.

'For the boys. I don't want them to go hungry on the drive down to London.'

'Have you used a whole loaf? There's enough here to feed twelve undercover detectives.'

'I know. I just wanted to be doing something. I don't like this job, Rave. This club of your dad's . . . Lee tells me not to worry, but how can I not?'

'You couldn't talk him out of going?'

'No. He says it's his best lead so far and he'd be a mug to ignore it. I'm glad Ol's going too, at least.'

Raven sighed. 'I wish he didn't have to.'

Tess put down her butter knife and went to give her friend a somewhat floury hug. 'How're you doing, love?'

Raven smiled. 'I'm fine, Tess, honestly. I mean I'm upset, obviously, but I'm resigned to it. Benjy and me wanted different things so it's for the best.'

'Did you want different things, or did you just panic because you felt like you weren't ready for the things?'

'What does it matter? It all adds up to the same outcome.'

'I'm sorry I wasn't there for you that night. If you'd texted I'd have cried off sick and come home.'

'There was no need for that. Ol was here to look after me. Anyway, I'm fine now.'

Tess released her from the hug. 'You are surprisingly fine. I thought you'd be even more gutted than usual this time.'

Raven shrugged. 'Maybe I'm just becoming inured to man-related emotional meltdown. I ought to be used to it by now.'

There was a knock at the door.

'I guess that's Liam,' Tess said. 'He's a bit early.'

It wasn't Liam she found outside the flat, however, but Oliver. For some reason he had a huge bouquet of flowers clutched in his arms, and he was blushing furiously.

'Um, hi.' He peered out from behind his flowers. 'Oh. Tess, it's you. I thought you might be . . . never mind.'

'You're early, Ol. Liam's not here yet.' She blinked at the bouquet. 'What are those for?'

'Er, they're for Raven. I mean for you and Raven. I know you've been having a tough time lately, her breaking up with Benjamin and you discovering Ade's body. I thought they'd cheer you up.'

'Oh. Thanks, that was thoughtful.' Tess took the flowers from him. 'Come on in and I'll get them in water.'

Raven passed Tess as she was heading for the kitchen to find a vase.

'Look, Rave,' Tess said, nodding to the bouquet. 'Oliver brought us flowers.'

Raven smiled at Oliver. 'That was sweet of him.' She glanced at his smart black suit. 'You look very dapper in your civvies.'

'I was told to arrive looking smart and un-vicar-like,' Oliver said, running one finger under the collar of his suit. 'I am going undercover, after all.'

'It suits you, darling.'

'Um, do you want to take Roger for a walk before Liam gets here, Rave?' Oliver said. 'I need to talk to you about something.'

'Fine by me,' Tess called from the kitchen. 'I have to finish making your sandwiches.'

'I hope you're hungry, Ol,' Raven said with a laugh. 'All right, we'll go down to the park.'

*

When Raven had clipped on Roger's lead, she and Oliver wandered towards the park, which the police had finally allowed to be unlocked.

'Are you sure you want to do this undercover thing?' Raven asked. 'You don't have to.'

'I'm not sure I'll be much use, to be honest. I doubt Liam needs a bodyguard, especially of the weedy and lanky variety. But if it'll reassure Tess . . .'

Raven reached out to squeeze his hand. 'Just look after yourself, OK? Make sure you know where the exits are and you've got emergency services on speed dial, and text me or Tess as soon as you get out.'

'I promise.'

They'd reached the park now, and Raven bent to let Roger off his lead.

Oliver rubbed his neck awkwardly. 'Look, Rave . . . we never did get a chance to talk the other day.'

She smiled. 'It was a bit difficult when we were smuggling you out in the dead of night, wasn't it? You might find this hard to believe, darling, but waking up with naked vicars in my bed is a relatively rare experience.'

'I tried to call you.'

She sighed. 'I know. I thought a day or two to process might do us both good.'

'You don't regret it, then?'

'I don't, and you shouldn't either. I'd say it was just what we needed after our most recent breakups. It gave my self-esteem a real lift.' She smiled at him. 'Funny. Before that night I'd have said you were about as far from my type as you can get, but we seemed to work pretty well, didn't we?'

'But we're not, um . . . I mean, it doesn't . . .'

Raven laughed. 'Don't worry, darling, I'm not going to frogmarch you to the altar or anything. I'm really not vicar's wife material.'

'Right. So it was just . . .'

'Rebound sex, I suppose,' she said with a shrug. 'We've been friends a long time. I think we can deal, don't you?'

Oliver felt a bit dizzy. He'd been angsting over this for the past three days, but Raven acted as though what happened between them had only marginally more significance than a game of tennis. He didn't generally mix in circles where people took such a casual attitude to sex.

'This isn't something I make a habit of, Raven.' He lowered his voice. 'In my world it's kind of, er . . . frowned upon, you know?'

She shook her head. 'The Church needs to get over this weirdness about sex. If it was so shameful then God wouldn't have made it such fun, would He?'

'The more progressive bishops tend to leave it to their priests' discretion, but a lot of my parishioners are distinctly . . . less progressive than that. If we were engaged, or even just dating, it wouldn't be as bad. But drunken one-night stands are not a good look for vicars.'

'We weren't that drunk.'

'I'm not sure that doesn't make it worse, to be honest.'

'Well, what could they do about it, these parishioners? They can't sack you.'

'It could undermine my position as their parish priest – maybe even to the extent I'd feel compelled to resign. Apparently it's already widely known that my parents are sex maniacs. This is really not what my career needs.'

'It's not like you've never done it before, though.'

Oliver closed his eyes. 'I haven't *done it*, if you must know, since around 2012.'

'You're kidding! Not even with Tammy?'

'Not even with Tammy.'

'But you were dating her for months.'

'We were . . . waiting. That was the idea, anyway.' He sighed. 'And then there was you.'

She patted his arm. 'In that case, darling, I'm even more flattered. And there's no need to worry, I won't tell a soul about it. I just want you to know, before we agree never, ever to discuss it again, that I had a simply marvellous time. I'd never have guessed you were so out of practice.'

Oliver managed a smile. 'As riddled with angst as I've been, it did feel like something I needed. I think I can make my peace with it, if we agree it was a one-off.'

Actually it had felt like more than something he needed. When Oliver had found his lips on Raven's that night, it had just felt . . . right. It had always felt easy to hold off from sex in his past relationships, but being with Raven had felt so natural, it hadn't even occurred to him to fight it. He'd just gone with the flow.

'I promise my lips are sealed.' Raven drew an imaginary zip across them, then bent to get the scampering Roger on his lead. 'We'd better head back. Liam'll be waiting for you.'

'Right.'

'Who was it?' Raven asked as they walked back.

'Hmm?'

'Back in 2012?'

'Oh.' Oliver rubbed his forehead. 'No one you know. Someone I met at college.'

Raven grinned. 'Hey. I found out something new about you.'

'I should think you found out quite a few things.'

'You've got a Leeds United tattoo on your left shoulder.'

He grimaced. 'Noticed that, did you?'

'When did you get that done?'

'For something we were never, ever going to talk about again, we seem to be talking about it a heck of a lot.'

'The ban only starts when we get back to the flat. You have to answer all my questions until then.'

He sighed. 'I got it when I was sixteen. You know, that year? It wasn't too hard to find an artist who didn't bother to check IDs.'

'I didn't think you were that die-hard a fan.'

'I didn't get it for me.'

'For Archie?' she said in a softer voice.

'Yeah. The footie was always our thing. Don't tell anyone, will you?'

'As on all other matters, even torture shall not drag it from me.'

Liam was waiting when they got back to the flat. He was holding a suitcase in his arms, looking rather bewildered while Tess bustled about.

'Hiya.' Oliver nodded to the case. 'What's in there?'

'Sandwiches, apparently.'

'Not just sandwiches,' Tess said. 'Also a wide range of snacks. You'll need to have full bellies for battling evil.'

'You see, this is what happens,' Raven said to Liam. 'You tell her she can't help so she overcompensates by going all mumsy on you.'

'Do you boys know your cover story?' Tess asked.

'I'm Carlton Walton-Lord, financier and eldest son of former member Dominic.' Liam nodded to Oliver. 'The Rev here is my younger brother Will, a doctor.'

'Is there a reason you're named after characters from *The Fresh Prince of Bel-Air*?'

Liam shrugged. 'Just my tribute to a quality programme.'

'Why am I a doctor?' Oliver asked.

'Because they like people with important or influential jobs.'

'Yeah, but I'm already a priest. That's quite important, isn't it?'

'Given the nature of the club, I doubt they'll be mad keen on admitting men of God into the ranks.'

'I don't like having to lie, Liam.'

'This is in the name of fighting evil, though,' Tess pointed out.

Oliver frowned at her. 'This is the second time you've dragged me into one of his investigations using that as an excuse.'

'You really don't need to come,' Liam said.

'Yes he does,' Tess said firmly. 'I know I've got a reputation as a sceptic, but if these guys really do what they claim to do . . . I'll just feel better knowing Oliver's with you, that's all.'

'You're sure you don't mind, Oliver?' Liam asked. 'I don't think there's going to be anything genuinely dangerous. These guys are probably just trying to be edgy with their robes and symbols. I'd bet good money that after lighting a couple of black candles and chanting something meaningless in Latin, they spend the night knocking back expensive booze and guzzling Ferrero Rocher.'

'No, Tess is right,' Oliver said. 'I don't like the idea of you getting into something like that with no backup. I'll feel better for keeping you company.'

'Well, if you insist.' Liam raised an eyebrow at Tess. 'And while we're away, you're going to be . . .?'

She rolled her eyes. 'Doing nice, safe desk research. Definitely not inviting any potential murderers round for tea and cakes.'

'That's what I like to hear.'

*

Five hours later, Liam pulled up outside a car hire firm in Fitzrovia. Oliver was asleep in the passenger seat.

'Oliver,' Liam whispered. 'We're here.'

Oliver grunted, wiping some drool from the corner of his mouth. 'This is the club?'

'No, this place hires out luxury cars. I booked us a chauffeur-driven Rolls.'

'A Rolls!'

'Well, yeah. If we're masquerading as wealthy landowners, we have to look the part. We're Walton-Lords now, remember?'

'Raven's an actual Walton-Lord and she drives an old Fiat,' Oliver pointed out.

'Real rich people can get away with that. When you're faking it, you have to try a lot harder.' Liam turned to look at him. 'We won't be able to talk in front of the chauffeur. Anything you need to ask, you'd better do it now.'

Oliver shook his head. 'Is this what it's like to be you?'

'Sometimes.'

'Suddenly I'm full of appreciation for the priesthood as a career. What do I do when we get there?'

'I'm not one hundred per cent on what'll happen but I did find a few scrappy details,' Liam said. 'At the bookshop they'll pretend they've never heard of the place, more than likely. I'll improvise a bit of chat, then I can show them Ade's card and our fake IDs.'

'You got us fake IDs?'

'We've got a driving licence each as Carlton and Will. I'm hopeful that should get us in. After that just follow my lead, OK?'

'OK,' Oliver said, looking bewildered.

Liam hoped Oliver wasn't going to blow their cover. This was obviously well out of the country vicar's comfort zone. Still, he had enough superstition to be grateful for some holy company tonight, all the same.

'I think it's best if you let me do most of the talking,' he said to Oliver.

'Fine by me.'

'Good. Just keep your ears open and let me know if you hear anything significant.'

Once in the Rolls, they travelled in silence. Half an hour later the chauffeur pulled up outside their destination and got out to open the door for them.

Sibley and Sons second-hand bookshop didn't look much like the facade for an exclusive gentlemen's club – although of course that was the whole point of a facade, Liam supposed. It was a faded establishment down a side street in Soho: the sort of place that included the word 'antiquarian' on its signage but was really only one step up from an Oxfam. A few tatty hardbacks gathered dust in the window.

If you weren't specifically looking for the place, you'd walk past it without a second glance.

The chauffeur looked puzzled as to why anyone would hire a luxury Rolls Royce to take them to such a rundown establishment.

'You may go,' Liam said, trying to get into character by summoning the sort of proud, definitely-better-than-you tone Carlton Walton-Lord might use. The chauffeur, apparently accustomed to this sort of treatment, gave a respectful nod.

'Are you sure this is the place?' Oliver asked doubtfully as the Rolls pulled away.

Liam took out the card Leonie had given him. 'It's the right address. Let's go in.'

Inside, an unshaven man in a grease-stained Motörhead T-shirt was sitting with his feet on the counter, eating Chicken McNuggets and reading the *Racing Post*. He didn't look like the doorkeeper for a gentlemen's club, Satanic or otherwise.

It was a dark, dusty place, books piled everywhere in no sort of order. Liam looked around for any sign of a door that might lead to a secret room, but all he could see was books. He and Oliver approached the man at the counter, who ignored them.

'Ahem,' Liam said pointedly.

The man grudgingly lowered his paper. 'Yes?'

'Perhaps you can help me. My name is Carlton Walton-Lord. This is my brother, William.' Liam paused fractionally to see if the surname resulted in any glimmer of recognition, but the man's gaze had already wandered longingly back to his *Racing Post*.

'Well?' he said.

'We're looking for a book. Somewhat rare, I understand. *The Grimoire of Truth*.'

The symbol the club used as its logo, the Sigil of Lucifer, had originally been taken from that work, and Liam watched for any reaction. The man only looked rather bored, however.

'Never heard of it, mate,' he said. 'There's a Waterstone's round the corner. I'd try them.'

He reached for his newspaper, but Liam slapped his hand down on it.

'I believe my late father was a customer here,' he said, trying a different tactic. 'Dominic Walton-Lord. Perhaps you know the name.'

'Must've been before my time. Sorry.'

'When he died, my brother and I inherited some of his papers.' Liam produced the black card Leonie had given him. 'Does this look familiar?'

The man glanced at it, and this time his face showed a slight flicker.

'Can't say it does.'

'That's your address, isn't it?'

'Must be a misprint,' the shopkeeper said, although Liam noticed he didn't bother to read the text. 'There's been a bookshop on this site for over a hundred years.'

'So you don't know anything about this place? The Fifteen Club?'

'Never heard of it.'

'What about this symbol? Do you recognise it?'

'Looks like a meaningless squiggle to me.'

Liam hesitated, wondering what to do. He'd relied on the card to get them in. Was there a secret password? Or did this guy genuinely not know anything about the club? Maybe they really had come to the wrong place. But then Liam was sure he'd seen the shopkeeper react when he'd presented the card.

The man had picked up his *Racing Post* and gone back to ignoring them.

'Right,' Liam said, his squared shoulders slumping. 'Well, thanks for your help.'

'No worries,' the man muttered, absorbed in his paper.

'Wait,' Oliver said. He looked at the man behind the counter. 'Um, did you know Ade Adams? The disc jockey?'

The man looked up sharply. 'Ade Adams?'

'Yes.'

'Know the name, don't I? He's been in all the papers.'

'He was a friend of our father's.' Oliver glanced at Liam. 'In fact, he was my godfather.'

Did Satanists give their children godfathers, Liam wondered? Or . . . devilfathers? Oliver's fresh approach did seem to be working though. The man was now regarding him curiously.

'Is that so?' he said.

Oliver nodded. 'He and our father were both members of this club, I understand.'

The man stared at him for a long moment. Eventually he turned to Liam.

'What was that book you boys were after?' he said. '*Grimoire of Truth*? You know, we might have a copy in stock. It'll be with our rare volumes in the back room. I can take you in to have a look if you want.'

Liam smiled gratefully. 'That would be perfect. Thank you.'

Chapter 22

'Right,' Tess said to Raven when the boys had left. 'Come on, sidekick. We've got work to do.'

'When did I get recruited for sidekick duties?'

'You're the only sidekick I've got left.' Roger glanced up from his bed and Tess smiled. 'Apart from you, Roger. We're a crime-solving dream team.'

'What do you want me to do, polish your mouse for you? It doesn't take two of us to trawl Wikipedia.'

'Three of us.'

'Roger won't be any help. His computer literacy's shocking.'

'I wasn't referring to Roger,' Tess said. 'And we won't be trawling Wikipedia. I've had a better idea.'

Raven frowned. 'Are you breaking the rules? Liam said desk research and nothing more.'

'Well, what Liam doesn't know won't hurt him.' Tess shook her head. 'I wish the man would stop treating me like a consumptive Victorian maiden who's too fragile for this world.'

'He's worried you're going to rush headlong into something dangerous without thinking it through, isn't he? You know, because of how you always do that.'

'I do not! Anyway, there are a hundred safe, useful things I could be doing. Talking to Peggy, or following Leonie to see if she's carrying on with someone, or trying to find out who had a prescription for sleeping tablets—'

'Sleeping tablets?'

'Ade had some in his system at the time of death. Lee thinks they might've been used to drug him.'

'What are you going to do, break into the surgery and hack into the prescriptions?'

'I'm not going to do anything reckless,' Tess said. 'I arranged a fact-finding trip for us, that's all. I'd rather speak to an actual expert than get my data off the web.'

'What expert? And who's this third person you mentioned?'

'Kennedy.' Tess checked her watch. 'She ought to be here soon. We're going to see her sister.'

'Seana? What for?'

'This is her area, remember? Witchcraft, bonfires and all that. I asked if we could have a chat with her, since Liam's keen to figure out the message in all this heavy-handed symbolism the killer's laid on.'

'I don't think he'd like you getting too hands-on, Tessie.'

'Well, he's not here, is he?' Tess sighed. 'Besides, I have to do something with myself. I need to take my mind off what the lads are up to.'

'I know, me too,' Raven said. 'You don't really think the club does sacrifices and things, do you?'

'Liam's probably right and they're just trying to seem edgy and mysterious with all the occult symbolism, but I don't like it. Those guys have got power – enough to cover up the sort of thing Ade liked to get up to, I'm guessing. Who knows what else they might be hiding?'

Raven shuddered. 'I'll be glad when the boys are home safe again.'

'So will I.'

'So what have you and Liam found out about Ade's history? Did you trace his other ex-wives?'

'One of them,' Tess said. 'Wife number three was a woman named Katrin Eckhardt. German. Ade met her in Munich while he was presenting a roadshow for the World Cup. Much younger than him, of course – she was barely twenty when they married.'

'Of course.'

'They were married a couple of years, then he left her for Sarah. Katrin moved back to her native country and started a family there with her second husband. Ade paid her maintenance but she hasn't been back to England since they divorced, so it doesn't look as though she's in the frame.'

'What about his other wives?'

'Sarah's no longer with us, of course. His second marriage, that was to Peggy, happened while he was working for Heartbeat FM in Leeds, when he was just beginning to be a name – it wasn't until his late thirties that he really started becoming well-known. Hopefully Liam can weasel any relevant information from her.' Tess shook her head. 'I wish he'd let me help. I'm so much better at that stuff than he is.'

'Well, he won't, and since I'm one hundred per cent on his

side, it's no good crying to me about it,' Raven said firmly. 'What about his first wife?'

'She's the real mystery. I've got a wedding date from a small announcement in the newspapers but that's it. Lily Gish, her name was.'

'Anything about her online?'

'Oh, there's plenty about Lilian Gish – just not the one we're interested in. She shares a name with a silent film star from the 1920s, which means that when you search for her, all you get is stuff about the actress.'

'You think that's a coincidence?'

Tess shrugged. 'Could be. Or it's a fake name, which throws up even more problems.'

'There's really nothing about her online?'

'Only the marriage announcement. Ade was pretty small time when they married, just a hospital radio DJ, so it didn't get any press. I can't find anything out except that the wedding took place in 1983, when she was in her late teens.'

Raven curled her lip. 'Yuck. Another seedy age gap.'

'Naturally.' There was a knock at the door. 'That'll be Kennedy.'

Seana Hamilton lived eight miles away in Paignley, a village on the outskirts of town. The three women piled into Raven's ancient Punto and set off.

'Thanks for sorting this out, Kenn,' Tess said. 'You're sure your sister doesn't mind?'

'Are you kidding? She loves having an excuse to talk about her favourite subject.' Kennedy smiled fondly. 'It's the only time she comes out of her shell. Seana's so shy normally.'

'You guys are really close, aren't you?' Raven said.

'I suppose we are, now. We weren't as kids – well, we never knew each other as kids, with the age gap. I was only little when Seana left home to go to uni. It was when I was more grown up that we really bonded.'

'That must be so nice,' Raven said wistfully. 'I always dreamed of having a sister when I was a kid. Mari was sweet and Grandmother did her best, but they were so much older than everyone else's parents. It was lonely being an only child.'

'I suppose it must be more like having another mum, when there's a big gap,' Tess observed to Kennedy.

Kennedy laughed. 'Yes, but you've got it the wrong way round. I'm definitely the mum. If it wasn't for me I don't think Seana would ever eat a square meal or have a clean shirt to put on.'

'Really?'

'Yeah, she's a mega genius but she's like a big kid. Nose always stuck in her books so she barely notices the outside world. It's such a struggle to get her to leave the house.'

'Was she always that way?'

'As long as I can remember. She suffers terribly with anxiety. It was really for my sister's sake that I moved back up north – not that I didn't miss the place, but I worried about her struggling on her own. Nick does his best but he's got his kids to occupy him, and his big, important job. I've only got Seana.' She leaned round to look at Tess. 'You never explained what this research trip was in aid of. Why the sudden interest in medieval folklore, Tess?'

Tess hesitated, wondering how much to reveal. It wasn't

common knowledge that anyone other than the police was investigating Ade's murder, or even that it was murder.

'I'm curious about the circumstances surrounding Ade Adams's death,' she said at last. 'The witch. The bonfire. All that bizarre stuff. It feels sort of symbolic.'

Kennedy shuddered. 'Oh God, don't. I still see his awful face every time I close my eyes. It was ghoulish, wasn't it?'

'I bet if you'd known then what we know now, you wouldn't have bothered trying to save the bastard's life,' Raven said, her brow knitting. Emotions in the village were still running high as more women came forward to tell their stories about Ade's grooming and abuse. Kennedy, however, tactfully refrained from replying.

'I thought it was a prank that went wrong,' she instead observed to Tess.

'So the police have been giving out, but there might be more to it. I found some tarot cards the night Ade died. It felt like they might be linked.'

Kennedy frowned. 'Tarot cards?'

'Yeah. Here, see for yourself.'

She handed her phone to Kennedy so she could look at her photos of the cards. Kennedy swiped through with a puzzled look.

'You found these?'

'Yes, by the body.'

'Do the police know?'

'They've got the originals but I couldn't help investigating them for myself.' She summoned a smile. 'You know I could never resist a mystery, Kenn.'

Unlike Tess's other friends, Kennedy didn't do the worried frown thing and warn her to leave it for the police. She only nodded. She had that sort of brain too: unable to avoid pulling at a thread once it had come loose.

'Did you talk to Peggy Bristow?' she asked.

Tess nodded. 'She told me what the cards might mean in a reading, but I thought your sister might be able to help too. There's a flavour of something ancient and occult about it all that I want to get to the bottom of. Maybe it's nothing, but it could point to something more sinister than a prank that went wrong, couldn't it?'

'It's a good idea to check it out,' Kennedy agreed.

Raven shook her head at Kennedy. 'You shouldn't encourage her. She gets far too involved in this stuff. You should've seen her this spring, sniffing around like a bloodhound trying to solve Aunty Clemmie's murder. She'll get herself into trouble one of these days.'

'No, I get it. It's hard to let it lie once you start asking questions. And who knows? Maybe we can point the police in the right direction, if we find anything out. That'd be pretty satisfying, being the ones to solve it.' She laughed. 'If Roger and Oliver were here we'd be just like the Famous Five.'

Tess gave her a gratified nod.

'Here we are,' Kennedy said as Raven's satnav announced they'd reached their destination. She nodded to a small cottage with an unkempt front garden, the curtains all closed, although it was only midday. 'Looks like she's forgotten we're coming. I might've guessed.'

They got out of the car and Kennedy knocked at the door.

Seana answered a moment later, wrapped in a huge woollen cardigan and with a distracted expression on her face.

'Oh. Kennedy.' She gave her a vague smile. 'Hello, my love.'

'Did you forget our appointment, Sean?'

'I suppose I must have. I was writing a paper and I . . .' She cast a puzzled look at the sky, as if surprised to find it was daylight. 'I must have lost track of the time. Do you want to come inside?'

'Yes, please. I brought Raven and Tess to talk to you about witches and things.'

Seana's face brightened. 'Oh yes, of course. Come in, all of you.'

Chapter 23

Kennedy followed her sister in, tutting as she examined the place. Seana's desk, which sat in one corner of the dark, untidy living room, was littered with papers, empty coffee cups and unwashed plates. There was no TV: just shelves and shelves of books, on all sorts of subjects. Most were on various aspects of history and folklore, but Tess noticed there were a number on medicine and anatomy too.

'We'll get these curtains open for a start,' Kennedy said, going to the window. 'Have you been working all night again?'

Seana blinked in the daylight. 'What day is it?'

'Thursday.'

'Then I suppose I must have been.' She smiled an embarrassed, apologetic little smile. 'Sorry.'

'Don't apologise. I know you can't help it.'

Seana looked at Raven and Tess, lurking about awkwardly as this exchange occurred. 'Oh. I suppose you want to sit down. Sorry, I always forget to ask the right things. Do go ahead.'

Tess glanced at Raven and they took a seat.

Kennedy remained standing, looking at the plates on her sister's desk. 'When did you last eat?' she asked Seana.

'I don't know. Yesterday, perhaps.'

Kennedy shook her head. 'And I'll bet it was a ready meal. You need to look after yourself, Sean. I left some stew for you in the freezer.'

Seana smiled apologetically again. 'Sorry. I forgot.'

Kennedy shivered. 'It's freezing in here.' She turned to Tess and Raven. 'I'm going to get the heating on, then I'll make some tea and defrost a proper meal for Seana. You three have a chat. It won't take me long.'

She piled up the plates from Seana's desk and marched off towards the kitchen.

'She makes such a fuss,' Seana said to Tess and Raven in a conspiratorial whisper. She had a very girlish face, although she was in her mid-forties: a little like a painting, with round apple cheeks and intelligent but innocent green eyes. She had the pallor that came of spending too much time indoors, however, and the bags under her eyes suggested far too little sleep.

Tess glanced at Raven. 'Um, we were hoping to talk to you about something you said at the bonfire. You were talking about fire. How it's one of the most ancient and powerful symbols.'

'The bonfire,' Seana said distantly as she took a seat opposite them. 'Oh yes, I remember. That awful dead body. It was horrible, wasn't it?'

'The police think it was an accident, but we're not so sure,' Raven said.

Seana frowned. 'You don't think it was a murder?'

'It could be. Ade Adams wasn't a popular man.'

'No,' Seana said, her voice once again taking on a vague quality as her mind wandered elsewhere. 'I don't suppose he was.'

'There are some elements of what happened that seem sort of folklorish, which is why I thought you might be able to help,' Tess said. 'The fact his body was discovered on top of a bonfire. The outfit he was wearing. And there were other things – a symbol on a card he had, for example: the Sigil of Lucifer. Fire, witches, the devil . . . it feels like it could almost be a message.'

Seana's eyes had kindled with interest as she listened. 'Well, there's the traditional connection between witchcraft and devil worship, of course,' she said. 'The two have always gone hand in hand.'

'Can you tell us more?' Raven asked as Tess took out a pad to make notes.

'In medieval and early modern Europe, it was popularly believed that witches drew their power from a diabolic pact. That's why the practice came about of tying up suspected witches and throwing them into a lake to see if they floated, which I'm sure you've heard of. A witch was supposed to have rejected her baptism in order to do a deal with the devil, so the baptismal water would therefore reject her.'

'And if it didn't, they'd drown.'

Seana nodded. 'In a lot of cases, yes. Witches were usually believed to be women, although this wasn't always the case – in some European countries, men accused of witchcraft outnumbered women. But in this country and others, it was definitely women who bore the brunt of witch hysteria. Claims about their practices grew ever more lurid. Witches were said to attend the nocturnal Sabbat, where they would have intercourse with the devil and kiss his anus.'

Raven blinked. 'They'd do what?'

Seana smiled. 'I know, it sounds ridiculous. Many of the claims about what happened at the Sabbat were obscene or macabre. Infanticide, with the sacrifice of newborns to the devil. Cannibalism. Bestiality. Artists and writers of the time really let their imaginations run wild. It seemed like they were perpetually trying to outdo one another with more outlandish claims.'

'Witches didn't actually do those things though, surely,' Tess said to Seana. 'I mean, sacrificing newborns and such.'

'Mostly those ideas just fed into the general hysteria. Behind much of it you can sense the very male fear of female sexual desire, especially when that wasn't linked to procreation. There's a reason post-menopausal women were targeted by witch-hunters. A woman with sexual desire and no capacity to produce offspring was a frightening thing to those with a vested interest in upholding the status quo – men, in other words.'

'And we still encounter that attitude today,' Raven said. 'It's not uncommon for someone to insult an older woman by referring to her as a witch.'

Tess glanced at Raven. 'Ade referred to his ex-wives as a coven, remember?'

Raven nodded. 'Just what I was thinking.'

'Yes, it's the same misogyny at the heart of it,' Seana said. 'That isn't to say that some of these dark, fevered fantasies didn't become a self-fulfilling prophecy, though. There will have been people who, hearing the rumours of how witches practised their art, believed they could gain diabolic power through human sacrifice or cannibalism.'

Raven shuddered. 'Devil-worship, you mean?'

'There were certainly attempts to practise black magic. Most people executed for witchcraft were harmless apothecaries or other community members, however, whatever they were made to confess under torture.' Seana scowled. 'Such ridiculous confessions. Sailing across the ocean on a sieve and other nonsense. It's shocking they haven't all been granted a blanket pardon.'

'How many witches make a coven?' Tess asked.

'A minimum of three, and we've Shakespeare to thank for the fact most people think of that number. A coven can have any number of members, though. Thirteen was often considered optimal, but three has powerful occult associations too.'

Kennedy came back in with a tray of hot drinks. 'Your stew's defrosting,' she said to Seana. 'I'll heat it up before we leave, or you'll only let it go cold while you're jabbering.'

Seana smiled at Tess and Raven. 'My sister knows my bad habits too well.'

Tess took her mug of coffee and held it in her two hands. The chill was starting to disappear from the air now Kennedy had turned the heating on, but it was still very cold.

'Learnt anything useful?' Kennedy asked, sitting down with her chamomile tea.

'A bit more than I wanted to know about the witchy practice of kissing the devil's bum,' Tess said. 'I probably won't look at Peggy Bristow the same way again. Still, it's fascinating.'

'Anything that links to Ade Adams's death?'

'I'm not sure yet.' Tess glanced at Seana. 'What about the bonfire? Does that have any connection with witches?'

'Oh, yes,' Seana said. 'The communal fire links to every sort of magical practice, whether black magic or white. As I told you before, it's the most ancient of totems for us as a species – both giving life and taking it. In some ancient civilisations, it may even have been worshipped as a god. Of course, for witches it would conjure images of the infernal flame and their master the devil.'

Tess took printouts of the three tarot cards she'd found from her notepad and passed them to Seana.

'What about these? Do they mean anything to you?'

Seana looked through them. 'Well, tarot isn't really my area. It's actually rather recent, although practitioners often make claims about ancient antecedents. There's no proof of those, however. Decks may incorporate symbolism from European folklore, but there's no record of them being used for divination before the late eighteenth century.'

'Oh.' Tess felt disappointed there wasn't a stronger link between the cards and the other elements involved in the murder. 'Well, my tarot expert tells me they can stand for any number of things. The Sun might mean positivity or joy, but it could also represent beginnings or endings, or fire. The Devil stands for our decadent impulses, and the Judgement card represents spiritual rebirth.'

'Sorry, I don't think I can help you,' Seana said. 'They all link to elements of what we've been discussing, but that could be the same for any card in the tarot. The meanings have to be layered and vague, don't they? That's how readings work: people find the meaning best fitting their situation.'

'I suppose so.' Tess took out a final printout, this time showing the symbol used by the Fifteen Club. 'Do you recognise this? It's called the Sigil of Lucifer. It's from an old spellbook, *The Grimoire of Truth*.'

Seana frowned as she examined the symbol. '*The Grimorium Verum*,' she murmured. 'Yes, I know it. An eighteenth-century Italian manuscript, although the author claimed a more ancient source originating with King Solomon. Well, they always do. The appeal to antiquity; that's what buys it legitimacy.'

'What about the symbol?'

'I can't tell you much about it off the top of my head, but I've a book in my bedroom that might help – *Symbols of the Occult in Literature, Magic and Folklore*. You'd be welcome to borrow it.'

'Could I?'

'Of course. I'll fetch it for you.'

'Thank you.'

She disappeared upstairs to look for the book. Meanwhile, Kennedy drew the tarot printouts to her.

'It sounds like you've spent a lot of time trying to figure out what these mean, Tess,' she said.

Tess nodded. 'I've googled the hell out of it, and Peggy gave me a load of information, but I can't work out what the murderer might have been trying to tell us with them. It's like your sister said – there are so many layers of meaning that they could stand for anything.'

'Anything to be learnt from the cards themselves? Physically, I mean? I take it you did see the originals.'

Tess frowned. 'Good question. I hadn't thought about that. Well, they were . . . sort of warped, as if they'd been in Ade's pocket for some time, but glossy, as if they were new. Peggy said the deck was unusual, so possibly they were custom-made.

'Custom printing just those three would make sense. A deck with three cards missing would be a pretty incriminating thing to have knocking around.'

'That doesn't tell us what they mean, though, does it?'

'No.' Kennedy sipped her tea thoughtfully, gazing at the cards. 'Unless . . .'

'Unless what?' Raven asked. 'You look like you're having a brainwave, Kenn.'

'I might be. I was just thinking, what if the cards mean exactly what they say they do?'

Tess frowned. 'I don't get you.'

'What if it's not about what they symbolise in the tarot but about what they *are*?' Kennedy laid her hand on each in turn. 'The innocent child. The lecherous old devil. The last judgement.'

'What, you mean—'

'I mean it could be all about the pictures, couldn't it? Ade Adams, this devilish figure who got away with abusing underage girls for decades, finally meeting his judgement day.'

'Peggy did say that was what made the pack unusual,' Tess murmured as her gaze lingered on the images. 'She says usually they carry the name of the card. She'd never seen a deck with the pictures alone.'

Tess drew the Sun card to her and looked at the child smiling atop its white horse. The child, the devil . . . and the final judgement. Could it be so simple? Was that what the killer wanted to tell them – that Ade had been an abusive monster who'd deserved what he got? If exposure as well as murder had been their ultimate goal, it would make sense that they would leave a clue on the body to point the police and public towards exactly what Ade's crimes had been – and exactly why he was dead.

Chapter 24

Oliver peeped out from under his cowl as he and Liam followed a fellow robed figure down a dark corridor deep in the cellars of Sibley and Sons. Whoever had decorated the place had pulled out all the stops when it came to capturing that medieval dungeon look. There were iron brackets with skull motifs attached to the bare stone walls, burning large black candles with mysterious insignia etched on them.

This didn't feel right. He was a priest, for goodness sake! How would his parishioners react if they found out that their friendly village vicar – hot on the heels of a one-night stand with his best friend and the rumours of his parents' sexual shenanigans during Bible study – had joined a devil-worshipping secret society?

But what was the alternative? Ignoring Tess's plea for help and letting Liam go alone, possibly to face the very darkest forces while Oliver hid in his nice, safe vicarage? What sort of priest would that make him? What sort of Christian?

Tess Feather, though, honestly. You offered to do the woman one little favour and the next minute you were joining the bloody Illuminati.

Oliver had tucked a small New Testament into his pocket before setting off, to give him courage in the face of whatever he might encounter here. He couldn't get at it now thanks to the huge red robe that enveloped him, but he touched his hand to his hip, taking comfort from the little oblong underneath his clothing.

At the end of the sinister corridor was a large arched door. It was ancient oak, with black iron fittings. Of course it was.

'Before you enter, you must make a solemn vow on the Satanic Bible that nothing you see or hear tonight will be shared outside of this room,' intoned their guide. 'The names of our members are not to be shared, either inside or outside this hall. Our practices are not to be shared, nor any documents, spells, chants or other powerful incantations and rituals. Any breach of confidentiality will be visited by the foulest and most unnatural punishments the darkest parts of your imaginations can devise.' He held out a large black book. 'Swear. To our Lord and Master.'

Liam lay his hand on the book and swore without hesitation. 'To our Lord and Master.'

'Do you pause?' the guide with the booming voice said to Oliver, observing him hang back.

'Er, no. My hand's just . . . a bit sweaty. I don't want to leave marks on your nice book.' Oliver pressed his eyes closed and laid his left hand on the Satanic Bible, pressing his right to the small volume concealed in his pocket. 'I swear. To *my* Lord and Master.'

The guide didn't seem to notice the amended wording and started unbolting the door. Oliver kept his eyes closed, wondering what horrors might be behind it. A torture chamber? A Satanic orgy to surpass the most fevered imaginings of Hieronymus Bosch? Voldemort's lair? A door like that had to be hiding something pretty sinister.

He felt a nudge in the ribs. 'It's all right,' Liam whispered. 'Come on.'

Oliver opened his eyes and blinked. The inside of the club had a very different vibe from the outside. It was luxurious, with a lot of mahogany, red leather and old oil paintings. Huge chandeliers hung overhead. It was exactly how Oliver would have imagined a swanky gentlemen's club. There were no black candles or skulls here. Most of the men, of whom there were twenty or so, had their cowls down as they chatted and sipped glasses of champagne. Their guide removed his hood too and turned to smile at them.

'Sorry about that,' he said brightly, in an entirely different voice to the one he'd been using outside. 'We have to do things properly when we introduce prospective members. Tradition, you know.'

'Of course,' Liam said.

The man clapped his hands to gain the attention of the room. 'Gentlemen and . . . gentlemen, may I introduce our guests? Tonight we have two applicants for the position of Novice, both close relatives of deceased former members. This evening you may know them as Brother Twelve and Brother Nine. Junior Warden, can you pour our guests a glass of fizz?'

'Certainly.' A bespectacled man with the air of an accountant stood up. He pushed a glass of champagne into each of their hands and ushered them into chairs around the large central table.

'New fish, eh?' he said cheerily, taking a seat beside Liam. 'It's been a long time since we welcomed any Novices.'

'That's right,' Liam said. 'Our father was—'

The man held his hand up. 'Oh. No names. The Grand Master's strict about us being discreet. I mean, it's fair enough really, isn't it? We are supposed to be a secret society.'

Oliver glanced around the table. There were a few faces he recognised among the uncowelled revellers. A senior cabinet minister. The owner of a major online retailer. A reality TV star. A soap actor. Apparently members of the Fifteen Club came from all walks of life – as long as they carried fame, power or wealth.

Liam had noticed the famous faces too.

'But surely everyone here knows who the others are,' he said to the Junior Warden.

'Well, yes, we *know*. But we don't *say*.' The Junior Warden lowered his voice. 'At least, not officially, but there are a lot of us who take the opportunity to do a bit of networking. All got our livings to make, haven't we? The Grand Master turns a blind eye if we're discreet about it. Here.'

Oliver saw him slip a business card into Liam's hand. Liam read it, then passed it to Oliver. It read *Colin St Leger – Wealth Management Specialist*.

'Tax loophole guru to the stars,' Colin St Leger said proudly. 'Do you boys have cards?'

'No. Sorry,' Liam said. 'I didn't realise we were allowed to bring them.'

'Was it someone here who introduced you?'

'Actually our father was a member.' He lowered his voice. 'Dominic Walton-Lord.'

'Is that so? Well, Dom's something of a legend around here.'

Oliver leaned round, interested in spite of himself. He knew Raven was upset about her father's association with the club. Perhaps here was an opportunity to learn something that might help her make her peace with it.

'Did you know him?' he asked Colin, the Junior Warden.

'No, before my time, but my uncle was a member then. He had some stories to tell. Dom and Ade used to have everyone in stitches with their double-act routine at the annual Lupercalia Beano.'

Liam looked up. 'Ade Adams?'

Colin bit his lip. 'Sorry. Senior Brother Six, I ought to have said. Anyway, they performed an incredible tribute to Morecambe and Wise, I'm told.'

Oliver took a sip of champagne, his head spinning. He'd anticipated many things when it came to going undercover at a Satanic gentlemen's club, but Morecambe and Wise tributes hadn't been one of them.

'Did you know A—Senior Brother Six well?' Liam asked.

Colin looked a little wary, as if suddenly remembering these were strangers. 'Not well. A little.'

Liam laughed. 'Don't worry, we're not the cops. He was family, that's all – well, sort of. He was my brother's godfather.'

Colin looked at Oliver with interest. 'Is that right?'

'Er, yes,' Oliver said. 'We were very . . . close.'

Oliver became aware of a middle-aged man in a green robe on his left, listening to their conversation with a drunken smirk on his face. He smiled vaguely back at him.

'Well, Ade was a good sort,' Colin said, topping up his champagne. 'Very unfair, all that stuff in the papers.'

'He was still a member when he died?' Liam asked.

'Yes, he was here a few weeks before it happened. Shame. Great shame.' Colin helped himself to an olive from a bowl. 'Women, right? Out for what they can get.'

Liam nodded. 'Easy to slander someone when they can't speak up. I always knew he didn't do it.'

'Oh no, he did it all right. Don't believe everything you read in the papers, though. Those girls wanted it, whatever they're saying now.' Colin leered unpleasantly. 'Then as soon as there's the chance of making some easy money, off they go crying to the papers. As if a girl of sixteen doesn't know exactly what she's doing. They'd have been long married off at that age four hundred years ago, while they were still prime breeding stock. The older they get, the less use they are to anyone.'

'Er, yes,' Liam said, although Oliver saw him suppress a grimace. 'They certainly had it right back in those days.'

The man next to Oliver nudged him in the ribs. 'Tell you what though, Brother,' he said in a slurred voice. 'Sixteen was just the tip of the iceberg.'

Oliver lowered his voice. 'There were younger girls?'

The man nodded. 'As young as twelve, some of them. He was a dirty old bastard, Senior Brother Six – I mean, no offence to your family. If he hadn't been one of us he'd have been ruined long ago.'

'So the club covered it up?'

'We always look after our own – while they're alive, anyway.' The man laughed drunkenly. 'The Old Gent sees to you after that. He certainly saw to Ade Adams.'

Liam nudged Oliver. 'Um, Brother... Thingy. The Junior Warden's going to introduce me to some people. Will you be OK here?'

Oliver cast a wary look at the green-robed man on his left. 'I suppose so.'

The man beside him topped up his wine unsteadily, then filled Oliver's glass for him. 'Junior Master Two,' he said chummily. 'What do you go by?'

'Er, Brother Nine. I think.'

'Nice to know you, Nine.' He sipped his wine thoughtfully. 'My old man was a Nine when he was a Novice. That would've been back in the sixties, when he was a big name in panto. Taught me everything I know, Dad did.'

'What is it you do, if you don't mind sharing?' Oliver was sure the man's face was vaguely familiar.

'Children's entertainer,' Junior Master Two said. 'The face of preschool primetime, me. Known professionally as Johnny Guffaws.'

That was it. Oliver had seen the man on magazines and children's merchandise. A veteran of kids' TV, the man was usually in full clown makeup, pretending to ride a puppet emu. A lot of the kids who came to Messy Church were fans of his. It made Oliver shudder to find someone like that in a place like this.

'What do you do?' Johnny Guffaws asked, reaching once again for the champagne bottle.

'I'm a priest,' Oliver said absently, his thoughts elsewhere.

Johnny frowned. 'A what?'

Oliver winced. 'Er, a Satanic priest, I mean. Black Masses and so on. Obviously that's on the side. Professionally I'm a surgeon.'

Johnny looked impressed. 'Satanic priest, eh? And a doctor too. You'll go a long way in this club, young man.'

'Oh. Great.'

Oliver glanced at Liam, making friends in a group of semi-familiar faces on the other side of the table. Liam knew what questions to ask to find out more about Ade's death, presumably. Oliver was thinking of Raven, however, and what he could find out about her dad.

'Did you know my father?' he asked his new friend. 'I don't know his rank. Dominic Walton-Lord.'

'Oh yes, I remember Dom. He was Steward for a time. He wasn't with us for long – too young when we lost him – but he made an impact all the same. Always joking around.' He grinned. 'A real charmer too. We used to do a ladies' night, back then, but they stopped them. You can't trust a woman to keep her gob shut, and some of the lads here get through wives like Smarties. Ade Adams seemed to have a new one every year.'

'Did Dominic bring his wife? I mean, my mum?'

'Yeah. Eva something or other. Model – gorgeous-looking

girl. Legs all the way up to her backside. Always wonder what happened to her.'

'What was she like? She left when I was young so I don't know much about her.'

'Strong. Ambitious. If she'd been born a man, she'd have joined herself and been Grand Master within a month. She had the sort of personality where if she told you to do something, you snapped to it without a thought.'

'Ambitious in what way?'

'In her career. She wanted to be an actress, see. Wanted Dom to use his connections here to get her on the West End stage.'

'Did he?'

Johnny shrugged. 'Died before he had the chance, I think. Still, if Eva wanted to perform in the West End then that'll be what happened. She always got what she wanted.'

Oliver glanced at Liam. As interesting as this information might be to Raven, he should probably remember his mission.

'What about my godfather?' he asked. 'Did Ade bring his wives to ladies' night?'

'The German girl came to one or two, I think. We'd stopped the ladies' nights before the last couple, though.'

'What about his first wife?'

'Never met that one,' Johnny said. 'All I know is she was a friend of your mum's from stage school. Foreigner. She'll have been a looker, no doubt, if Ade took up with her. I don't know how he did it. He treated his women like crap, but he always seemed to have them hanging around.'

A member in a golden robe with his cowl up – the Grand Master, presumably – had risen and started lighting candles, which Oliver sensed was the prelude to some sort of ritual. He pressed one hand to the New Testament in his pocket.

'How does this work?' he asked Johnny. 'I mean with the . . . the Old Gent. Do we, you know, call him forth or whatever?'

Johnny had knocked back another glass of wine and was once again topping up his glass. 'Well, he's always present in spirit. Wherever a few of us gather in his name, there he is in our midst.'

'I believe Jesus said something very similar,' Oliver murmured. 'Don't we have to make a pledge or something before he accepts us as one of his disciples?'

The man shot him a woozy look. 'Didn't you say you were a Satanic priest?'

'Well, yes, but . . . we're an unusual sect. I imagine things work a little differently here. Do you, um . . . sacrifice things?'

There was a huge gong mounted on the wall. The room fell silent as the Grand Master struck it with a stick. The lights lowered, and a pentangle traced in UV paint became visible in the centre of the table.

'You're about to find out,' Johnny Guffaws whispered. 'Watch and learn, Brother Nine. Watch and learn.'

Chapter 25

As soon as the ritual was over, Oliver made his excuses to Johnny Guffaws – now practically under the table – and found a quiet part of the room where he could take a moment to be by himself. The act of worship hadn't been particularly frightening – in fact, it had been rather ridiculous – but he was definitely ready to leave. Hopefully it wouldn't be long before Liam had all the information he needed. He was much better at this undercover lark than Oliver, smiling and being charming with some of the other Brothers, but there was a weary look in his eye that suggested he, too, would be very glad to get out of here.

In fact it was half an hour before Liam tore himself away from Colin St Leger and his braying, awful friends to make a beeline for Oliver. Silent, discreet waiters had started to emerge with silver trays bearing expensive-looking food. Three huge five-bird roasts in an orange sauce passed by Oliver's shoulder.

'Come on,' Liam muttered under his breath.

'Are we going?'

'Yes, we're going. We're getting out of here and we're going to find a pub.'

Oliver let out a low whistle of relief. 'Praise the Lord. How do we get out?'

'There's a fire escape up the stairs by the Gents; I spotted it earlier. I doubt they'll notice us leave now the food's coming out.' Liam glanced at the Grand Master, who'd fallen asleep in his chair. His cowl had slipped down to reveal he was one of the presenters on a popular home improvement show. 'Most of them are sozzled now anyway. I'll go first, then you follow in a few minutes. If anyone asks, tell them you're going for a fag. I've noticed a few of them sneaking out for a smoke or a snort so I doubt they'll ask questions.'

Oliver nodded and Liam headed for the fire exit. Oliver waited a few minutes before sidling off in the same direction. No one stopped him, or even seemed to notice him much.

When he reached the alleyway outside, he pulled off his robe and threw it to the ground. Then he leant back against the wall beside Liam and breathed deeply.

'Thank God we're out of that.' Liam took off his own robe and pushed it into a nearby bin.

'You said it,' Oliver agreed fervently. 'Did you mention something about a pub?'

'First one we find that looks distinctly non-Satanic and ordinary. Come on.'

'We'd better text the girls,' Oliver said. 'You don't think those guys will come looking for us, do you?'

'Are you kidding? They can barely walk.' Liam shook his head. 'Those guys aren't Satanists. That was just a drinking club for some of the worst people I've ever met, with a couple of pentangles chucked in to make it seem mystical. Spoilt City boys, trust fund kids and child rape apologists. What a shower.'

'That Latin incantation they made us chant was gibberish,' Oliver said as Liam tapped out a text to Tess. 'Just nonsense words that sounded good.'

'I didn't know you had to learn Latin in the Church of England. Isn't that a Catholic thing?'

'I did a course on Duolingo.' Oliver finally relaxed enough to smile. 'The second verse was the dummy placeholder text they use in typesetting. I distinctly recognised the line "Lorem ipsum dolor sit amet". It's gibberish.'

'They've just chucked together a load of occult symbols, some made-up Latin and a few random ideas about witchcraft and Satanism. It's a bit pathetic really. Little boys making believe they're doing something more significant than just getting sloshed and stuffing their faces.' Liam nodded to a cosy-looking pub with coloured Christmas fairy lights around the door, glowing with welcome – the Flying Pig. 'This place isn't bad; I've been before. Come on, Rev. I'll buy you a drink.'

'Call me Oliver.'

'You don't like Rev?'

'I don't mind it around the village, but my friends call me Oliver.'

Liam smiled. 'All right, Oliver it is.'

'Will we drive back tonight?' Oliver asked as they approached the bar.

Liam ran a hand over his forehead. 'As desperate as I am

to get far, far away from that place, I'd better not. I had to have a couple of glasses of fizz, for the look of the thing. I'll book us a pair of rooms at a hotel. Leonie's paying our expenses.'

'OK.'

Liam scanned the bustling pub, a faraway look in his eyes.

'Do you miss London?' Oliver asked.

'Not really. I was just remembering how Tess took me here on our second date. She bought me a cheese toastie.'

Oliver laughed. 'The last of the great romantics.'

'Given the price of toasties down here, it was quite romantic.'

'You like Tess a lot, don't you?' Oliver said quietly.

'More than she's ever likely to believe,' Liam replied with a sigh. 'What're you drinking, Oliver?'

Oliver selected a beer and when they'd both been furnished with a pint, they found themselves a seat.

'Well that was a waste of time,' Liam said. 'I can't believe Ade's murder could be connected to that club. Those pissheads were the worst excuses for Satanists I've ever seen.'

'It wasn't a total dead end. We found out a few things.'

'Such as what?'

'That it was the club who covered up Ade's abuses.'

'We didn't need to come down here to find that out. I'd already guessed it.'

'Still, the Fifteen Club has got a lot of power. I think you're right that they probably didn't arrange the murder, though.'

'Certainly not for any occult reason. That lot wouldn't know a genuine Satanic ritual if it bit them on the arse.'

'I can't see any reason they'd have murdered Ade in that very public way. It could lead to exposure, and if the club's existence leaks out then it's going to end a lot of careers.'

'You're right. If the club had done it they'd have arranged it discreetly and passed it off as an accident, not tried to draw maximum attention to abuse they'd been covering up for years.'

Oliver lowered his voice. 'That awful children's TV presenter said that what we know about Ade is just the tip of the iceberg.'

Liam frowned. 'There've been eight women come forward to accuse Ade of grooming and abuse so far. He thinks there were more?'

'More, and younger. Girls as young as twelve.'

Liam pulled a face. 'That's nasty stuff.'

'I know.' Oliver paused, remembering something. 'Actually, my mum hinted at the same thing.'

'What did she say?'

'She made a comment about "that poor child", in relation to Ade. I thought she was referring to Leonie, but when I said so my mum said that wasn't who she meant. Then she totally closed up, as if it was some big secret. I wondered if there were other girls in the village who Ade had attempted to groom. Younger girls, maybe.'

'It's certainly possible.'

Oliver sipped his beer, wondering whether to tell Liam what he'd found out about Raven's parents. He hated the thought of his friend's family getting dragged in. Then again, you never knew what could be significant.

'I found out something else tonight,' he said. 'About Ade's first wife.'

Liam paused with his beer halfway to his lips. 'What, Lily Gish?'

'I guess, although he didn't mention her name. Johnny told me she was a friend of Raven's mum, Eva. They were both aspiring actresses apparently; went to stage school together. Oh, and he thinks she was foreign, although he didn't mention what nationality. Do you think that's relevant?'

'Perhaps.' Liam took out a notebook and wrote it down. 'Thanks, Oliver. And thanks for coming tonight.'

Oliver smiled. 'For all the use I was to you. Still, it made Tess feel better.'

'Rubbish. We'd never have got in if it wasn't for your quick thinking, not to mention you found out possibly the only useful information we got tonight.' Liam put down his pen. 'And now we're out, I don't mind admitting I was pretty nervous. I appreciated some godly company.'

'Well, that's my job,' Oliver said, feeling rather gratified.

Liam's phone buzzed and he glanced at the screen.

'Text from Tess,' he said. 'Apparently the girls have had a productive day too. She thinks she's made a breakthrough on those tarot cards.'

'I don't know how I'm going to tell Raven this stuff about her parents,' Oliver said with a sigh. 'Another connection to Ade Adams, through her mum this time. It's going to upset her.'

'Do you want me to tell her?'

'No. I have to do it.'

Liam regarded Oliver curiously as he sipped his pint. 'You, Tess and Raven have been mates a long time, haven't you?'

'Nearly all our lives. Why?'

'Isn't that a bit unusual?'

Oliver shrugged. 'I suppose. Most people within the Church tend to form a social circle from that same faith background. The fact my closest friends are a pair of unbelievers is occasionally commented on. But my route into the Church was a bit different from my peers. I had a relationship with Tess and Raven long before I discovered my faith, and they were there for me at the darkest point in my life. A lot about who I am might've changed since we were kids, but I'd never turn my back on those two.'

'I actually meant it's unusual that your best friends are both women. Hasn't that ever led to . . . you know, things?'

'Things?'

'Well. They're women who like men, you're a man who likes women . . . complications can arise in friendships like that. Feelings.'

'Er, no.' Oliver picked up a beer mat and started folding it to give him an excuse to drop eye contact. 'No, there's nothing like that.'

'I did wonder if you and Raven might have a history.'

'Why did you think that?'

Liam shrugged. 'Just a vibe. As Tess reminded me recently, you weren't always a vicar.'

'I wouldn't have been her type. Raven likes beefy, confident, handsome men – the sort who come with muscles and a gym membership. Besides, we're old friends.'

'That doesn't rule out becoming more.'

Oliver squinted at him. 'Is this laddish banter? I'm a bit out of practice.'

Liam smiled. 'If you like. You want me to change the subject?'

'Please.'

'Why was your route into the Church different to your peers? Or is that private?'

'I don't mind talking about it,' Oliver said, grateful to move the conversation on. 'I didn't have a strong faith as a kid. We weren't even a churchgoing family, which is unusual for someone who goes on to become a priest – just weddings and Christmas. But I lost my big brother young from complications related to Down syndrome. He was eighteen, I was sixteen.'

'I'm sorry,' Liam said quietly. 'And finding your faith helped you through it?'

Oliver laughed grimly. 'Not until I'd worried my parents half to death and nearly killed myself in the process. I was so angry at the unfairness of it that my behaviour became self-destructive. I fell in with a bad crowd of older lads, started smoking stuff I shouldn't, drinking too much . . .'

'Who, you?'

Oliver smiled. 'Hard to believe, right? I've got a criminal record and everything. Shoplifting and joyriding.'

Liam shook his head. 'You're a dark horse.'

'If it hadn't been for Raven and Tess, I don't know if I'd have come through it. Them and Reverend Springer, who was our vicar back then.' Oliver paused, remembering what Mikey had said about the old vicar being there for him too.

'He was a good man. He helped me find comfort and peace in a place I never would have thought to look for it. Saved my life, probably – spiritually and literally. That's the sort of parish priest I aspire to be.'

'I never knew you had so many layers, Oliver.'

Oliver shrugged. 'We've all got a past. I mean, look at Tess.'

'Tess?'

'Yeah. You'd never guess now what her life was like growing up. The sort of family she came from.' Oliver finished his beer. 'I was lucky to have friends who didn't give up on me when I went through my wild phase. I could so easily have ended up like Mikey.'

'Mikey?'

'Tess's eldest brother, Mikey Feather.'

'Oh. Yeah, she's mentioned him once or twice.'

'Mikey was always a rogue – well, it runs in the family. But when Leonie left him, he really went off the rails. Ended up getting a two-year GBH sentence for attacking a man he thought she was seeing behind his back – the wrong man, as it turned out. All the Feathers were petty criminals, but after the GBH sentence Mikey got into harder and darker stuff. The sort you don't easily find your way back from. That could've been me, if things had turned out differently.'

'Tess's brother . . . is Leonie Abbott's ex,' Liam said slowly. 'The one she left for Ade all those years ago.'

'Well, yes.' Oliver frowned. 'Didn't she tell you they went out?'

'She told me Leonie was in a band with one of her brothers.'

'Caleb. She was, but it was Mikey she was dating. Tess really didn't tell you that?'

'No. No she didn't.'

'Oh. Then I probably shouldn't have said anything. I wonder that she never mentioned it, though. It's hardly a secret.'

'So do I,' Liam said quietly. 'So do I.'

*

When they arrived back in Cherrywood the next day, Liam dropped Oliver outside the girls' flat.

'Are you not coming up?' Oliver asked when Liam showed no sign of getting out of the car.

'No, I've got another job to do. I'll let you debrief them.'

'Right,' Oliver said, feeling puzzled. 'Bye, then. We must do this again sometime. I mean go for a pint, not infiltrate a Satanic society.'

Liam smiled, although his face carried a distracted look. 'Definitely. Thanks for keeping me company, Oliver. It's been . . . enlightening.'

Liam drove off, leaving Oliver to knock on the door of the flat. As soon as it opened, Raven hurtled into him, nearly knocking him down the steps. She was closely followed by Tess, with Roger providing a chorus of barks to add to the festival atmosphere.

'Oh, thank God you didn't get sacrificed or have to kiss the devil's bum,' Tess said breathlessly.

Oliver blinked. 'Um, what?'

'It was a whole thing once, apparently.' She peered round him. 'Where's Lee?'

'He's got a job to do. He asked me to debrief you.'

'That's annoying. I wanted to tell him what we found out from Seana. Come on in, then.'

Oliver followed them inside. Raven seemed unwilling to let him go, slipping her arm through his and guiding him to the sofa next to her.

He laughed. 'Don't worry, Rave. I'm not going to run away.'

'Well, we've been worried about you, darling. Was it very awful? What happened?'

'It wasn't much fun,' he admitted. 'We found out a few things, though. Also we may have done some male bonding, which was a novelty for me.'

'You guys are best mates now?' Tess said.

He smiled. 'Don't worry, I still love you two best.'

'I should hope so. Tell us what you found out.'

Oliver cast a wary glance at Raven. He'd been pondering on the journey home how much he ought to say about her parents' relationship with Ade Adams. In the end, he'd decided to keep it to himself. It could only upset her, and there was no need for her to know it.

'Well, it seems that we've only seen the tip of the iceberg when it comes to Ade's abuse,' he said. 'More girls, and younger – as young as twelve, apparently.'

Tess pulled a face. 'Eurgh. Seriously?'

'Yeah. The club members were pretty terrible Satanists, but they were deeply unpleasant people.'

'Terrible Satanists how?'

'They weren't really Satanists at all. It was like the spooky club you set up in your Wendy house when you're a kid: all secret passwords and scary-looking symbols, but no real understanding of what they mean.'

'Really?' Raven looked somewhat relieved by this.

Oliver nodded. 'All they really do is get drunk and stuff their faces – that and do each other favours. They managed to keep Ade's activities out of the press when he was alive. Still, I can't see them having any connection with the murder itself. Lack of motive, lack of means, lack of opportunity.'

Tess smiled. 'You sound like Liam, Ol.'

'Only temporarily. I'll be very happy to finish my stint as a detective and get back to being a country vicar.'

'Did you find out anything else?'

'A little bit about Ade's first wife. She was an actress, apparently. My source thought she might have been foreign, although he never actually met her.'

'That's worth knowing. Did you tell Lee?'

'Yes, I filled him in afterwards.'

'Funny he didn't come with you,' Tess said. 'I was sure he'd want to talk to me. I've got the results of the research he asked me to do.'

'Perhaps he's planning to catch up with you afterwards.' Oliver stood up. 'Right. I'm going to have a shower and transform magically back into a vicar. See you later, girls.'

Raven followed him to the front door.

'Hey,' she said, touching his arm. 'I really was worried about you, you know.'

He smiled. 'Thanks, Rave. I was thinking about you too.'

'Did you hear anything about my dad while you were there?'

'I found out what I could for you. Apparently he was the life of the party, and very charming to the opposite sex on ladies' night,' Oliver said, trying to be as truthful as he could without saying anything to upset her. 'Like I said, those guys weren't proper Satanists – it's really just a dining club with delusions of grandeur. I don't think you need to worry that he was into anything really dark.'

'I wasn't worried.'

He smiled. 'Yes, you were.'

'OK, perhaps a little,' she admitted. 'Still, to be friends with Ade Adams . . . do you think my dad knew what Ade was into?'

'Possibly not. The club's got rules about not sharing personal information, although some members are a bit lax about it.'

'Well, thanks for trying to find out more for me. It means a lot that you made the effort.' Raven stood on tiptoes to kiss his cheek. 'Bye, Oliver.'

'Yeah.' He watched the door close. 'Bye, Raven.'

Chapter 26

'Three days later Liam was sitting in his office, staring morosely at the list of still unanswered questions relating to the Screaming Ade Adams case. Considering he'd been on the job for nearly five weeks, it was a depressingly long list.

Just his luck that the Fifteen Club had turned out to be a bust. Liam had invested a lot of time trying to find out more about that place which hadn't been justified by the information he'd gained. Like everything about this case, it had just left him with more questions than answers.

Another lead had gone up in smoke since his trip too. Before heading down to London, Liam had called up an old contact who was one of the best missing person tracers in the biz and asked him to see what he could find out about Angela Campbell. Liam had supplied a file of everything he knew about her, including a photograph and details of her career, plus his own observations on the things about her that didn't add up.

Liam's contact hadn't turned up anything new under the name Angela Campbell, which, as Liam had expected, was a false identity. What he had discovered was an old theatre playbill – and that had been enough.

Liam would probably have skimmed over the photograph if he'd seen it in any other context, never noticing that the young woman in heavy stage makeup was one and the same as the flame-haired middle-aged journalist. But once he'd examined it more closely, he'd realised it was certainly her – and the name underneath had made it abundantly clear that the reason Angela Campbell was hiding her true identity probably had nothing to do with Ade Adams. A quiet conversation with her at home one evening, and a promise of his discretion, had confirmed that fact. Which meant that when it came to lead suspects, Liam was back to square one.

He read down his list of questions again, wondering where to look next. He didn't want to spend any more time investigating something that would turn out to be a dead end.

Whose key was used to unlock the park?
When was Ade drugged, and why?
When was Ade killed?
Who would have access to Valium and/or digoxin?
Does Leonie have a lover, and if so who is he?
Why did Ade agree to open the Guy Trail?
How did Ade's marriage to Peggy end?
What is Peggy's alibi for the day Ade died?
Where is Mikey Feather? Does he have an alibi for Ade's death?
Did Ade abuse another girl or girls in the village when he lived here?
Where is Ade's first wife, Lily Gish?

He really ought to know more than this by now.

Liam had tried finding out more about Lily Gish but there was nothing significant. The woman was a ghost. How old would she be now, if she was still alive? Fifty-seven? Fifty-eight?

Ade must have known where she was though, mustn't he? Tess said Ade had complained about maintenance payments to his ex-wives – called them a coven of witches. Assuming that meant three, of whom one was Peggy Bristow and one Katrin in Germany, the third must be Lily Gish. Perhaps Leonie knew her whereabouts.

Liam glanced at the names pinned to his whiteboard. What did he know about each of them?

Well, there was Mikey Feather. Career criminal and teenage sweetheart of Leonie Abbott. Did time in jail for attacking a man he believed to be messing around with Leonie, not realising that the man he really wanted was Ade Adams. Could he have decided to correct that mistake, all these years later? And where the hell was he?

Next on the list was his client, Leonie Abbott. Just eighteen years old when she'd left her family to run away with the married lover who'd promised to make her a star. Drug user, prone to casual sex with strangers, filled with hatred for her husband yet unable to break free of him. She certainly had a motive, and a somewhat shaky alibi. Could she and her unknown lover have planned it together?

And then there was Peggy Bristow. Something in his copper's gut kept drawing his gaze back to that little card on his whiteboard. He couldn't help feeling Peggy might be the key to all this.

The problem was, there were so many others with a reason to want Ade dead. Women all over the country had come out of the woodwork to accuse him of abuse, and according to Oliver's informant at the Fifteen Club, there could be many more – perhaps even in this village.

Liam wished Tess was here to bounce ideas off. They always came up with more answers together, and she was good at making connections. He'd been avoiding her calls ever since he got back from London, hurt that all this time she'd been keeping key information from him.

I bet you'd even suspect me, wouldn't you? Tess's words of a week ago rang in his ears. And Liam had joked that he would, if she ever gave him reason to. Of course he'd believed she never would.

He knew he had no right to take the moral high ground, after the way he'd treated Tess during the Porter case. So she'd lied to him to protect her brother. A brother she presumably loved in spite of his criminal career, and wanted to keep out of the line of suspicion. Wasn't that what anyone would do to protect a loved one? Lying to Tess for his own selfish ends had been far worse; Liam knew that. And yet, the fact Tess had chosen her brother over him still stung. There were very few people in his life that Liam had trusted implicitly. In fact there had been none – none except Tess Feather. He really felt they'd been able to move on from Porter, at least in terms of their working relationship, and build a bond based on respect and trust. Partners in spirit, if not yet in name. Friends who always had each other's backs. Now that trust been shaken, and as hypocritical as he knew it to be, Liam couldn't help feeling hurt.

His gaze drifted back to Mikey Feather's name. That was the other avenue he had been exploring. Mikey, he'd discovered, had recently completed a sentence in Strangeways for car theft, but he had certainly been in the Cherrywood area at the time of the murder – several people had seen someone answering to his description in the nearby town, and Liam had discovered that a Michael Feather had just finished a temping contract at a warehouse there. However, when he'd visited the address the warehouse had on file for him – a local hostel – Liam discovered Mikey had moved on, leaving no forwarding address.

There was a knock at the door, and Liam jumped up to throw a sheet over his whiteboard before calling for them to come in. For a moment he hoped it might be Tess, but it wasn't. It was Leonie.

'I got your expense receipts,' she said, getting straight to business. 'A London hotel; hire of a Rolls. I hope that means you went to investigate that club of my husband's and not that you've been gallivanting around town on my money.'

'Sorry. I know it wasn't cheap, but I had to impress those people. It's not the sort of club to let you in if you roll up in an Astra.'

'Well, luckily for you I can afford it.'

Leonie took a seat. She wasn't her usual glam self today. In grey sweatpants and an oversized hoodie, it was unlikely anyone would recognise her as the immaculately dressed and made-up TV star Leonie Abbott. She took out her vape and held it between her fingers, although she didn't switch it on.

'Did you find out anything?' she asked Liam.

'I'm . . . still processing it.' He took in her wan, tired features. 'Are you all right?'

'I'm fine.' She rubbed a hand over her forehead. 'Cold turkey, that's all. I'm trying to get clean. I can't live in the shadow of what Ade did to me all my life – none of us can.'

'You mean his former wives? I understand there's a few of you.'

'His wives. The girls he abused. Their families. We were all his victims. Well, now he's gone and I for one am moving on with my life – without the use of substances.'

'I'm glad to hear that. Can I get you a coffee or anything?'

'No thanks. I'm off that as well.' She followed his gaze to the dormant vape in her hand. 'This too, although I like to hold on to it for emotional support purposes. I actually came to tell you that the police have dropped the case against me, so I'm going to let you go.'

Liam blinked. 'Oh.'

'I'll pay you the full fee, but to be honest I really don't care who killed my husband. As long as I'm off the hook, that's all that matters.' She stood up. 'Thanks for all your hard work, Mr Hanley. I understand it was partly thanks to the information you shared with your police contact that the case against me was abandoned. That being so, you've earned your fee just as much as if you'd solved the murder.'

'No problem,' Liam said. 'So you don't want to know who did it, then?'

'Whoever did it can get away scot-free with my blessing. I should think there are at least a hundred suspects, based on what's come out about Ade since he died. The police will probably never pin down the real killer, and to tell you the truth I'm glad. I suppose it must have been to do with some poor girl he molested.'

'Very likely.'

She held out a hand and Liam rose to shake it. 'Nice working with you. If I'm ever asked to recommend a detective, I'll be sure to send them your way.'

'Just one question before you go,' Liam said. 'I'd like to put something to rest that's been on my mind. Do you know what became of your husband's first wife – Lily Gish? I'm assuming he was paying her maintenance. Apparently he mentioned it before he died.'

Leonie frowned. 'Lily? I think you've made a mistake. Ade's first wife wasn't called Lily.'

'That might have been a stage name.'

'Yes, that's possible. I understand she was an actress.'

'So I'm told,' Liam said. 'Do you know her real name?'

'I don't remember, sorry. All I know is that she was a Shakespearean actress – quite a successful one. Ade wasn't paying her maintenance, though, whatever he might've claimed. He loved to make these misogynistic cracks about the women in his life bleeding him dry, but it was just talk. His first wife had her own income.'

'Then you've got no way to contact her?'

'No.' Leonie squinted at him. 'Why would you need to? I just said the case is done.'

'It isn't to do with the case. I . . . discovered a connection to an acquaintance of mine. But never mind, if you don't know.'

'All right. Well, thanks again. I'll transfer the rest of your money when I get back.' She smiled awkwardly. 'Sorry about that whole black eye business.'

'Don't worry about it, I've had worse. Good luck with the new album and the cold turkey and . . .' He glanced at her wan, sickly features. 'And everything.'

When she'd gone, Liam sat in silent contemplation.

Leonie wanted him off the case. She'd just paid him fifty grand to be off the case. Why? As much as she had loathed her husband, surely she wanted to know who killed him. Was she trying to protect someone she'd discovered was involved – her lover, perhaps?

And there was something else he'd noticed too. Something she probably thought she'd concealed well, but Liam was good at noticing small details. That's why he'd gone into this racket.

Well, Leonie could try and take him off the case but his brain sure as hell wasn't going to let that happen; not while there were still questions to be answered. He'd been paid fifty grand to find out who murdered Ade Adams and he fully intended to earn it.

Liam looked again at his list of people of interest. The names whirled around in his head, like atoms trying to connect to one another then breaking apart. *Mikey Feather. Angela Campbell. Leonie Abbott. Lily Gish. Peggy Bristow . . .*

There was one person on the list he knew where to find, anyway. And actually, now he thought about it, Liam had always fancied having his tarot cards read.

*

'Where's he going, then?' Tess muttered as she peeped between the blinds, watching Liam stride down Cherrywood main street.

'Who?' Kennedy asked from the sofa.

Since Liam was ignoring her and Raven had point-blank refused to hear another word about Ade Adams, Tess had decided to invite Kennedy round to bounce a few ideas off. Kenn had made a good sidekick when they'd gone to chat with Seana, and Tess had been impressed at her insight into the tarot cards. The more she thought about it, the more she suspected Kennedy was right – it wasn't the cards' meaning in the tarot that was important but the images themselves. The child, representing Ade's victims. The devil, of course, was Ade himself: a monster who'd destroyed many lives. And then the final judgement – Ade's death, and the exposure of his crimes to an unforgiving public. Taken at face value, the cards pointed to exactly what Ade had done and the motive for his murder. They were as clear as any note.

Tess turned to Kennedy. 'Liam Hanley. He looks like he's going somewhere.' She paused a moment, then added, 'He's been investigating Ade's murder on behalf of his widow.'

Well, why shouldn't she tell? Liam wasn't speaking to her, so when it came to investigating she was on her own.

Tess could only assume Raven had grassed her up about the visit to Seana – at any rate, Liam seemed to know that she hadn't honoured her pledge about leaving the practical stuff to him. That had to be the reason for him ghosting her. And since Liam was refusing to talk to her, she had an enthusiastic prospective sidekick right here who was keen to help.

'Where do you think he's going?' Kennedy asked. 'To interview a suspect?'

'Well, he could just be going to the shops. Still, he looks very purposeful.' Tess sat back down.

'Maybe we should go investigate something too,' Kennedy suggested.

'Maybe we should. There's only so far you can get with curtain-twitching.' Tess reclaimed her coffee from the table. 'It's nice to have a friend who's enthusiastic about crime-busting. Rave just rolls her eyes at me.'

'Oh, I love it. At Christmas, me and Seana always go to Nick's and we do a family murder mystery game.' She laughed. 'I've got a reputation for getting overly competitive. I love working out whodunnit.'

'Me too. I like watching all the old mystery programmes and trying to work it out before the detective does.'

'That's exactly what I was doing when you called, funnily enough. I'd just got it all worked out when the phone rang. Had to be the paramedic who examined the body.'

'Well, now you've got a real mystery to solve.'

'If my expertise can be any use, I'm more than happy to help.'

'That reminds me,' Tess said. 'Kenn, you don't know who in the village uses Valium, do you?'

Kennedy smiled. 'Come on, Tess. You know I can't tell you that.'

'I suppose not.' She sipped her coffee thoughtfully. 'You'd need to give someone a fair bit to knock them out totally, wouldn't you?'

'At least five times the maximum dose, I should say. More, if you wanted to be sure of it.'

'Would that be difficult to get hold of?'

'I couldn't prescribe it in those amounts. It's addictive, so it has to be carefully controlled. Even doctors aren't able to get their hands on doses that size, in case we're popping pills on the sly.'

Tess fell silent, her coffee going tepid in her hands as she thought this over. Eventually, she went to peer through the blinds again, checking to see if Liam had come home yet. Perhaps it was time she had it out with him in person, if he was going to childishly insist on keeping up the silent treatment.

'Hello,' she murmured.

'Is it Liam?'

'Angela Campbell, heading up Royal Row. And looking a bit furtive, if you ask me.' She glanced at her friend. 'Are you up for some hands-on sleuthing, Kenn?'

'I thought you'd never ask.' Kennedy got to her feet. 'Where are we going?'

'If Liam's right, Angela's hiding something. If we're lucky, she'll lead us to exactly what that is. Come on, before we lose her.'

The women grabbed their coats and hurried out. It was a bright, chilly December day, a crusting of frost twinkling on the grass that still lay in shadow. Angela was just visible in the distance, heading in the direction of Cherrywood Hall.

'Oh,' Tess said, disappointed. 'Looks like she's just going to see her pony. That's no help.'

'She's not wearing her riding things, though,' Kennedy pointed out.

'Going to give Meg her feed, I suppose. Still, we're out now. We might as well follow.'

They headed up Royal Row, Angela now quite small in the distance.

'We need to look nonchalant or she'll realise we're following,' Tess murmured. 'Pretend we're chatting.'

'She does look a bit furtive, doesn't she?' Kennedy observed as Angela cast a glance over her shoulder. Luckily she didn't seem to register them, lingering by a lamp post as they pretended to read a poster for the Women's Guild Christmas fair.

'Mmm. I wonder what she's up to?'

Tess wondered if Angela might pass Cherrywood Hall and continue to some other destination, but she turned right into the grounds. She didn't head for the stables, however, but made her way towards the small pagoda near the Chinese gardens. There was another figure, waiting there expectantly as if a meeting had been arranged.

'Who is it?' Kennedy said as they lurked under a group of trees near the gates.

Tess squinted at the small, spare figure with a head of grey hair. 'It's Candice.'

It all looked very odd. As far as Tess knew, Angela and Raven's grandmother were the most casual of acquaintances: friendly enough to exchange pleasantries at the Women's Guild or village events like the *Macbeth* performance, but not what you'd call bosom pals. Yet now they had their heads together in close conference. Surely Candice wasn't involved in this business too?

The two talked earnestly, as if about something very momentous, although Tess was unable to make out the words. She and Kennedy continued to lurk near the trees.

'Can we get any closer?' Kennedy asked. 'We might be able to hear what they're saying.'

'Not without being spotted.' Tess took a last look at Angela and Candice, deep in conversation. 'We'd better go, before they notice us hanging around.'

Tess was silent as they walked back to the flat, turning something over in her mind.

'You look like you're pondering the mysteries of the universe,' Kennedy said. 'You don't know what that was all about, do you?'

'I don't, but . . . I did remember something. It seemed so insignificant at the time, but now . . .'

'What is it?'

'You remember that night at the *Macbeth* dress rehearsal?'

'Oh Lord, wasn't it awful?' Kennedy said with a groan. 'Seana still hasn't forgiven me for making her sit through it.

I don't think I understood the term "overacting" until I saw what Angela was capable of.'

'That's exactly what I'm wondering,' Tess said. 'No one can be that much of a ham without realising it, right? Surely if you're that cheesy, you know about it.'

'Do you think so?'

'Do you remember Les Dawson, Kenn?'

Kennedy frowned. 'The comedian? Not really, but I'm aware of him. My dad was a fan.'

'So was my grandad. Dawson used to do these sketches where he'd play the piano so badly it was comical. I remember my grandad saying, you have to be a very good pianist to play that badly. I'm starting to think Angela might be just as good an actress as Dawson was a musician.'

'How do you mean?'

'Liam thinks Angela's been lying about who she is. Apparently there's no record of her having worked on the papers she claims to, not to mention that she sporadically develops an American accent sometimes when she shouts,' Tess said. 'It takes a good actress to perform a part that well. Maybe it takes a pro.'

Kennedy frowned. 'Did you say Ade Adams had been married to an actress?'

'Lily Gish. And no one knows where she is now.'

'But what's Candice got to do with all of this?'

'I'm not sure, but there was a passing comment she made at the dress rehearsal that I glossed over at the time. Right before Angela came over to ask what we thought of her performance, Candice observed to us that it wasn't her best work. But how would she know, right? This is the first time Angela's ever been in a Cherrywood Players production.'

'You think Candice must have seen her act before?'

'Well, there's obviously some connection. They looked a lot closer than casual acquaintances, didn't they?' Tess's brow knitted. 'And I'm planning to find out what that is.'

Chapter 27

To Liam's surprise, Peggy answered the door on the first ring. He'd spotted the doorbell camera and suspected the door would remain firmly closed when she saw it was him.

'You've taken your time,' she said. 'The police were here weeks ago.'

'I've been exploring other avenues. I didn't realise you were waiting on me.'

'Well, you're here now.' She peered round him. 'Where's Tess?'

Liam felt rather perplexed by this turn of events. It hadn't occurred to him that Peggy had been expecting him. 'Er, it's just me,' he said.

'Oh. Well, I suppose you ought to come in.'

Peggy led him to the kitchen, where a checked cloth had been thrown over the table. On it were objects relating to her art: the obligatory crystal ball; assorted crystals; her tarot pack.

'I suppose you saw me coming, did you?' Liam asked, nodding to the crystal ball.

'That's just for atmosphere. I don't offer scrying.'

'Scrying?'

'Crystal ball gazing to you.' Peggy ushered him to a seat and sat down opposite. 'Let's get this over with, then.'

'You're surprisingly cooperative. I thought you'd slam the door in my face.'

Peggy shrugged. 'You may as well know the same as I told the police.' She squinted at him. 'You really ought to have brought Tess, you know. She balances you out.'

'I don't want Tess getting involved,' Liam said, in a harsher tone than he'd intended.

Peggy raised an eyebrow. 'Trouble in paradise?'

'We're not partners. Besides, you never know—' He stopped.

'You never know what?'

'Who you can really trust,' he finished quietly.

Peggy regarded him curiously. 'Well, if you're here to interrogate me I hope you're going to make it worth my while,' she said.

He smiled dryly. 'Do I have to cross your palm with silver?'

'You can cross it with a tenner. That'll cover a standard three-card tarot spread.'

Liam sighed and fished the money from his wallet. Peggy stashed it in her cash box and passed him the deck of cards.

'Shuffle,' she ordered. 'Make sure you're thinking about the question you want answering.'

'The first question I want answering is about you and Ade Adams,' Liam said as he obediently started shuffling. 'You were his second wife?'

'That's right.' Peggy went to flick the kettle on. 'I was twenty when we married in 1986.'

'He was older, I presume.'

'By twenty years. He was working for Heartbeat FM in Leeds. I'd just got myself a cleaning job there. I was naive then. Naive enough to think I was in love with this older married man who bought me presents and told me I was beautiful.'

'Did he leave you for someone younger? That seems to have been the pattern.'

'No,' Peggy said quietly, not turning from the kettle. 'I left him.'

'Why?'

'Because I didn't want my child to grow up in a house with that man.' She turned to look at him, her eyes moist.

'I had no idea you had kids.'

'The baby was given up for adoption. I wasn't in any state to be a mum then – not after what I'd been through with Ade.' Peggy sighed. 'I hope my baby boy had a good life.'

'Did Ade know? About the baby?'

'Absolutely not. I was lucky enough to be able to get away before he ever knew I was expecting. That was the only luck I did have in the time I was with him.'

'I'm sorry,' Liam said quietly.

'It was a long time ago.' Peggy slid a mug of tea to him and nodded to the cards he was shuffling. 'You can stop whenever it feels right. Don't forget, you need to be thinking about the question you want answering. Not for this case. For yourself.'

'Right.'

Liam shuffled the cards for a little longer while Peggy turned down the lights and lit some candles and incense sticks. The repetitive action was rather soothing, and he found his thoughts wandering to Tess. They often did when he didn't keep them tightly reined in, but now they were tinged with sadness.

'I think I'm done,' he said, putting the deck down.

'Well, let's see what we have.' Peggy drew three cards and laid them face down.

'How does it work?' Liam asked.

'The cards represent past, present and future. Their meaning ought to guide you to the answers you're seeking.'

She turned over the first card. Liam looked at it dreamily, his brain foggy from the sweet, pungent incense.

Peggy's deck was very different to the cards Tess had found, with an unusual design featuring old medical and botanical diagrams. The first card showed five bottles of poison in the midst of a blue-flowering plant. The artwork was a little creepy, but rather beautiful too.

'What does it mean?' Liam murmured, swept along in spite of himself.

'The Five of Elixirs represents something from your past: an old wound recently reopened, perhaps. Grief, or possibly heartbreak – either your own or that of someone close to you. Something that's preventing you moving forward.'

Something like his previous relationship with Tess, the sudden ending of which had left her broken-hearted and Liam bereft. The betrayal she couldn't get over. His hurt about the lie she'd told, choosing loyalty to her brother over the relationship they'd been building since he'd come to Cherrywood . . .

Peggy smiled at his thoughtful expression. 'Well, your turn. What's next on your list?'

'Hmm? Oh. Right.' Liam tried to pull himself together. 'What was your relationship with Ade after your marriage ended? Did you still hear from him?'

'More often than I wanted to. He paid me maintenance, which meant he still felt he owned me long after our relationship ended. Adrian was needy, and when he couldn't get what he wanted from his current wife or mistress he'd go running to one of the previous ones. He needed to be loved, you see, like so many narcissists.'

'What did you do when he contacted you?'

Peggy sighed. 'You'd think I'd have hung up on him, wouldn't you?'

'But you didn't.'

'I couldn't. I relied on the money he sent, even after I married Ian. I humoured Ade – even pitied him at times. He seemed like a pathetic figure. I didn't know what he'd done to all those girls or I'd have starved before I took a penny of his.' She turned over the next card. 'Let's see what your present holds, shall we?'

The picture was of four knives, on a bed of white flowers.

'The Four of Blades,' Peggy murmured.

'Um, is that bad?'

'It's . . . telling. If the Five of Elixirs represents an old wound, then this card suggests an urgent need to heal that wound.'

She glanced up to meet his eyes. 'There's something in your life that needs to be repaired, Liam Hanley – something you're failing to deal with. And until it is repaired, you won't be happy.'

Liam stared at the card for a moment.

'So, my turn,' he said at last. 'Had you seen Ade before his death?'

Peggy smiled tightly. 'Now here's where it gets tricky. But the police don't think I'm a person of interest, so I may as well tell you.'

'Tell me what?'

'I did see Ade. I saw him that day – the day of the bonfire.'

Liam sat up straight, blinking at her through the smog of incense. 'You saw him the day he died? You could've led with that, Peggy.'

She shrugged. 'You ask, I answer. That's how interrogation works.'

'What time did you see him? Where?'

'Here.' Peggy sipped her tea calmly. 'He'd had a row with the most recent Mrs Adams and stormed out. All her fault, he told me – it always was, according to him. It must have been early when they fought. It wasn't even light when he turned up on my doorstep, demanding a drink and a listening ear. It was the first time I'd heard from him in years.'

'And you let him in?'

She nodded. 'As a favour to the girl really. I know what he's like when he gets in a rage. I thought if I let him get it out of his system, he might have calmed down by the time he went back to her.'

'What time did he leave?'

'No more questions yet. It's my turn.'

Peggy turned over the final card – the future card. The image on this one was particularly macabre: a stack of skulls with flowers growing from the eye sockets, with a swarm of bees flying overhead.

'The Tower,' Peggy said quietly. 'One of the Major Arcana. A fire card.'

'What does it mean? I'm guessing a pile of skulls doesn't suggest a lottery win and a date with Miss Universe.'

Peggy smiled. 'I've made a believer of you at last, haven't I?'

'No. It's just . . . interesting.'

'The Tower is not a positive card,' Peggy admitted. 'It represents destruction. If you don't resolve the problem raised by the past and present cards, then sometime in the future you're going to find yourself standing in the ruins of all you've been working and hoping for.'

Liam felt his heart sink. 'Oh.'

'Now, don't worry,' Peggy said soothingly. 'The future is a shadow, that's all – an outcome that may come to pass if the problem is left unresolved. If you take steps to address it, however, you might see a different outcome.' She put the cards back into the deck. 'Besides, I know you're a sceptic. None of this can apply to you, of course.'

'Of course.' Liam was silent for a moment. 'So . . .'

'Ade left around ten a.m.,' Peggy said, her tone brisk as she put her cards away. 'He was quite drunk by then. I don't know where he went afterwards. If you'd like me to account for my movements for the rest of the day, however, I'm happy to do so. The police have checked my alibi and are satisfied.'

'Had he taken anything? Besides vodka, I mean. I'm aware he was a cocaine user.'

Peggy shook her head. 'He told me he was off the stuff, on the advice of his doctor. Heart issues, I believe. He hadn't used it in a month.'

Liam frowned. 'Is that right?'

'So he told me.'

Liam had been convinced the digoxin that killed Ade must have been administered by making a switch with his cocaine, since the two white powders would be indistinguishable. If that hadn't been a possibility, then how had it been given? And why hadn't Leonie mentioned that her husband had stopped taking cocaine? She must have known.

'He didn't take anything else?' Liam asked as Peggy stood up to extinguish the incense and candles.

'He was puffing away on his vape. Stank to high heaven – like Vicks. When I knew him he was on forty menthol fags a day. He obviously still needed his nicotine fix.'

'That's all?'

Peggy nodded. 'Is that everything? Not to rush you, but I'm expecting a customer.'

'One more thing before I go. Do you know where your key is for the park gates?'

'Of course. It's on the ring where I keep all my work keys.'

'Can I see?'

Peggy shrugged. 'If it gives you any joy.'

She left the room. When she came back in, she was carrying a large bunch of keys. Peggy worked as a cleaner for most of the public buildings in Cherrywood, and as such had keys to half the village.

'Which one is it?' Liam asked.

Peggy showed him a key with a blue plastic cover. 'This one. Why?'

'It hasn't been removed? You haven't lent it to anyone, or noticed it missing?'

'No. It's been in the same place it always is, the drawer in my bedside cabinet.'

'Was it there after Ade left?'

'Of course. Not that I looked, but it was certainly there when I took the bunch to work at St Stephen's the following Monday.'

'You checked, did you?'

'Well, no, but I'd have noticed if it was missing.'

'Right.' Liam stood up. 'Thank you, you've been a big help. And, er, thanks for the reading.'

'My pleasure. Just you make sure you heed it, all right? You've been given a timely warning, Liam. It could help you avoid disaster, if you act now.'

Liam nodded and started towards the door. He paused with his hand on the knob. 'One last thing,' he said. 'Do you sleep well, Peggy?'

Peggy, who was now leaning over her crystal ball giving it a wipe with the duster, looked up. 'I'm sorry?'

'How do you sleep? All right?'

She blinked. 'Well enough. I'm an early riser but I usually

get a good six or seven hours. Why the concern for my sleeping habits?'

'I just wondered if you took anything to help with that.'

'Only Horlicks. Why?'

'Oh, no reason. Thanks, Peggy.'

As Liam left the house, he spotted Tess and her doctor friend Kennedy on the other side of the street. He hesitated, thinking about the dreamlike tarot card reading Peggy had insisted he have and that macabre card with the pile of skulls: the Tower. He crossed the road.

'Hi,' he said.

Tess gave him a curt nod. 'Hi.'

'I've . . . been to see Peggy.'

'Good for you.' Tess paused. 'Find out anything?'

'Nothing you need to know about.'

Tess shook her head, frowning. 'What the hell is up with you lately?'

Kennedy tapped her elbow. 'Tess, I'm going to go. This looks like something you two need to discuss privately.'

'Wait,' Liam said. 'It was actually you I wanted to talk to, Doc.'

Kennedy blinked. 'Me?'

'Yeah. I just wondered if you knew anything about a drug called digoxin.'

'Oh,' Kennedy said. 'Yes, a little. Better known as digitalis. It's used for cardiac problems.'

'How easy would it be to access in lethal amounts?'

'In the case of digoxin, a lethal amount would be quite small. Anyone prescribed it could have enough to kill, as could chemists and healthcare professionals. You could even make it, if your chemistry's good.'

'Make it?'

'Digitalis is extracted from the purple foxglove. Very hard to synthesise but relatively straightforward to extract if you've got the equipment and know-how. Is that related to Ade's murder?'

Liam shot a look at Tess. 'Who told you I'm working on Ade's murder, as if I didn't know?'

Kennedy smiled awkwardly. 'Sorry. Tess thought I might be able to help, that's all. I'll see you both later.' She walked off in the direction of her place.

'Well?' Tess said when Kennedy was out of earshot. 'What is up with you, then?'

'Nothing,' Liam said, trying to sound like he meant it. 'I've just been busy, that's all.'

She shook her head. 'I can't believe you're being like this, just because I went to talk to Seana. It was hardly dangerous, was it? She's not even a suspect.'

'You think that's what I'm upset about?'

'Well, aren't you?'

'No, Tess. I'm upset because . . . because you lied to me.'

'About arranging to go and see Seana Hamilton? I didn't lie, it just . . . didn't seem that important.'

'Not that. You lied to me to protect a suspect. Someone who I know was in the area at the time of the murder, and who's already done time for an assault intended for Ade Adams. Didn't you?'

'What? Lee, I don't know what you're talking about.'

'Come on, Tess! You told me on more than one occasion that you couldn't remember the name of Leonie Abbott's ex-boyfriend – do you remember?'

'Oh. Him. Well, yes, I might've—'

'And then I discover that not only do you know his name but he's family. Your brother. Isn't he?'

Tess looked bewildered. 'Mikey? He's here?'

'Yes, Tess, Mikey's here. But I presume you knew that.' Liam turned to go.

'Lee, wait! Don't go. Let's talk about this.'

He paused at the sound of Tess's voice. An image appeared in his mind of that tarot card, the Tower, the one that represented his future – his future with Tess, the reading had seemed to say. He hesitated for a second. Then he shook his head and strode off.

The top skull on the tower started to wobble.

Chapter 28

Oliver was staring blankly at his laptop when the vicarage's landline phone rang.

He'd been trying to write a sermon while he waited for another visit from Nick. It was for the family Christingle service and he'd chosen 'Doing the Right Thing' as a suitably child-friendly topic, but the words weren't coming easily.

Twice lately, Oliver had discovered that doing the right thing wasn't as black and white as he could wish it to be. A few days ago, he'd tried to do the right thing by doing what objectively might seem like a very wrong thing when he'd accompanied Liam to the Fifteen Club. And then last week there had been what happened with Raven. His visit to the Fifteen Club had been the right thing to do – it would have been both cowardly and unchristian to let Liam go alone – but it had still *felt* wrong. And with Raven . . . with her it had been just the opposite. Of course it had been wrong to give in to temptation like that with his old friend. And yet it had felt completely right, at the time. If Oliver couldn't get his head around what was right and what was wrong, how on earth was he supposed to preach about it to the kids on Sunday?

And then there was Mikey. Oliver still hadn't spoken to him about Archie so he could start to move past his anger.

Sighing, he closed the laptop and got up to answer the phone.

'Hello, love,' his mum said.

He should've known it would be her. Hardly anyone called him on the landline except his parents.

'Hiya, Mum. How are things?' Oliver felt a sudden worry. 'Er, the park home's OK, isn't it? You're not coming to stay again?'

'Everything's fine. Can't a mother ring her son without him worrying? I just wanted to check what to bring for Christmas dinner other than the turkey and a couple of puddings.'

'Honestly, you don't need to bring anything.' Oliver could already picture his parents arriving on Christmas Eve with a twelve-person feast in the boot of the car. 'I've got a turkey crown in the freezer and a list of everything else I need to buy. I'll get everything prepared and ready before the evening service, ready to go in the oven. You can put your feet up for once.'

'Oh, nonsense. You can barely manage to feed yourself properly, Skinny Minnie. Besides, you'll be working all morning.'

'I want to do it though, Mum. There'll be time, if I get everything oven-ready the day before – after all, it's just the three of us. I won't feel like a proper grown-up until I've made at least one family Christmas dinner on my own.'

'Well, all right, if it really means that much to you. I promise I'll just bring a few things.'

Oliver sighed in resignation. 'A few things' meant at least two courses and a mountain of snacks. But he knew from experience that it was no good trying to talk her out of it.

'So. Any new young ladies in your life?' his mum asked archly.

Oliver winced. 'I only broke up with Tammy last month, Mum.'

'Tick tock, Oliver. You're not getting any younger, you know. You won't always have your mum around to cook you Christmas dinner.'

'I'm supposed to be cooking you Christmas dinner.'

'Well, let's not split hairs.' His mum's tone became solemn. 'You'll have seen the latest, I suppose.'

Oliver frowned. 'The latest what?'

'About Ade Adams. I always said he was a dirty old devil. You see, that was truer than I ever knew.'

'Mum, what are you talking about?'

'You really don't know?' his mum said in surprise. 'It's been all over the news. Your dad's whatchamacallit has been pinging all day.'

'Um, his what?'

'That tablet thing you got him. It keeps bringing up breaking news alerts about it. Haven't you seen them?'

'I set my mobile to do not disturb while I tried to concentrate on my sermon. Has another woman come forward?'

'Even more shocking than that.' His mum lowered her voice. 'It turns out there was a reason he managed to keep it out of the papers – all those little girls, I mean. Apparently Ade Adams was a member of some secret club. Very shady business. Devil worship and all sorts, they're saying. Says in the paper it could go all the way to the top – politicians and Lord knows who else. I think we're in for a lot of revelations in the next few weeks.'

So Ade's membership of the Fifteen Club had made the papers! Oliver experienced an overwhelming sense of relief.

He'd been wrestling with his conscience ever since he'd come home, feeling that something ought to be done about that place. As ineffectual as the members had been in the Dark Arts, they were still an unpleasant bunch and he hated the idea of them using their power and influence to do each other favours. After turning it over in his mind, Oliver had decided to write an anonymous letter tipping off the press and posted it to one of the big national papers. He guessed Liam wouldn't approve, since it might jeopardise his case, and there was also the risk of Oliver's involvement with the club being exposed, or the members themselves coming at him for revenge. But in this case, at least, his conscience had firmly pointed him towards the right thing to do.

'Does it say how they got the information?' he asked his mum.

'It just says "an anonymous source". Well, I'm glad of it.'

'So am I,' said Oliver fervently.

'I always knew Ade Adams must have friends in high places, after what he got away with. Shame it never came out into the open while he was still alive to answer for it.'

Oliver frowned. 'You mentioned that before. "That poor

child," you said. Were there other girls in the village who made accusations? I don't remember anything about it.'

'No, it'll have been before your time,' his mum said vaguely.

'But he only lived here for a year.' The doorbell rang. 'That'll be Nick. We've got a mentoring appointment.'

'All right, I'll let you go.'

'Wait,' Oliver said before she could hang up. 'What did you mean, Mum? Who's the child?'

'It's really not my story to tell. Forget I said anything.'

'But if it could help the people investigating then you really ought to tell the authorities.'

'So they can find Ade's killer? I'm sorry, Oliver, but I can't find myself caring a whole lot about whether they catch this murderer or not. I should think there are a lot of people who think an OBE would be a more appropriate reward for them than imprisonment.'

'Not just because of that. It'll help give closure to his victims, I hope. Not to mention that they might be entitled to compensation from his estate.'

'Like I said, it isn't my story to tell.' Annette paused. 'If you really think it's important for the police to know then I'd suggest you speak to your friend.'

Oliver blinked. 'Friend? Which friend?'

'You'd better get the door. See you at Christmas, love.'

Feeling bewildered, Oliver hung up and went to answer the door.

'Sorry for the wait,' he said to Nick as he ushered him

inside. 'I've just had my mum on the phone, threatening to fatten me up over Christmas. Do you want tea?'

Nick smiled. 'Get your kettle fixed, did you?'

'As soon as my mum and dad had gone home it started working again, funnily enough.'

'I'd love a cup. Thanks, Oliver.'

Oliver showed him into the study and headed to the kitchen, returning with two steaming mugs and a plate of biscuits.

'So what's the mentoring emergency this time?' Nick asked as he helped himself to a Jaffa Cake. 'Still struggling with your crisis?'

'No.' Oliver ran a hand over his forehead. 'I mean yes, but that's not why I asked to see you. I've got . . . another crisis.'

Nick raised an eyebrow. 'You're really going through the mill at the moment, aren't you?'

'Life does seem to be full of challenges,' Oliver admitted. 'I always thought I was good at resisting temptation. Apart from a weakness for white chocolate Toblerone, controlling my baser urges hasn't been a problem since I was a hormonal kid. But just lately, I seem to be wrestling with all of them. Anger, resentment . . .' He flushed. 'Um, lust.'

'OK,' Nick said quietly. 'Why do you think that is?'

'I'm wondering if I ever was good at resisting temptation, really. There I was congratulating myself on being able to manage it, but I wonder if it was only that the right temptations had never fallen in my way. I managed to control my anger because it had been so long since anything had made me truly angry – until this person came back into my life. And then . . .'

'I'm not here to judge,' Nick said. 'Only to help, if I'm able to.'

Nick's face was kind, open and warm, as Oliver liked to imagine the face of God must be. He took a deep breath.

'There was . . . an incident,' he admitted. 'I mean I've had girlfriends before, and there was the odd slip when I was young, but since ordination I've never had a problem with . . . that type of thing. I felt that I could wait – at least until there was the understanding of a lifelong commitment, if not until that had been signed, sealed and delivered. But last week . . .' He pushed his fingers into his hair. 'Last week it all fell apart. And the worst thing is, I can't even feel guilty about it.'

Nick leaned back in his chair. 'Oh?'

'I know I ought to. And yet it did feel . . . almost spiritual, at the time. At least, it didn't feel like a sin – like something I ought to fight.'

'I didn't know you were in a relationship.'

'I'm not,' Oliver mumbled, hiding his face in his mug of tea. 'She's a friend. A very old, close friend. She was upset about breaking up with her boyfriend, I was upset about breaking up with my girlfriend last month, and I suppose . . . one thing just led to another.'

'Does she regret it, this friend?'

'No. She doesn't have any faith. This sort of thing probably happens to her all the time.'

Oliver felt a stab in his gut when he said that. What was it? Jealousy? Wow. He was really racking up deadly sins.

'How does that make you feel?' Nick asked, as if reading his thoughts.

'I feel like . . . I guess, like I wish things were different.'

'Why? Is this someone you've regarded in a romantic light in the past?'

'Well, no, I . . .' Oliver stopped. 'I don't know.'

'So, why do you wish things could be different?'

'Because then we could—' Oliver stopped as the realisation hit him in a rush of light. 'Because then we could be together,' he finished quietly.

'You have feelings for her then, this woman?'

'I suppose I must have,' Oliver said in a faraway voice.

'Might she return them, do you think?'

'I . . . no. She can't do. Honestly, if you saw the sort of men she usually dates . . .' Oliver trailed off. 'She was just upset. Anyway, it doesn't matter how she feels, does it? As she said to me afterwards, she's not exactly vicar's wife material. Not to mention that she's . . . her background is unusual. Her family have certain expectations.'

'That might not be insurmountable, if there are feelings in the case.'

'But the other thing is insurmountable,' Oliver said. 'She doesn't have any faith, Nick. As friends we can get around that, but as anything more – it just wouldn't work.'

'It is a difficulty, I can see that,' Nick conceded. 'Still, if you're in love with this person – so much so that you find it hard to be around her without wanting to be with her – then perhaps you need to have a conversation. For the sake of your friendship, if nothing else.'

In love . . . The shock Oliver felt at hearing it stated so baldly was the emotional equivalent of sticking his fingers in a plug socket and switching it on. Could it be that? Raven, one of his best friends, and his exact opposite in so many ways. Perhaps that was what had blinded Oliver to his feelings for so long.

'I don't know,' he said. 'It might scare her. I don't want to ruin our friendship by making things weird.'

'You think you can hide how you feel until you're able to move on?'

'I guess I could try.'

'I'm not sure that's the healthiest solution, but you know the relationship better than I do.' Nick finished his tea. 'As for your conscience, I don't think you need to beat yourself up too much. It sounds as though the situation is somewhat complicated. I'd advise you to forgive yourself for this one slip, and vow to do better in future.'

'Thanks, Nick. I'll try to do that.'

Nick put down his empty mug. 'Is that all you wanted to speak to me about?'

'Yes,' Oliver said, lost in his thoughts. 'Thank you.'

'Then I'll leave you.'

Nick stood up, and Oliver roused himself.

Speak to your friend, his mum had said on the phone. He'd wondered if she meant Raven, or Tess, but she'd said what had happened with Ade had been before their time. Could she have meant not his absent friends but the one who had been knocking at the door – Nick Hamilton?

'Before you go,' Oliver said. 'I did want to ask you something.'

'Not another crisis?' Nick sat back down. 'While admittedly you do make a good cup of tea, for the sake of my time management you're going to have to spread them out a bit, Oliver.'

'It's not about me. It's about something my mum said – about Ade Adams. Another girl in the village he might have abused.'

'We talked about this, didn't we? I told you, I'd moved away by the time Ade Adams was living here.'

Oliver shook his head. 'My mum said this was something that happened before my time. I don't know how, or who was involved, since Ade wasn't living here then. My mum wouldn't tell me what she meant, but she suggested I speak to my friend – that meant you, I think. I'd told her you were at the door.'

Nick's face took on a guarded expression. 'Why me?' he said, although the nonchalant tone sounded a little forced.

'I was hoping you'd be able to answer that. Did you ever hear of anything – a girl of your generation, maybe, who was a kid here at the time? It's definitely worth passing any information along to the authorities.'

'If I knew anything significant, I'd have done so already. Although I don't see what good it would do now. The man's dead. He can't answer for what he did in his life, except to God.'

'You never know who else might have been involved in covering this up, though – people who are still here to answer for their crimes. And the women might be entitled to money from his estate.'

'Some might prefer their privacy over any amount of

money,' Nick said, getting to his feet. 'If one of the women who suffered under Ade Adams has chosen not to come forward, I'd presume that's because she wants to avoid going over a traumatic experience again. It's not for me or anyone else to make that decision on her behalf.'

Oliver rose too. 'You mean you do know of someone?'

'I was speaking hypothetically.' Nick reached out to shake his hand. 'Goodbye, Oliver, and good luck dealing with your crisis. As for Ade Adams, I sincerely hope the day will soon come when we won't have to hear his odious name ever again.'

*

'Interesting,' Tess murmured when Oliver had finished filling her in. 'So you think Nick knew something?'

'He was definitely being cagey,' Oliver said, sipping his mug of tea as he stroked a sleeping Roger. 'I'm sure he knew who my mum was talking about. I guess it was someone his age, but I don't know where she'd have got to know Ade. This must've happened back in the nineties – the peak of his fame. That was long before he had any connection to Cherrywood.'

'Yeah, he'd have been living down in London then.'

'Nick sounded properly angry,' Oliver said. 'Called Ade odious. He's always so calm and collected normally. Do you think there could be a connection to the case?'

Tess shrugged. 'Who knows? There's no shortage of women with similar stories. Still, anyone with a grudge against Ade and a connection to Cherrywood is worth investigating.'

'Nick's right really, isn't he? If this woman hasn't come forward, she obviously doesn't want to relive those memories. And what good will it do, in the end? Ade's already been exposed. There's no need for her to go through the trauma of revisiting her past.'

'But if it could help catch a killer . . .'

'If it's connected to the killer. It might be nothing to do with it.' Oliver finished his drink. 'Will you fill Liam in for me? I'd go round but I've got somewhere I need to be.'

Tess scowled. 'I can't. He's sulking with me.'

'Did you have a fight?'

'Oh, he . . .' Tess sighed. 'He's got the wrong idea about something. He thinks I lied to him about Mikey.'

Oliver blinked. 'Mikey?'

'Yeah. He was seen in the area at the time of Ade's death. God knows why – he hasn't been back here since Mum's funeral. Anyway, Liam thinks I've been covering for him.'

Oliver ran a finger under his dog collar. 'Um, why would he think that?'

'It's my fault,' Tess said with a heartfelt sigh. 'I didn't know Mikey was around. I haven't heard from him in years. But I did tell Liam I couldn't remember the name of Leonie's big ex.'

'I know. Sorry, it was actually me who spilled the beans when we were down in London. I didn't realise you were trying to keep it secret.'

'I wasn't really. You can't keep secrets like that around here; I should know that by now. He asked and I . . . I couldn't bring myself to mention it.'

'Why?'

She flushed. 'Well, I was ashamed, wasn't I? I mean, Liam's an ex-copper – one of the good ones. He's very big on right and wrong, and the difference between the two. My family . . . not so much.'

'You didn't want him to know about your family because you thought he'd judge you for it,' Oliver said quietly.

'I suppose.'

'I don't think Liam's that sort, Tess. He likes you for you. He doesn't care what your family are.'

'Doesn't he? And yet he's barely speaking to me.' She sighed again. 'I don't know why it matters so much to me that he approves of me, but I can't help feeling that way. Any advice from on high, Ol?'

'No, but you can have some from me.'

'Go on.'

'I reckon you ought to make Liam talk to you.'

She frowned. 'Make him how?'

'I don't know. He just seems like a man who'd appreciate being tackled head-on.'

Tess was silent for a few moments, lost in thought as she sipped her coffee.

'Another thing I'd love to know is who leaked that stuff about the Fifteen Club to the press,' she said at last. 'I guess that must've been Lee, but why? I'd have thought he'd wait until the case was wrapped up.'

'Oh. Yeah.' Oliver grimaced. 'Um, that was actually me as well. Sorry.'

Tess blinked. 'You wrote to the papers?'

'Yes. Anonymously, because I'd rather my congregation didn't know I'd been attending Black Masses on the side.'

'That was pretty risky, wasn't it? Those guys have got power.'

'I know.' He shivered. 'When I think of Johnny Guffaws being a member, when so many kids love him . . . it isn't right. I get that it was dangerous, for my career and my personal safety, but I had to do it.'

Tess gave him an impressed nod. 'That took a lot of guts, Ol.'

'I'm glad something good came of it, anyway.' Oliver prepared to leave, then paused. 'Er, how's Rave doing post-break-up?'

'Fine.' Tess smiled. 'A bit too fine, actually. I'm getting suspicious there might be someone else on the scene.'

'Already?'

'It is a bit soon. Not to mention that her rebound affairs usually end up making her more miserable than the break-up that inspired them. Still, she's seemed suspiciously jolly. I can't tell if it's genuine or she's masking her real feelings. I really thought she loved him.'

Oliver ignored another bite from the green-eyed monster. 'You think she is?' he asked. 'Masking, I mean.'

'Who knows? She's not giving anything away.' There was the sound of the front door opening. 'That's probably her. She's been to see her nan and Marianne.'

Raven stomped in, looking grumpy, and dumped a wad of leaflets on the coffee table.

Tess picked one up. 'Carpe Diem Fertility Services,' she read. 'Not the egg freezing thing again?'

'If it's not egg freezing then it's sperm donors and turkey basters. I swear, I've got leaflets for every private fertility clinic in the country.' Raven moved Roger aside to throw herself down next to Oliver. 'And there's worse. I had to tell Grandmother about breaking up with Benjy, obviously, so now I've got her trying to set me up with eligible bachelors left, right and centre.'

'Does she know any eligible bachelors?' Oliver asked.

'Loads, apparently, and I'm expected to boff each and every one of them until I'm in the club.' Raven pulled up a photo on her phone, which she passed to Tess. 'This is tonight's offering. Giles Twistleton. I never thought I'd find myself on a date with a Twistleton.'

'At least he's hot,' Tess said, examining the curly-haired young man in rugby shirt and chinos. 'If you have to shag eligible poshos, you might as well enjoy it.'

'You're not actually going, are you, Rave?' Oliver said.

Raven shrugged. 'Might as well. It'll buy me some peace, at least until after Christmas. And you never know, he might not be entirely awful.'

'Right.' Oliver stood up. 'Well, I'll love and leave you. I'm helping a parishioner move house.'

Tess smiled. 'You really do go above and beyond, you know. I've always said you were too good for this place, Ol.'

'Er, thanks. Bye, then.'

He was preparing to open the front door when he felt a hand on his shoulder. He turned to face Raven.

'Everything OK?' he asked.

'I was going to ask you the same question.' She smiled uncertainly. 'We're good, aren't we, Ol?'

'Of course.'

'Only you seemed a bit abrupt just now. I hope you're not rushing off because of me.'

'I'm not, honestly.'

'Because, um . . .' She hesitated. 'I don't want things to go weird. Between us, I mean.'

'They're not weird.' He forced a smile. 'Seriously, Rave, it's fine.'

'You promise?'

'I promise. Here.' He gave her a hug, and she wrapped her arms around him tightly.

'Still friends?' she whispered.

'As good friends as ever.' He held her back to look into her face. 'Rave . . .'

'Yes?'

'You know I . . . that is to say, I've always, um . . .'

'What?'

'You know I care about you a lot, right?'

She smiled. 'Likewise.'

'And I'd hate to ever not have you in my life. Do you know that?'

'Of course, darling.'

Oliver winced. 'Don't call me that.'

'What?'

'Darling.'

She blinked. 'But I call everyone that.'

'I know you do. Just . . . call me Oliver.' He kissed her forehead and let her go. 'I need to get going. See you, Rave.'

'Yeah. See you.'

The door closed. Raven disappeared. Oliver sighed as he walked away.

Chapter 29

Tess was driving home from a Christmas cake-decorating class the Women's Guild had organised, feeling distinctly middle-aged.

She'd enjoyed the cake decorating, but it was surely another irreversible step towards talcum powder, nylon support tights and Werther's Originals. She was certain that at her age, she ought to be out going to raves or something. Did people still go to raves? Well, anyway, she should be doing something more appropriate to her early thirties than decorating cakes and learning how to macrame. Even worse, Angela had lined up a bingo night for next month. And even worse than that, Tess was actually looking forward to it.

What she really wanted was to be giving her brain some exercise by helping Liam crack the Ade Adams murder. Even desk research was better than being shut out entirely. But Liam was still ignoring her calls.

The fact was, it wasn't just the case Tess missed. Now he was no longer coming into the pub or dropping into the flat to chat about his latest discoveries, Tess found the absence of

Liam's company had left a big hole in her life. Not that she'd ever admit that to him, obviously.

And then there was Mikey. Tess's brow knitted. So the prodigal brother had come back, had he? Looking for fresh hunting grounds, no doubt, after exhausting the criminal opportunities in Manchester. According to the last update she'd had from Caleb, Mikey had been working the Salford area twocking cars before his most recent conviction. She wondered he had the nerve to show his face here, after what had occurred on his last visit.

It must be . . . God, fifteen years ago. So long already. Mikey had been doing time for assault after he and his gang had beaten poor Craig Prewitt to a pulp, supposedly for seeing Mikey's girlfriend Helen behind his back. Craig had been innocent, of course – Ade Adams had been the real culprit, but as with everything in his life, he'd got away with it. Mikey had been not so innocent, or so found the judge who convicted him. Already with a criminal record for petty theft, graffiti and a number of minor offences, Mikey was handed a two-year custodial sentence. With good behaviour, he could've been out in just over one, but that hadn't happened – and the incident that had cost Mikey Feather another nine months of freedom was the same one that meant he hadn't set foot in the village or spoken to his sister since.

It was emotions rather than visual memories that washed over Tess as she thought back. Most of all, she remembered how alone she'd felt. Matt had left home. Dad had been inside, of course. Mikey had been serving out his GBH sentence. Caleb, poor lad, had broken down completely and been no use to anyone. The only person in the house who'd ever been able to keep it together in a crisis – who'd made sure the Feathers stayed a family, however dysfunctional they might be – had been their mum. Once she was gone, it all fell apart. Tess, seventeen years old, the youngest of them all, found the weight of everything landing on her shoulders. Organising the funeral, sorting out death certificates, speaking to coroners – things no schoolgirl should ever have to deal with. It had all fallen to her.

She'd been pleased when Mikey had been granted compassionate day release, but she hadn't expected much of him. All she'd needed was for at least one big brother to hold it together and support her at the funeral, so she wasn't facing this thing completely alone. Instead, Mikey had made a day that was supposed to be all about their mum all about him. The ridiculous escape attempt; the manhunt that followed. Tess blinked back tears as she remembered how anger and grief had almost incapacitated her. All these years later, she could forgive her brother anything except the way he'd denied her the opportunity to say a proper goodbye to her mum.

She slapped the steering wheel.

What the *hell* did he think he was doing, coming back here? Was he after scrounging from her, fifteen years after they'd last spoken? She didn't even know where he'd been staying. Sleeping rough, probably, if as per usual he didn't have a stolen penny to scratch his arse with. It was the worst possible time for him to turn up, with Ade's murder happening just when he showed his face. Of course it couldn't be connected – whatever else her brother might be, he wasn't a killer – but that was unlikely to hold much sway with the police. Mikey, already well established as a petty criminal when Leonie had left him, had moved on to bigger, more serious offences since then. He had a rap sheet as long as his arm, one item on which was grievous bodily harm against a man he'd taken to be Ade Adams. That put him clearly in the frame, if he had returned to the area at the time of the murder.

Tess found her thoughts turning again to Liam, with a degree of something like fondness. She liked to think of herself as a pretty independent person – she'd had to be. Fending for herself had become ingrained at an early age in the Feather household. Liam's constant attempts to keep her out of danger were frustrating to say the least, when she was perfectly capable of looking after herself. Still, it was nice to have someone who cared enough to watch her back.

Tess frowned as she turned towards Cherrywood. Just up ahead, illuminated by a streetlight as it passed, was a red Toyota Yaris with a very familiar numberplate.

'Speak of the devil,' she murmured to herself.

Tess watched Liam's car take a left, heading away from the village and towards Paignley, where Seana Hamilton lived. Where was he off to? Was he investigating? She still hadn't been able to fill him in on what she'd discovered the day she, Raven and Kennedy had visited Seana. He probably didn't think it was significant – she'd always suspected he was palming her off with a fluff job when he'd asked her to research the symbolism around the murder – but something told her it might be more relevant than he thought.

Oliver's advice came back to her. *Make him talk to you. He'd appreciate being tackled head-on.*

Making a snap decision, she pulled over into a lay-by and counted to five. After that, she guided her car along the same street Liam had just driven down. There were a few cars between them now, but she could still see him. Hopefully, if she kept her distance in the dark, he wouldn't realise she was following.

She'd expected him to take the road into Paignley, but Liam's car kept straight on. After ten miles, he showed no sign of slowing down. Tess was starting to worry he might not stop for hours. After all, it was the festive season. Perhaps he was going to visit family – if he had any family. Liam had rarely talked to her about his personal life, even when they'd been dating.

Five more miles, Tess told herself. Then she'd turn around and go home.

In fact it was another eight miles before Liam indicated to say he was taking the next right, and Tess was still following. She indicated too, then frowned as she watched him drive down a narrow dirt track. There was an illuminated sign at the top that read 'High Fell Camping and Caravan Park'.

A campsite? Was he going for a wintry weekend away? He always had been the outdoorsy type. Tess was going to feel a right tit if she'd followed him all this way just to find him pitching a tent and singing 'Ging Gang Goolie'.

She drove down the track and stopped in the visitors' car park. When she got out, she turned on the torch on her phone to look around. There was no sign of Liam's Yaris, which meant he must have booked a pitch and parked there. She'd have to look for him on foot. She hesitated, then as an afterthought grabbed one of the two small Christmas cakes she'd decorated and tucked it under her arm.

There were no tents on the campsite at this time of year, but there were a few static caravans that seemed to be occupied, and a couple of those little wooden camping pods. Tess soon located Liam's car, parked behind one of the smaller pods.

She paused at the door, wondering whether to knock. But she didn't need to bother. The door opened almost immediately, and a hand yanked her inside.

*

'What the hell are you doing here?' Liam demanded. He was on his knees, as if he'd been peering through the little porthole window in the door.

'I'm . . . on holiday.'

'Seriously?'

'All right, no. I followed you.' She held out her iced cake. 'But I came bearing peace-offering fruitcake.'

Liam ignored it. 'Why did you follow me?'

'Because I wanted to talk to you.' Tess knelt down by him, put her cake on the floor and peered through the porthole. 'What are you looking for?'

'That's classified.'

'Lee, come on.' She attempted a smile. 'You know, if you tell me, I might leave.'

'You won't though, will you?'

'No. Tell me anyway, though.'

He sighed and nodded to the caravan opposite. 'There's a woman in there. A tall, attractive woman in her early thirties with long brown hair.'

'You know, Lee, if you want a date there's apps for that.'

'Very funny. It's Leonie Abbott in one of her wigs, isn't it?' Liam said. 'I had a tip-off she'd be here tonight and while she isn't my hottest lead, I thought I'd be a mug not to see what I could find out. She's concealing something pretty major, if my guess is correct.'

'What's she concealing?'

He gave her a guarded look. 'Never you mind.'

'Do you think Leonie's here to meet the secret boyfriend?'

'That really doesn't concern you, Tess.'

Tess made herself comfortable, sitting cross-legged on the floor. While Liam seemed determined to be grumpy, he was at least talking to her. Actually, she rather enjoyed the challenge of getting him to open up again when he was in a sulk.

'Got some information for you,' she said.

'If it's about Oliver and that press leak about the club, I know. He texted me earlier to say he was the source.'

'Oh,' Tess said, nonplussed. She'd been looking forward to stringing that out. 'Are you annoyed with him?'

'No, I'm annoyed with you. All that does is confirm what

I knew already: that for every person who knows about a case, you lose a little bit more control. And there's you sharing it with every man and his dog in Cherrywood.'

Tess ignored his grumpy tone. She shuffled on her bum to stop it going numb. 'Did you find out anything new about Angela? Because, you know, she didn't turn up to our cake-decorating thing tonight, and the last time I saw her she was—'

Liam interrupted her. 'Angela's no longer a person of interest.'

Tess frowned. 'What?'

'She isn't involved in this. I'm sure of it.'

'How can you know that? She was your lead suspect last week.'

'Yes. And now she isn't.'

'But we know she's lying about who she is. And she was the one who invited Ade to the village, plus she had access to the park. She's got access to digoxin too.' Tess paused for dramatic effect before she unleashed her big idea. 'You know what? I reckon she's Lily Gish, Ade's first wife.'

'There's no proof of that.'

'She might be, though, mightn't she?' Tess said, refusing to let Liam's scepticism dampen her enthusiasm for her new pet theory. 'Lily was an actress, and I'm convinced Angela's awful performance at *Macbeth* was a screen – I bet that was why she arranged the early dress rehearsal and invited us all, to throw us off the scent. The ages match up too. Plus, get this: the night I went to the hall to meet Ade and Leonie, I distinctly remember Angela making a reference to Buster Keaton.'

'Well?'

'Well that's another silent film star, isn't it? Clearly she's a fan of the era. The sort of person who might choose a hero of the silver screen for her stage name. Not to mention that Angela was acting very cagily when I saw her sneaking off to Cherrywood Hall for a secret conference with Candice the other day.'

'Angela wasn't involved, all right?'

'How do you know?'

'How I know doesn't matter.' He fixed a stern look on her. 'Tess, I've said this to you a hundred times – we're not partners. So please, just leave and let me do my job.'

'You're not doing this just because you're angry with me about Mikey?'

'No,' he said quietly. 'Not because I'm angry. Because I'm hurt, Tess. I know I've got no right to be, after the way I treated you in London, but I can't help feeling it all the same. I thought . . . I suppose I thought we'd moved past the Porter case, or at least that our friendship had. I know Mikey's your brother and you love him, but it still hurts that you chose him over me.'

'What?' She laughed. '*What*? You think I chose Mikey over you?'

Liam didn't seem to hear her. His gaze was fixed on the soft light behind the curtains in the caravan opposite.

'I know it sounds pathetic as hell but I don't *have* anyone else,' he said in a toneless voice. 'I don't have what you've got, with Raven and Oliver and your little community in Cherrywood. There was only you, and you lied to me to cover for your brother. So yes. Even though I know it makes me the world's biggest hypocrite, I'm hurt.'

'So that's why you've been avoiding me. Rather than confronting it like a big boy and actually having a conversation with me, you went into a sulk.'

'I wasn't sulking. I just . . . needed some time to work out how I felt, that's all. What I ought to do about it.'

'You really think that's what was going on here?' Tess demanded, shuffling to face him. 'I promise you, I wasn't lying to cover for Mikey. Honestly, if I hadn't thought he was long gone I'd never have tried to hide the truth. I haven't spoken to my brother in fifteen years.'

He frowned. 'What?'

'You remember when we found those remains at Ling Cottage, you asked me if I'd ever seen a dead body? And I said I had – just once?'

'I remember. Whose was it?'

'My mum's,' Tess said quietly. 'I came home from school one day when I was seventeen. My two eldest brothers had left home, and Caleb, who was the next youngest, was out at work. Dad was in prison. There was . . . just me.'

'You found her?' Liam said in a softer voice. 'All on your own?'

She nodded. 'She used to drink too much,' she said in a choked voice. 'She had to, to keep it together enough to deal with the chaos of life in our family. That meant it happened sooner, I think.'

'Oh God. Tess, I'm sorry.'

Tess pressed her fingers to her temples. 'I was the youngest, but suddenly I had to be the adult. Caleb couldn't cope. Matt was on a job abroad and couldn't get back home. Mikey and Dad were in prison.'

'You took it all on yourself?'

'I was grateful for something to take my mind off things, to be honest. Keeping busy stopped me going insane. All I wanted was for the funeral to pass off without a hitch so I could say goodbye to my mum.'

'Didn't it?'

'No. Mikey saw to that. Dad couldn't get out but Mikey had a record of good behaviour so they granted him compassionate release. That's when he decided that rather than serve what would probably have been his last two months, he'd go on the run.' She swallowed a sob. 'I *needed* that funeral, damn him!'

'Did he get far?'

'Are you kidding? He barely got three miles before the cops picked him up. That's the last time we ever spoke.' She looked up at him. 'And you really think I want to cover for the bastard?'

'But then why did you lie?' Liam asked. 'You could just have told me about his connection with Leonie.'

'Because of you, you pillock. Because I was embarrassed. Ashamed to have you know the sort of family I come from, and the business we did.'

'What business was it?'

'Whatever business there was that required discretion,

some very shady contacts and a flexible approach to the law. If you needed something to fall off the back of a lorry round here, you can bet your arse it would be a Feather who did the pushing.' She lowered her gaze. 'I knew I couldn't hide it for ever, but I couldn't bring myself to tell you about it when you asked that first time. I couldn't bear to think you'd stop thinking well of me. I suppose I . . . I wanted you to like me. Pathetic, right?'

'Not in any way, shape or form is it pathetic.' Liam moved closer. 'You really thought I'd have cared about that?' he asked softly.

'Well, yes,' Tess said, flushing. 'You care so much about justice and all that stuff – enough to make it your job. You're a born policeman, Lee. I was born a Feather. Those two things have never been known to mix.'

'I'm not a policeman any more. These days I mix with who I like.'

'I thought maybe that you wouldn't want to know me, if you knew. It could affect your professional reputation, being linked to my family.'

'I don't care.'

'It might cost you clients.'

'I don't care about that either.' He stretched an arm around her. 'There's only one Feather I'm interested in, and she makes a pretty good partner despite her underworld beginnings.'

'Underworld might be overstating it. We weren't the mafia.' She looked up at him. 'Did you just say partner?'

Liam didn't answer.

'I went to see Peggy Bristow the other day,' he said instead, in a slightly dreamy voice.

'You told me. Did you learn anything?'

'She read my tarot cards. There was this tower – a tower of skulls . . .'

Tess blinked. 'OK. Is that connected to the case? It wasn't one of the ones on Ade's body.'

'Hmm?' Liam shook himself. 'Sorry. Yes. Partners was what I said.'

She smiled. 'I like that.'

'Tess . . . when you told me it wasn't as simple as I thought it was. Me and you. Was this what you meant – because of your family?'

'Yes,' she said quietly. 'I was so sure, once you knew . . . I thought it would change everything.'

'Then perhaps you don't know me as well as you think.' He took her hand. 'Tess, look. I know I let you down over Porter. But whatever I have to do to earn your trust again, I'll do it, all right? I won't lie to you again, if you can promise me the same.'

Tess looked down at her hand in his. 'I promise.'

'Partners, then? Together through thick and thin?'

She withdrew her hand from his so she could lick the tip of one finger and cross it over her palm, then held out her hand. 'Partners.'

He smiled. 'What's that all about?'

'Me and the boys used to do it when we were kids. It means a promise you can't break. You have to do it too, then we shake hands.'

Laughing, Liam copied the gesture and gave her hand a firm shake.

'What was it you said about a tower of skulls?' Tess asked.

'Oh, nothing. Just... the shadow of something that might have been.'

Chapter 30

Tess shivered, glancing out of the porthole to see if there'd been any developments across the way. 'It's bloody freezing. What time do you think this boyfriend is going to turn up, Lee?'

'Who knows? Leonie's lost her police tail but she's smart enough to be cautious still. Keep a bit of distance between them.' He glanced at her. 'You don't need to stay, you know.'

'Hey. Partners, remember? I'm not leaving until we've seen it through.'

'Well, get under the covers then,' he said, nodding to the bed behind them. 'I'll keep watch.'

'I didn't stalk you all this way just to have a kip.' She rubbed her hands together, trying to get some feeling back into the fingers. 'I want to savour the experience of my very first stakeout, thank you very much. Did you bring a Thermos?'

'Didn't think to.'

'Seriously, no Thermos? TV detectives always have them at stakeouts.'

'I'm sure your mate Jessica Fletcher has four different flasks with a choice of coffee, tea, hot chocolate or carrot and coriander soup. But I'm afraid all I've got is half a bottle of flat Pepsi Max.'

She shook her head. 'And you call yourself a pro.'

'Look, why don't you go home? I promise on my honour as a gentleman to update you the moment I learn anything.'

'Your honour as a *gentleman*?' Tess folded her arms. 'In that case I'm definitely staying.'

Liam sighed. 'You're a stubborn little donkey, Tess Feather. Hang on.'

He jerked the duvet off the bed and laid it across both of their knees.

'There we go. Nice and cosy,' he said.

He shuffled closer, and Tess didn't move away. After all, it was very cold. It made sense to share a bit of body heat.

'Christmas cake?' she asked, picking up the cellophane-wrapped fruitcake. 'We'll have to use our fingers.'

'Seems a shame to eat it when you decorated it so prettily. Mind you, I am starving.'

Tess unwrapped it and they each helped themselves to a handful of fruitcake, marzipan and icing.

'Food always tastes better on stakeouts,' Liam said when he'd finished.

Tess licked the icing remnants from her fingers. 'It does, doesn't it? Want any more?'

'No, we should make it last. At this rate it's going to be midnight before this guy turns up.'

'So, tell me everything you've found out since you've been giving me the silent treatment,' Tess said, trying to focus on the case and ignore the pleasant feeling of Liam's body against hers. 'I've got stuff to tell you too.'

Liam smiled. 'I have missed having someone to bounce ideas off. You go first.'

'Well, it isn't much but it might be significant. For a start, Kennedy had a brainwave about the tarot cards. She reckons – and I think she's right – that the cards aren't supposed to carry loads of deep symbolism.'

'Eh?'

'What I mean is, that wasn't the killer's intention when they planted them on Ade. They're just pictures, in the end – pictures that tell us why he was killed.'

'What, so . . .'

'The child, representing his victims,' Tess said, counting on her fingers. 'The devil, representing Ade himself. And the last judgement, representing his punishment – death and public exposure. The killer might have known very little about tarot – just seen the cards as a useful way to send those investigating a slightly cryptic message.'

'Slightly cryptic, but not too cryptic.'

'Right, so they could be sure we'd arrive at the correct conclusion.'

Liam looked thoughtful. 'You know, that never even occurred to me.'

'Nor me, until Kennedy pointed it out. Sometimes it's the simplest solutions that you can't see for looking.'

'I'm starting to build a picture of this killer. Someone who knows they'll be found but wants that to be on their own terms and in their own time. Someone who's been playing us from the get-go, giving us just as much information as we need.'

'You think so?'

'It's feeling more and more like we're pieces being pushed around a board. Or like mice being kept alive by a cat, toying with us until they decide it's time to strike.'

'I know what you mean. I thought at first that any killer who murdered someone in the way Ade was murdered must have more showmanship than brains, but now . . .'

'My thoughts exactly. Did you find out anything else on this visit to your academic friend?'

'Well, I learnt a lot about witches,' Tess said. 'How witch hysteria targeted innocent women because of fear around female sexual desire. It was fascinating.'

'Fascinating but irrelevant. Is that what you're saying?'

'I'm . . . not sure,' Tess said vaguely. 'I suppose so. Still, there's something nagging me about it.'

'What?'

'Something I can't quite put my finger on. Hopefully it'll come to me.' She roused herself. 'Well, come on then, your turn. What have you found out?'

'The club was a bust – I guess Oliver filled you in. Like I said, Angela was a dead end too.'

'Are you sure about that? I was convinced she must be Lily. I mean, everything seems to point to it.'

'I'm sure she's not.'

'Did you ask her?'

'No, but . . . some new information came to light.'

'What new information?'

'Well . . . I can't tell you. It doesn't have much to do with the case, but it is rather delicate. Out of respect for Angela, I'd rather not share it. Even with you, Tess – sorry.'

'You don't trust me?'

'It isn't that. This is Angela's secret, and since it isn't connected to the case, it's really up to her who she chooses to share it with. You'll know all about it when the time comes.'

'All right,' Tess said, more puzzled than ever. 'Does it absolutely rule her out of being involved in Ade's death?'

'It doesn't rule her out. But . . .' He hesitated. 'Let's just say that she managed to convince me.'

Liam seemed certain he was right, but Tess was far from convinced. If he hadn't asked Angela if she was Lily, how could he know she wasn't? She was the right age, she probably had an acting background, and Oliver's contact at the Fifteen Club had told him Lily was foreign. Well, wasn't Angela hiding an American accent? Liam clearly wasn't prepared to discuss it further, however. Tess parked it to ponder later when she was alone.

'Anything else?' she asked.

'I haven't been able to track down your brother. All I was able to find out is that he's been working as a packer in a warehouse in Cloverly Bridge. He's finished his contract now, though, and the address the company had on file for him was a dead end.'

Tess raised her eyebrows. 'Mikey's been working?'

'Is that unusual?'

'When the work's legit, then yes.' She frowned. 'Where is he, then? And what's he doing back? I never thought we'd see him within twenty miles of Cherrywood, after how he left the place.'

'Do you think it's connected to Ade?'

'Nah. If Mikey wanted to get his own back on Ade and Leonie, he's had plenty of time to do it before now. Anyway, my brother's not a killer.'

'Sure about that?'

'Positive. Mikey's an incurable crook, a selfish bastard and an utter waste of space, but I don't believe he could take a life.'

'He must've done some damage to this man he assaulted to get years for it.'

'That is true,' Tess conceded. 'Terry Braithwaite and those other thugs he hung around with will have egged him on, but if he could do it once then I guess he could again. Still, Lee, I really don't think he's the type to poison someone. He couldn't plan a murder in that cold, calculated way Ade's killer did.'

'Well, OK,' Liam said, although he sounded far from convinced. 'Like I said, I also went to talk to Peggy. Did you know that she's the only one of Ade's wives who left him? He was such a controlling bastard, none of the others seem to have dared – they just had to wait until they got too old for him. Which didn't take long, usually.' He pulled the duvet further up to cover their laps. 'Not only that, but she was with child at the time.'

'You're kidding! Peggy had a baby?'

'Given up for adoption, apparently,' Liam said. 'Peggy didn't want the baby to grow up with Ade as his father, and her mental state was so poor after leaving the man that she didn't feel fit to be a mum. She was only in her early twenties.'

'Poor Peg,' Tess said with feeling. 'What a traumatic experience that must've been.'

'Makes for a pretty good motive too, doesn't it? There's evidently a lot of regret over having to give up the child.'

Tess shook her head. 'How do you manage that level of cynicism? Are there exercises you have to do?'

Liam smiled. 'I'm only professionally cynical. I have to be, don't I? Exploring every possibility and all that. I'm actually a bit of a softie outside work.' He glanced at her. 'You should let me show you sometime.'

Tess decided it was safest to ignore that comment. She was very aware of Liam's legs pressing against hers under the duvet. Something about the addition of the cover made their relative positions feel far more . . . intimate.

'What else?' she asked.

'Now here's the really interesting thing. Guess who Ade was with on the morning of the day he died?'

'Not Peggy?'

'That's right. He spent the morning drinking vodka in his ex-wife's kitchen after a row with Leonie. She may have been the last person to see him alive – apart from his murderer.'

'You're kidding!'

'Nope. She was very cooperative, this time around. Told me everything quite happily.'

'So we're starting to build up a picture of Ade's last day on earth, aren't we?' Tess said. 'Let's walk it through.'

'Good idea. So, Ade is in his hotel room in the early hours of the fifth, probably around five a.m., when his wife rolls in.'

'Do you know where she'd been?'

'She claims she was out on the town, alone – a habit when she wanted to pick up men, although she didn't go home with anyone that night. Says she can provide witnesses, although I wouldn't be surprised if they were bribed and she was actually with the boyfriend. Anyway, Ade had been drinking and when she refused to account for her movements, the two had a blazing row.'

'That's when he stormed out.'

Liam nodded. 'Peggy said he turned up on her doorstep when it was barely light – that must put it at eight a.m. or earlier. She started feeding him neat vodka, hoping to calm him down before he went back to Leonie.'

'What time did he leave?'

'A couple of hours later, Peggy said. So the questions we still need answering are firstly, when was he drugged? Secondly, how and why did he climb the bonfire? And thirdly, when and how was he killed? I thought the digoxin might have been swapped for his cocaine, but according to Peggy he was off the stuff. Issues with his heart.'

'Hmm.' Tess fell silent.

'Any ideas?' Liam asked after a moment.

'Hang on. Just . . . don't talk to me for a minute. I'm trying to do detection.'

Liam obediently went quiet.

'All right,' Tess said after a little while. 'So, I saw this episode of *Columbo*—'

Liam shook his head. 'You and your cop shows.'

'No, but listen. There was this dentist, right, and he'd found out one of his patients was having it away with his missus. Obviously he decides to murder him, but to give himself an alibi he coats the poison with this slow-dissolving gel they use for dental painkillers or something and hides it under the guy's crown. Then the guy dies two hours later from what looks like a heart attack while his killer's in a room full of people. He used digitalis too.'

'What are you saying? We should be investigating Screaming Ade's dentist?'

'No, I mean . . . we know Ade was drugged, right? But if he'd been drugged in order to get him up the bonfire, that'd need at least two people to dress him in the witch costume and get him to the top. Very difficult to do without disturbing the pyre or anyone in the village hearing the noise. But if he climbed it himself, what possible reason could there be for someone to follow him up and drug him? Firstly, he'd see them coming and surely try to fight them off, again disturbing the pyre and making a racket. Secondly, if that person was also the killer then why drug him at all? Why not just administer the digoxin, plant the tarot cards and leave the body to be discovered hours later when everyone gathers for the bonfire?'

'So you're saying . . .'

'Supposing Ade was drugged *before* he climbed the bonfire?' Tess said triumphantly. 'If he'd been given a drug that was set to release later, that meant the effects wouldn't kick in until he was on top of the bonfire. Both Leonie and Peggy would have had the opportunity to slip him something, and perhaps others too, since we don't know all his movements after leaving Peggy.'

'Why would the killer do that?'

'Well, so that having once climbed the thing, he'd stay up there until the bonfire. They couldn't risk him sobering up, thinking better of the idea and climbing down. That'd ruin the whole plan.'

'And how would this time-release drug be given? I doubt either Peggy or Leonie were giving him dental treatment that morning.'

'Well...' Tess floundered for a moment. 'Maybe... maybe it was disguised as a vitamin pill or something. I guess you could create a capsule from concentrated Valium that looks like the others and coat it in some sort of time-release substance.'

'We're getting a bit theoretical here, Tess. Neither Leonie nor Peggy is a trained chemist, and it must take skill to create a pill like that. Not to mention that I doubt these time-release things are something you can predict to the exact second, whatever happens in *Columbo*. There's a chance Ade could conk out before he reached the top of the bonfire, and then the plan goes up in smoke. Plus, that still doesn't answer the question of why the killer wouldn't just skip the Valium and go straight for the deadly poison like your evil dentist did.'

'All right,' Tess said, feeling rather put out at the squashing of her second brilliant theory of the night. 'It was just an idea. I don't see you coming up with any amazing suggestions.'

'Come on, don't sulk,' he said, giving her a squeeze. 'I'm

not shutting it down. It's a good theory, or the germs of one. All I'm saying is that it doesn't answer all our questions. Let it percolate and see what develops.'

They both jumped at the sound of a car pulling up, and scrambled for the porthole window.

'Here we go,' Liam breathed. 'Let's see who's paying Leonie Abbott night-time visits, shall we?'

The door opened on the driver's side, and Tess inhaled sharply as a man got out.

'No,' she murmured. 'That's not right. It can't be right.'

It was Oliver.

Chapter 31

Oliver examined the rusting rental caravan in front of him.

It wasn't much of a place. Long past its best. Still, it was a start for them.

He took a cardboard box from the boot of his car. Mikey got out of the passenger side and joined him.

'Thanks for this, Oliver,' he said, clapping him on the back. 'I won't forget it. I reckon you and Springer must be made of the same stuff to help out a wrong 'un like me.'

'Mikey, that might be the nicest thing anyone's ever said to me.' Oliver placed the box containing Mikey's few possessions into his arms. 'Just stick with it, eh?'

'I won't let anyone down this time. If I do, there can't be any way back.' Mikey nodded to the battered caravan. 'Will you come in and meet Bels? I know we can trust you to keep your gob shut.'

'About what?'

'You'll see,' Mikey said, a little mysteriously.

'Hang on.' Oliver put a hand on the man's shoulder. 'Before we go in, there's something I need to say to you.'

Mikey blinked. 'OK.'

'Look, I . . . I owe you an apology. When you first turned up, I think it's fair to say I wasn't very happy to see you.'

'Don't I know it?' Mikey said, rubbing his jaw. 'Still, if it'd been anyone else I'd have got worse, I guess. Our Tess would've kneed me in the nads soon as look at me.'

'That's not what I wanted to apologise for. To be honest, it's more a confession than an apology.' Oliver closed his eyes. 'The thing is, I tried to do the right thing. Give you the help you needed to make a fresh start. I did it because it was my duty as a priest and it's what Reverend Springer would've done. Because . . . because I knew it was what my brother would've wanted me to do. But I couldn't *feel* it. Deep down, I think I really wanted you to fail.'

Mikey didn't look angry, as Oliver had anticipated he might. He only looked rather puzzled as he put the cardboard box down at his feet. 'But you were the one who told me to keep on fighting,' he said. 'Gave me all those pep talks about not letting myself and Bels down.'

'I said what you needed to hear, because they were the right things to say. But my feelings didn't always match the script.'

'So you were lying? Didn't think you lot were allowed.'

'It was more that I was trying to force my emotions to match what was coming out of my mouth. The problem was, I knew what the right thing to do was but I couldn't get over my anger. I thought that was all about Archie, and the way you used him.' Oliver took a deep breath. 'But I've been thinking a lot lately. About feelings, and duty, and right and wrong. And actually, it was never really that. Really it was fear feeding the anger, because I knew I could so easily have followed the same path you did.'

'When Archie died, you mean?'

'Yeah. If Reverend Springer hadn't shown me there was another way, my life might have been very different. In a way, I always felt like you represented that alternative future. You turning up reminded me of how that felt – that a darker side was still part of who I was – and that scared me.'

'All right,' Mikey said, blinking. 'That's deep stuff, Rev. Why are you telling me?'

'I just wanted to confess, and say sorry.' Oliver held out his hand. 'I hope you and Bels have got a happy future ahead of you, Mikey. This time I really do mean that.'

'You're not still angry, then?' Mikey said as he shook Oliver's hand.

'Not any more. I hope you can understand why I felt that way.'

'Sure,' Mikey said, his eyes taking on a faraway expression. 'I remember how I felt when the screws told me my mum had died. God, I hated the world. All I wanted was to run away. Stick my head in the ground like an ostrich and hope when I pulled it out everything would've gone back to how it was years before. Hated myself mostly, for giving her all that stress in her last couple of years. Not that it helped me change myself for the better, mind. I've not got the strength you have. It took Bels to do that.'

'That was why you ran?'

'Guess it was. To me, Mum's death meant . . . no way back, you know? Bloody stupid thing to do. But it's in the past now, along with all the other bloody stupid things I've done.' He nodded to the caravan. 'Come on. I want you to meet Bels.'

Mikey unlocked the caravan with a small key and ushered Oliver inside.

It was a small caravan. There was a compact living area, with a table and corner sofa that folded down to make a bed. At the far end was a kitchen, and there was a door that probably led to a bathroom.

'It's not much, but it's home,' observed a familiar female voice behind him.

Oliver turned and stared at the woman on the sofa. She had long brown hair today and she was dressed in a very different style than the last time he'd seen her, but he still recognised her instantly.

'Leonie?'

She smiled. 'Call me Helen. Hi, Oliver.'

'You, um . . . you remembered my name?'

'I always did. I remembered all of you that night, in spite of the state I was in.' She curled her lip at the memory. 'It seemed wise to put on an act. I didn't want anyone to draw a link from me to Mikey. If Ade had found out . . . well, God knows what he would've done.'

Mikey sat down beside her. 'You can take that off now, Bels,' he said in a gentle voice Oliver had never heard him use before, nodding to Leonie's wig. She did so, and he gave her a kiss.

Oliver was still feeling rather dazed. 'So . . . you're Bels?'

Leonie smiled. 'That old nickname. Only Mikey ever

called me it. Hell's Bells, you know – for Helen? It reminds me of when we were kids. The girl I was before Ade dug his talons into me.' She shook her head. 'God, what a fool I was! I thought it was worth it. That fame and wealth would be worth turning my back on my family, my friends, my home. On the boy I'd promised to marry.'

'None of that,' Mikey said, turning her face to his for a kiss. 'We're moving on, remember? We both made stupid choices. Anyway, the wedding wasn't cancelled. It was only postponed for a little while.'

'You two were engaged?' Oliver said, sinking dizzily on to the sofa.

Leonie nodded. 'We decided to keep it quiet. We knew nobody would take it seriously; a couple of daft kids, in love for the first time. Still, he asked and . . . I said yes. Gave me a sweet little ring he'd saved for weeks to buy, which I ought to have realised was worth more than all the expensive jewellery Ade gave me to get into my knickers. If it hadn't been for him, Mikey and me would have been happy, I think.'

'We are happy,' Mikey said, drawing her against him.

'But how did you, um . . . I mean, how did it happen?' Oliver asked.

'It was fate, I suppose,' Leonie said, smiling fondly at her fiancé. 'You might say I catfished him.'

'You did what?'

'I can't use social media under my own name now – stage or real. I'm hardly Kylie but I still get my share of obsessive fans, and then there was my controlling husband. I had a Facebook account under a fake name that I used to keep in touch with the few people I knew – one that Ade thankfully never found out about.' She glanced at Mikey. 'I did used to think about you, Mike. Wonder if you'd forgiven me. One day, after a few drinks and a particularly big fight with Ade, I thought I'd look you up.'

'She didn't tell me who she was, at first,' Mikey said to Oliver. 'She sent me a friend request, we interacted on our timelines, and gradually started chatting privately. Started to build a bond. I told her where I was and how I'd ended up there. The sort of life I'd led. She told me about the drugs and struggles with her mental health. Then she broke the news that she was married. Told me the husband knocked her about, and she was planning to leave him just as soon as she had the courage. We were planning a future together long before she finally confessed who she really was. I couldn't believe it when I found out she still loved me after all this time.'

Oliver smiled. 'That's a sweet story.'

'I'm just glad she found me again,' Mikey said, looking at Leonie. 'Bels saved me, Oliver. I'd never have had the strength to keep straight if it wasn't for her.'

Oliver glanced around the tatty caravan. 'I don't mean to be intrusive or anything, but don't you live in a mansion, Le—Helen?'

Leonie laughed. 'Are you suggesting I move my ex-con lover in just weeks after my husband was bumped off? I mean, it might boost my album sales but I'm not sure the police would look too favourably on it. The whole reason we've been trying to keep our relationship low-key is in the hope they won't find their way to Mikey.'

'Wouldn't it be better just to come clean?'

'With my record?' Mikey looked around the caravan proudly. 'No, this place'll do until we can be together properly. I don't want to live in a mansion, and certainly not one Ade Adams helped pay for. I can just about manage to pay my share here, once I get another job.'

'Is that why you came back to Cherrywood?' Oliver asked. 'Because you knew Leonie was coming here?'

'Yeah, partly, although I knew we'd only get the odd stolen moment while she was still with Ade. I liked to be close to her, though, and I thought it'd be somewhere I could find the help I needed to get straight.'

'From Reverend Springer, you mean.'

Mikey smiled. 'Or not, as it turned out.' He stood up. 'Now, how about a cuppa before you drive back, Rev? You have to say yes, since you're our first houseguest.'

Oliver was about to agree when the door burst open and a red-faced creature came flying in with Liam hot on its heels. Tess flew at Mikey, pushing him against the wall of the caravan so hard that it made the rickety old thing rock.

'All right, you son of a bitch,' she growled. 'What the hell do you think you're doing back here?'

'Tess, for God's sake!' Liam glanced apologetically at a horrified Leonie, who'd risen from the sofa. 'Sorry. I tried to keep her away until she'd calmed down, but, er, that didn't work out.'

'Tess,' Mikey said in a choked voice – mainly because his sister had her hand against his throat. 'Where did you come from?'

'Me? Where did *you* come from? I swear, Mikey, if you had anything to do with Ade's murder . . .'

'Come on. I'm not a murderer. You must know that.'

'I thought I did. I thought "not taking a life" was the ridiculously low bar you'd set yourself when it came to basic human decency. That, however, was before I found out you were shagging Ade Adams's missus on the side.' She turned to glare at Oliver. 'And you! What's your role in this? Have you been hiding him from me?'

'I didn't have any choice,' Oliver said, flushing deeply. 'He asked me not to tell anyone he was back when he came to me for help.'

'You . . . Judas, Maynard!'

'It's my job, Tess. If it makes you feel any better, I've been on fire with guilt about it.'

'Not enough to tell me the truth, clearly.' She looked back at Mikey. 'Where've you been staying?'

'Er, Ling Cottage?'

She shook her head. 'He's been putting you up as well? Bloody hell, Oliver, what other secrets have you been hiding from me?'

Oliver thought about Raven and hoped the additional flush in his cheeks would be lost in the general pinkness of his shame.

'Stop, please!' Leonie said. She had turned very white. 'I can't . . . please. I can't cope with this.'

She stumbled dizzily and Liam stepped forward to catch her before she fainted.

'Tess, for God's sake!' he said. 'Stop it, can you? You're upsetting her.'

Mikey managed to push Tess away and darted to Leonie's other side so he and Liam could support her to the sofa.

'Bels?' he said softly, sitting down beside her. 'What's wrong, love? Do you need a doctor?'

Tess blinked. 'A doctor? Is she sick?'

'It's nothing about six months and a significant reduction in stress wouldn't fix,' Liam said. 'That's right, isn't it, Leonie?'

'Call me Helen,' she mumbled. 'Can someone bring me a glass of water? My vape too, please.'

Tess, who looked more bewildered than angry now, went to get a glass from the tap in the kitchenette. Mikey handed Leonie her vape from the table.

'I just like to hold it,' she murmured to no one in particular. 'Like a . . . a security blanket.'

Tess's gaze fixed on the vape as she returned from the kitchenette.

'What?' Leonie said, seeing where her eyes were directed.

'Nothing. Just a thought.' She handed Leonie the water and turned to Liam. 'Did you say six months?'

'That's my estimate. Perhaps Helen or your brother might like to confirm – assuming the baby is his.'

Oliver stared. 'Baby! There's a baby?'

'There will be.' Mikey glared at Liam. 'And yes, of course it's mine. I'd thank you to watch your mouth, whoever you are.'

Leonie smiled weakly and put a hand on his arm. 'It's OK, Mikey. The man's just doing his job.'

Mikey looked worried. 'What is he, a cop?'

'A PI. I hired him to investigate Ade's murder. Then I unhired him again.' She looked at Liam. 'I knew you couldn't let it drop.'

'Why did you want me to?'

'I didn't, really. I just didn't want to be involved any more. Like you said, I don't need the stress. If you chose to go rogue, well, I'd made my peace with that. It's going to come out eventually, and I'd rather it was you who got the glory.'

Liam shook his head. 'If you don't mind me saying, you guys aren't being very discreet. Secret liaisons, and involving the reverend here. You're lucky it was me who showed up tonight and not the cops.'

'We had to involve somebody,' Leonie said. 'And there haven't been many secret liaisons – not since Ade died.' She squeezed Mikey's hand. 'But sometimes I just needed to be with him, you know?'

Liam squinted at her. 'That night with me at the hotel . . .'

'That was for Ade's benefit. I knew he was watching my every move. I had to keep up the pretence that everything was normal, didn't I? He already suspected I was seeing someone. If he'd known for certain, he wouldn't have stopped until he found out who it was.'

'That was why he laughed like that. Why he seemed almost happy when he caught you out. If you'd turned me down that night it would've confirmed all his fears, I suppose, about you having fallen for someone else.'

'Exactly.'

'What happened at this hotel?' Mikey demanded, casting a suspicious look at Liam.

Leonie smiled. 'Nothing, thank God. I've never been so pleased to have my suspicion confirmed that the man who'd been chatting me up was one of Ade's stooges. Naturally I had to throw that punch, though, or Ade would've seen right through me.'

Liam rubbed the area around his eye. 'You couldn't have pulled it?'

'What, and have you getting suspicious? I can see you're not a man to let something drop.'

'You three had better leave us,' Mikey said, glancing at his fiancée's pale face. 'Bels needs to rest now.'

Leonie leant back against the head cushion and closed her eyes. 'Liam'll want to ask you some questions first,' she muttered.

Liam nodded. 'She's not wrong. Do you mind telling me where you were the day Ade Adams died, Mr Feather?'

'What day did he die?'

'Saturday the fifth of November, sometime between eight a.m. and six p.m.'

'I was at Ling Cottage.' Mikey frowned. 'Look, if you're implying I had something to do with this—'

'I'm not implying that, but I still have to ask. Was there anyone who can vouch for it?'

'Bels had been round the night before, but she left early to be back when Ade woke up. Then . . . no. I was trying to keep it quiet I was up there, wasn't I? No one knew except Oliver, and I only went out when I had to work.'

'Thank you.' Liam stood up. 'Come on, Tess. Oliver. I think we'd better let Helen rest.'

Oliver nodded and stood up. 'Well, it's certainly been an eventful evening,' he said to Mikey.

'Yeah. Thanks for helping me move,' Mikey said with a weak smile. He stood and followed them to the door. 'Um, Tess?'

She turned to fix a cold look on him. 'Yes?'

'I . . . It's good to see you, all right?'

'You'll forgive me if I don't say "likewise".'

'Look, about Mum . . .'

Tess glared at him, and for a moment Oliver worried she was about to pin Mikey to the wall again. As different as Tess was from her brothers, in some respects she was pure Feather.

'Don't you dare talk about Mum to me,' she growled.

'I just want you to know I never meant what happened to happen, OK? I didn't plan it and it wasn't because I didn't care. I know I've been a selfish bastard, but that wasn't it. I was just . . . overwhelmed by it all. Tried to run away from losing her; reset things somehow. I guess it was a sort of panic attack. Can you understand that?'

'You think I didn't feel like that?' Tess demanded. 'You think I wasn't desperate to run away, hide under the covers and make it all disappear? I was seventeen, Mike.'

'No, I . . . I know you must've been. But you were strong. You were always stronger than the rest of us.'

'I was strong because I had to be. Because none of you bastards ever gave me a choice.' Tess turned away from him. 'Just go back to your girlfriend and your baby and forget you saw me, OK, Mikey? That's the best I've got for you now.'

Without another word, she walked out.

Chapter 32

'And what time do you call this?' Raven demanded when Tess emerged at eleven a.m. the next morning and joined her in the kitchen.

Tess groaned, rubbing her temples. 'Oh God, please don't. I've got a drama hangover.'

'You want breakfast?' Raven nodded to a couple of pans on the hob. 'I've done a fry-up. I thought you might appreciate something more substantial than Coco Pops.'

'I thought I could smell something unfamiliar and delicious. This must be the first time you've cooked for us since . . . you were born. How'd you know where everything was?'

'I soon found the things I needed once I'd hunted around. So, sunny side up or sunny side down for your eggs?'

'Er, sunny side up, please,' Tess said, taking a seat at the breakfast bar. 'What's happened? Have you been body-swapped with Nigella?'

Raven shrugged as she started dishing up. 'I just thought it was time I started experimenting with proper-grown-upping.'

'This isn't to do with your date with that posh eligible type last night, is it?'

'Oh, I changed my mind and cancelled. It's too soon after Benjy to have the energy for dating, especially when Grandmother's hovering around demanding to know if I'm pregnant yet.' She put a plate loaded with bacon, eggs, beans, sausage and fried bread down in front of Tess.

'Wow,' Tess said, blinking at it. 'Hey, if you keep on like this I might have to marry you myself.'

Raven smiled as she sat down beside her. 'Sweet-talker.'

'So what brought on this attack of domestic goddessing?' Tess asked as she tucked in.

'I just thought, if I'm so lucky as to stumble over another nice guy silly enough to want to be with me, I want to be someone worth being with, you know?' Raven said with a shrug. 'I mean, not that I'm planning to become a tradwife or anything, but I'm thirty-one. It's high time I learnt to fend for myself, and for any smaller folk who might come along one day.'

Tess smiled. 'You haven't quite written off procreation, then?'

'Not entirely. I could be convinced, with the right partner. Although the Angela lifestyle still has a lot of appeal.'

'Ugh. Angela,' Tess said, rubbing her temples. 'I'd forgotten about the case.'

Raven frowned. 'She isn't a suspect, is she?'

'Liam says not, but I've got a few questions for her that I wouldn't mind getting some answers to.' Tess looked at her. 'I thought I was forbidden from discussing the case with you.'

Raven sipped her coffee. 'That was before you replaced me with Kennedy Hamilton. I refuse to be ousted in favour of another sidekick.'

'You ousted yourself.'

'Well, now I demand to be unousted. And I demand to know everything that happened at this stakeout you texted me about.'

Tess smiled. 'Kennedy is an excellent sidekick, but I must admit, I'd rather solve mysteries with my best friend than anyone else.'

'Aww. I know that's the crispy bacon talking, but still.' Raven gave her a squeeze. 'Come on then, fill me in. Did you find out who Leonie Abbott's been banging on the side?'

'That was a total shocker. You'll never guess.'

'Who is it?'

'Mikey Feather.'

Raven stared at her.

'Say that again,' she said at last. 'I think I might have bacon fat clogging up my ears.'

'It's Mikey. My brother Mikey.'

'But . . . how is that even possible?'

'They must have reconnected while he was inside, I suppose. Apparently he's been in the area for ages.' Tess gave a grim laugh. 'A shock though that was, I got an even bigger one when the car pulled up and Oliver got out.'

Raven's eyebrows shot up. 'Oliver!'

'Yeah. I genuinely thought for a few seconds he must be

the lover, until Mikey climbed out too. Can you imagine, our Ol a secret sex fiend?'

Raven shrugged. 'You never know. He might surprise you.'

'Not that much.'

'What did Ol have to do with it all?'

Tess's brow knitted. 'He's a right little Lando. He's been hiding Mikey up at Ling Cottage. And me here in blissful ignorance while he never said a word.'

'Why would he do that?'

'Oh, some sort of noble vicar duty or something. He's been helping him get back on his feet after his last stretch. Can you believe it, after what Mikey did to Archie?'

'I can believe it.' Raven smiled fondly. 'He'd always try to do the right thing, even if it was a struggle. That's what makes him Oliver.'

Tess chewed a mouthful of fried bread thoughtfully. 'Yeah. I suppose it is.'

'So how long will it take you to forgive him?'

'I'll probably manage it in a day or two.' She shook her head. 'Mikey, on the other hand... Honestly, I felt like throttling him. I half did. All I could think about was the funeral. God knows what sort of father he's going to make.'

Raven blinked. 'Father?'

'Yeah. Leonie's about three months' pregnant.'

'Bloody hell!'

'I know.'

'So they didn't have anything to do with the murder, then?'

'Liam thinks probably not, but the police might believe otherwise if they find out about them. Mikey's got a record that includes assault against a man he mistook to be Ade Adams, he's been sleeping with Ade's wife and now she's having his baby. And we know Leonie was desperate to leave Ade. Finding out she was pregnant would just have added a ticking clock element.'

'Well, what do you think?'

'Honestly? I don't know. Estranged as we are, I would like to believe my brother wasn't capable of taking a life. But after fifteen years, how well do I really know him?'

'He wouldn't have done it like that, though, would he? Surely if Mikey wanted someone dead, he'd just . . . I don't know, stab them or something.'

'But he's with Leonie now. She's a clever woman, and a good liar too. If they were in it together, who knows how they might have planned it?' Tess tossed a piece of bacon rind to a hopeful-looking Roger. 'I did have a thought, though.'

'What is it?'

'Last night, I was telling Liam about this theory I'd come up with about the drugging. I thought the Valium might have been administered before Ade climbed the bonfire, and coated with something that would delay release until he was up there. That way, the murderer could be sure he wouldn't sober up and climb down again before they'd seen the plan through.'

Raven nodded. 'Sounds like a strong theory.'

'Lee didn't think so. He picked it to bits. But supposing . . .'

Tess fell into a brief, thoughtful silence. 'Supposing Ade drugged himself?'

'Eh?'

'Supposing the murderer had laced something they knew Ade was going to take when he reached the top of the bonfire with a drug to make him pass out? That would work, right?'

'You mean like cocaine?'

'According to Peggy Bristow, he was off the drugs. All except one. It seems he couldn't quite break his long-standing nicotine addiction.'

'So . . .'

'What if the Valium had been added to the fluid in his vape?' Tess said triumphantly. 'It came to me last night, when Leonie was twiddling hers. We know he puffed on the thing constantly, and he had a long wait on top of the bonfire before he could spring his prank. Of course the first thing he'd do is turn his vape on to get his nicotine fix. That menthol stuff he liked would probably cover any difference in smell or taste, and the slow release means he'd lose consciousness gradually, so he'd be less likely to cry out or fall forward. It makes sense, right?'

'It's an excellent theory, darling. Did you tell Liam about it?'

'Not yet. He'll only pour cold water on it, because it still doesn't answer the question of why anyone would drug Ade in the first place. The killer could just as easily have laced his vape juice with something lethal, then it would have been job done.'

'That is a point. Why risk having to go back to finish the job?'

'And who could have finished the job, when the park was locked? Only a handful of people had keys, and of them, only Angela Campbell was seen going in that afternoon.'

Raven shook her head. 'It can't have been her.'

'That's what Liam says, but there are so many unanswered questions. I thought she might be Lily Gish, this mysterious first wife of Ade's. She's the right age, and there are other similarities.'

'No. I can't believe she'd have been married to someone like Ade. She's too smart.'

'Well, there must have been some connection. Otherwise why would he have agreed to judge the Guy Trail?' Tess looked up at Raven, her eyes glittering as the thrill of the chase took hold. 'I think we ought to go and see her. Do a bit of sleuthing for ourselves, since Lee's making such a shoddy job of it.'

'He won't like it.'

'Tough. He said last night that we were partners. That means I get to call a few shots too.'

She sighed. 'If it's going to help get Angela off the hook, all right. Let me get my coat.'

*

Ten minutes later, the two women were knocking on the door of Angela's cottage.

'Oh. Hello, girls,' she said when she answered.

'Er, hi.' Tess thrust out the second of her cake-decorating

efforts, the first having been reduced to a pile of crumbs during her stakeout with Liam. 'I brought you this.'

Angela looked at it in surprise. 'That's very kind.'

'I thought you might like it, since you missed the cake decorating.'

'Sorry about that – imminent deadline, unfortunately.' She paused, waiting to see if they'd leave, but Tess stood firm. 'So . . . would you like to come in for some tea?'

'Thank you.'

They followed her down the passage to the living room.

Raven nudged Tess. 'How're we going to do this then?' she muttered under her breath. 'Thanks for the tea, and by the way, did you do a murder?'

'We'll think of something,' Tess muttered back.

Angela's front room was a riot of colour, with boldly patterned Bohemian furnishings. There was no television, and no sofa either: just a handful of large cushions scattered on the floor. There was also, Tess noticed, an absence of any family photographs. The only pictures on the wall were a painting of Angela's beloved horse, Meg, and an old playbill for a production of *As You Like It*.

'Aha,' Tess murmured when she saw it.

Angela blinked. 'I'm sorry?'

'I was just admiring your playbill,' Tess said, nodding to it. 'I see you're a long-time Shakespeare fan.'

'Oh, yes. He and I go way back. A friend of mine left that to me recently in her will.' Angela nodded to the floor. 'Do pull up a cushion. I'll boil some water.'

Tess went to examine the playbill more closely while

Angela was out of the room, hoping to see the name Lily Gish, but there was no joy. The female lead had been a woman called Rose Blanchet, and the photo beside her was no one Tess could identify. Disappointed, she sat down beside Raven.

'Well?' Raven whispered.

'No Lily Gish.'

'See? I told you Angela wasn't involved.'

They fell silent again as Angela came back in with a tray of hot drinks. 'I'm afraid Earl Grey is all I've got,' she said in an apologetic tone. 'I don't entertain very often.'

'That's fine,' Tess said.

Angela sat down cross-legged opposite them. 'Now, is this a social call or did you come to offer your services for front of house for *Macbeth* next week? We could use additions to the ticket-punching rota.'

'Er, no. I mean, I'm happy to help, but that isn't why we came.'

'Oh. Well, what can I help you with?'

'Well . . .' Tess cast a glance at Raven.

'Um, we kind of had this theory,' Raven said.

'A theory? What about?'

Was it Tess's imagination or did Angela look faintly worried?

'It's about Ade's murder,' Raven said.

Angela raised her eyebrows. 'You two have been doing a bit of crime-busting, have you? Well, go ahead and tell me this theory.'

'It's Tess's theory really,' Raven said, sounding slightly

desperate now as she realised she was at the point of no return. 'She thought . . . that is, it seemed possible that you might, um . . .'

'Might what?'

'Are you Lily Gish?' she blurted out.

Angela blinked. 'Lilian Gish? The film star?'

'No.' Raven's cheeks had turned red. 'That was the name of Ade Adams's first wife. Tess thought . . . at least, she believed it was possible you might be her. I said you weren't, but . . . we wanted to ask you in person.'

'Lily Gish.' Angela's eyes had taken on a faraway expression. 'Lily. Yes, I remember that name.' She roused herself. 'Why on earth would you think I'd been married to Ade Adams?'

'Well, he did come to the village as a favour to you,' Tess said, feeling seven shades of awkward. Trust Raven to just drop it on the woman like that! 'And we know . . . That is, it's clear you're hiding your real accent and you're probably American, and you'd be the same age, and no one knows who she is or where she went to, so it just seemed . . .' Tess trailed off. 'Sorry. I hope you aren't offended.'

'No.' Angela's eyes were gazing into the distance, as if lost in the past. 'No. I'm not offended.'

'Well?'

'Well what?'

'Are you her?'

'I'm not Lily.' Angela gazed for a moment longer before her eyes unclouded. 'Excuse me. I just need to make a telephone call. There's someone I'd like to be here.'

'Um, OK.'

Angela went to the landline phone mounted on the wall and dialled a number.

'Hi,' she said when whoever was on the other end answered, and suddenly her accent sounded quite different, with a mellow Bostonian drawl. 'I figure it's time. Are you free?' She paused, then nodded and hung up.

'We'll just have a little wait,' she observed in her strange new accent. 'Can I bring you girls more tea?'

'Um, that's OK.' Raven was staring at her as if hypnotised; as if seeing her for the first time.

They waited in silence for whoever Angela had summoned to arrive. Tess couldn't think of what to say, and Angela had lapsed into thoughtful silence. There was nothing to do but sip the dregs of their now cold tea and wait for a knock at the door.

That came five minutes later. Angela stood up to answer it. She came back in, followed by a man.

Tess blinked. 'Lee?'

He shook his head. 'You just couldn't take my word for it, could you?'

'Sit down, Liam,' Angela said.

He claimed a cushion on Tess's other side. 'Are you sure you're ready to do this?' he asked, looking up at Angela.

She shrugged. 'I would have liked a little longer, but Fate's forced my hand, it seems.'

'I don't get it,' Raven said. 'Forced your hand to do what?'

'Well, let me answer your questions first. I'm sure Mr Hanley here will be interested in the answers, and since he's been generous enough to keep my secret, I wanted him to be here for them.' She took down the framed playbill and handed it to Tess. 'This lady is Lily Gish,' she said, pointing to the photograph of the female lead.

'But it says Rose Blanchet.'

'Yes, she was French originally. Rose was her name when we met at stage school, and she used it in early productions before she decided to reinvent herself. Still, she was always Rose to me.' Angela smiled at the playbill. 'This was the first time we ever worked together. A tiny little theatre, but we had some wonderful audiences.'

'I was convinced you must be the same person,' Tess murmured. 'Where is she now?'

Angela sighed. 'Gone. As I said, she left me that playbill in her will – a memory of happy times together. It's two months since she passed.'

'I'm sorry,' Raven said automatically. 'What did she die of? She can't have been very old.'

'Fifty-eight,' Angela said. 'Cancer of the spine. I think she wanted to go in the end. When he phoned to deliver the bad news, her son told me that she'd been flushing some of her meds. Poor Rosie, she deserved better.'

Raven glanced at Tess. 'So she couldn't have had anything to do with Ade's murder. She must have died not that long before he did.'

'She certainly couldn't,' Angela said. 'She was very frail those last few months. Couldn't move without the aid of a wheelchair. I'm sorry, detectives, but if that's where your thoughts were tending then I'm afraid it's a dead end.'

'You said she had a son,' Liam said. 'Would we be able to get in touch with him?'

'For what reason?'

'Nothing that'll intrude on his grief. I'd just like to know if there was anything in what she left behind that might relate to Ade – documents, photos, that sort of thing. I'm running depressingly short of leads again.'

'But I was sure . . . I mean, if Ade didn't have any connection to you, why would he come to the village?' Tess asked Angela.

'There was a connection. Like I told you, he was a friend of my late husband's. Not someone I knew well, but enough to give me an introduction.' She smiled grimly. 'What I did know about him, though, was something that meant I could be pretty sure he wouldn't turn down any request for a favour from me.'

'You knew,' Tess murmured. 'You knew he was a member of that dodgy club.'

Angela nodded. 'It was actually Rose's suggestion I ask him. I was surprised – she mentioned him so rarely, I'd half forgotten they were ever married. They had a pretty acrimonious divorce. It was the effect of the cocktail of drugs she was on at the end that she was able to speak of him so lightly, I suppose. She suggested to me that Ade's celebrity in Cherrywood – or rather, his notoriety – would sell more tickets than the two-bit panto star I'd been planning to ask.'

'You said you'd use your press contacts to get Cherrywood a celebrity,' Liam said. 'But it was your personal contacts you made use of in the end. Because you don't have any press contacts, do you, Angela?'

'Not many,' she admitted. 'I'm not a journalist by background, of course. The editor of the paper I worked for briefly in Glasgow was a former lover and when I explained what I wanted to do he gave me a job; helped me build a new identity and cover story. I owe him a lot. Anyway, it turned out I'd rather a talent for the work.'

'I don't get it, though.' Raven took the playbill to look at the photo of the late Lily Gish/Rose Blanchet. 'If you're not Lily then who are you, Angela? Why did you need a new identity?'

Angela smiled rather sadly. 'Your grandmother would be able to tell you that. She's been very good to me since I came to Cherrywood. Or your friend Mr Hanley here.'

Liam shook his head. 'You know it has to be you.'

Raven stared. 'Grandmother? Grandmother knows about this?'

'I thought she must do,' Tess said. 'I spotted you two in the summerhouse at Cherrywood Hall. Plus she said something the night of the *Macbeth* rehearsal that made me think she'd seen you act before.'

Angela laughed. 'Yes, significantly better than I did that night, although it was many years ago that her son brought her to see me perform. She was the only person in the village who would be able to recognise me by sight, even if I don't look much now like the girl I was at twenty-five. I thought she might bawl me out when I showed up at her door, but Candice is a kind woman in her stern way.

She did feel for me, once I'd laid my heart and soul at her feet.'

Tess felt a sudden sense of foreboding. 'You say your name's on that playbill?' she said.

'One of my names.' She nodded to the playbill in Raven's hands. 'You'll find it right at the bottom, Raven. I only had a chorus part.'

Raven's eyes skimmed to the bottom line. 'Eveline Russell,' she read.

'Yes. My stage name. But when I married your father, I was still known as Eva Russo.'

Raven stared at her. All the colour drained from her face.

'I'm sorry,' Angela said quietly. 'I'm so sorry, Raven.'

'You . . . you're my . . .'

'I'm afraid so.'

Angela started to approach her, but Raven jumped to her feet and took a step back. 'But . . . you left me,' she whispered. 'You . . . you *sold* me.'

'That isn't true. Your grandmother can back me up. I never got any money.' Angela gave her a pleading look. 'I was twenty-five, Raven. I'd just lost my husband in that horrible accident. I was suffering with depression. I left you because I knew I couldn't care for you – never because I didn't want you.'

Raven's eyes were wet, but her expression was hard. 'That was thirty years ago,' she said in a low voice. 'Do you want me to believe that you were depressed all that time? You certainly sounded like you were having a lot of fun in all those stories you told me.'

'There were other stories. Stories I didn't tell you.' Angela sighed. 'I wanted to come to you. I was afraid I'd left it too late. I suppose it was Rose getting ill and my heart problems that made me think, you never know how much time you're going to have. That was when I concocted this ridiculous plan to create a new identity and move here, where I could get to know you. Candice helped me.'

'Why would she do that?'

'Because she'd always felt rather sorry for me, I suspect. Marrying into a family like the Walton-Lords was never an easy thing – she knew that first-hand – and to be married to someone like your father, who was himself an overgrown child . . .' Angela met her eyes. 'He wasn't a bad man, Raven. I know you worry about that. He could be selfish, yes – he'd been raised to be, like so many over-indulged children. But that foolish club he was in with Ade was no more to him than a boys' hideout, I promise you.'

'I don't believe this,' Raven whispered. 'I can't . . . I just can't deal with this. Tess, where are you?'

Tess, who had been waiting quietly until her help was asked for, stood to put an arm around her friend. 'Here, Rave. Shall I take you home?'

'Yes. Please.'

Tess started guiding her from the room.

Angela put a hand on Raven's arm as they passed. 'I did love you, Raven,' she said quietly. 'I know you don't believe that, but it's true. If your dad had lived . . . everything would have been different.'

'Don't.' Raven shook the hand from her arm. 'Just . . . don't touch me.'

She held her head erect as Tess supported her out of the door, not looking back.

Chapter 33

'How's the patient?' Oliver asked Tess when he arrived at the flat the following afternoon.

Tess had filled him in over the phone the evening before, and they'd agreed to take it in turns to babysit Raven while she came to terms with the life-changing news of her mother's presence in the village.

'Still struggling with it all,' Tess said with a sigh. 'I don't know if it's more the fact Angela tricked her into building a relationship or the abandonment issues from when she was a kid. I always suspected she'd taken it a lot harder than she ever told us.'

Oliver shook his head. 'So Angela Campbell is actually Eva Russo. I can hardly believe it.'

'I know.' Tess gave him a look. 'There seem to be long-lost family members popping out of the woodwork all over the place.'

'Don't make that face. I had to help Mikey. Believe me, it wasn't easy for me.' Oliver put a hand on her shoulder. 'You know, he really does mean it. Now he's got Helen and a baby on the way, he's got more motivation than ever to want to go straight. I bet he'd appreciate some family support while he tries to find his new place in the world.'

'Why should I give him support? He's done nothing to deserve it.'

'We don't always show kindness to others because they deserve it. We do it because they need it.'

'Save it for a sermon, Oliver. I don't want to hear it, OK? As far as I'm concerned, I have no brother. I mean, apart from the other two.'

'You'll have a niece or nephew in six months, though. I'm assuming you're not visiting the sins of the father on them, are you?'

Tess's brow unknitted a fractional amount. 'All right, I know it's not the baby's fault. I'll . . . send Helen a christening mug or something.'

'I think some more hands-on support might be appreciated. Will you think about it? For me?'

'No. You're in the dog house. But . . . for the baby I'll think about it, if it'll stop you sermonising at me.'

Oliver smiled. 'I knew you'd do the right thing.'

'That's you. You're a bad influence. Or a good one, which is infinitely more annoying.'

'Eva Russo,' Oliver said again in a vague voice. 'I assumed she must be Italian.'

'So did Raven. A lot of Americans have got Italian ancestry, though, haven't they? I feel stupid for not thinking of that earlier.' She nodded to Raven's bedroom. 'Our patient's tucked up in bed with Roger, trying to read.'

'Has she been crying?'

'No. I don't think she can. It's been too big a shock for her.' Tess cast a worried look at Raven's bedroom door. 'I don't like leaving her. Are you sure you're fine with me going out?'

'Don't worry, Tess. I think after all these years, I know how to get Raven through an emotional crisis.'

'She's never had an emotional crisis like this one. I'm worried about her.'

'We'll see it through. We always do.' Oliver pecked her cheek. 'Off you go. I'll take care of Rave.'

'We won't be long. Liam's arranged to visit the son of this Rose Blanchet. He's very happy for us to have a look through her things, apparently. We'll be two hours, tops.'

'Reckon you'll learn anything new?'

'Probably not,' Tess said with a sigh. 'It'd be helpful if we did, though. We seem to have hit a brick wall again, now Angela's no longer prime suspect and Rose-slash-Lily has shuffled off this mortal coil. I'd like to believe Mikey wasn't involved, for old time's sake.'

'Well, good luck. We'll see you in a little while.'

When Tess had gone, Oliver knocked on the door of Raven's room. A choked 'Come in' summoned him.

Roger wagged his tail when he entered, and Raven gave a damp laugh. 'Let me guess,' she said. 'Tess has got me on suicide watch and called you over to babysit.'

'Nothing so severe, but she did think you might like some company while she was out.'

'I really don't need minding, Oliver. What I need is to be left in peace to work things out.'

'All right. I'll sit in the living room and watch some TV until Tess comes home.'

She sighed and flipped over the corner of the duvet. 'No you won't. Come on, get in.'

'You sure that's a good idea? You remember what happened last time.'

'I thought we weren't mentioning that.' She nodded to the sleeping dog by her legs. 'It's all right. We've got Roger to chaperone.'

Oliver smiled and climbed in next to her. He put an arm around her shoulders. 'Want to talk about it?' he said softly.

She rested a head on his shoulder. 'I don't know.'

'Well, give it a try and we'll see what happens, eh?'

'I thought I'd made my peace with it all,' she mumbled as Roger snuggled against Oliver's leg, making himself at home between these two nice, warm humans. 'When I was a kid I was pissed off, you know? Angry at my dad for getting killed in that stupid, pointless way, and even more so at my mum for selling me off. But when I grew up, I just became . . . resigned to it, I suppose. That was how my life began and there was nothing to do but accept it.'

'But you didn't, did you?' Oliver asked quietly, stroking her hair.

'Not really.' She gulped back a sob. 'I think the worst thing is that I *liked* her. I really liked her. I thought she was the sort of person I wanted to be – clever, confident, fun, successful. Turns out she's just my screwed-up mum, who's made no better use of her life than I have of mine.'

'Do you know that? Or are you projecting insecurities about yourself on to her?'

She gave a damp laugh. 'What, are you a shrink now?'

'Just a keen observer of human nature. Well?'

'Maybe I am. I can't help it. I always worried I'd never make it as a mum, or be able to hold down a healthy relationship. Knowing Angela's failed at both those things too just makes it . . . so much harder.'

'She came here because she wanted to have a relationship with you, Raven. The way she did it was misguided, but there was a genuine wish to have you in her life. Perhaps if you opened yourself up to that, it could bring both of you a little peace of mind.'

Raven burst suddenly into tears.

'They had to come,' Oliver said. 'Go ahead, let it out.'

'I just feel . . . so helpless,' Raven gasped.

'I know. I would too. I mean I did – that's just how I felt when Archie died. And what I learnt from that was to lean on your friends and the people you trust. Don't be afraid to let yourself need them for a little while. It's the only way to get through it.'

Raven sobbed into his shoulder for a while. Oliver handed her a clean handkerchief, which made her laugh for some reason.

'What?' he said.

'Nothing. You're just the only person I know under sixty who still carries a hanky.' She blew her nose on it, then laughed again at the initials *OM* in the corner. 'Monogrammed too. You're such a grown-up, Ol.'

'Gee, thanks.'

She looked up at him with red-rimmed eyes. 'Thanks for looking after me,' she whispered.

Her face moved closer, and gently Oliver guided her lips away.

'Sorry, Rave,' he said quietly. 'It doesn't work that way. You can't just use me when you need me.'

'I . . .wasn't.' She blinked on fresh tears. 'I wouldn't.'

'It's OK. You're upset and not thinking clearly. Just . . . let's keep things simple, eh? If we don't, we're going to make a mess of everything.'

She leaned against his shoulder. 'It did feel simple at the time. Don't you think it did?'

'That doesn't make it a good idea to repeat it.'

'It's never been like that before,' she said wistfully.

Oliver blinked. 'Really?'

Raven laughed. 'You sound very pleased with yourself about it.'

'Well. I don't get many compliments on my performance in the bedroom. I mean, I haven't had much opportunity to gather feedback.'

'You get the full five stars on TripAdvisor from me, darling.'

He winced. 'Please don't call me that.'

'Why? You never minded before.'

'You probably need some time to yourself,' Oliver said, pushing aside his share of the duvet. 'Get a little sleep. I'll be in the other room if you need me.'

She frowned. 'Oliver? What's wrong?'

He turned his face away. 'This is hard for me, Rave. I mean, I like you. And when you're near me . . . I forget that I shouldn't like you as much as I've started to realise I do.'

Raven stared at him. 'Look at me,' she said softly, guiding his face to hers.

'I know it couldn't ever be . . . a thing,' he said, pressing his eyes closed. 'Me and you. It was stupid of me to let my guard down when I've managed so well all these years. I'm sorry. I shouldn't have told you. You've got bigger things than me and my daft feelings to worry about.'

'I never . . . Oliver, I never knew . . .'

'It's OK. Just forget I told you.'

'It wouldn't be easy,' she said, as if to herself. 'Your job. Your faith.'

'And your grandmother.'

'She's getting too panicked to be picky, but I think she'd still prefer someone with a name like Giles Twistleton to be my ultimate match.' Raven laughed. 'Can't you picture it, though? Me, hosting the vicarage garden party.'

'And me, riding to hounds or whatever your people do.'

'Tea with the bishop. The Sunday School picnic. No doubt I'd disgrace myself after too much elderflower wine and end up dancing on a gingham blanket waving my knickers in the air.'

'And I wouldn't have you any other way.' He kissed her hair. 'Never change, Raven.'

Raven fell into a thoughtful silence for a moment. 'It wouldn't be easy, would it?'

'No.'

'Nigh on impossible.'

'I think you're right,' Oliver said, feeling his heart plummet.

'But if it's all the same to you . . .' She looked up at him with an expression in her eyes he hadn't seen there before. 'If it's all the same to you, I'd rather like to give it a go.'

Oliver stared at her. 'Say that again.'

'I mean, if you would,' she said, suddenly shy.

'You'd really want to do that? Be with someone like me?'

'Oliver, all my life I've dreamt of being with someone like you. Someone kind and caring and considerate, who loves me despite the car wreck I am. I'm starting to realise just how dim I've been that I couldn't see my perfect guy wasn't just someone like you. He actually *was* you.'

'But . . . the men you've been out with were all . . .'

'Arseholes?' she said with a wry smile.

'Big, I was going to say. In a muscly, gym-bothering sort of way.'

'Yeah, big arseholes. I feel like ever since I was a kid I've been searching for this mythical unicorn: a good man. And all the time there was my best friend, hiding in plain sight.'

'I'm not dreaming, am I?'

Raven reached up to plant a soft kiss on his lips. 'What do you think?'

'Oh . . . God.' Oliver pressed his eyes closed, his conscience wrestling with his other senses, prodding him to do the right thing. 'No. You're upset. You've had a shock. You're not making rational decisions.'

'Oliver, this is the most rational decision I've made in my

life. It's so fiendishly sensible, I'm starting to wonder if it's really me making it at all and not Tess.' She put one finger under his chin. 'Open your eyes.'

Oliver opened his eyes.

'Now kiss me, then tell me yes or no. If it's no, I understand. But kiss me first, so I can remember the one time I came this close to being happy.'

'Can I say yes and then kiss you?'

She smiled. 'Even better.'

'Then, yes.' He claimed her lips for a kiss. Roger thumped the bed with his tail, as if to give his blessing.

'It really won't be easy,' Oliver whispered when they broke apart. 'We'll have to keep it quiet for a while. It's going to be a big shock for people. I don't know how my parishioners are going to react to me seeing someone from outside the faith, and as for your grandmother . . .' He shuddered. 'The upper classes don't still go in for that flogging business, do they?'

'Only for their own entertainment.' Raven kissed him again. 'All right, if that's what you want. We can keep it quiet, at least until we've worked out how to break it to everyone.'

The unspoken words in that sentence, Oliver felt, were *and until we've seen if it can actually work*. But he was bouncing on a fluffy pink cloud at the moment, and he pushed gloomy thoughts away.

Raven claimed his lips for another kiss.

'Will we tell Tess?' he asked when they broke apart.

'We'll certainly tell her first,' Raven said. 'But . . . maybe not quite yet.'

'Um. Rave?'

'Hmm?'

'About . . . the other thing.'

'Sex, you mean.'

'Er, yeah.' Oliver rubbed his neck. 'You know, we really shouldn't. I mean, we did, but . . . we shouldn't.'

'You mean you shouldn't.'

'Well, yes, but I thought you might struggle on your own.'

'You think so, do you?' She smiled at the expression on his face. 'All right. If that's what it takes.'

'You'd be happy with that?'

'I wouldn't exactly be happy, because I really fancy you. But if it's important to you, that's OK with me.'

Oliver smiled at her. 'You'd really do that for me?'

'Of course. Your faith's important to you, and if this is part of it then I'll respect that, just like I'm sure you'd always respect the things that are important to me.' She reached up to kiss his ear lobe. 'Besides, you'd be surprised how much fun you can have in bed not having sex.'

Oliver felt his cheeks turning a fetching shade of pink. 'Er, yes. I think I probably would.'

'That's allowed, isn't it?'

'I believe it's entirely at the individual churchgoer's discretion.' He pulled her to him. 'So come here.'

It was a long time until they came up for air.

'I suppose Tess will be back soon,' Raven murmured.

'Yes. I should probably leave, otherwise I'm going to give the game away with my big guilty face.'

'I don't want you to, though.'

'We'll see each other soon.'

She smiled. 'A clandestine affair. I've always wanted to have one of those. It ought to be rather fun, don't you think?'

'I don't know. I've never got the hang of clandestine.' He pushed off the duvet. 'Think about what I said, Rave. About your mum.'

She scowled. 'Why did you have to bring her up? We were having such a nice time.'

'I just think you ought to talk to her. Not now, but when you've had time to come to terms with everything. I think it could help you – both of you.'

Raven shook her head. 'Half an hour into a new relationship and already exploiting boyfriendly privilege.'

Oliver smiled. 'I like hearing you call me that.'

'Strange, isn't it? I thought it'd be weird but it isn't at all. Fits the lips perfectly, it seems to me.'

'Just like this.' He leant down to give her a goodbye kiss. 'I'll see you soon, Rave. Think about it.'

Chapter 34

'How's Raven doing?' Liam asked when Tess met him for the trip to Rose Blanchet's home.

'Not great,' Tess admitted as they both got into his car. 'I guess she'll come to terms with it – she tends to be pretty resilient. Whether she'll want a relationship with her mum is another matter.' She shook her head. 'What possessed Angela to do it like that? If she'd been up front from the off, I don't think Raven would find it nearly so hard to accept. Now there's a double sense of betrayal – the abandonment as a baby and the deception now as an adult.'

Liam started the engine. 'I suppose she was worried Raven would reject her outright. This way, she was able to build a bond with her before she revealed her true identity.'

'That's only made it worse, though. Raven really admired her. Now she feels completely betrayed.'

He shrugged. 'I didn't say it was a good idea.'

'Well, I hope to God she wasn't involved in Ade's murder, for Raven's sake. Rave's already got a relative she never knew she had doing time for quadruple murder. Finding out she's got killers on both sides of the family is not going to help her get over her insecurities about her genes.'

'Does she have insecurities?'

'She reckons she's genetically predisposed to screw up. It's not all fun and games, being from a family like the Walton-Lords.' Tess glanced at him in the rearview mirror. 'When did you know?'

'Not so long ago,' he said as he indicated to take the road into Paignley, where Rose Blanchet's son David lived. 'I thought the same as you as first. That all the signs pointed to Angela being Lily Gish. It was only when an old contact turned up a photo of her as a young woman on stage that I realised who she really was. That stage name, Eveline Russell – it didn't take me long to remember why that sounded familiar.'

'You could've told me.'

'Why would I? I confronted Angela and she admitted it, then asked me not to tell anyone. I advised her to come clean to Raven, but at the end of the day it wasn't my business. Since it didn't have anything to do with the case, I thought it was up to Angela how and when she revealed it.' He glanced at her. 'Besides, I wasn't talking to you.'

She smiled. 'You do know how to throw an impressive sulk, I'll give you that.'

'Well, I'm glad to have you back on the case, despite the stunt you pulled with Angela yesterday. Can you at least try to remember to run these things by me before you go in all guns blazing?'

'Sorry. I just couldn't understand how you could rule her out so quickly and thoroughly. You know I hate unanswered questions.' Tess stared thoughtfully at the car ahead, which had a Christmas tree strapped to its roof. 'She couldn't be involved, could she? She does have that connection to Ade through her late husband. There might be a motive we don't know about in their shared pasts.'

'On a purely personal level I don't believe she's involved, but like you said, we can't completely rule it out.' He shook his head. 'We're getting dangerously short on leads, Tess.'

'I know.'

'The problem is, no one who might have been involved has got a full set when it comes to the holy trinity of means, motive and opportunity. Leonie and your brother have got a motive and Leonie, at least, had the opportunity to drug her husband if, as you think, the drug was administered with a time delay somehow—'

'Oh! I had an idea about that,' Tess said. 'I wondered if the Valium might have been in Ade's vape. Then it wouldn't kick in until he sparked the thing up on top of the bonfire, which given his nicotine addiction seems pretty likely. What do you think?'

'Yeah,' Liam said slowly. 'That's good thinking. I think that could well be it.'

'Not going to pick it apart?'

'No, it fits perfectly – I mean, other than the fact we still don't know why the killer didn't administer the poison outright or when and how Ade was murdered.' He smiled at her. 'I told you if you let that idea of yours percolate something would develop, didn't I? Well done.'

Tess flushed under the praise. 'Thanks.'

'Anyway, let's say you're right. Leonie might have had the

opportunity to lace his vape juice. So might Peggy. But as for the murder itself, that's trickier, isn't it? Peggy has the means to get into the park, but she's got an alibi for the time of the murder. Leonie could have accessed the park, but even in one of her famous wigs, could she bank on not being recognised coming through the village on the day of a sold-out event when it would be busiest? In any case, why stagger it when they could have lethally poisoned the vape to begin with?'

'What about Angela?'

'Means and opportunity are both present – she had a key to the park, and she's the only person seen entering alone the day Ade died. There might be a motive we're unaware of from somewhere in their shared past. But I don't see how she could have been the one to drug him if it was done the way you think.'

'Two people working together? One drugs him, then when he's in place and unconscious, the other one finishes him off while their partner in crime makes sure they have a rock-solid alibi?'

'My thoughts had tended that way too. I still don't think the plan was to ultimately cover it up, but doing it that way would buy them time.' He glanced at her. 'I know you won't want to hear this, Tess, but I'm afraid the only pair with a solid set of motive, means and opportunity between them is Leonie and your brother.'

Tess shook her head. 'It can't be them.'

'Why not? Leonie's a clever woman who justifiably hated her husband, and your brother's clearly devoted to her. You might not believe he's a killer, but he's got violence in his past and a long career on the wrong side of the law. Under the influence of the woman he loves, with a baby on the horizon and Leonie's increasing desperation to break free of Ade, who knows what he might be capable of?'

Tess was silent. She didn't want to say it, because if she did that might make it real, but she knew Liam was right.

'Well, let's see what we turn up at this place,' she said as Liam stopped the car outside a large bungalow in a pleasant-looking cul-de-sac. 'Perhaps whatever remains of Lily Gish can furnish us with another lead.'

The man who opened the door was quite young: perhaps around Liam's age, a little older than Tess herself. He had a tired, washed-out look, although he summoned a weak smile.

'Good afternoon,' Liam said, shaking the man's hand. 'Is it David?'

'That's right.'

'Thank you for agreeing to see us. I know this is a difficult time for you.'

Tess nodded. 'We were very sorry to hear about your loss.'

'If it's going to help to solve a murder I suppose it's my duty, although I'm afraid you're going to find Mother's papers and things to be of little help. Come in, please.'

David ushered them inside.

'Her room is rather a mess, I'm afraid,' he said. 'I was her only child, and her carer at the end. It's difficult when you don't have an extended family to help you deal with everything that needs to happen after a death.'

Tess nodded in sympathy. 'I know.'

David opened the door to a bedroom and they followed him in.

'It's going to be a bleak Christmas, just me.' He cast an absent glance around the room, with its piles of papers and other paraphernalia. 'Mother said that when she was gone she wanted me to start living my own life. It's rather hard to remember exactly how, I'm finding.'

'I'm so sorry.' Tess said gently. 'It sounds as though you were close.'

'We were all each other had, except for Mother's little online circle.' He nodded to a laptop on a desk. 'I suppose she was what you'd call a silver surfer, except she wasn't really old enough. She was so frail at the end, it was easy to forget she was still relatively young. Only fifty-eight when she went.'

'She had a lot of friends online?'

'From all over the world. I was glad of it. It meant she still had some quality of life, even after she became completely housebound.' He looked at Tess. 'I don't suppose you'd like to see a photograph?'

'We'd love to.'

He beamed at her and took out his phone.

'This was at the end,' he said, pulling up a photo of a frail-looking lady in a wheelchair who smiled for the camera. 'See that grin? She was in so much pain but she never lost her sense of humour.' He nodded to a photo on the wall showing a curvy young woman in a professional pose, smiling seductively. 'And that was while she was still on the stage.'

'She's very beautiful,' Tess said. 'Talented too, I hear. Her friend Eva showed us one of her old playbills.'

'Yes, she had quite a career. I've found piles of old programmes and posters and things.' David looked bewildered for a moment. 'I don't know what on earth I'm going to do with them all. Some sort of museum, perhaps . . .'

Liam had wandered over to a table where there were assorted medical items, including an oxygen mask and various bottles of pills.

'This is her medication?'

David nodded. 'I can't think what to do with them. I don't suppose it's safe to throw them out. I'll have to speak to the doctor.'

Liam picked up a bottle to show the label to Tess. It was digoxin.

'That one was for her heart,' David said. 'Nothing was working properly at the end. She used to joke that if I shook her, she'd rattle.'

'Did she ever have visitors?' Tess asked.

'Not often. There were one or two friends from acting days, like Eva. Like I said, she'd formed some strong friendships online, and a few of those within travelling distance came to visit her to say goodbye. The only regular visitor was our friend Seana.'

Tess frowned. 'Seana? Not Seana Hamilton?'

David brightened. 'That's right. Do you know her?'

'A little. Her sister's an old schoolfriend. How did she know your mum?'

'They met when Mother used to help at the food bank in

our community centre. Honestly, she's a wonderful person, Seana. She always brought Mother something when she came to visit – some little treat she knew she'd like. I thought she might stop coming when Mother died, but she still stops by regularly and takes me out to eat. She says it's the only thing she sets her alarm for.'

'That's kind of her,' Liam said. 'How often did she visit your mother?'

'Once a week. More often when it got closer to the end. Sometimes she'd bring her brother or sister, which Mother liked because she could complain to Kennedy about her doctors. I can't tell you how grateful I am to them all, especially Seana. It can be a very isolating experience, watching someone you love die when you haven't got any family to share it with.'

Tess nodded soberly. 'I can imagine.'

'It's very public-spirited of you to agree to help us,' Liam said. 'A lot of people think some sort of medal is in order for Ade's killer in lieu of a prison sentence, given what we now know.'

'Oh, he was a horrible man,' David said, his brow furrowing. 'Deeply, deeply unpleasant – wicked, really. Still, people can't go around taking the law into their own hands. It's only one step from vigilante justice to mob rule, and then where's society?'

'You sound as though you knew him,' Liam observed. 'Ade, I mean.'

'I never met him, but Mother used to talk about him sometimes. Did you know it was her who got him his big break? When they met he was only on hospital radio.'

'Is that right?'

'Yes. She started making a name for herself on the stage and she built up some contacts. She helped Ade get a slot on local radio and it grew from there.' David sounded angry now. 'And what thanks did she get? It turned out the whole time he'd been seeing some other woman behind her back.'

Liam nudged Tess. 'Peggy,' he mouthed.

'He was a very cruel man – psychologically cruel,' David went on. 'Not that Mother talked about it much. She didn't like to mention his name, except sometimes when she was on a lot of pain relief medication she'd start talking about him. But I heard enough to make my mind up.'

'It seems to have been a pattern,' Tess said. 'We've spoken to a number of Ade's ex-wives, as well as his widow. There's a history of cruelty and infidelity, and in nearly every case he left his wife for someone else.'

'Well, Mother was well rid of him. She met my father a year later, and they had a happy marriage for as long as we had him.' He gestured to the papers lying around. 'But murder's murder, no matter how bad the victim may have been. If there's anything here that can help with your investigation, you're welcome to it.'

'Thank you,' Liam said.

'Would you like some tea while you hunt around?'

'That would be lovely. Just a black coffee for me.'

'White tea, please,' Tess said.

David nodded and left the room.

Chapter 35

'Well,' Liam said in an undertone. 'Food for thought there. Your friend Seana seems to pop up in some unlikely places.'

Tess shrugged. 'She and Rose were neighbours. It's not too much of a stretch that they would have been friends. Seana hasn't got any of your big three, has she? No motive, no means, no opportunity. It's probably a coincidence.'

'Probably. Odd, though.'

'Well, what about the digoxin? You remember what Angela said, that Rose had stopped taking some of her meds. Long enough to squirrel away a lethal dose of heart medicine, maybe.'

'Yes, that's something to consider.' Liam glanced around the room. 'Come on. Let's have a good hunt before Norman Bates gets back.'

'Don't be cruel. The lad misses his mum. I think he's sweet.' Tess approached the desk and started sifting through some documents. 'Seems to me the most likely reason for Seana's visits here is a crush on David. He's evidently smitten with her.'

'Could be.' Liam looked round from the papers he was

flicking through. 'Nothing but old theatre programmes here. You found anything?'

Tess picked up a photo. 'Here's a wedding shot. It's not Ade, though. Must be the second husband.'

Liam went to a cardboard box by the bed and drew out a large, leather-bound volume. 'What's this?'

'Looks like a photo album.'

He glanced at a sticker on the front. '1997 to 2001,' he read.

Tess put the wedding photo back. 'Any more?'

'Yeah, about a dozen. All labelled.' He glanced at her. 'What year were Ade and Lily married again?'

'Um . . . 1983, I think?'

'And he married Peggy in 1986.' Liam rifled through the albums, finally withdrawing an aged-looking volume. 'Here we are. 1982 to 1986. Let's see what we can find.'

He brought it over to the desk so Tess could take a look at it with him.

The door opened and David entered with a tray of drinks.

'Here you go.' He handed Tess her mug and put Liam's down on the desk. 'Anything useful?'

'Not yet,' Liam said. 'We were just going to have a look through this album. I hope that's OK. I noticed the label covered the years your mum was married to Ade.'

David nodded. 'You're very welcome to look at anything that might help.'

Tess hoped he might leave again so they could speak freely. However, he hung around with his mug of coffee, providing a running commentary on the photos as they flicked through.

'There's Mother in a play with Eva,' he said, pointing to one photograph. 'They were at stage school together, you know. And here she is playing Lavinia in *Mourning Becomes Electra*. She got a standing ovation on closing night.'

'No photos of Ade at all,' Liam observed as he turned the pages.

'I suppose Mother destroyed them. As I said, she hated to be reminded of her first marriage.'

Liam reached the end of the book.

'Any use?' David asked.

'I don't think so,' Liam said, not quite managing to conceal his disappointment. 'That covers the time they were married, so I can't imagine any of the other albums are going to be of help.'

'Shall we go?' Tess said. 'It seems like Rose has pretty much expunged all memory of her marriage to Ade. We don't want to intrude on David's time if it's a dead end.'

'Yes, I suppose we should.'

'I'm sorry it wasn't more use,' David said.

Liam glanced around the room. 'We'll take one last look if that's OK, just to make sure we haven't missed anything.'

'Of course. I'll go get dinner on, if you don't mind – Seana's going to be joining me later. Just give me a shout when you're done.'

He left the room.

'I don't think we're going to find anything, are we?' Tess said. 'The album was our best hope.'

'I just want to be a hundred per cent sure there's nothing else.'

Liam wandered around the room, glancing into boxes and sifting through piles of playbills and other paraphernalia from a long career. Finally, he bent to look under the bed.

'Hello.' He pulled out another cardboard box. 'What's this?'

Tess went to have a look. 'Looks like more photo albums.'

Liam drew one out and looked at the label. 'Not albums. Scrapbooks. This one's labelled "David's Baby Book".'

Tess smiled. 'Aww.'

Liam flicked through it. 'Lock of hair, milestone dates, first drawings and so on. Wonder what's in the others?'

He pulled them out one by one. Apparently Rose Blanchet had been a keen scrapbooker, keeping volumes for productions she'd been in, her second wedding day and other key life events.

'Now then,' he said as he drew out a book. 'What do you think the label is on this one?'

'What?'

'It just says "Ade".'

Tess moved closer so she could see the book. 'Go on, open it.'

The scrapbook was filled with items relating to Ade: photos from events he'd attended, press cuttings about his career and fundraising, a marriage notice from when he'd tied the knot with Katrin, and later with Leonie.

'This is odd,' Liam murmured.

'Yeah. If Rose was so traumatised by her marriage with Ade that she destroyed all photographs of their life together, why go to the effort of saving these?'

'Not only that. The dates.' He passed the book to her.

'These are from long after Rose and Ade were divorced. If she hated him, why was she saving cuttings? She wanted to forget all about him, didn't she?'

'That's what David seemed to think.' Tess flicked through the pages of the scrapbook. She stopped to curl her lip at a press cutting about some sort of hospital fundraiser, with a photo of Ade surrounded by a crowd of beaming staff and patients. Some of them were very young. 'Look at them, gazing at him in adoration. It's sickening he was never found out when he was alive.'

'So it seems Rose Blanchet was borderline stalking the man,' Liam said. 'Why?'

'Hard to say, now she's not here to ask.'

'Hmm. That sort of obsessive behaviour doesn't suggest any positive mental state.'

'Maybe not, but she's dead, isn't she? There's no way Rose could have been—' Tess stopped.

'What?'

'This photo, in the hospital,' she said in a low voice.

'What about it? Ade did a lot of fundraising for Leeds Royal. He started his career there on hospital radio.'

'Yes, but . . . this is from 1991.'

'Well?'

Tess looked up at him, fire in her eyes. 'Lee! This is it!'

'Tess, I'm really not following you.'

'You remember Oliver's mum hinted that Ade had abused a girl in the village before and it had been hushed up? She told Oliver it was before his time, and we couldn't work that out because Ade only moved to Cherrywood around 2007.'

'I remember. And?'

'And, Oliver spoke to Nick Hamilton about it and he was dead cagey. Ol thought it must be someone from his generation who didn't want it to get out.'

'Where are you going with this, Tess?'

She pointed to a teenage girl in the crowd of staff and patients in the photo, smiling shyly as she tried unsuccessfully to hide herself behind the woman in front. 'Who's that, Liam?'

Liam squinted at the grainy photo, then looked up at her with wide eyes as the truth dawned. 'Oh my God!'

'Exactly,' Tess said. 'Seana Hamilton.'

Chapter 36

Tess looked Liam up and down when he opened the door of his office three days later.

'You're a bit overdressed, aren't you? It's rural am-dram, not the Royal Opera House.'

He shrugged, straightening his bow tie. 'Theatre's theatre. I don't want to look like a slob.'

'Or, you know black tie looks good on you and you're trying to find any old excuse to wear it.'

'Blame society and its unfair dress codes. No man should need an excuse to look good.' He scanned her red cocktail dress. 'You look pretty good yourself. Very festive.'

'Thanks.' She lowered her voice. 'So, did you find out anything?'

'Yeah. You'd better come in.'

Tess followed him to his office, where a large photo of Seana Hamilton now occupied the central spot on his suspects board. What mainly caught her eye, however, was an oil canvas of Ben Nevis that had appeared on one wall.

'Wow,' she said, blinking at it. 'Any more of this frivolous decoration and the place is going to start looking almost homely.'

He smiled. 'Do you approve?'

'Very much.' Tess nodded to the bare bulb overhead. 'Tell you what, I'll get you a lampshade to go with it for Christmas.'

'You spoil me, you know.'

'Does that mean you're staying, then? Not going back to London?'

'Yep. I signed a new tenant for my office space down there. Sorry, you're not getting rid of me just yet.'

Liam sat down at his desk. Tess took the seat opposite.

'So tell me what you found out about Seana,' she said.

'It was her in the photo,' Liam told her. 'I was able to find out from the hospital that she did work experience with them for three weeks when she was in Year Nine. Ade was frequently there at that time as the celebrity face of a fundraising campaign for their children's ward. I'm assuming that's where he found the opportunity to groom her.'

'I noticed Seana had a number of medical books among her volumes of folklore the day we went to visit her,' Tess said. 'At the time I assumed they might have been Kennedy's.'

'Have you talked to Kennedy about it?'

'Sort of. I mean I couldn't just ask her outright about her sister's association with Ade Adams, obviously, but I was able to get out of her that Seana had aspirations of becoming a doctor when she was young, just as her little sister eventually would. Then she had to take a year off school due to health problems and her interest shifted to folklore.'

'What health problems?'

'Kenn didn't say, but I wondered if they were mental rather than physical. Abuse like that could have triggered a breakdown, right?'

'Definitely.'

'I always assumed Seana was likely autistic. She's got a lot of traits. But some of them – chronic anxiety, isolation, tendency to dissociate – could also go hand in hand with PTSD, couldn't they?'

'That was my thinking too.'

'So she did have a motive.'

'Plus the means – if, as her book collection suggests, she still took a lively interest in medicine on the side. And who do we know of who was a close friend of Seana Hamilton's, who had an equally strong reason to want Ade dead and who had access to a lethal dose of the drug that killed him?'

'You think Rose was involved?' Tess asked.

'It makes sense, doesn't it? She may well have decided, since she was dying anyway, that it was time to rid the world of her evil ex-husband's presence. Don't forget what Angela told us – that Rose was the one who suggested she invite Ade Adams here to open the Guy Trail.'

'Rose and Seana. Two people working together, like we said,' Tess murmured. 'Seana does have an alibi, though. She and Kennedy were both with the Guy Trail committee on the fifth, buttering sandwiches. Plenty of people saw her.'

'I don't know if that's what you'd call watertight. She was in the vicinity of the park, and Angela may well have left her key lying around, or forgotten to lock up one time. Would anyone have noticed if she took a longer than usual toilet break in order to sneak off to the park and finish off a drugged Ade on top of the bonfire?'

'I suppose it's possible,' Tess conceded. 'What about the Valium? Assuming it was administered via Ade's vape, when would Seana have had an opportunity to have interfered with it? It must have been done that morning. And how was she able to get her hands on a dose big enough?'

'I admit, I haven't got an answer for that yet. Still, I think we're definitely on the right track. Is Seana going to be at the *Macbeth* performance?'

'No. She didn't want to go without Kennedy, and Kenn decided one dress rehearsal was more than enough.' Tess sighed. 'She's going to be devastated if her sister was involved with this. Nick too, but Kennedy and Seana are particularly close. I almost wish we'd never looked in that damn scrapbook.'

'It's murder, Tess. People can't be allowed to just get away with it, no matter what the justification.'

'I know, I know. I only wish things were different, that's all.' She stood up. 'We'd better get to the village hall. Curtain's at half-seven.'

'Are we waiting for Raven and Oliver?'

'Oliver's helping with refreshments so he'll be there already. Rave couldn't face it, she said. She's avoiding Angela. Kennedy's going round to sit with her; I'm still not happy leaving her on her own while she's upset.'

'All right.' He stood up and offered her his arm. 'To the theatre, then, fair lady.'

Tess smiled as she took it. 'Just remember. It's not a date, OK?'

'Of course not. Partners, that's all. Of the strictly professional variety.'

'Like Holmes and Watson.'

'Exactly.'

'I'm Holmes, though, just to be clear.'

When they arrived at the hall, the auditorium was already full. While Cherrywood Players productions were notorious for being dire, there was also little else to do in the village at night so they usually sold out. Tess had heard rumours in the pub that Guy Cartwright was running a book on whether the latest offering would be better or worse than their last attempt at Shakespeare the previous year, as decided by a consensus of impartial judges on the front row.

'There's one thing I can't understand,' Tess whispered to Liam as they claimed their seats.

'Why people are such gluttons for punishment that they keep coming to these things?'

'No, I mean about the case. Supposing it was Seana and Rose, working together. How could either of them have known he'd put on that ridiculous witch's outfit and climb up the bonfire? I mean, if we're assuming he planned to play a prank, how did Seana know that would happen?'

He shrugged. 'Maybe she put him up to it. There could have been a window between him seeing Peggy and climbing the bonfire. What if it was Seana he was with?'

'That doesn't make sense, though. He had a pre-existing relationship with Peggy. She was his wife.'

'Yes, apparently he often expected one of his ex-wives to provide him with emotional support when he couldn't get it from the current one.'

'Right. The young girls he abused, on the other hand, seemed to be tossed aside and forgotten once he was done with them. Do we think he just happened to bump into Seana and she said, "Hey, remember me, you dirty old bastard? How about passing your vape over for me to have a fiddle with and then dressing as a witch and climbing up a bonfire?"'

'Er, yes?'

'And then she stole Angela's park key so she could nip down and murder him later on?'

'All right, all right, so we've still got questions to answer.' The lights had started to fade. 'We'll talk about it later. It's starting.'

'"That poor child",' Tess murmured. 'That's what Oliver's mum said to him.'

'Well? She might have heard rumours about it around the village, mightn't she?'

'She'll have got it directly from Moira Hamilton, I should think. They were close friends.'

'Then what of it?'

'There's just something about the wording. Why child? Why not girl?'

'What's the difference? Seana was a child.'

'I suppose so,' Tess said absently. 'It just feels like an odd choice of words.'

The curtains had started to open, and a woman in the row in front turned to give Tess a dirty look.

The three witches capered around the deserted ballroom, just as they had done at the dress rehearsal, chanting in couplets. There was no hamming this time, however. Angela – or Eva, as Tess knew she ought to get used to calling her – seemed to have decided that since her secret was out to the only person she'd ever really cared about hiding it from, she might as well give the performance her all. Tonight she was spot on: just the right blend of chilling, macabre and insane. It sent a shiver down Tess's spine. She could see what must have drawn audiences to any production starring Eveline Russell, back in the day.

'Wow,' Liam whispered. 'What a performance. I think I just lost a tenner on Guy Cartwright's book.'

Tess watched the capering witches, letting her mind wander. All sorts of thoughts were swirling around her head. Things she'd seen, things people had said. Her brain kept coming back to one of the tarot cards on Ade's body: the Sun card, representing the innocence and happiness of childhood. She thought about Peggy, and the child she'd been forced to give away. About Angela and Raven, estranged for so long. About Leonie, and the baby she and Mikey had invested all their future in. About the young girls Ade had robbed of their childhoods. About the day they'd been to visit Seana, and what she'd said about witchcraft and fertility. It all seemed to be linked, somehow. Mothers and children . . . the child on the white horse under a flaming sun . . . *that poor child* . . .

'Suppose it wasn't two people working together,' she murmured to herself.

Liam nudged her. 'Tess, shush.'

Tess stared at the prancing witches on the stage, mesmerised. Ade had referred to his ex-wives as a coven, that night . . .

Three witches in a coven. Three tarot cards on the body. The power of three . . .

If it was me, I'd feel like I had to know. Suddenly, Kennedy's words the day of the Guy Trail opening came rushing back into her brain. *It's hard not to be curious about someone who contributed half your DNA.*

Tess jumped to her feet.

'Liam, we have to go,' she whispered urgently.

He blinked. 'What? But it's just started.'

'We have to go, Lee!'

'Why?'

'Because I know who killed Ade Adams, and it wasn't Seana Hamilton. We have to get back to my flat, now.'

Chapter 37

Tess tore along the main street at breakneck speed, Liam hot on her heels.

'I mean, I didn't think it was that bad,' he panted as he tried to keep up with her.

'Don't joke, Lee. If I'm right about this – and I'm sure I am – Raven might be in danger.'

'Tess, what on earth is going on?'

'How do you get enough Valium to knock out an adult man, when it's so carefully controlled even doctors can't get hold of it? Through prescriptions for multiple people, that's how. How do you make sure your plan goes off without a hitch? By having several people all playing their parts. And why do you drug someone when you could kill them outright? Because when people work together to plan something like that, one of you – just one – has to be the actual killer.'

'OK, explain.'

'If you've already decided which one of you is going to slip the victim the fatal dose – as a right and a privilege, as the person with the greatest claim – you can't risk that going wrong. So, you drug the victim first – or in this case, you make sure the victim drugs himself – so that the designated killer can administer, first-hand, the poison that's going to end his life.'

Liam frowned. 'You don't mean . . .'

'Yeah,' Tess murmured. 'You know, she even tried to tell me. All this time, she's been sending us messages, drip-feeding hints. She told me, the day we trailed Angela, that in the mystery programme she'd just been watching, the murderer was the paramedic who first examined the body. And she seemed so far removed from the murder that I was blind to it, this whole time. It was only when I started thinking about Seana, and how all the connections fitted together . . .'

Liam shook his head. 'Kennedy Hamilton. Why, though? Revenge for what happened to her sister? And who was she working with?'

'I've got ideas about both those things. Just hurry up, can you? Raven's currently sitting at home entirely oblivious to the fact the babysitter I've assigned her is a killer. You can understand if that's top of my list of priorities.'

They ran the rest of the way to the flat and burst into the living room, Tess first with Liam behind.

Raven looked round to blink at them. 'Tess? What're you doing back? And what's with the dramatic entrance?'

'Rave, are you OK?' Tess said breathlessly.

'Yeah. We were just sharing a bottle of Echo Falls and watching *Love, Actually*. Why would you think I wasn't?'

Tess glanced at Kennedy, sitting beside Raven on the sofa with Roger across their legs and looking about as un-killer-like as anyone could. For a moment, she wavered. She'd been so certain she'd been right, but now, confronted by the sight of her old friend in the mundane setting of the flat, sipping cheap wine and watching a Christmas film, it all felt rather unreal.

'I think she means because of me,' Kennedy said quietly. She put down her wine, dislodged the snoring Roger and stood up to smile at Tess. 'I knew you'd work it out in the end. I'm glad it was you, Tess.'

Raven shook her head. 'Can someone please tell me what on earth's going on?'

'Ade Adams was your father,' Tess said in a low voice to Kennedy. 'Wasn't he?'

Kennedy nodded soberly.

'When did you find out?'

'Six months ago.'

'The day of the Guy Trail opening, you said you'd find it impossible not to be curious about someone who had contributed half your DNA.'

'Yes,' Kennedy said. 'It would have been better for me if I hadn't had that curiosity. The more I found out about my father, the more disgusted I felt, knowing he was part of me.'

Raven looked beyond bewildered now. 'Hang on. Ade was your father?'

'Just a moment.' Kennedy reached into her pocket, and smiled at the look on Liam's face as she drew out her phone. 'Oh, don't worry. I'm not going to do anything foolish or desperate. I'm not a psychopath, Liam.'

'Who are you calling?' he asked.

'I need to send a message to some friends. That's if you don't mind hosting, Tess?'

Tess nodded.

'I'd appreciate it if you didn't call the police just yet,' she said, sitting back down and reclaiming her wine as if she hadn't just confessed to being involved with a murder. 'I'll tell you our story, but I would appreciate ten minutes or so to make some arrangements. Seana will need to be provided for. My sister's really quite helpless without proper care. That's what Ade did to her.'

Tess sat down in the armchair and Liam took a seat in the other one.

'You mean your mother,' Tess said quietly.

Kennedy nodded. 'Poor soul. And all the time there I was, a constant reminder of what had happened to her. Can you imagine what it's like, to discover the only reason you're in the world is because your father groomed and raped your mother?'

Raven, who'd recoiled to the far end of the sofa and had been watching her old friend in the fascinated horror of someone who's just seen them in a whole new light, rather surprised Tess now by reaching over and rubbing the self-confessed killer's back.

'Oh, Kenn,' she said softly. 'I'm so sorry.'

Kennedy smiled sadly. 'And you thought you had dibs in the screwed up parents stakes, right?'

'How did you find out?'

'It was pure chance really. I was looking for a new hobby and I decided to take up genealogy. If I'd told Nick and Seana they'd have tried to talk me out of it, I suppose, but I didn't – I thought it would be nice to surprise them with what I could find out about the family tree.' She sighed. 'I half wish I hadn't, now. Ignorance was bliss, as they say. Still, it's done.'

'How did that give you a connection to Ade?' Tess asked.

'I did one of those DNA test things to help get me started. I couldn't understand it at first. I kept getting all these matches to cousins in New Zealand, although we've got no family there, while my dad's brother, who'd also done a test, was showing up as a great-uncle. Well, eventually I worked out what was going on. That was shock enough, discovering my parents were actually my grandparents, but then when I started following the New Zealand connection I found an elderly paternal aunt . . . you can probably guess the rest.'

'Ade's sister,' Liam said. 'Did you tell Seana?'

'How could I? It could have broken her. She's got no idea I know who she really is. No, I went to the only person I thought could give me answers – the only one I knew with a connection to Ade.'

'His ex-wife,' Tess said. 'Rose Blanchet.'

Kennedy nodded. 'She was a close friend of my sister's, and it turned out Seana had confided the whole story to her – how she'd been groomed by Ade when she was fourteen, and her parents had pulled her out of school to hide the pregnancy until they could pass me off as their own. Rose didn't want to tell me at first, but I insisted on knowing. When she showed me her scrapbooks, all the information she'd collected on Ade and his abuses, I felt physically sick.'

'So that was when you hatched the plan to kill him.'

'Actually the plan was already in motion, months before

I learnt who my mother and father really were. Rose had long wanted her last act in this life to be delivering Ade to his final judgement, but she was very frail and she couldn't do it alone. She'd already started bringing people together online when I went to see her.' The doorbell rang. 'That will be the first one.'

Tess went to answer the door, suspecting she knew who she was going to find on the other side, but she still felt a jolt of surprise when she opened it to Peggy Bristow.

'Tess. I'm told it's time.'

'Er, yes.'

'Well, I'm glad. I was getting quite weary waiting. Kennedy had hoped it would be you and not the police.'

Tess wasn't sure what to say to this. She turned and led Peggy into the living room.

Peggy smiled when she noticed Liam. 'Well, young man, I'm glad to see you here. I take it that means you heeded the warning in your cards.'

Liam nodded. 'Peggy. I'm not glad to see you here, but I'm not really surprised.'

'I didn't think you would be.' She smiled warmly at Kennedy. 'Hello, sweetheart.'

Kennedy stood up. 'I'm sorry, Peggy.'

'Oh, nonsense. We all knew it was coming. It's what we agreed to – no crime without punishment. I actually find myself rather relieved.'

They embraced before Kennedy took her seat again.

'Oh. We need more chairs,' Raven said, taking refuge in the practical. 'I'll bring in the beanbags from my room.

Peggy, you can have my seat.' She stood up and hesitated. 'Er, would anyone like a glass of wine?'

'I must say, this is the most civilised murder confession party I've ever attended,' Liam murmured to Tess.

'Yes, why not?' Peggy said. 'Thank you, Raven. After all, it might be some time until we can enjoy the finer things in life again.'

'Was it worth it?' Tess asked.

'It'll be worth every second of lost freedom,' Peggy said vehemently. 'If you'd known Ade the way I did, you'd understand why.' She smiled at Raven as she came back in with a glass of wine. 'It's strange, isn't it? The police were very quick to arrest me on suspicion of Clemmie's murder, although she was a kind, dear old soul I wouldn't have hurt for the world. Yet when it came to Ade Adams, a man I had every reason to hate, they let me off without a pause.' She sipped her drink. 'And I'll tell you why. Because I was a drop in the ocean, that's why. One out of hundreds – maybe even thousands – who hated Ade Adams with every fibre of their being. That man was a monster, and while I don't think I'm a natural-born killer, I'll never regret playing my part in taking him out of this world.'

The doorbell sounded again.

'There's the third,' Kennedy said. 'The last of our little coven. Tess, would you show them in?'

Chapter 38

This time, Tess wasn't sure who to expect. Could it be Angela, after all? That could be devastating for Raven, but for personal reasons she didn't much care for the alternative.

'Oh,' she said dully when she opened the door. 'So it's you.'

Leonie nodded. 'Sorry, Tess.'

Mikey was there too, holding her hand tightly. He smiled awkwardly at Tess.

Tess ignored him and turned to Leonie. 'Was he involved in this?'

She shook her head. 'He knew nothing about it until yesterday when I confessed everything. I couldn't risk Mikey getting another strike on his record.'

Mikey kissed her hair. 'Don't worry, Bels. I'll be here for you, whatever happens.'

Tess gave a resigned sigh. 'You'd better come in. We're having quite the pre-arrest party in here. I'm thinking of sending out for a Domino's.'

They headed inside. Leonie squeezed on to the sofa next to Kennedy while Mikey pulled one of Raven's beanbags over to sit beside her.

'So,' Liam said. 'I was right to suspect you.'

Leonie smiled. 'I knew you were good. You know, the plan was never to get away with it. Hiring you was a way of staying in control, and making sure everything we wanted to get out about Ade found its way into the public domain. We could influence you in a way we couldn't the police.'

'That's why you sent me on that wild goose chase down to London.'

'It was a good way to buy time, but it wasn't a wild goose chase. I suspected it must be his ridiculous secret society that had prevented Ade being exposed all those years. I hoped if I encouraged you to investigate, we could make sure they got their comeuppance too.'

'You've got Oliver Maynard to thank for that. He investigated with me and anonymously tipped off the press.'

Kennedy nodded. 'I'm glad it was him. That feels fitting.'

Leonie took Kennedy's hand and gave it a squeeze. Kennedy smiled at her and took Peggy's on the other side.

'Well, here we are,' she said. 'The witches of Cherrywood. Our little coven.'

'That was always a joke between us, when we first started talking online,' Leonie said. 'Ade hated women, and he particularly hated the women in his life. Hated the fact they had power over him. He used to joke about his ex-wives being a coven of witches. He meant it as an insult, of course, but we decided to claim it as our own.'

'There was Rose too, as I'm sure Kennedy has told you,' Peggy said. 'She was more of a Mother Superior than a member of the coven, since she was very sick by that point. She hated

Ade, as we all did, but she'd been smart about it and directed that hatred where it needed to go. She'd kept a complete dossier on Ade: everywhere he'd been, everything he'd done. She always intended to expose him, when she was sure she had enough evidence that even his pals at that faux-Satanic boys' club wouldn't be able to sweep it under the carpet. Then she found out her time was coming to an end, and Ade's celebrity had sunk so far that there was no way she could guarantee he'd be exposed the way he deserved to be. That was when she put the coven together.'

'Who did she approach first?' Tess asked. 'Er, Raven, do you want to fetch more drinks? Orange juice for Leonie, I think.'

'I was the first person she got on board,' Leonie said. 'I'd been wanting to leave Ade for years, but I knew what he'd do to me if I ever tried it. Worse, I knew what he'd do to Mikey. I signed up without hesitation.'

'I was next,' Peggy said. 'Rose had considered Seana for the last member, but we could tell she wouldn't have it in her, poor soul. So it was going to be Katrin in Germany we approached, but then Fate stepped in and Kennedy came to us. Once Rose had told her the story behind her conception, she agreed to become the third and final member of the coven.'

'That must have been hell for you, Kenn,' Tess said softly. 'Hearing the whole story.'

'It was pain beyond belief,' Kennedy said. 'It made me sick to my stomach to think Ade was a part of me. Still, I don't think I really thought of myself when I signed my soul on the dotted line, so to speak. I only thought about Seana. Ade ruined her life, and she's the sweetest person you could ever meet. My sister's worth ten of me.'

'You can't think this is what she'd have wanted,' Liam said.

Kennedy smiled. 'You seem to believe this was a practical decision, made after weighing up all the pros and cons. It wasn't, I can promise you. It was driven purely by anger, and a sense of the stinging unfairness of it all. Ade Adams was an old man who was going to die peacefully in his bed, probably, with his reputation spotless and no justice for his many victims.' She met his eyes. 'How would you feel, Liam? If it had been your sister he abused, or your daughter – what do you think you might be capable of?'

'Not murder.'

'Really? Could you swear to that?' She took her wine from the table and sipped it calmly. 'Don't underestimate your dark side. It might surprise you one day.'

'That was why you did it? The unfairness of it?' Tess asked.

'Yes. And no. I think as much as that, it was a need to . . . to exorcise him, I suppose. It made me sick to think he was a part of me – a child abuser and a rapist. Until you've known what it feels like to find something like that out about yourself, I don't think you can ever truly understand.'

'So when Annette Maynard talked about a poor child, it wasn't Seana she meant,' Tess said. 'It was you – Ade and Seana's baby. Wasn't it?'

'I suppose it was. I imagine my mother – that is to say, my grandmother – shared the story with her in an unguarded moment. They were close friends.' Kennedy sighed. 'It's going to be a terrible embarrassment to Nick. He's such an upright man. I hope he can understand and forgive me, one day.'

'That was what the Sun card represented. Not the children Ade abused, but one specific child. You.'

'Yes.' Kennedy smiled. 'You know, Tess, I was disappointed you didn't work the cards out earlier. In the end I just had to tell you. It was frustrating watching you stumble around trying to work it out.'

'Why use tarot cards?' Liam asked.

'It felt like it fitted, since we'd decided to think of ourselves as a coven,' Leonie said. 'We also thought it would buy time by acting as a screen for Peggy. You know, sort of a double bluff. Since everyone in the village knows Peggy reads tarot, the last thing you might expect is her to put herself in the frame by leaving some at the scene of the crime.'

'Who did plant them?'

'I did,' Leonie said. 'I slipped them into the witch's pocket the week before Ade was killed.'

'That was risky.'

'Oh, I was in disguise, of course. You forget, Liam, that I'm used to hiding in plain sight – my marriage taught me that skill, at least.'

Liam touched the eye she'd once blackened for him. 'I didn't forget'

'It was the first time I'd been back to Cherrywood since I left with Ade. It felt odd being back here after all that time, but I wanted to play my part after the others voted against me doing the deed itself.'

Tess raised an eyebrow. 'You had a voting system?'

'Oh yes, we were very democratic,' Peggy said. 'When it came to who was to perform the act itself, it was a case of deciding who had the greatest right. We voted for Leonie at first, as Ade's current wife. Her suffering was the freshest. But when she found out she could be expecting a little one, we vetoed that – we knew that whoever carried out the act would likely bear the brunt when it came to sentencing. So, Kennedy's claim was considered to be the next strongest. Ade was her flesh and blood, after all.'

Kennedy shuddered. 'I wish you wouldn't remind me, Peg.'

'That made it nice and easy for you,' Liam said. 'I think I can see how events played out. Everyone playing their part, right?'

'So on the day of the murder itself . . . Leonie, you got the ball rolling, I suppose?' Tess asked.

She nodded. 'I knew how to get Ade riled up. I stayed out all night, then rolled in pretending to be drunk in the early hours. Taunted him with his impotence and other things I knew would strike at the jugular, and took my bruises valiantly. I knew he'd go running to the nearest source of an ego massage.'

'You,' Tess said, looking at Peggy. 'You drugged Ade's vape fluid?'

She nodded. 'It was easy enough. Kennedy had told me how to prepare the cartridge. All I had to do was wait until he was in the bathroom and swap them over.'

'Where did you get enough Valium?'

'We all had a share in that,' Leonie said. 'On an individual basis prescriptions are carefully controlled, but with three of us pooling resources, we were soon able to get the amount we needed.'

'And the digoxin, I suppose, came from Rose.'

Kennedy nodded. 'It wasn't difficult for her to slip some tablets to me one day when I visited her with Seana. I took them home and condensed them into a single capsule.'

Liam looked at Peggy. 'And you, I think, must have suggested the idea of a prank to Ade.'

'Naturally. Oh, he went mad for the idea. He was drunk enough to think it could be the key to reviving his fortunes, the old fool. There'd been a popular prank on his godawful television programme involving a scarecrow that had apparently gone down a storm, and I promised to arrange for the press to be there when he revealed himself. I walked him down to the park myself, to make sure he didn't have a change of heart. Took him down the snicket and over the bowling green where we'd be least likely to be spotted, let him into the park, helped him change clothes with the witch, drew his lipstick smile on for him, removed the ladder after he'd climbed the pyre and then finally I locked the gates behind him.'

'So he couldn't have got out even if he had sobered up,' Tess said.

'Not without calling for help. Anyway, as soon as he reached the top of the bonfire he switched on his vape – I knew he would. I could smell the damn thing while I was removing the ladder. He'd have been unconscious shortly after and stayed that way until he was discovered that evening.'

Liam glanced at Kennedy. 'And that's where the doctor here comes in.'

Kennedy nodded. 'I knew I'd be called for as soon as you'd got him down. I'd hidden the digoxin capsule in a tub of chewing gum.'

'That's right, I remember you chewing gum that night,' Tess said. 'I also remember that you pushed under Ade's chin when you were giving him CPR. It struck me at the time that I'd never seen anyone do that before, but I was distracted trying to keep time for you humming "Nellie the Elephant".'

'Yes. I'd hidden the capsule under my tongue so I could slip it into Ade's mouth under the pretence of giving CPR. All I had to do then was make him bite down on it. It was a large dose so he'd have been dead long before any paramedics arrived to examine him.' Kennedy sagged back against the cushions, looking suddenly weary. 'I wouldn't take it back. Ade Adams deserved everything he had coming to him. I only wish I could have done it years ago, and perhaps prevented what happened to my sister – my mother – happening to any other poor girls.'

Tess glanced at Mikey, who'd stayed silent throughout, holding on to Leonie's hand as the women told their story. What was going to happen to him now? Could he really stay straight, if the person that had been keeping him going was in prison?

'Sorry, ladies, but I'm going to have to call my police

contact now,' Liam said. 'I understand why you did it, and I suppose I can't say that if I'd been in your circumstances I wouldn't have felt the same. Still, you knew it had to come to this.'

'Yes.' Kennedy roused herself. 'Just give me a few minutes. I need to call my brother and sister and speak to David Blanchet. Then we can all finish our wine while we wait for the police.'

She left the room with her mobile. It didn't occur to Tess, or seemingly to anyone else present, to accompany her. Somehow they knew instinctively that Kennedy wasn't going to run. She was going to wait for the police, calmly tell her story, just as she had tonight, and take the punishment that was handed to her with resigned serenity. All the women would.

When Kennedy came back in, she was a little paler and her eyes were damp. However, she showed no sign of emotion as she sat back down.

'It's done,' she said. 'Nick and David will keep an eye on Seana. David's planning to invite her for Christmas, which will be nice as I know she's sweet on him. I did ring my sister to tell her I might be going away for a little while, but I didn't tell her why. Nick's going to explain what happened when it all comes out. I didn't want to do it over the phone, when she had no one with her. Liam, please go ahead.'

Liam nodded and left the room to call Della.

'I'd appreciate it if someone could look after old Nelson for me,' Peggy said. 'Poor soul, he does seem to get through mistresses.'

'Of course.' Tess looked at her brother. 'What's going to happen to you?'

'I'm going with Bels,' he said firmly. 'They won't get rid of me. I'm going down to the station too.'

Leonie smiled and squeezed his hand. 'That's sweet, Mike, but I'm probably going to prison. You can't go there with me. Just promise me you'll stay straight and wait for me, will you? Our future's postponed for a little while, that's all.'

'Maybe not. You might get a suspended, in your condition. You didn't do it, did you?'

'No, but I was as much a part of it as the others, which means I'm likely to be looking at a murder charge. Even if it's conspiracy to murder, that's hardly a wrist-slapping offence.' There was the sound of sirens outside. 'Well, it sounds as though they're playing our song. Ladies, shall we get our coats?'

The police arrived soon after, and Tess and her friends watched as with quiet dignity the unlikely trio of killers was led away.

Chapter 39

'Another season, another murder,' Oliver observed when he, Tess, Raven and Liam convened for a post-murder-solving drink at the Star later that evening. 'Would I be tempting Fate to firmly wish this might be the last one in Cherrywood for at least a hundred years?'

'It's certainly a case that's going to stay with me,' Liam said, sipping his pint. 'I'll never forget that image. The three of them, holding hands as they were led away.'

'It's hard not to sympathise, isn't it?' Raven said. 'Ade caused so much pain, to them and to so many others. What Kennedy said, about never underestimating your dark side . . . it did make me think "There but for the grace of God".' She glanced at Oliver. 'Is that wrong?'

'What, compassion?' He reached over to give her hand a squeeze. 'No, Rave. Compassion is never wrong.'

'Do you think that's true, what Mikey said?' Tess asked Liam. 'Might Leonie get a suspended sentence?'

'She might be looking at a more lenient one, considering her condition. Especially given the abuse her husband put her through.'

'I hope so. I'd hate to think of her in prison and pregnant, and I really don't trust him to keep straight without her steadying influence.' She shook her head. 'Sounds strange, doesn't it, that my brother's so-called steadying influence is likely to be sent down for conspiracy to murder? But he definitely needs her.'

'You're doing him a disservice, you know,' Oliver said. 'Mikey's got some inner strength. He just had to work on finding it. I think the prospect of being a dad is going to straighten him out more than you think.' He paused, staring into his pint. 'I made a decision tonight. About Ling Cottage.'

'Oh God, you're not going to live in it, are you?' Raven asked.

'Not me. I'm going to give it away. To Mikey and Leonie – I mean, Helen. They're going to want peace and quiet when she gets out, far away from their old lives. The cottage is perfect.'

Tess frowned. 'You're going to give it to Mikey? You want Mikey living here, in the village?'

'Yes. I've made my peace with it.' He glanced at her. 'How about you?'

'I would like to have a relationship with the baby,' she admitted grudgingly. 'Mikey . . . we'll see how he acquits himself.'

The door to the pub opened and Angela entered with some of the survivors of the *Macbeth* performance. She smiled uncertainly when she noticed Raven, then made her way to the bar.

'Hang on,' Raven said. 'I'll be back in a minute.'

The other three watched as she joined Angela at the bar and pulled her to one side. They talked for a moment, then after what looked like a brief but awkward silence, Raven held out her hand. Angela beamed as she shook it.

Oliver smiled. 'Well, that looks like progress.' Raven looked over and beckoned to him. 'It seems like I might be wanted. I'll get a round in while I'm there, eh?'

'Thanks, Oliver,' Liam said.

He and Tess watched as Oliver joined Raven and Angela at the bar.

'There's something going on between those two, isn't there?' Liam observed to Tess.

'Yeah. They think they're so sneaky I haven't noticed, but Oliver gives off guilt pheromones I can smell from five miles away.'

'What do you reckon? Can it work out?'

'They'll have a lot of challenges to face. Very different backgrounds. Very different beliefs.' Tess smiled as she watched her two friends, chatting to Angela at the bar. 'But you know, I think they could be exactly what each other need.'

'Go on, then, say it,' Liam said as he finished his pint.

'Say what?'

'You know what. I've been waiting for it ever since the police left.'

She grinned. 'All right. How does it feel having me crack another of your cases?'

'I knew you couldn't help yourself.'

'Well?'

'It feels . . . great.' Liam took an envelope from his pocket. 'Here.'

'What's this?'

'Open it and see.'

Tess drew it out and stared. 'Twenty-five grand! Liam, this is a cheque for twenty-five grand!'

'That's right. Half my fee for the Ade Adams case. You deserve it just as much as I do – more, probably.'

'Do you know how long it takes me to earn that kind of money?' She shook her head. 'I can't take this.'

'Course you can. That's how partnerships work, isn't it?' He nodded to the envelope. 'There's something else in there.'

Tess reached inside and drew out a small, rectangular card. It was very similar to the ones Liam gave his clients, with the Cherrywood Investigations and Gardening Services logo printed at the top. But it wasn't Liam's name underneath.

'Tess Feather. Private Investigator,' Tess read. 'Um. What?'

'I want to make it official, Tess,' Liam said softly. 'Hanley and Feather, partners in crime-solving. What do you say?'

'You mean it? Really?'

'Really. I ordered your cards the day after our stakeout. I realised then that I couldn't do it alone.'

Tess hesitated, looking at her name on the card.

'You can still keep up your singing,' Liam said, sounding worried when she didn't say yes right away. 'And your pub job too, if you really want to. But things might start taking off for me now, with all the media attention solving the Ade

Adams case is likely to get, and you've been a big part of that. I want you to keep working with me, and I'd really like to make it official.'

Tess was still staring at the card.

'I can't prune,' she said at last.

Liam frowned. 'What?'

'I can't prune. When it comes to gardening, you're on your own.'

'Um, all right.'

'And there's to be no more of this treating me like a delicate Victorian maiden rubbish. I want to do my fair share of the legwork. No more Wikipedia-trawling while you're undercover having all the fun.'

'All right, I think you've proved yourself on this case,' he said, smiling. 'I did think, that night you had your brother pinned to the wall of his caravan by the throat, that I'd got it the wrong way round trying to keep you out of danger. It's really the rest of the world I ought to be protecting from you.'

'Damn straight.'

'Mind you, you'll have to promise you'll work on developing an appropriate sense of jeopardy and not rush off to murderers' houses for a pot of tea and arsenic the minute I leave you unsupervised. Partners means partners, OK? No mavericking.'

'Also, it's Feather and Hanley,' she went on, ignoring that remark. 'It sounds better with my name first. Alphabetical, you know?'

Liam laughed. 'Fine by me. So, have we got a deal?'

Tess shrugged. 'I think I can stand to work with you again.' She licked the tip of one finger, crossed it over her palm and held out her hand. 'It's a deal.'

Liam smiled as he copied her. 'Good to have you on board, partner.'

Acknowledgements

Thanks once again to the team at Headline and my editor Bea Grabowska for all their hard work, as well as my agent Hannah Todd for her advice and support. I'd also like to thank my friend Antony Shenton for kindly answering my questions on some of the medical aspects included in this story.

'My new favourite cosy crime series!'
★★★★★

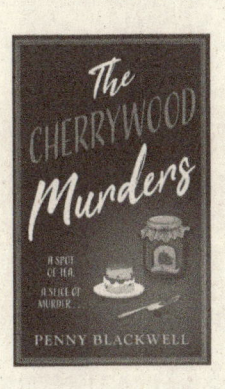

A DOLLOP OF JAM. A SPOT OF TEA. A SLICE OF MURDER...

It has been a year since Tess had to trade the hustle and bustle of London life for pulling pints and moonlighting as a Cher impersonator in a backwater country pub.

The sleepy Yorkshire village of Cherrywood would always be home, but a return to rural life wasn't *quite* the path she'd paved for herself. Still, being back with her oldest friends, Raven and Oliver, was a definite upside and she was beginning to settle into the slower pace.

That is until Clemmie Ackroyd, a stalwart member of the community, is brutally murdered. Ruled a robbery gone wrong, it's an open-and-shut case for the police, but something isn't quite adding up for Tess.

Then an unexpected face from the past shows up in the village, pointing fingers, and Tess finds herself resolving to get to the bottom of Clemmie's death – even if that means getting up to her neck in jam, Jerusalem and deadly secrets at the Women's Guild...

Available to order

ACCENT